St. Petersburg Noir

EDITED BY JULIA GOUMEN & NATALIA SMIRNOVA

Published by Akashic Books
©2012 Akashic Books

Series concept by Tim McLoughlin and Johnny Temple
St. Petersburg map by Aaron Petrovich

ISBN-13: 978-1-61775-101-1
Library of Congress Control Number: 2011960950
All rights reserved

First printing

Akashic Books
PO Box 1456
New York, NY 10009
info@akashicbooks.com
www.akashicbooks.com

ALSO IN THE AKASHIC BOOKS NOIR SERIES

FORTHCOMING

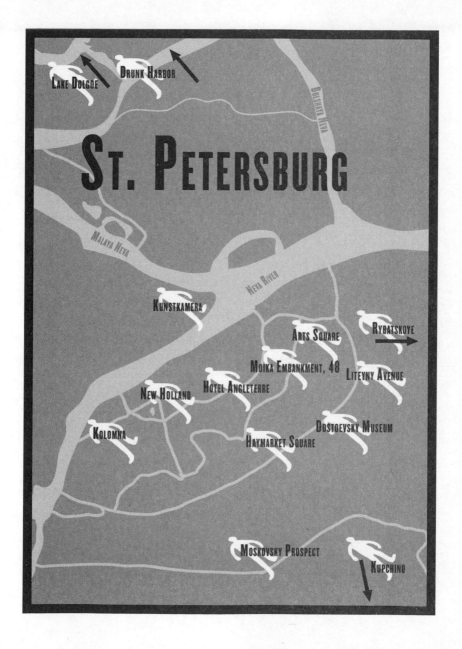

TABLE OF CONTENTS

PART III: CHASING GHOSTS

INTRODUCTION
INESCAPABLE ANGUISH

W hen you think of the most noir city in Russia, the name that springs to mind is St. Petersburg. This link between the place, its character, and the genre has become quite paradoxically the biggest challenge for the authors in this anthology, who must balance their work with the city's rich noir tradition and at the same time transform daily criminal headlines into a literary experience.

Indeed, the tradition of noir writing in St. Petersburg features the greatest names of Russian literature. Most obviously, one thinks of the nineteenth century: Fyodor Dostoevsky (you can hardly find a more obvious noir spirit than in *Crime and Punishment*'s Kolomna settings, where Raskolnikov kills an old lady with an ax), Alexander Pushkin (my grandmother likes to recall how scared she was walking home in the city before World War II following the Mariinsky Theater's opera performance of Pushkin's "The Queen of Spades"; and "The Bronze Horseman"—a long poem about a disastrous flood—is one of the creepiest stories in Russian literature), and *Petersburg Tales* by Nikolai Gogol. More recently, the early twentieth century contributed to the city's noir tradition with Andrey Bely's novel *Petersburg*; followed later by the absurd, bleak writings of Daniil Kharms and Mikhail Zoshchenko.

Speaking of the latter two—Petersburg somehow nurtures ironic, satirical, and darkly humorous interpretations of reality. The darker and harsher life gets, the more humorous its interpretations tend to be. Indeed, only at a Petersburg house party could writers argue enthusiastically over the most efficient way to get rid of a corpse (with the deceased taking vodka shots next to them, vividly participating in the discussion). This anthology is no exception: in Andrei Kivinov's story, for instance, a dead body comes to life only to die again in an ironic salute to Gogol.

The origins of this rich noir tradition come from the city's history, its urban landscape, and even the weather, as Petersburg's climate undoubtedly affects local character. What morbid thoughts can freezing winds from the Baltics bring along? Which emotions swirl inside a person struggling through snowdrifts in the streets? How can one remain positive when the long-awaited northern "summer" offers less than a dozen sunny days?

St. Petersburg is an *intentional* city: established by the czar's will as the inverse of Moscow's old-style ruling, and an outpost to guard the country's expansion to the north. But the initial purpose of the city has faded, and dwellers of St. Petersburg live in a place of broken grandeur incongruent with daily routine. Its denizens seek to move beyond the city's limits—sometimes through cheap alcohol (as in Sergei Nosov's "The Sixth of June"), sometimes with the help of drugs (check out Andrei Rubanov's "Barely a Drop").

Yet the conflict between the grandness, the imperial indifference of the city's architecture, and its dwellers remains painful. Each stone and monument in the city center breathes of history and purpose—while locals are like exhibits of the Kunstkamera: oddities gathered for examination or research, the purpose of which remains unclear. (This conflict has been elegantly examined in Eugene Kogan's and Alexander Kudriavtsev's stories.) Enriching the city's already vast postmodern treasury, the authors of the anthology bring monuments and museums to life: a bust of Pushkin takes on flesh and color in Lialin's "Paranoia"; college students become material for new taxidermy projects in Pavel Krusanov's "Hairy Sutra."

Crime in Petersburg fiction is traditionally of a metaphysical nature. With a history densely filled with dark crimes, the city's atmosphere is saturated by a poisonous miasma coming from the swamps upon which it is built—an ideal condition for ghosts to haunt the landscape and folklore. Quite a few contributors have introduced ghosts or spirits into their stories.

St. Petersburg is famous for its canals, rivers, embankments, and bridges. This romantic landscape offers poetic comparisons to Venice in Italy, but also implies fluctuation, unsteadiness, fluidity that diffuses the local character and its morals. Since Pushkin, water has contributed to the gloomy and desperate atmosphere of the city: in his poem "The Bronze Horseman," a flood kills the protagonist's beloved girl, driving the hero insane. Water becomes a character in Lena Eltang's "Drunk Harbor," and is also prominent in Kurchatova and Venglinskaya's criminal tale, Anna Solovey's theatrical drama, and Vadim Levental's classic mystery investigation.

But reality, as often happens, proves more horrifying than any invented images. Crowded communal apartments in Kolomna (the statistics shock: in 2011 the number of citizens residing in such projects exceeded 660,000), drug abuse, sexual violence, and mandated killings in Russia's "criminal capital" become a regular routine and give rich material for artistic interpretation. It is not surprising that many national TV crime shows have been set in St. Petersburg—including *The Streets of Broken Lamps*, now in its twelfth season, *Gangster Petersburg* (2000–2007), and *Deadly Force* (fifty-seven episodes in five years; the show is based on Andrei Kivinov's script), to name a few.

Dark, grim, and terrifying—these stories concoct a unique noir space of the city, mapping a very untouristic route for those who dare to explore its narrow streets, haunted shadows, and the intricate web of its black water.

The city's inescapable anguish will seize every reader of

these stories, resonating to the maddening clopping sound of the Bronze Horseman.

Julia Goumen & Natalia Smirnova
St. Petersburg, Russia
May 2012

PART I

Gangsters, Soldiers & Patriots

TRAINING DAY

BY ANDREI KIVINOV

Kupchino

Translated by Polly Gannon

Rise and shine, Eagle Scouts! You've got a report."
Leaving the door to the rec room open and not waiting
for us to wake up, Evseyev returned to duty. I wasn't
asleep anyway. I was just lying there with my eyes closed on top
of an ancient, disintegrating overcoat spread out on some chairs
I had pushed together. That was in contrast to Farid Ismagilov,
the Tatar, snoring loud enough to wake the dead. I still hadn't
learned to fall asleep at three in the afternoon. That was under-
standable: I didn't have enough practice. Although the idea of a
postprandial nap made sense. If there's an opportunity to sleep
during the day, use it. That way, at night, you won't keep yawning and nodding off if something happens. Farid, over there, was
a guy with a lot of practice.

I got up off the chairs and put on my brown shoes. The
standard-issue black ones didn't fit me, so I had to settle for civilian ones. The officers frowned on them, but the civilian population didn't give a damn, so I wasn't worried. No big deal, it's
not like shoes are your uniform cap. I straightened my tie, then
nudged Farid, still sleeping on the bench.

"Mister Driver, we've got a report to check out. Let's get
going."

Farid woke up, rubbed his eyes, and yawned, exhaling a lethal reek of bacon and garlic. A Muslim, he scarfed down bacon for lunch despite the injunctions of the Koran. They called him Driver because he drove the official kozel jeep. In his free time, that is, when he wasn't sleeping. Rank: sergeant; age: thirty-three; disposition: Nordic, sometimes gloomy, with a slight chance of showers. Inclined toward mild, daily drunkenness. Whether he was an athlete or a good family man, I didn't know yet. Rooted for the Rubin Kazan soccer team.

"We'll check it out later. It's our legitimate quiet time."

"Yeah, but felons don't get a quiet time."

Evseyev, the duty officer, was playing a game of erotic Tetris on an office computer, forming a naked minor on the screen. Or, in his words, drawing up a duty roster. This drawing up of a roster was not easy: every time Evseyev got above knee level, he had to start all over again. It irritated him to no end. His assistant was fastidiously interrogating a reticent drunkard who smelled of piss. He steered the man toward the "aquarium" (the drying-out tank) with a gentle kick, and sprayed apple-scented air freshener around the room.

"So, what's with the report?" Farid said, kneading his neck.

Without glancing up from his "duty roster," Evseyev handed us a piece of paper covered with what looked like chicken scratch.

"Here's the address. The paramedics called. Dead on arrival. Forty-two-year-old male. Asphyxiation. Allegedly choked on meat dumplings. Go take a look. If anything seems suspicious, call and I'll send the operative. And if there's no sign of foul play, do the usual routine."

The usual routine. It was my first day on duty, and I had no clue what the routine was. I mean, I knew it in theory—I had taken a three-month course for police investigators—but instructions and regulations were one thing, "the usual routine" was something else. I didn't let on, naturally. I nodded and took the address as though it was something I did every day. If worse came to worst, Farid would tell me what to do. He'd been in the department more than ten years. He'd give me a shoulder to lean on.

When we went out into the courtyard, the weather was doing its best to discourage any sort of work ethic. It was like being in a thriller. Gray thunderheads, spitting rain, slithery mud, a screaming wind. Indian summer had given way to an abrupt early winter. I have to say that in St. Petersburg there's no real spring, summer, or fall. It's one eternal season of early winter. Even in the July heat people escape from here to warmer climes. You've just got to put up with it and not start howling when some Lexus speeds by, splashing you with dirty water. Because St. Petersburg is the president's hometown.

Sopping wet leather shoes were no match for the standard-issue leather kersey boots. But they hadn't given me those. Said there was a shortage of kersey leather in the country, and that kersey boots had gone out of style a long time ago, anyway. Not flashy enough, I was told.

Farid chased away a filthy crow sitting on the hood of the kozel and, cursing, tightened the metal wire around the bumper that fastened it to the body of the jalopy. The kozel was even more experienced than the driver. It had lost part of its engine in gang wars. Its gear box and suspension had been severely wounded, and its scratches and battle scars were too numerous to count. It had received a medal of honor for "Endurance," undergone treatment in the field hospital, and continued to serve under the proud moniker of *G-Wagen,* which some witty cynic had spelled out in black paint on the yellow hood.

After he had tightened the wire, Farid loaded himself into the vehicle and passed me a hand crank. I stuck the crank under the bumper. Mustering up all my strength, I grabbed the handle with both hands and gave it a turn clockwise. Nada.

"Harder," Farid said. "It's not a beer bottle."

"You shouldn't have stopped the engine."

"If you gave me more gas, I wouldn't have to."

Our jalopy started up on the fourth attempt. The joyful roaring of the engine resounded through the courtyard, its blue exhaust filling the air. I dropped the crank under the seat and jumped in. We were rolling. Finally.

We didn't have too far to go. Our precinct was based in Kupchino, a Petersburg bedroom community, settled at one time, according to legend, by merchants. Or maybe not. In any case, nowadays the people who lived here were just the same as the people living in any other part of Petersburg, and probably the entire country. The places we inhabit have no bearing on the way we think and live. That's a proven fact.

Our precinct covered fifty hectares, all told, and it counted about 100,000 people. They lived mainly in Khrushchev-era buildings—architectural monuments unprotected by either the government or UNESCO. The people who lived in them were responsible for their upkeep. The ones who didn't drink. I had only spent a few weeks here as a police inspector when I understood that was a clear minority. Very clear.

In addition to watching over the populace, my tasks included regular twenty-four-hour on-call duty. I had to go with the driver to all kinds of events that were not distinguished by any significant criminality: domestic violence, drunken brawls, petty vandalism, and other amoral phenomena that disrupted the peace of ordinary citizens. Naturally, my job was not just to go there, but to react quickly and adequately, adhering to the letter of the law, if possible. And if not—*not* adhering to it.

As I already mentioned, today was my debut; or, rather, my training day. Like any other novice, I was nervous. Thank goodness, before lunch it all went as smoothly as could be. No mass riots or technogenic catastrophes. A few scuffles between neighbors, and a fight in a café where a crusading customer refused to pay for an order that he had already more than half-consumed. Ismagilov had dealt with all these incidents without much effort. He never even pulled out the Jedi baton, a product of some factory's rubber division, from his broad belt. The fight was broken up and the brazen customer was shaken down for a few rubles with the use of the magic words "detention" and "downtown." Usually the Star Wars began after six in the evening, when the weary proletariat returned home after its labors and grabbed any means at hand for letting off steam and reducing stress. I was hoping that today wouldn't produce many marvels. You can't put too much strain on a lieutenant's shoulders that have yet to be tested, or on the brain of someone fresh out of engineering school.

I had never had to file paperwork on a murder—not when I was in college, or even in the service—so I was feeling some emotional anxiety. I just wasn't used to procedures like this. Actually, I had no experience whatsoever. They had taken us on a field trip to the city morgue during our training, but I pretended I was mortally ill and copped out of it. I had no desire to examine internal organs in their natural state. I'd rather look at a picture in a textbook on forensic medicine, or, better yet, not see it at all. Now I was reaping the questionable rewards of my own squeamishness. Farid didn't seem the least bit bothered by it. He'd seen it all in his ten years with our outfit. It was all still ahead of me, though. But there was nothing you could do about it. I had chosen this path myself when I decided to devote my younger years to fighting domestic crime, and, if I was lucky, to getting a place of my own in the bargain. It was cramped living in one small apartment with my parents and brothers.

Not long ago I had been at a funeral. A relative on my mother's side, an eighty-seven-year-old man, had died. We stood by the coffin in the morgue to say goodbye, everyone crying, of course. A few other coffins containing the deceased surrounded us. Suddenly, a seriously drunk fellow burst in, looked around, and then, pushing aside all my relatives, cried out, "Goodbye, Mama!" and flung himself into my dead relative's crossed arms. In spite of the tragic pathos of the moment, everyone standing around the coffin broke into laughter, myself included. After that everyone started crying again, but not like before. Laughter through tears; a patch of light, a patch of darkness . . .

Next to a shopping center Driver slowed down and dashed out to buy cigarettes in a little dive with the nostalgic name 3.62. I seemed to remember that was how much a half-liter of vodka cost when I was a kid. Farid had a discount there—he checked out their daily scuffles. By the door a soaking wet beggar sat in the rain on a piece of cardboard, exhorting the public through a megaphone to donate money to him for bread. He amplified his voice without shame or timidity, like a guide on Nevsky Prospect inviting tourists on a canal boat ride. "Hurry up, hurry up! Just one piece of bread! Don't pass up your chance to help the needy. You won't be sorry in the next world!"

Coming out of the dive, Farid the Muslim sinned against the Koran yet again. Instead of extending charity as he was supposed to according to the one of the five pillars of Islam, he chased off the beggar. He called it "checking his license."

Our multicultural duo sped over to a nine-story building that rose up just behind the shopping center. A few minutes later the G-Wagen screeched to a halt by the entrance, next to an ambulance with a sleeping driver in it. Farid turned off the engine; leaving an empty cop car with the engine running wasn't advisable. There were always people willing to take it for a spin. This wasn't Beverly Hills, after all. Better to let the inspector spin the hand crank one more time.

I noticed a large warning sign on the moldy wall of the building:

DON'T STAND UNDER THE BALCONY
DUE TO THE DANGER OF IT COLLAPSING!

Thanks to the residential supervisor for his concern. Next year the word "balcony" would have to be replaced with the word "wall."

We ducked into the entrance hall. It was so leaky and damp it seemed to be raining inside the building. I went up in the ramshackle elevator. Farid walked up to the fifth floor. They say that after a certain incident he had become "elevator shy." Once, some big bosses decided to check on how one of the then-inspectors was dealing with a routine domestic violence call. The bosses were big in the literal sense too—two of them two-hundred-pounders at the very least. The inspector was also not given to shunning God's bounty, judging by his amplitude. Plus Farid himself. The higher-ups didn't want to walk all the way up to the last floor, so they all squeezed into the elevator together. The elevator up and ground to a halt halfway; it couldn't cope with the load. To add insult to injury, not one of them was carrying a cell phone or a walkie-talkie. They called out to the residents for help. Like, "We're police, we're responding to a call, we're stuck! Call the repair service!" "Ah, the pigs? Well, you got just what you deserve!" It's no secret how ordinary citizens view us, in spite of the heroes on TV. Some of them even started jeering. "We're going to rip off your car while you're in there sweating!" Farid nearly had a stroke. They stood there in complete darkness between the fifth and sixth floors for nearly two hours, praying that the cable wouldn't snap. Since then Farid refuses to set foot in an elevator, even in his own building. He takes the stairs, and only the stairs. Besides, it's good for the heart.

The apartment where the drama was being played out was a completely ordinary, no-frills, working-class affair. Two small rooms, a kitchenette, and a narrow hallway. The deceased was lying on a bed in the room closest to the entryway, where his wife and son had carried him. His wife—his widow, rather—wasn't sobbing, as I would have expected. She sat silent at the head of the bed and stared at her husband. She was in shock.

A paramedic filled us in. The wife and son had been watching TV, while the head of the family was in the kitchen eating. He was a construction worker and was grabbing a quick meal; the construction site was next door, and it was cheaper to eat at home. He was running late, and swallowed a dumpling whole, it seemed, without chewing it. When he was choking, trying to cough it up, he fell and broke a plate. When the wife and son ran into the kitchen, he was writhing on the floor, clutching at his throat. The son rushed to the telephone, the wife tried to extract the dumpling, but it was lodged there and wouldn't budge. Asphyxiation. The paramedic had no doubts about the cause of death. An accident. He had removed the dumpling from the dead man himself.

After leaving us their number, the paramedics rushed off on another call. I went into the kitchen. A broken plate on the floor, a few stray dumplings in the corners—those were the only traces of the incident. I would probably agree with the paramedic that it seemed impossible to contrive an accident like that, to "make it happen" on its own. And there was no reason to, either. I was young and inexperienced, of course, but just by looking at the wife I could state with certainty that homicide was out of the question.

The son came into the kitchen: a kid, about sixteen, pale as a wall poster bleached by the sun. "I'll clean it up now," he said, nodding toward the shards.

"Don't do that. Go get the neighbors. We need two witnesses. And get your father's ID too."

While he was trying to talk the neighbors into coming over, I called Evseyev and reported the situation.

"Question the next of kin, and cough up a report for sending the body to the morgue," the duty officer said. "And get back here on the double. More reports are about to start pouring in. I'll send someone to pick up the body."

That was about what I had planned to do. Cough up a report and question the relatives, as they taught us in the training course.

I went back into the hallway. Without entering the room, I asked the widow to help her son find the documents. The woman nodded and left. I stood in the doorway, unwilling to go in and be face-to-face with the dead man. Like I said, I wasn't used to it. It's one thing at a funeral, but another thing entirely in domestic circumstances. I wasn't squeamish or suspicious, I didn't believe in the living dead, but I couldn't shake those zombie movies from my mind. Maybe I could just draw up the report right here in the doorway? I thought. It's not a murder, after all. There's no need to search for evidence or find fingerprints. Especially since they already moved the body from the kitchen into the room, disrupting the original circumstances of the incident . . .

I peered at the dead man. He was clothed in the dark-green jacket that construction-site foremen usually wear. He must have really been in a hurry, since he didn't bother to take it off while he was eating. Poor guy. The paramedic had wrapped a bandage around his head and jaw, like someone with a toothache. Suddenly I imagined that the fellow was about to sit up, take off the bandage, and smile, saying that it was all a joke and everyone was invited in to finish off the dumplings.

"What's holding you back?" Farid's voice sounded somewhere behind me.

"I'm just not used to it, that's all."

"Aw, c'mon, he won't bite." He entered the room calmly and leaned over the builder's face. "It's as clear as day. He died all by himself. Nothing to be afraid of."

Sure. He won't bite . . .

The neighbors arrived: two old ladies. As you'd expect, both of them shaking their heads, "what-a-pity" and "woe-is-me." I asked them to come into the room and observe the examination. I sat down on a stool by the head of the body and took out an official form. If this had been my hundredth case, I wouldn't have been nervous. I could have filled the thing out with just my left hand in five minutes. But a debut is a debut, so the whole thing took about forty minutes. I didn't want to show my inadequacy. Recalling the instructions they gave us during the course, I began describing the circumstances from the general to the specific, as clearly and legibly as possible, and without making any spelling errors. This wasn't exactly easy. First, I'm no Leo Tolstoy, and second, a dead man lying right next to you doesn't exactly inspire confidence. I couldn't find the right words. I kept losing my train of thought, so I ended up describing the clothes the dead man was wearing twice. I had no time to do it over, and you weren't allowed to cross things out, so I just left everything as it was. Farid checked in on me a few times and tried in annoyance to hurry me up. The old lady witnesses patiently carried out their duties as citizens, whispering about what a wonderful neighbor he had been, although sometimes he took a drop too much. I could have done with a little drink myself. Just a tad—for the confidence.

When I was done with the report, I dismissed the neighbors and went into the other room to question the wife. That took another forty minutes. The woman was in a sort of stupor, understandably enough. She answered in monosyllables. After she signed the report without even reading it, new characters appeared on the scene.

There were two of them. Both wore baseball caps and dark green canvas jackets that looked like firemen's suits. The older one, who looked about forty, carried a roll of black plastic under his armpit. The second one, about ten years younger, was holding a folded stretcher like a spear. They looked like the Tin Man and the Scarecrow. A glitter in the eyes and a faint but familiar smell pointed to the presence of low levels of alcohol in their blood.

"Hello, ma'am. We're from the morgue," the first one said. "We're here for the deceased."

The widow nodded.

"May we take it?" This question was addressed to me.

"Yes, we're all done here."

"Where is he?"

"The next room."

The two turned around and disappeared into the hallway, where Farid's voice could be heard.

"You're fast today."

"Yeah, it's the third stiff since morning. They're dropping like flies."

While they were attending to the body of the builder, I explained the formalities of ordering a funeral to the widow, although I didn't actually know a thing about it. Then I drafted a cover letter for an autopsy and took it to the orderlies. They were already carrying the body out. They had tied an oilskin tag with a number on it to the wrist, and for some reason had removed the bandage around the jaw. It was a sorry sight. The widow stayed behind in the room, probably afraid she would break down. The son held the door.

Farid asked them to tow-start our G-Wagen. They agreed. After they had carried the dead body out onto the landing, they returned to the apartment and called the widow.

"Our condolences, ma'am," the older one said, removing his baseball cap and smoothing down his unwashed hair. "Maybe we should drink to his memory? Just a shot or two? So that everything will go smoothly, like it should. So we'll be able to deliver the body safely and all that . . ."

The widow nodded again in silence and went out to the kitchen. The orderlies followed behind. We stayed in the hallway.

"Won't you have some?" she said, poking her head out.

"No," Farid answered. "We're on the job."

Then he whispered to me that I shouldn't get drawn into such things, even though I wasn't planning on it anyway. We said goodbye to the widow and her son, expressing our condolences again, and went downstairs. The weather had deteriorated even further and reminded me of someone in a critical stage of fever. The death throes were about to begin. We got into the jeep and waited for the Tin Man and Scarecrow. Their black van with a yellow stripe was a more reliable means of starting the engine than the elbow grease of a young police inspector. It was worth waiting for. Evseyev wouldn't miss us.

The orderlies didn't waste much time at the spontaneous memorial service. Five minutes later they brought out the builder and loaded him in the corpse-mobile. The alcohol content in their blood had increased significantly, but the fellows weren't in the least worried or ashamed about it. It wasn't likely that the traffic police would stop their particular vehicle.

While we were preparing the tow rope, the tall one informed his partner that they had one more client to pick up in the neighborhood, and they wouldn't go to the morgue just yet. They would pick them all up and deliver them wholesale. This would be easier and more economical. Apparently, their gasoline supply was intermittent, like ours.

On the way back I dreamed about the warm rec room, a cup of hot tea, and a game of backgammon with Farid. But I had to bury my dreams. That evil Evseyev, apparently frustrated in his attempts to construct the naked minor on the computer screen, was waiting at the door with another body for us. In the park a dead fellow with no signs of violent death was sitting on a bench, scaring the passersby. Probably a junkie. Probably OD'd.

Onward, gentlemen—on with the inspection and the report. If anything looks suspicious, call the operative.

Thank god Mister Driver hadn't stopped the engine, so I didn't have to expend my valuable muscle power. I shouldn't have to waste it on things like that anyway. There was not a single line in my job description that said that a police inspector is required to start up the official vehicle manually. Then again, I wasn't going to get very far in my brown shoes.

There didn't seem to be any foul play here, either. Nothing criminal anyway. The experienced Farid recognized the poor guy immediately. A local junkie with an unhappy personal life who had been shooting up for three years. The doctor confirmed it was an overdose. A dirty syringe was lying in the grass nearby. It was unlikely that someone had shot up his buddy. Not that sort of a guy. It was self-liquidation.

While I was sitting in our G-Wagen kozel drawing up the second inspection protocol of the day (which went a lot more smoothly than the first), a familiar black van with a yellow stripe pulled up. Long time no see!

"They're sure prompt today," Farid remarked. "Sometimes you wait for six hours, and the stiff just lies there on the ground getting soaked in the rain. Though it's all the same to him at that point."

The Tin Man managed to stay on his feet without any help, but the Scarecrow had to support himself with the stretcher. I wasn't judging the guys. Theirs was a unique profession, unpleasant; you needed a way to reduce the tension or you wouldn't make it. And it had been a hard day. One memorial service after another. That's probably why they didn't recognize us right away. Once they did, they started griping.

"They're keeling over left and right! Dropping like flies. We didn't even get a lunch break. What do you have for us now?"

We pointed to the body. Scarecrow dropped the stretcher in

front of the bench, sat down beside the junkie, and lit up a cigarette. The seat was uncomfortable, and while his partner was ty-
ing on the tag, he leaned over to rest on the shoulder of his dead
companion on the bench. He was zonked. Picking up the dead
was nothing like beating the odds to get to the Emerald City.

When the tag had been fastened, the orderlies—cigarettes
still hanging from their lips—loaded the junkie onto the stretcher
and hauled it over to the van. *We're off to see the Wizard, the wonderful Wizard of Oz* . . . Their movements were hardly light and
agile, but they did manage to bundle the body into the back of
the van, where it took its place among its brothers in misfortune.

"Back to the Corpse Motel, Valek?" Scarecrow asked his older
partner, who apparently carried the weight in their symbiosis.

"Not yet. Palich will bust us. He'll know we're drunk and
open his big mouth. By nine he'll be outta there and we can go
back. We can say the battery went dead. Jump in, we'll go grab
some dinner and call to find out if there are any more runs to
make."

"Whatever you say."

Apparently, as supervisor of the morgue, Palich commanded
the respect of the personnel.

When I handed Valek a copy of the death-scene report and
the cover letter, I tried peering into the back of the van. There
was nothing to see, though. The front seat was screened off from
the back by a thick black cloth. It was just as well. What's the
point of knowing what's in store for you? I hoped it was a long
time before I'd find out.

Valek got behind the wheel, turned the ignition, and the van
waddled slowly off down the narrow park road.

"I have a feeling that's not the last time we'll be seeing them
today," Driver said, his eyes following the van.

"Who knows? Today may be the thirteenth, but it's not Friday. It's Tuesday."

"All the same, it's the thirteenth."

On the way back, we swung by the shopping center to pick up a drunk from the cop stationed there, at the request of Evseyev, who had called us on the walkie-talkie. The drunk turned out to be that same beggar as before. The breadwinning megaphone was fastened around his neck with a sturdy chain, so no one could take it from him. The beggar didn't put up any resistance. It was all the same to him. Unlike ours, his shift was over.

I don't know whether Evseyev ever finished the game of erotic Tetris, but Farid and I didn't get to battle it out over backgammon that night. Reports rained down on us thick and fast. There were family dramas, complaints about noisy neighbors, drunken brawls with the use of sharp objects or cutting implements. There was even a runaway—or a *crawl*away—of a six-foot-long boa constrictor, from the apartment of a rich eccentric. Naturally, we didn't go after it; we sent the owner to EMERCOM.

I just kept on trucking, and, in contrast to my experienced partner, didn't whine, driven by my sense of duty and the dream of moving away from my parents and into my own apartment. The whole time I was counting the hours to midnight, when the thirteenth would give way to a more auspicious date on the monthly calendar.

But the dark powers wouldn't give up. They're not called dark powers for nothing. They delivered their final blow just five minutes before the finish line. Evseyev, their trusty messenger, breezed into the rec room just when we were arranging the pieces on the board.

"Quit loafing, you two—we've got another stiff."

"Aw, gimme a break! This day can go shove it!" Farid said. "Let us play at least one game!"

"Your game can wait. Doesn't look like homicide . . . The wife came home and found her husband dead in front of the door. Looks like she's been drinking. Maybe she even killed him herself. Go check it out. If there's any sign of foul play, I'll send the operative. Here's the address."

That was the third time today we were hearing about the operative.

The courtyard, rain, the jeep, hand crank . . . In a month I'd be ready for some kind of pull-starting engine contest.

The address was in the farthest reaches of our precinct, next to the railroad embankment, in one of the barracks built after World War II by German prisoners. Back then they were barracks, that is. Afterward they repaired them and slapped a bit of plaster on the walls, and offered it to the ex-cons returning from a hard-labor lumber camp who didn't have a place to live. A homey little spot that had earned the name *Blue-Light District* because of its plentiful bashed-up inhabitants, with all manner of bruised faces and shiners. It wasn't a favela in Rio, of course, but strangers were well advised not to set foot there. Locals either, as a matter of fact. It might be hard to find your way out with a shiner that all but blinds you.

We had already been to the district once today about a duel fought by the local "nobility." We separated them when the gentlemen had just squared off to fight, having chosen their weapons (broken bottles, or "roses" as they call them). High society, in other words.

This time I grabbed a flashlight, just in case, since the electricity had been turned off in most of the barracks because of unpaid bills. I prepared myself mentally to come face-to-face with real crime.

The jeep kept a steady course, somehow coping with the absence of a real road. We reached the barracks without incident. Farid was chewing out his beloved Rubin soccer team for losing to Barcelona. "Isn't it time for them to take a short vacation? The coach too. Fifteen days in the drying-up tank should do it.

To get them moving again. Their bosses pay them big bucks, and they don't even bring in a penny. I understand losing to Zenit— but to Barcelona?"

The buildings didn't have any numbers on them, but Farid knew the area like the back of his hand. He could have found any address blindfolded.

"Which pad?" he asked.

"Number eight."

"Third floor," he said automatically, turning off the engine.

We got out of the warm vehicle. The three-story structure appeared black against a still-blacker sky. Fantastic. All we needed was some lightning, a flock of crows, a peal of thunder, and, in the background, an airplane plunging to earth, leaving a trail of smoke in its wake. It was a good thing I brought the flashlight. Candles or torches gleamed here and there in the dark windows. The age of nanotechnologies. Kupchino, St. Petersburg, Russia in the twenty-first century . . . At least the landline still worked, since someone had managed to call the police.

I entered the building first, lighting the way and scaring off the rats. I won't go into any detail about the smells that assaulted us. I'll just say that week-old garbage smelled like Dolce & Gabbana in comparison. On the first landing we were greeted by some petroglyphs, with the message *Dead hedgehogs go north*. The artwork of young junkies—I recognized the elevated style.

The middle-aged woman who had called the police met us at the door. Sitting on the floor. Leaning against the wall. With a half-empty bottle of vodka in her hand. I tried to get her to tell me what had happened. She tried to answer me, but her tongue wouldn't obey her. She had been at the bottle for quite awhile already. Not to mention the stress of the situation. It's a wonder she could dial the number at all.

While I was busy trying to bring the woman to her senses, Farid turned on his own flashlight and ventured into the apartment to take a look. He didn't stay long. Thirty seconds later he was back, crossing himself. Farid the Muslim was crossing himself!

I shone the flashlight directly in his face. It looked like it was made of stone. What had he seen in the apartment? Dismemberment?

"Alex," he said in a hollow whisper. "There's . . . in there . . ."

"What?"

"The builder."

"What builder?"

"The one from earlier. The same one. I'm seeing things. For my sins. Allah is punishing me for my sins."

I had no idea what he was talking about. What did he mean, *the same one*? What sins? Since when did Allah make sinners hallucinate? Pushing aside the babbling wreck of a driver, I boldly went into the apartment, where no policeman had gone before, and noticed that instead of a lock, the door was held shut by the sash of a housecoat tied to the doorknob.

The dead body was lying in the hallway, a few feet away from the entrance, facedown. He was wearing a khaki work jacket. I was already less nervous than I had been in the morning. I was getting used to things. Without feeling any squeamishness I lifted up the head of the already cold body by the hair and pointed the flashlight square in his face.

Then I crossed myself too. I did it without even thinking, and just about dropped the flashlight. It was the builder who had choked on the dumpling, the one I had written up so scrupulously in my morning report. There was no mistaking it. I examined his hand. The oilcloth tag was still hanging on the string.

I stood up, wiping the sweat from my forehead. Just take it easy, I told myself. Two people can't share the same hallucination. Even if Allah really wants them to. Shining the flashlight in front of me, I walked on further. The two-bedroom apartment looked like the interior of a Berber's desert tent. A minimum of furnishings, maximum of cockroaches, dirt, and empty bottles. The bathroom had no door, which theoretically wasn't the end of the world. Not long ago I had been in the castle of some high-born nobleman. He had several bathrooms, all with glass doors. They say it's fashionable. Good design. Especially good for the noble guests and girls in love with the nobleman. It's a place for them to show off their fancy undies. There was probably design in this bathroom too.

I didn't trip over any more dead bodies. I tried to find papers or IDs that would tell me who lived here, but I was unsuccessful. More than likely they didn't even have any. I went back out to the landing. Farid was sitting next to the woman and staring dully into the darkness.

"Get up, buddy. Allah has forgiven you. For the time being. It really is our builder."

Farid stirred. He said, "You're sure?"

"Yup. He's wearing the tag."

"What's he doing here?"

"Stopped by for a visit. Wanted some beer to wash down the dumpling."

I bent over the woman. She had conked out and was snoring loudly through her broad nostrils.

"Do you have any idea what's going on?" Farid said.

"To be honest, my head's gone into a tailspin. She said that it was her husband. But one guy can't have two wives. This may not be the West, but it's not the Orient. And even if he's her husband, he couldn't have come here on his own. He's friggin' dead."

"I agree. Dead men don't walk."

"We'll have to call the duty officer. Explain the whole thing. Have Evseyev call the morgue and get in touch with those block-head orderlies."

"Go ahead."

"Let's get her inside first."

Farid got up off the floor. We grabbed the dame by the arms and dragged her into the first room, steering clear of the builder in the hallway. She seemed to weigh about two hundred pounds. Cursing, we hauled her up onto a three-legged couch. I found a red telephone dating back to the Comintern era in the other room, so I called Evseyev and explained the situation. As I had suspected, he was completely baffled. He told me to stop messing with his head and to return immediately to the department.

I would have been baffled too.

"What are we going to do?" Farid asked predictably.

"No idea. But I'm not writing up a report on him. I've already done it once."

Farid lit up a cigarette. I bummed one off him and started to smoke too, even though I'm a health nut. We were silent for a while, thinking about the unusual circumstances we'd found ourselves in.

"We can't leave him here," Farid said, breaking the silence.

"Are you suggesting we take him to Evseyev? That'll make him happy."

"No, we'll drop him at the morgue. It's not far from here, next to the hospital."

"What do you mean by 'drop him'?"

"We'll load him into the glass and take him there. He's a tough guy, he won't fall apart."

I still hadn't quite figured out all the police jargon, and I had no clue what "glass" could mean here. But I didn't let on.

"Will he fit?"

"We packed eight in there once."

"And what are we going to tell them at the morgue?" I pressed.

"That the body's been registered, they've got the papers, so they should take him. If they don't, we'll just leave him on the doorstep."

On one hand, the prospect of taking care of a stranger's corpse didn't inspire enthusiasm. On the other hand, I wanted to get to the bottom of this and find out how the poor builder had ended up in the Blue-Light District. Curiosity won out.

"Okay, let's do it."

The lady muttered something and turned her face to the wall. Farid glanced around the room, went over to the window, and jerked down a single curtain, stained and discolored. When we went back into the hallway, he asked me to lift up the body and then shoved the curtain under it.

"It should hold."

We grasped the corners of the improvised stretcher and at the count of three elevated the body off the floor. The curtain started ripping, but didn't split. Farid took the lead and stepped out onto the landing, the flashlight lodged under his armpit.

"I wonder," I said, trying to lighten the mood, "how much they pay the orderlies for this little task."

"Maybe they do it for love, not money," Farid replied. "I'm so fed up with my relatives saying, *Why do you bother being a cop? There's no money, no respect in it.* And I figure, how am I going to live as a civilian? I don't even have a car. That's how those orderlies figure too, probably. Money isn't everything, you know. Watch out, here's a step missing. Don't trip."

From somewhere on the second floor, a woman's shrieking cackle rang out, and I almost let go of the curtain. Man, this really was like something out of a B-movie thriller. Dead hedgehogs go north.

I found out what the "glass" was when we emerged from the mildew and stench of the entryway into the fresh air. It was just the area in the back of the jeep for detainees. It was designed for two people. Or sometimes eight. Maybe even more. In any case, the builder would have plenty of room.

We placed him carefully in the rear of the vehicle, and Farid piled the curtain in next to him.

"We'll have to treat the backseat with chlorine tomorrow," he said, closing the glass. "Or we might catch something."

He got behind the wheel and lit up a cigarette. The smoke deodorized the jeep better than any disinfectant could.

"In the old days, when I worked out in the country, I used to drive all the stiffs around in the glass," Farid said with an air of nostalgia.

"Why was that?"

"It was a mess. There was just one morgue for the whole county. And the morgue-mobile only served the town. There was just one car for the rest of the county, and it was always broken. So I had to deliver the body myself, if it was more or less fresh. You can't expect the relatives to bring the body to an autopsy. I remember once we were delivering this guy. Not a homicide. Heart attack. First, we had to swing by the department to get some papers stamped. I stepped out to drink some tea. And across from the department was the drying-out tank."

Farid stepped on the gas, swerving to avoid a water-filled pothole.

"I don't want the engine to die. The alternator is already on its last legs. Right, so what was I saying? . . . Their boss often borrowed drunks from ours. Just for the numbers. Our boss didn't mind—it created more breathing space in the aquarium. On that day there wasn't a single drunk, though. The boss at the drying-out tank begged ours, *C'mon, just give me one, or I'll never be able to leave here.* Our boss was a real card. *Sure,* he said, *take that one in the glass out there, they just brought him in.* A minute later the sergeant comes out of the tank with his nightstick, opens the glass, and barks, *Get out!* The stiff doesn't answer, naturally.

The sergeant shouts again, *Didn't you hear what I said, you goon? I said get out!* Silence. Then the sergeant bashed him over the head with his stick. Then gave him another one in the chest. The dead guy fell out of the jeep. The sergeant was about to pick him up, when he noticed that the sot wasn't breathing anymore. He runs to the duty officer, his eyes popping out of his head, and shouts, *Your drunk out there expired!* The duty officer says, *What do you mean,* expired? *You killed him with your stick! Everyone saw it. We'll have to call the district attorney.* The sergeant makes a break for the door and takes off running. They tried to catch him for two months, but he finally turned himself in. Was exhausted from hiding out in cellars and barns. They forgave him, saying it was only the first time. He's never taken a nightstick into his hands since."

We started driving up the overpass. Farid stepped on the gas once more so he could make it up the incline, but the wheels started spinning on the wet asphalt, and the engine conked out.

"Goddammit!" he barked, smashing his fist against the steering wheel. "The tires are bald. And I forgot to shift into four-wheel drive. Okay, out you go."

He put the emergency brake on and passed me the hand crank. I sighed and climbed out into the rain. But the engine wouldn't turn over—not on the third try; not even on the tenth. Either I was too tired, or the jeep was. Farid, cursing up a storm, climbed out too.

"The morgue is just a stone's throw away. Just over the bridge there."

"What do you suggest we do?"

"We could push it to the middle of the bridge. It'll start when we coast downhill."

"We'll have to stop someone to help us. We can't manage by ourselves."

There were no cars in sight, what with the late hour and all. It was getting close to one in the morning. When my uniform was sopping wet and my shoes felt like I had fishbowls on my feet, a traffic cop driving a Lada drew up alongside our jalopy.

"What's the problem, boys?" the round-faced lieutenant asked, rolling down his window.

"Won't start. Will you help us push? Or pull us, maybe?"

The traffic cop reluctantly got out from behind the wheel and walked around our jeep. "Why are you knocking yourselves out? Put that prizefighter back there to work."

"He can't. He's not feeling well," Farid explained.

"Well, who's feeling good right now? Hey, buddy!" The lieutenant tapped on the glass. "The officers are out here bustin' their asses in the rain, and you're in there chillin'. You scared of a little work?"

"Let him be," Farid said dismissively. "It's like trying to squeeze water from a stone."

"Well, make him get out, at least. It's extra weight. Listen, buster, move your butt."

"Don't," I said, stopping the lieutenant, who was reaching out to open the door. "He's a wild one. He'll get away, and we'll have to chase him all over again."

We finally got the jeep started up, but we had to cut the engine again at the morgue. Farid and I went up to the back entrance and rang the bell. While we were waiting for someone to come, I read a soggy printout that hung on the left side of the door:

Funeral Home
Cheap. Discounts for Wholesale Customers.

Wholesale? Buy three coffins, get one free? Are you friggin' kidding me? They might as well say, *All incoming are free.*

Footsteps sounded from inside, and a light went on in the peephole.

"Who's there?"

"The police. We brought a client," Farid said, pointing to his cap.

The lock and bolt jangled and the door opened. A whiff of something both foul and sweet-smelling escaped outside and enveloped us. An elderly man with a handgun was standing in the doorway. He looked like the night watchman. When he had convinced himself of our good intentions, he tucked the handgun back into his belt.

"Live ammo?" Farid asked.

"Tear gas," said the watchman. The smell of beer suggested that the pensioner wasn't just catching some z's on the job. "Who did you say you brought?"

"A client," I answered. "Where should we unload him?"

"No, no, boys," he said, shaking his head. "We're closed. You'll have to register the person at eight a.m., please, those are the rules. Palich will be here, and you can hand the body over to him. Go on now."

He didn't seem in the least surprised that we weren't transporting the corpse in the official morgue-mobile. Apparently corpses arrived in all kinds of things.

"Look, mister, he's already registered," Farid protested. He didn't seem to relish the prospect of driving the builder around in the jeep until eight in the morning. "We already handed him over to your fellows at eight this morning. Here, look at the tag on his hand!"

"How come you have him then?"

"Found him on the road. I don't know, maybe he fell out or something. Long story short, Pops, this ain't no grocery store you've got here. Don't give me that eight-to-nine business. Show us where to unload him."

The watchman stared mistrustfully at our wet faces and asked us to show him the body. We did. When he had to admit we were telling the truth, he shrugged and nodded.

"All right, bring him in. I guess they really did lose him. Drunken morons."

Then we repeated the trick with the curtain, as a result of which the long-suffering builder was moved to yet another resting place.

"Take him into the freezer," the old fellow ordered us when we had entered the kingdom of the dead. "It's this way."

Thank God we didn't have to go far, or else I might have gotten a hernia or a ruptured navel. The watchman flung open wide doors and turned on a switch.

"Go ahead. Put him in that empty spot."

We were struck by a wave of cold. Here it was—the penultimate stop on the road to eternity. The grave would be the terminal station. To be honest, if I had ended up here in the morning, my nervous system would probably have given out. But now my nervous system had adapted somewhat, insulating me from any deep psychological perturbation. I had never been in a place like this. The watchman wasn't fazed in the least. For me, however, the tables and shelves overflowing with the dead made a strong impression. Especially considering the fact that the appearance of many of them was far from aesthetically pleasing, and some of them had died in far from natural circumstances. There was one, for example, whose leg was no longer even attached to its body. It immediately reminded me of that little Hollywood gem I had seen on the box not long before, *Resident Evil*. People just like this guy suddenly up and came to life again. Not only that, they started forcing themselves on ordinary citizens, striving to get their fill of fresh meat.

The fluorescent lamps in the freezer cast an unnatural light, turning the dried blood on some of the bodies a bright red. Memories to last a lifetime. At a moment like this the only thing I could do to cope was to repeat Farid's mantra to myself: *They won't bite.* Really, what did I have to worry about? They were simply dead people. Dead for good. They can't harm the living. They just lie there. And there they stay. When you see them in some thriller or an action film, no one rushes to turn off the TV. Farid there—he didn't show a trace of emotion. But it set my teeth on edge. It could have just been the cold, though. My feet were already completely numb.

Some of the corpses were fully clothed. They had most likely been brought in not long before and still hadn't been worked over. Farid found an empty space on the farthest table. With his free hand he nudged aside an old woman who was already lying there, then heaved the legs of the builder onto it. After that he helped me with the rest of him. He didn't pick up the curtain.

"Done," he said.

Turning around, he bumped into a stretcher that was leaning against some of the shelves. It clattered down onto a bucket with a mop.

What happened next made my feet and my blood burn hotter than any sauna or any amount of vodka ever could. If I had been a heart patient, the whole incident would have ended with yet another death certificate. For starters, I experienced a tremendous burst of adrenaline. A maiden parachute jump must be pure pleasure compared to what I felt. And I'm pretty sure I lost every last one of my marbles, at least temporarily. The next thing I did was cross myself multiple times, without even thinking about it, for the second time that day. Farid did too, by the way . . . As did the watchman, whose face was the color of an aging bruise from a billy club. So this is what you're like, Ms. Schizophrenia. Well, hello there.

One of the corpses that had been lying peacefully on the table nearest the door suddenly stirred, and then uttered a hoarse expletive. After this it sat up on the table, steadying itself on its neighbor—the junkie we had picked up earlier in the park. I couldn't make out the face of the resurrected one, but I had no burning desire to do so, either.

After crossing myself once more, I froze. My right hand moved automatically to my holster, though I knew from watching those zombie movies that you can't kill them. Farid staggered into the farthest dark corner of the freezer and waited, muttering something about Allah. Now the fiend will look around and notice us, raise his stiff arms up in front of him, groan, and start moving toward us for fresh blood, I thought. And then we'll turn into zombies too, and go back to Evseyev. Boy, will he be happy. Why am I even thinking about that? What's the point in thinking at all?

I raised my gun, because I didn't know what else to do at such a tragic moment in my life. What would you have done if you were in my place? Picture this: a corpse has come back to life in the city morgue. *Hello, I'm back!*

The dead man dangled his legs over the edge of the table and turned toward me . . . My finger rested on the trigger.

An avalanche of life-affirming curses coming from the watchman saved me from a fatal mistake. I won't quote him here. I'll just say that at that moment they worked better than any magic spell of Harry Potter. I realized that the watchman no longer feared for life and limb. Literally or figuratively. He recognized the corpse.

A second later I recognized him too. Or, rather, I recognized his canvas jacket. And when he raised his red calf-eyes to me, I knew it was him. Scarecrow. One of the orderlies. The junior partner.

"Dudes, what are you doing here?"

I put my gun away without answering. Farid seemed to come to life again too.

The watchman just kept up the barrage of curses. "How did you get in here, you son of a bitch?" He dragged the orderly off the table and shoved him up against a cooling pipe. "Are you trying to get me sent up, you miserable pig?"

"Where's Lenka?"

"Who the hell is Lenka?" the watchman roared.

"My wife. Is she here too?"

"We're all going to end up here someday," Farid said prophetically, shaking the blood off his jacket, which had rubbed up against some gangster with a shotgun wound.

The watchman dragged the orderly out of the freezer into the warm corridor. We were right behind them, in case someone else decided to come back to life.

The watchman sat the zombie-wannabe down on a wooden bench in the hallway and subjected him to an emergency purification ritual, threatening him with the gas pistol. We didn't interfere. Judging by the turns of phrase, Mister Watchman had clocked in a few hours in a KGB basement.

"Why are you going off on me?" the orderly said in his own defense. "Just give me a beer. Our shift was over, and I asked Valek to drop me off at home. Ask him yourself . . . Hey, guys, where have I seen you before?"

The former KGB officer didn't give us time to answer. "I'm the one asking the questions around here! How did you end up in the freezer, you enemy of the people?"

"How should I know?" Scarecrow coughed loudly, putting his hand to his heart.

"What do you remember? Tell me now or I'll lock you up in the freezer again!"

"Wait a second. Let me think. So, we picked up the lady from Kupchino to bring her over here . . . I got into the back of the van. Thought I'd lie down for a while to take a snooze. I was dead beat, hadn't eaten anything all day. Valek said he'd wake me up when we got here, and then take me home. He had to drive the van to the garage . . . But where is he now?"

I turned to Watchman. "Did you see them unload the van?"

"No. I only get here at eleven."

"Is there someone who helps them carry in the bodies? From the van to the freezer?"

"No, there's not enough help here. They do it themselves. That's what they're paid for. And they don't have to carry the corpses far when they go through the back. Before he had a partner, Valek did it all by himself. He slung the corpse over his shoulder—and into the freezer he went. He's a strong fellow, for someone who drinks."

Suddenly it all made sense to me. You didn't have to be Sherlock Holmes to figure this one out. Tin Man tried to wake up his partner, but it was the wrong guy. He kept poking and tugging at someone wearing the same kind of jacket—the builder. In the end, he couldn't wake him up, and he unloaded the van himself; but he unloaded it after he dropped off his partner at home. Understandably, he didn't even wake up. He was dead to the world. But no big deal, Tin Man just slung him over his shoulder and took him up to the apartment. The door wasn't locked; it was held shut by only a sash. He opened it and dumped Scarecrow (who was actually the builder) in the hallway, propping him up against the wall. Then he said goodbye and left. The wife was too drunk to realize the corpse wasn't her husband. She called the police and had her private memorial service right away.

"Where do you live?" I asked Scarecrow, just to make sure. "In number eight?"

"Yep . . . How did you know?"

"We stopped by today. Your wife invited us in."

There was still one thing I didn't understand. Wouldn't Valek have noticed that the body of his partner was pretty cold and stiff when he dropped him off? But then it depended on how many "memorial services" they'd had that day, and there seemed to have been plenty.

Farid seemed to have figured it all out too. But there was something else bothering him.

"How does Valek drive the van in that condition?"

"Oh, that's no problem at all," said the watchman. "Valek can be falling-down drunk when he tries to walk, but as soon as he gets behind the wheel he sobers up fast. Experience."

Evseyev's hoarse voice could now be heard barking out of the jalopy. Duty officer demanded we contact him.

"Let's go, we've done our part," Farid said, motioning to me.

"Dudes, can you give me a lift?" Scarecrow asked, his eyes still closed. "If I go on foot I won't get there until morning. My wife must be worried."

"Nah, she took a sedative," Farid said by way of comfort. "And don't forget your curtain in the freezer."

When he was showing us out, Watchman nodded to Scarecrow, still standing in the corridor, and said softly, "Valek doesn't have any luck with partners. They're all saboteurs. Do you know what the last one did? He took the van at night, covered the yellow stripe over with black electrician's tape, and made money picking up people at the train station. Turned it into a jitney. They fired him. People like that should be summarily executed . . . That would get the country back on its feet."

I couldn't get to sleep that night. If you spend the whole day picking mushrooms, you'll start seeing enormous milk mushrooms and orange caps as soon as you go to bed. If you sit in one place with a fishing rod for five hours, you'll have visions of a float bobbing up and down. That's just how the brain works. I had hardly closed my eyes when I started seeing gloomy corpses. Of course, I jumped up from the makeshift bed (chairs pushed together) and looked around the room in terror. I couldn't see anyone except for the peacefully sleeping Farid, so I tried once again to fall asleep.

At around six in the morning the indefatigable Evseyev came into our room. He still hadn't won his computer game.

"Alex, you've got to make a run over to number eight again. To that orderly from the morgue. The paramedics called about some nonsense going on over there. His wife jumped out the window. From the third floor. She fractured almost every bone in her body, but she's still alive. He came home drunk half an hour ago, apparently, wrapped up in a curtain. She saw him and started shouting, *Get thee gone, Satan!* Then out the window she went. I don't like the looks of it. I'm afraid he might have chucked her out himself, and he's trying to pin the blame on Satan. Swing by the place, in any case, and see what you can find out. If it's something serious, I'll call the operative . . ."

THE SIXTH OF JUNE

BY SERGEI NOSOV

Moskovsky Prospect

Translated by Polly Gannon

I was told to forget about this place. Not to come here, ever. But here I am.

A lot has changed, there's plenty I don't recognize. It could have changed still more, on an even grander—*planetary!*—scale, if I had kicked opened the bolt on the door and burst into the bathroom back then.

I hope I don't have to explain for the ten thousandth time why I wanted to shoot Boris Yeltsin.

Enough is enough.

Since I got out, I haven't been to Moskovsky Prospect even once. Tekhnologichesky Institute metro stop was where I disembarked, and then my feet took me where they wanted to go. Everything is close to here. To the Fontanka River it's six minutes if you walk fast. The Obukhovsky Bridge. Tamara and I lived not in the corner building, but right next to it—number 18 on Moskovsky Prospect. Hey, check this out! A restaurant called The Lair. There didn't used to be any lairs here. There used to be a grocery store, where Tamara worked behind a counter. I went into The Lair to take a look at their menu. Bear meat is their specialty. Oh well.

If this is a lair, it would be fair to call the room in the apartment above The Lair, where Tamara and I used to live, The Nest. And if things had worked out differently, there would be a museum now in our nest above the lair. The Museum of the Sixth of June. But a museum was really the last thing on my mind.

I walk into the courtyard. There, with the help of a hoist that raises a worker up to the height of the third floor, a poplar tree is being dismantled in stages. The worker amputates the thick branches with a chainsaw, piece by piece, cut by cut. I used to view that tree with great respect. It was tall. It grew faster than the others, because it didn't get enough sunlight in the courtyard. I used to sit under this poplar in '96 and '97, smoking on the rusty swings. (Today the playground is filled up with wooden blocks.)

This is where I met Yemelianych. He crouched down one day on the edge of the sandbox and, opening up a small vial, downed an infusion of hawthorn berry. I wanted to be alone, and got ready to leave, but he asked me about my political convictions. We got to talking. We shared a lot of the same ideas. About Yeltsin, as was to be expected (everyone talked about him in those days), and about how he should be killed. I said that not only did I dream of doing it, I was ready to do it for real. He said he was ready to do it too. He said that he had been the commander of a platoon of intelligence agents in a certain African country, the name of which he didn't have the right to say out loud. But soon he would, and then everyone would know. I didn't believe him at first. Yet there were details. Lots of details. It was impossible not to believe him.

I told him I had a Makarov (two years ago I had bought it in the empty lot behind Yefimov Street). Many people had firearms back then—those of us who had them hardly tried to hide it. (Well, Tamara didn't know. I hid the Makarov under the sink behind the pipes.) Yemelianych said that I'd have to go to Moscow. That was where all the important events happened. There were more opportunities there. I said my windows looked out on Moskovsky Prospect, and official government delegations often passed along that route. It was significant that the year before I had seen the presidential cortege from my window. Yeltsin was visiting St. Petersburg, since it was getting close to election time. We'll wait. We should wait until he comes back.

But, Yemelianych said, you can't shoot him from the window. They have armored cars.

I knew that. I said that was not what I was going to do.

You have to do it another way, said Yemelianych.

So that's how I got to know him.

And now the poplar will be gone.

Yemelianych was wrong when he said that I got together with Tamara solely because of the view onto Moskovsky Prospect. That's what he thought at first. That's what the investigator thought too. Ridiculous. First of all, I knew myself that it made no sense to shoot out of the window. Or even to leave the house and run to the corner, where the government corteges slowed down to turn onto the Fontanka Embankment. It made no sense to shoot at an armored car. I'm not a complete idiot. I'm not nuts. Although, I must admit, I do let my imagination run away with me sometimes. Sometimes, I have to say, I would see myself running over to the car that had slowed down at the corner, aiming at the glass, shooting, and my bullet hits just the right weak spot, and all the bulletproof glass . . . and all the bulletproof glass . . . and all the bulletproof glass . . .

But that's just first of all.

Second of all: I loved Tamara. It was just by chance that her windows faced Moskovsky Prospect.

By the way, I didn't rat on Yemelianych. I took all the blame.

* * *

I'm not supposed to think about Tamara.

I won't.

I met her . . . well, what difference does it make to you?

Before that I lived in Vsevolozhsk, outside St. Petersburg. When I moved into Tamara's place on Moskovsky Prospect, I sold my apartment in Vsevolozhsk and invested the money in a financial pyramid scheme. There were tons of pyramid schemes back then.

I loved Tamara not for her beauty—of which, to be honest, there was none—and not even because when we had sex she called loudly for help, shouting out the names of her former lovers. I don't know myself why I loved her. She gave me love in return. She had an excellent memory. Tamara and I often played Scrabble. Tamara always beat me. Seriously, I never tried to lose on purpose. I told her lots of times that she should be working in a bookstore on Nevsky Prospect, where they sell dictionaries and the latest novels, not at the fish counter in a grocery store. People don't read much nowadays. Back then everyone read a whole lot.

Like I said, my legs took me here all by themselves. Sooner or later, I would have come here anyway, however much they told me not to think about it.

It's just that in those two years that I was living with Tamara, the poplar grew. Poplars grow fast, even the ones that look like they're fully grown. And when you see something slowly changing before your very eyes in the space of a year, or a year and a half, or two, you figure that you're changing too, along with it. So it was changing, and so was I. And everything around us changed, and definitely not for the better. Except for that tree, which just continued to grow. Long story short, I didn't understand that I had anything in common with that tree. I only realized it just now, when I saw the worker cutting it down. And just by chance I had to stop by this address at the very moment they were cutting down the tree! And all those memories started up in me right then. The ones I'm not supposed to think about.

Her wages were miserable. Mine too. (I used to occasionally fix TVs—old Soviet models with tubes. People still had them, but by the sixth of June, 1997, people didn't even want them fixed anymore.) Anyway, we lived together.

Once I asked Tamara (when we were playing Scrabble) if she would take part in an assassination attempt on Yeltsin.

"In Moscow?" she said.

"No, when he visits St. Petersburg."

"Oh, when is that ever going to happen?" she said. Then she asked me how I was going to do it.

"Like this," I said. The big black cars speed down Moskovsky Prospect. Before they turn onto Fontanka, they generally slow down (because they have to). Tamara runs out in front of the car, falls to her knees, and raises her hands up to the sky. The presidential limousine stops, Yeltsin, curious about what's going on, gets out and asks who she is. And there I am with the handgun. *Bang, bang, bang, bang . . .*

Tamara said that, luckily, I didn't have a gun. Of course she was wrong, because, luckily or not, the Makarov was still under the sink behind the pipes in the bathroom. And there were twenty bullets too, in a plastic bag. But Tamara didn't know a thing about it. She was convinced that no one would stop, anyway, if she threw herself in front of the cortege. And if the presidential limousine stopped, Yeltsin wouldn't get out. That's what I thought too: Yeltsin won't get out.

I just wanted to test Tamara, to know whether she was with me or not.

Then he asked me, shining a light in my face: did I love Tamara?

For some reason, not only the head but the entire bunch of investigators wanted to know the answer to this question. Yeah, I loved her. Otherwise I would never have held out for two years on that noisy, stinky Moskovsky Prospect, even if I had only one passion—to kill Yeltsin.

In fact, I had two passions—my love for Tamara and my hatred for Yeltsin.

Two uncontrollable passions. Love for Tamara and hatred for Yeltsin.

And if I didn't love her, would she really have called me "honey," and "loverboy," and "snookums"?

A lot of people wanted to kill Yeltsin back then. And a lot of them did. In their heads. 1997. The year before that there had been elections. Please, no historical digressions. I've had it up to here with those already. Is there anyone who doesn't know how they counted the votes?

I used to chat with a lot of people in the buildings surrounding our courtyard at 18 Moskovsky Prospect, and every single person denied they voted for Yeltsin in '96. And that's just in one courtyard. What if you take the entire country? I didn't vote. Why vote when you didn't have to?

They did an operation on him, an American doctor remade the heart vessels.

Oh, I'm supposed to forget about this.

I forgot.

I'll shut up.

I'm okay now.

So . . .

So I lived with Tamara.

The papers had recently discussed the possibility of his death on the operation table.

I remember how in one paper, I forget which one, they warned me and others like me against making a life strategy based on expecting him to die.

But I don't want to go into the motives of my decision.

As for Tamara . . .

Haymarket Square is a stone's throw away—at the end of Moskovsky Prospect. They had chased away most of the black-market dealers by then. But you could always sniff out a grapevine that led you straight to a dealer, depending on what kind of dealer you were looking for. In this case—someone selling the thing that goes *bang!*

That's the kind of dealer I found in the vacant lot where Yefimov Street runs into Haymarket Square.

Anyway, it wasn't that Yemelianych supported me in everything—but we were always together. He drank too much, though, and really rotten stuff. He bought it at the kiosks by the Vitebsky train station.

One day he said that he had a whole organization behind him. And that they wanted to take me in.

In our organization, he was one step higher than me, and so he knew others—from our organization, that is. I only knew Yemelianych. He lived in the building next to mine, in number 16. His windows faced the street crossing, and if Yeltsin showed up, he could take better aim. But we didn't plan to shoot at the car. Why shoot at it when it was armored? That's nonsense. That's both suicide and undermining the whole idea. But I said that already, didn't I?

But here's what I haven't talked about yet: we had another idea.

June of 1997 rolled around. On the fifth of June, Yemelianych told me that Yeltsin was coming to Petersburg the next day. I already knew. Everyone who had even the slightest interest in politics already knew.

The president wanted to celebrate the 198th birthday of Pushkin in Petersburg.

Alexander Sergeyevich Pushkin. Our national poet.

I was anticipating the assassination attempt.

Yemelianych told me that the leaders of our organization were laying down a plan. Tomorrow evening, the sixth of June, the president would go to the Mariinsky Theater, formerly the Kirov Opera and Ballet. Someone would take me backstage beforehand. Yeltsin would be sitting in the front row. After that, it would be like when they killed Stolypin.

The only difference would be that I would come out onstage.

The weapon I would use I had bought myself, with my own money, not the money of the organization that Yemelianych was more involved in than me.

But I wasn't thinking about any career ladder.

And what about Tamara? She was already sick of the name Yeltsin. She asked me not to talk about him. Let me tell you something, though: she was afraid that my hatred for him would crowd out my love for her. And she was sort of right. She was right to be afraid. I remember my hatred for him more than my love for her. But I loved her, all right . . . Boy, how I loved Tamara!

I have a good memory too.

Gosha, Arthur, Grigorian, Ulidov, some Vanyusha, Kuropatkin, and seven more . . .

First names, last names, nicknames. I didn't hide anything.

I didn't name Yemelianych, and I didn't betray the organization.

Yemelianych wasn't Tamara's lover.

Them? I betrayed all of them. Why did she have to yell out their names like that?

In the beginning the investigators thought she was an accomplice. They were interested in the network of relationships.

Let them try to figure it out themselves if they want.

It's not my business. It's their job.

In the little park opposite, I met someone from the building next door. Yemelianych pointed him out to me, said they were neighbors.

Yemelianych's neighbor was a writer. With a beard, in a Sherlock Holmes cap. He was often there sitting on the bench.

I think he was crazy. When I asked him whether he could kill Yeltsin, he answered that he and Yeltsin lived in two different worlds.

I asked him: who are you with, the masters of culture? He didn't understand the question.

No, I remembered. I remembered how at the end of Gorbachev's perestroika a large group of writers went to Yeltsin in the Kremlin to show the president their support. And there wasn't a single one among them who would even pitch a glass ashtray at the man! Forty people—that's a lot! And no one probably even checked them for weapons. Anyone could have brought one in. So now I ask: Valeriy Georgievich, why didn't you bring a handgun and shoot Yeltsin? No answer. And I ask: Vladimir Konstantinovich, why didn't you bring a handgun and shoot Yeltsin? No answer. And I ask the others—there were forty of them!—no answer. No answer! No answer from any of them!

And this one, the one with the beard in the park, tells me he wasn't invited.

And if you had been, would you have shot Yeltsin?

Who gets to to be invited? What did you have to write to be invited, so you could shoot Yeltsin?

What do you write, and who needs it, if everything keeps going along just as it is, predetermined by the powers that be?

Sometimes I wanted to become a writer myself. Yeltsin must have needed supporters, and he must have invited new ones to the Kremlin, and I would be one of them—with a handgun in my pants under my belt—and do you think I wouldn't reach for it at the sound of "Dear Fellow Russians," and that I wouldn't do it?

Oh, for that I would write! I would write anything just to be invited!

As for the handgun: I kept it in the bathroom, behind the pipes under the sink.

Tamara didn't know.

Though I told her a million times that he deserved a bullet in his stomach, and she sort of agreed.

Yemelianych I didn't betray, and I didn't betray the organization that was behind him.

The investigation went another route.

Gosha, Arthur, Grigorian, Udilov, some Vanyusha, Kuropatkin, and seven more . . .

I added the writer with the beard too.

It was the morning of the sixth of June. I was still at home. In my mind I was getting ready for the evening's exploit. But I didn't think about fame and glory.

At nine o'clock I was supposed to get a call. Nine, nine fifteen, he didn't call. Why didn't Yemelianych call?

At nine thirty I called him.

He didn't pick up for a long time. Finally he did. I heard a familiar voice, but I realized that Yemelianych was drunk as a skunk. I couldn't believe my ears. How could this be? Yeltsin was already landing! What is your problem? How could you do this? Relax. Chill. Everything has changed. What do you mean, changed? Why? There's not going to be a performance, says Yemelianych. *The Golden Cockerel* is dead. The opera, I mean. (Or the ballet?)

I screamed something about betrayal.

Cool it, Yemelianych said, get ahold of yourself. There will still be another chance. Just not today.

I was stir crazy the whole morning.

The grocery store underneath us was closed for fumigation. They had been spraying for cockroaches since opening that day, and the salesgirls were dismissed early. Tamara came home smelling of chemicals.

On Moskovsky Prospect, I forgot to say, there's a lot of traffic. It's always noisy. In the two years I shared the place with Tamara I learned to live with it.

I was in the room. I remember (although I'm not supposed to remember) that I busied myself watering the plants. Cacti, to be exact. Tamara was taking a shower. Then suddenly it went quiet outside our windows. Though there was still sound coming from the bathroom—the shower. But outside it was quiet. The traffic had stopped.

That could only mean one thing. They were clearing the road for Yeltsin. He had flown in already, and would soon be at our crossing. I knew he was flying in. Of course I knew. According to our original plan, I was supposed to take him out at the opera (or was it a ballet?).

But now the ballet was canceled. (Or was it the opera?)

The Golden Cockerel, Yemelianych said.

Anyway, I'm at the window. All is quiet on Moskovsky. Cops are posted on the far side of the road. No traffic at all. They're waiting. And here comes a cop's Mercedes (or bigger than a Mercedes?) to make sure everything's ready for the president's cortege to roll on through. They always check everything beforehand.

All the same I had to get the gun and head outside. A voice inside commanded me. And another voice inside said: Don't grab the gun, just go outside and take a look, the gun won't work, you know that.

All the same I decided to take the handgun. But Tamara was in the shower.

Tamara bolted the door when she took a shower. She had started to do that in April. She thought that if the shower made a noise it would turn me on—like I'd be out of control. It wasn't like that. Well, not the way she imagined, anyway.

See, we had this one nearly inexplicable episode a couple of months before.

Since then she had started to lock me out.

But I was talking about something. What does the bathroom have to do with it?

Oh, yeah, so I remembered about the hiding place, and ran to the bathroom and banged on the door. I shouted, Open up!

Again? Tamara yelled (pretending to be mad). Get lost! Calm down!

Open up, Tamara! There's not a second to lose!

Get lost! I won't open up!

But she didn't know I had a gun hidden behind the pipes.

What if she had known?

What did she know, anyway? What was she thinking? She didn't know a thing about me. She didn't know I wanted to kill Yeltsin. And that the hiding place was in the bathroom.

And if I was really so turned on by the sound of the shower, wouldn't I have broken down the door? After that time in April I had a lot of opportunities to break into the bathroom when she was in the shower, but I never smashed the bolt. Plus, she was provoking me (I realized it later on) on purpose.

Anyway.

I would have smashed the bolt, if a voice inside me hadn't stopped me—a second one, not the first. Calm down, it said. Go outside and act all cool and casual. The gun won't be of any use to you. The plan has changed. Go outside and take a look. Just hang out there. Until he passes by.

I ran outside in my bedroom slippers, so as not to waste another second.

I ran out of the building but slowed down to a normal pace in the courtyard. I walked out onto the sidewalk. Yeltsin hadn't passed by yet. There were people strolling down the sidewalk. Just as they always did. A few people stopped and looked into the distance. Far away, behind the Obvodny Canal, the Triumphal Gate was visible, a memorial to the war with Napoleon.

Usually, when government dignitaries were passing through, they closed the streets at least ten minutes beforehand, so there was still time.

From the Fontanka Embankment side, they had blocked off traffic. There were cars waiting there. I couldn't see them from where I was, though.

It was strange to gaze across the empty street. The emptiness was alarming, somehow. There wasn't a single parked car. They had towed them all away.

Another police car whizzed by. It turned from Moskovsky to the Fontanka—to the left, that is. There was plenty of room there.

It was no secret that Yeltsin would drive along that route. It was the only route.

I peered up at the roof of the Railroad Engineering Institute. Were there snipers anywhere?

There didn't seem to be.

* * *

My situation was this: On my right hand over the Fontanka River was the Obukhovsky Bridge. Across the street was a park, a traffic light, and a cop's sentry box. A historical site—a tall milestone in the shape of a marble obelisk—in the eighteenth century the city boundary followed along the Fontanka here.

I remember every second of the events that followed. Here they come—they are getting closer, driving down Moskovsky. The presidential limo wasn't first in the cortege, but the first car had already reached me, and then slowed down—there was a left turn coming up ahead. I'm looking, of course, at the president's car. And others are looking too, not just me; other bystanders and people just walking by. And I'm looking and thinking, Is that really him in the car? Or is it just a decoy? A decoy in a real armored car? And then I see his hand. It's definitely his, waving slightly in mute greeting—behind glass, in the backseat—and who's he waving to, if not me? Sure it's me! That was when he was right in front of me.

Putting on the brakes. Slowing down. (There's a turn up ahead.)

Then something completely improbable happens. Someone's shadow intercepts him. I couldn't figure out who it was at first, a woman or a man. And when I saw that it was a woman, I thought, Could it be my Tamara? Did Tamara pick up my hint?

My heart started pounding, thinking about Tamara.

But how could it be Tamara, when she was in the shower? Of course it wasn't her!

Then something even stranger happened—the car stopped. And others behind it. The whole cortege. And then the strangest thing of all: he got out.

The door opened, and he got out!

It was the sixth of June, 1997.

* * *

He stood about ten paces from me, and that woman was standing there too—about fifteen paces away!

Pretty unbelievable, but that's how it was. He got out of the car and went up to her!

And all his minions started to get out of their cars and go up to the woman in solidarity with him.

The mayor! He got out too!

And Chubais!

What, you don't know Chubais? I'm not supposed to think about him. But how can I forget him? How can I forget?

And bystanders who just happened to be there, they started to go up closer to him too, and I went with them . . . Without thinking about it, along with them, step by step—closer and closer—to him!

It was like the way it used to be, before!

In the old days, when he—it happened a few times, actually—mingled with the people! At a factory, in the market, on the street, somewhere else . . .

He mingled boldly with the people.

I heard—we all heard—their conversation.

A woman of about forty. She stopped the presidential cortege. You're not going to believe this, but she talked about conditions in the libraries.

She said: There are big problems with the libraries, I'm a teacher, I teach Russian literature and language, and I know very well how matters stand, Boris Nikolaevich. And what's more, Boris Nikolaevich, librarians and teachers, not to mention doctors in the polyclinics, have very low wages.

And he answered her: That's not right, we have to fix this.

And his assistant said: We'll definitely fix the problem, Boris Nikolaevich.

And I thought: Where's my gun?

I didn't have my gun with me!

And suddenly she tells him who she is: My name is Galina Aleksandrovna, I live on 9–11 Maklina Street in a room that I share with my grown boy . . . The building is in terrible shape, I live in a communal apartment . . .

And he tells her: We'll give you a new home.

And the assistant tells her: We'll take care of everything.

And this was all happening right in front of me! I was there! And I didn't have my gun!

Other people also started to ask him things, but they were more vague and confused. He wasn't interested in them.

I wanted to ask him something too: Boris Nikolaevich, is it true you're going to the ballet tonight? (Or the opera?) I still hadn't lost hope. But just then a broad back blocked me off from the president.

But even if I had asked, they wouldn't have told me a thing.

The investigator, by the way, was kind enough to show me a newspaper: Yeltsin, it turned out, laid a wreath at the Pushkin monument on that day.

Then the president put his heavy body back in the car. And all his minions and assistants ran to get into their cars. And the whole cortege started to move, and turned from Moskovsky onto Fontanka.

The teacher stood there and watched them drive off. Journalists from the president's press corps surrounded her. A lieutenant-colonel asked us to clear the road.

Soon the traffic was moving again on Moskovsky.

And I snapped out of it.

I stood under the traffic light in my slippers and thought that fate would never give me another chance like that. Why hadn't I broken down the bathroom door? But could I really have guessed that something like that would happen, and that he would get out of his armored car?

I could have! I could have foreseen it!

Coulda shoulda woulda.

I saw myself shooting the president. I saw him fall. I saw the expressions of shock on the faces of the bystanders who couldn't believe they were freed from the tyrant.

I could even have saved myself. That wasn't my aim, but I could have dropped the gun and run into a back alley to escape.

I could just see myself running into the courtyard at number 18 and crossing it. The ones who were smart and alert would race after me, then think, What kind of an idiot is this? There's a dead end there . . .

Me, an idiot? No, you're the idiots! How about the passage on the left? There's a pretty wide opening between the blind wall and the corner of a five-story building. So I run past the poplar that they hadn't cut down yet, and I head left, and now I'm already in an oblong courtyard that doesn't have a single entrance into the building, not counting the doors to the former dry cleaners . . .

How's about that, eh? There are two ways out of here—through the courtyard at 110 Fontanka, or through the courtyard at 108 Fontanka, past the concrete ruins of an ancient outdoor bathroom. Better through 108. No one is expecting me on Fontanka! Or I could race up the stairs to the roof, it's amazing to walk on the roofs here! You can make your way all the way to the Tekhnologichesky Institute metro stop climbing from roof to roof. Or I could scramble up a blind brick wall, that's an idea, onto the sloping roof of a structure they added on to the veteran's hospital . . . Through the hospital grounds I could get to the passage leading to the Vvedensky Canal real fast. Or over the fence—to Zagorodny Prospect, from the other side of the block.

I could easily get away.

Or I could stay. I could give myself up. I could say: Russia, you're saved!

Oh, they'd erect a monument to me! Right there in the park across from Tamara's building. Right next to the marble milestone, nineteenth century, by the architect Rinaldi.

Only I don't need a monument. And I don't need a memorial plaque on Tamara's apartment building.

You don't know how much I loved Tamara!

You can't imagine how much I hated Yeltsin!

And I missed my chance. I wandered through the city, over to Haymarket, then along Gorokhovaya Street. When I was crossing the wooden Gorstkin Bridge, I wanted to drown myself in the filthy waters of the Fontanka. Wooden posts poked out of the water every which way (they guard against the spring ice floes); I looked at them and wondered how I could go on in this life.

I should have drowned myself! It would have been much better.

I don't remember where else I went, I don't remember what I was thinking exactly. I don't even remember whether I stopped into that lowlife pub on Zagorodny. The investigation proved I was sober. But I felt like I was out of my mind.

One thing I know for sure: I'll never forgive myself.

It doesn't get dark at night in June in this city, but I felt like it was dark, or maybe it was just my eyes that made everything that way. I remember that I came home. I remember that Tamara was watching TV. I didn't want her to hear the shot, I wanted to shoot myself in the courtyard. I went into the bathroom, took the gun, loaded it. I hid it under the belt of my pants. I stared at myself in the mirror.

My face looked horrible. When I shoot myself it will look still worse.

I decided not to say goodbye to her. And then she came out of the kitchen, where she was watching TV, and that's when she said it to me.

She said it to me.

She said: Where were you? You missed it all. Do you know what happened? You won't believe it, it's all over the news! Guess what happened today right under our window! A teacher stopped Yeltsin's car! She lives in a single room with her grown-up son, and Yeltsin promised to give her a new home!

I froze.

You all keep giving Yeltsin hell, Tamara said, and he promised to give her a new home.

Fool! Fool! Fool! I shouted.

And I shot her five times.

I didn't try to hide anything, and during the first interrogation I admitted that I wanted to kill Yeltsin.

They took me away somewhere. I was questioned by high-ranking officials. I told them about the gun, about the pipes in the bathroom. I named all the names, because they thought that I killed an accomplice. Gosha, Arthur, Grigorian, Ulidov, some Vanyusha, Kuropatkin, and seven more . . . plus the writer guy with the beard.

Only Yemelianych I didn't give away. And the organization behind him.

At first they didn't believe me that I acted alone, and then they stopped believing anything at all.

Weird. They could have believed me. Back then they were uncovering assassination plots right and left. The security service reported it. Even before me, I remember, they uncovered a gang from the Caucasus. They took them right from the train in

Sochi before they could get to Moscow. One potential killer hid in some attic in Moscow, he had a knife with him—he confessed during the investigation. I don't know what ever happened to him. They wrote about it in the papers. It was on the radio.

But about me there was nothing. Not a word.

Everyone heard about the teacher, Galina Aleksandrovna, who lived on Maklina Street and stopped Yeltsin's car on Moskovsky Prospect. But about me, nothing. Not a word.

I still don't know for which African country Yemelianych fulfilled his international duty.

Professor G.Y. Mokhnaty, MD, respected me. He treated me well. But it wasn't easy, I kept thinking about a lot of things.

He recommended that I just forget about those years.

I live in Vsevolozhsk with my disabled father, whose second wife died. I have a father. He's an invalid.

Sometimes we play Scrabble. My father can hardly walk, but his memory is as good as mine.

This is the first visit I've made to St. Petersburg in a long time. I'm not supposed to be here. They recommended that I not come here anymore.

I regret that everything happened like it did. I didn't want to kill her. It's all my fault.

But how can I explain to anyone how much I really loved Tamara? If you've loved someone even a little bit you'll understand. She had so many good qualities. I didn't want to. But it was her too. She shouldn't have. Why did she? To say something like that with all her good qualities! You can't be such a complete fool. You can't. Fool! A complete fool! Fool, fool, I tell you!

WAKE UP, YOU'RE A DEAD MAN NOW

BY VADIM LEVENTAL

New Holland

Translated by Ronald Meyer

Everything finally started coming together when I was walking across the Lieutenant Schmidt Bridge. In a word, I was pretending that my nose itched, but I was actually sniffing my fingers (sometimes you happen to suddenly sense a forgotten smell so clearly that it's as though it's not a matter of memory, but rather that those same molecules suddenly landed on your snotty nose)—and then my phone rang.

It was raining buckets, the zipper on my jacket got stuck, no choice but to hold the umbrella under my arm and hunch over so I could undo my jacket and get my phone from the inside pocket, and so I pushed the button like a spastic, pressed the phone up to my ear, and heard Stepanych say, "What's new?"

I told him there was nothing new. He mumbled a few more words to the effect that nothing much was new with him either, that something's moving along, but so far nothing definite. Then he asked: "Did you tell anybody?"

I said no, and Stepanych hung up with the words, "Well, make it there then."

I put the phone back in my pocket, pulled up the zipper with a jerk, and walked on, cursing under my breath. The wind was blowing rain under the umbrella, the vans rumbling over the metal joints of the bridge splashed arcs of water in their wake, and I took an envious look at the enormous white ocean liner that had arrived from God knows which country, where they certainly didn't have anything like this horrid weather—but that wasn't the point really; I'd forgotten the smell. It had been erased from my memory, all that was left was cold logic: a young boy, who had caught the scent of his first girl on his fingers, had walked across this very bridge, moving away from her sweet, almost childlike face—but the particulars of that indistinguishable face disappeared as quickly as the seventeen years in three steps.

Therefore, it wasn't just the rain that put me in a rotten mood. I needed to find shelter for a bit, but there wasn't any place in this damned part of the city—an eternity passed before I happened upon some door: turned out to be a nightclub. It wasn't anything special. It wasn't busy yet, so I took a seat at the bar and waited for a chance to order something: the girl behind the bar (whose face would have been cute without that spur-of-the-moment piercing) was talking away with her girlfriend across the counter. I couldn't see the girlfriend very well—the way the bar was constructed blocked my view. I waited and waited, and then I lost my patience and grumbled something rather sharply, and then the girl reluctantly turned in my direction, while her girlfriend leaned over to get a look at me.

A minute later, with a glass in my hand, I was already thinking what I should say—I wanted her to lean over again, I didn't get a good look the first time. But I couldn't come up with anything better than to ask: "Why Toasted?"

"What?"

"Why is it called Toasted? What, do you eat toast here?"

The girl behind the bar looked ironically in the direction of her interlocutor and turned her back to me: from the twinkling darkness, rumpled hundred-ruble bills stretched in her direction demandingly.

"There are two types of people," her girlfriend leaned over once more to make certain that I was listening, and once more I didn't manage to get a good look at her, "some ask whether we eat toast here, and the others what we toast to."

She then walked off in the direction of the stage and flew up there like she owned it, though I didn't have a chance to be surprised—my phone started ringing, not the one in my jacket, but the one in my jeans, and that meant that it was time. I quickly said where to wait for me, drank down my bourbon in a single gulp, and walked outside; the girl was settling in behind the keyboard, I managed to hear her begin to finger the keys as I fiddled with my umbrella: it seems the rain was pouring down even harder.

And here was my single error in all of this: I had managed to forget that in Piter the way from point A to point B is never the same as from B to A, and I ended up on the cheerless, narrow embankment a good deal earlier that I needed to. I took shelter in the doorway—it smelled, as it always does, but when you smoke it's not so noticeable. I smoked a couple of cigarettes, pacing back and forth from an ink-black corner on one side to the corner on the other side, which was a blackish brown in the flickering streetlight in the courtyard, until the phone in my jeans started vibrating.

"Well, I'm standing across from a big archway." I told him that he needed to drive slowly around New Holland.

"New Holland? What's that?"

I explained that the dark patch to his right was New Holland; that seemed to make him happy.

"And so where are you then?"

His car whizzed by a couple of times; the headlights picked out the fish eyes of the puddles and the wet tentacles of the bushes on the other side of the ditch—he wasn't being tailed. The third time I stepped out from my cover in advance and, after opening my umbrella with a loud smack, I walked over to his vehicle—turned out he has a Lexus. The guy was uncommonly sociable and seemed pleased with life.

"Why sit in the back? Want to come up front?"

I declined.

"Where are we going? Want to stay here for a bit? Or drive around? Go figure, I've been living in this city for twenty years and didn't know it was called New Holland."

The man was impeccable—suit, leather seats, and chocolate laced with cocaine. He even had a business card: *Financial Analyst*. I chuckled when he held it out to me.

"Basically, as far as your situation goes . . ." He somewhat cheerfully but with a great deal of confusion started to explain about my situation, who he called and who he talked to; I didn't know any of the names. "To be honest, they laughed at me when I told them. Like, *Do you need Gazprom too?* and so on. And I started to have doubts myself, like maybe it was a practical joke or something." He kept glancing in the rearview mirror, trying to get a good look at me, but I knew where to sit. "Basically, there was a call this morning. They said that maybe there is something, but, like, they want to hear something definite and so on and so forth. Andrei Petrovich—does the name mean anything to you? Me neither. He said he was Andrei Petrovich. Basically, the way it's going to work . . ." He started to explain with visible pleasure how much money he wanted.

Through the tinted window you could only see the pale corners wrapped in a gloomy shroud—streetlights, windows, stop signals—whirling, turning, turning—and I thought that's how the pale luster of stolen gold (you know, the gold is always stolen) would look from the porthole of a submarine gliding along the bottom of the sea.

"So should we talk tomorrow?" He stopped the car at the same gateway where I got in.

I had already grabbed hold of the door handle, but I thought that I should say something, even if he didn't believe me.

"If you want my advice," I said, "disappear as quickly as possible. Throw away your cell phone, change your clothes, abandon your car, and take a commuter train as far away as you can. It would be best if you didn't even stop by your place."

"What??"

What else did I need to explain to him? The door softly swooshed closed behind me; I was about to open my umbrella, but it turned out that the rain had stopped. He revved the Lexus, then the car jumped forward and hurtled away through the puddles.

I turned around: in front of me, wrapped up in a greasy velour coat, stood a little old woman—and when she raised her head (it was bald, that head; wisps of hair hung here and there, but it appeared more like mold that had set in from dirt and damp), I would have cried out, if fear and loathing hadn't left me dumbstruck, because she had tenacious and greedy eyes, one of which she winked at me, after twitching her nose as the Lexus drove away—and I almost let out a groan, in any case some sort of wailing sound began to arise from under my ribs, but the old woman had already passed me by and was scurrying away. Her hands were folded behind her back, and her raggedy empty bag swung back and forth.

Cold, black waves of terror washed over me one after the other. To find myself in the emptiness and darkness of an apartment would have been like death. I needed a crowded, noisy place as much as I needed air to breathe—the terrible old woman's eyes kept dancing in front of me. I flinched. All I could see was the predatory, damp darkness.

The rhythm of my gait, the senseless snatch of conversation— "We'll think about it"—made my heart begin to thump as if it had broken loose from a chain. It suddenly occurred to me that because of all the scrambling around I did today, I seemed to have forgotten to take my pills, and so I should take them—but the main thing was that maybe there wasn't anything particularly terrible in that effing simple old woman from Kolomna. Nevertheless, the glass door of Toasted was lit up, and it would have been silly not to drop in.

Turned out she sings. The evening was coming to an end— that's probably why she was singing something dreamily melancholy. I managed to drain half a glass in the time that she kept repeating a hundred times: *"When you die asleep your dreams will keep on going . . . When you die awake you just die . . ."*

Later, when she got down from the stage and took the seat next to me, to get the conversation going (and she turned out to be very, very pretty: an exquisite face with wide eyes, sculpted cheekbones, and determined, thickly painted lips) I asked her about the song. She turned toward me, took a sip from her glass, and said: "It's a Buddhist song. About the right way to die."

I think that I'm only now beginning to understand what she had in mind; but then I simply didn't pay any attention—I was much more taken with the movement of Nadya's lips. She asked me what I did, I said that I was a private investigator (and jokes about a hat, cigar, and the femme fatale), I asked her how old she was ("You look sixteen, but when you sing—it's like you're thirty-five"), then we walked around (it was clearing up in the city, and it started to look like an antique silver damask; I was forced to admit that I hadn't been in the city for more than a decade, so I didn't know where you could go now to get a decent bite to eat), she kept asking me about London, and I kept trying to make her talk: I wanted to hear her voice again and again, all night long—finally we ended up on Repin Street and decided it was stupid for her to try to find a taxi and take her God knows how far.

I'd like to meet the man who wouldn't have mentally undressed her if he found himself in my shoes. But when we were heading up and I tried to kiss her, she slipped away and said that she wasn't going to sleep with me. I sighed and made a farting noise with my lips (we were drunk), but no means no, all those schoolboy games—an hour on the T-shirt, an hour on the bra, an hour on the pants, an hour on the panties, and an hour and a half to persuade her to spread her legs, and then to be too fed up to want anything besides giving her a smack on the head—no, no, that's not for me; I poured myself a cognac, showed Nadya where the bathroom was, and went to bed. As I was falling dead asleep, I remembered that I still hadn't taken my pills.

II

Next morning I found her lying next to me in bed ("Sorry, there weren't any sheets anywhere, and you were already asleep . . .")— but how could I help myself from making a pass at Isolde in the morning, and what kind of Tristan am I with a hangover? She plunged deeper into sleep, I went to the kitchen to squeeze some juice, and I had almost a full glass when the phone started ringing and I remembered that I was supposed to meet Yura. I walked over to the window, moved the curtain aside, and saw that he was circling the column as he explained that he had already been waiting five minutes. I told him to calm down and sit on the bench for another ten minutes, finished squeezing the juice, put a glass by Isolde's bedside and my spare set of keys next to the glass—you see, I like sentimental gestures.

I wasn't trying to be clever when I told Stepanych that I didn't want to go to Piter—it's terrifying and dangerous, though to some degree there was a plus-side as well: Yura. Yura was wearing a suit now, and it looked like an expensive one (he didn't sit down, but waited for me standing), but there was a time when he wore ripped jeans—it was his style, to get out of his father's car wearing ripped jeans. (The ripped jeans weren't the style, they were simply ripped jeans.) I was waiting for the wonder of recognition—the same whimper and joy with which my heart greeted the Rumyantsev Garden with its gloomy, forgotten column and empty summer stage, and the littered backyards of the academy, and the view of the shipyards: a flock of steel-blue birds which had alighted on some carrion—but no, Yura was simply a benevolent operator, and it's frightening to share memories with people like that. I gave him the photographs and envelope. As we were getting ready to part, I told him "Thank you," and he said, "I haven't done anything yet," but I thought that there was something to be grateful for—the fact that he didn't stop to see if it was all there. Yura left; I was still sitting on the bench, smoking. A cold wind was blowing, the sky was clear, like porcelain. Given the chance, I would have burst into tears at the impossibility of dissolving without a trace in the icy, still transparency of Petersburg.

Stepanych called me precisely at that moment.

"Listen, Stepanych, you told me yourself to sit on my ass quietly and not show myself. To let you know if they start following me. And now you ask me what I'm doing? I'm sitting quietly on my butt."

He burst out laughing. "You're a chip off the old block. He'd lie there with his legs raised for several months too, and then he'd move like a whirlwind, you couldn't keep up with him."

I didn't say anything.

"Excuse me. I liked your dad a lot . . . Well, if something comes up, call me."

I hadn't been gone for long—I went out to buy some oranges and a fresh baguette—but when I returned my bed was made and the glass had been washed. It was disgustingly quiet in the apartment, and to keep from hearing this silence (it's funny, but Stepanych was absolutely right: the main thing for me now was to wait for the call from the guy in the Lexus—I didn't doubt for a moment that he would shrug off my warnings), I went to bed. On the pillow next to me lay several of her hairs, I gave them a good sniff and it seemed that maybe, just maybe, the pillow really did still carry the sweet secret of Isolde's scent.

I hung out at Toasted every night (even Miss Piercing stopped turning her nose up at me), so it's quite possible that certain events got shuffled around in my memory, either on that same day, or altogether: that night I woke up with the sense that I wasn't completely awake and made my way to the club as though I were in some sort of milky fog (while I was sleeping, the wind pounded the rain, and once again it was drizzling), and what's more, while I was walking I even glanced a few times at my palms, to make certain that I wasn't walking in my sleep— somebody had told me that you can't look at your own palms in a dream. It was probably that night, just after I'd taken a seat at the bar and stuck my finger in the bottle, when her voice announced from the stage that among us there was a private detective and that she was dedicating her performance to him—and after that she sang for an entire hour "Sway," "Put the Blame on Mame," "Amado mio," and for some reason "Quizas, Quizas, Quizas." I was intimately familiar with all of them—down to the last note. That evening or some time later she sang "the Buddhist song about the right way to die" again—I'm not sure when. In any case, it was definitely one of those evenings, because I wouldn't have remembered it from hearing it the first time.

Occasionally she would come down from the stage and sit with me, but we didn't drink as much as we had that first night—not that night, or later on. All the more so as that night I ended up getting my call, I went outside to talk (the guy was mumbling with exaggerated bravado; I understood at once that everything had come together, and without even thinking I set up another meeting in the Rumyantsev Garden), and after that I never went back to the club; as I was saying goodbye to the "financial analyst," I noticed the bald old woman on the other side of the street.

At first I automatically took several steps in her direction, but then I lost sight of her for a moment. When she appeared again, I began to catch up with her—I needed to get a look at her face, but I felt a bit awkward: maybe it wasn't the woman. I walked for a fairly long time; the opportunity to get a casual look didn't present itself—she wasn't hiding her face, it simply didn't work out. In the end, she disappeared, she suddenly dove into a gate or a door; after taking a look around, I heaved a deep sigh as I straightened myself: I could just make out the archway of New Holland in the violet darkness.

As I was crossing back across the bridge (maybe I had sobered up, or maybe it was on account of the old woman—in any case, I was in a real shitty mood) it occurred to me that New Holland and the Rumyantsev Garden could be (or to be more exact: had always been) the heads of two screws with which my Petersburg had been joined to nonexistence, to the Neva. New Holland—empty, overgrown, almost in ruins, with its cyclopean triumphal arch—it might be that it was the only thing left of imperial, Rome-like Petersburg, and it would only take a greedy bat with his shitty investments to get to it to build some disgusting Hamburger Bahnhof for the whole city, with a gnashing sound, to become set loose from this swamp and, listing to one side, take on water, and float out into the open sea.

Later Nadya laughed, as if to say, *Do you always give a girl the keys to your apartment right away instead of giving her your telephone number?* I said I only did it when the girl knew the right way to die, but the compliment seemed to fall flat. That was the next day, when I photographed her. After the meeting in the Rumyantsev Garden, which I observed from the kitchen window, I understood that I needed photographs of her. A black BMW with tinted windows pulled up, the pale financial analyst got out from the backseat. At first he walked around the column, then he started to phone (the phone on my table blinked silently). After twenty-five minutes he glanced in the direction of the car, nodded, and slowly walked back, but just a few steps away from the vehicle he jumped up and took off running in the direction of Repin Street. The car doors slammed shut twice, the guy made an angry gesture with his fist, and as he flew down the street, he came crashing down headfirst on the curb. The Beemer pushed off with a quiet swoosh.

I photographed Nadya first in the club—on the stage, at the bar, and she came out dark on a dark background, the thing wasn't cooperating (I hadn't bothered to read the instructions)—and then later in my apartment; there I managed to get her unawares in the bathroom flooded with halogen light on the background of ceramic tiles as white as teeth—just the thing. She slammed the door shut with a crash, and I chose the shot in which she had just turned around and hadn't had time to open her mouth— and I dialed Yura's number. First I dictated the license plate number of the Beemer, and then I asked how the document was coming.

"It'll be taken care of tomorrow, why?"

"I need another one."

"What the fuck! Do you want to be Sovereign of the Seas as well?

"My dear boy, don't worry, I know the price. The premium for fucking with your head is an extra 50 percent. Well?"

Yura heaved a sigh and said that he would try. "Exactly the same kind?"

"No, it's for a girl."

"I should have known, people don't change," Yura burst out laughing.

The noise from the water in the bathroom had stopped, so I quickly finished what I had to say to Yura and threw the phone down. Nadya was beautiful, like a newly born Venus, and she even let me kiss her, but when I tried to slide my palm under her bathrobe, she pulled away and said that she didn't sleep with cheeky private detectives.

"So who do you sleep with?" What else was there to say?

"Only with those who know the right way to die," she said, and then stuck her tongue out at me.

I had completely forgotten about my pills—I'd remembered several times, but reluctantly: I was enjoying this sensation of self-control and concentration, and I needed to keep feeling like that: it was a winning combination, but only if I played my cards right. Moreover, I just wasn't up to taking them; in the evening I fell asleep on the same bed as Nadya (but alas not under the same sheet), and in the morning I woke up next to her—that's just how things turned out.

The keys stayed with her once again—I left before light, before dawn, in order to catch Yura, and she and I didn't meet until evening at Toasted. Coming back from Yura's, I got lost in the Kolomna streets which are as straight as pipes—I deliberately decided to return on foot: at first it was amusing, I didn't ask directions on purpose, the streets and the river twisted around, came together (I probably hadn't sobered up completely). The Pryazhka flowed into the Moika, the Moika pretended to be the Kryukov, the Kryukov ran off to one side, it seemed like several hours had passed, I was deeply agitated, cursing under my breath—when I finally dragged myself to the apartment, Nadya was already gone, and I collapsed on the bed, putting the phone down nearby. On the pillow lay her hairs, just like the day before yesterday.

I had night sweats, tossed and turned from one side of the bed to the other, and only at Toasted that night—Miss Piercing kept giving me a hard time, and among other things claimed I'm lying when I say that I'm a private detective, private detectives don't just sit around drinking in bars all day long; on the contrary, Nadia retorted, that was *all* they did, and she sang a bit of "As Time Goes By," but I nevertheless had to answer the question about what I was investigating (the loss of a document from a leading company's managerial file, I duly reported to the ensuing serving of her giggles)—did I remember that earlier in the day I had been wrenched from sleep by Stepanych's phone call and he'd told me to be ready for anything, and kept stressing that his guys, who were sitting there waiting like a fire brigade, would be on the move as soon as the alarm was sounded.

"We can't get by without the guys?"

"Maybe in your Berlins and Londons you can get by without the guys, but here you snooze you lose, or as the Germans say, *In die grossen Familien nicht with the beak klats-klats!* (I at once recalled how as I child all those generals with whom my father had business would make me feel sick with their stupid jokes.)

Miss Piercing kept pestering me, and I didn't understand why, until—it seems it wasn't that night—I asked her almost out of nowhere whether she was into women, and it turned out that I hit it on the nail. After Stepanych's call (or to be more precise, after I remembered it in the club) I saw with the clarity of an advertising photo of a resort flooded with sunshine that the main thing for me was not to come unhinged.

An additional complication was that I had become restless, I couldn't sit still, I was rushing up and down streets, checking whether I was being followed (I covered my tracks: I'd walk through courtyards, transfer from one trolley to another, go around in circles), or I'd try a bit of shadowing myself—from time to time it seemed like I glimpsed that ill-fated old woman. I was tormented by the certainty of what was taking place and at the same time by the suspicions aimed at me, and this vile murk was cut through here and there by moments of fruitless illumination: so, I understood that by sending me away, the old man, of course, wanted to protect me from the necessity of thinking about the company (he evidently took it as his and only his personal hell), although he talked about a PhD, but even he had hardly formulated for himself the main thing—that he wanted to get me out of the cold trap of Petersburg, even at the cost of being obliged to remain in it forever; after all, the old man had taken the position that the only way for him to leave Petersburg was a bullet fired from the barrel at a speed of 350 meters a second.

It was easier at Toasted. Miss Piercing and I engaged in banter, I'd point out some girl—"She's pretty, isn't she?"—and she'd wave me away (and when she got really wrecked, she'd become candid: "Beauty is in the movement of the soul, and they all have cellulite instead of a soul"—while trying not to look at Nadya), while Nadya and I got drunk, then went for a stroll, and off to my place.

I slept with Nadya the sleep of the dead (she unfailingly and good-heartedly declined my ritual solicitations), and in the afternoon the vile old woman was catching up to me in my dreams—in the worst of these I was riding with her in the backseat of a car and was afraid to turn toward her because I didn't want to give myself away, but I couldn't help it and started to steal furtive glances at her: she remained indifferent, didn't budge, and from her nostril appeared the squirming end of a transparent brown worm brought out by the rain, it slowly knocked against her lip, first here, then there, gathering together and unfurling the rings of its segments—it was precisely from that dream that Yura's call jolted me awake, and, still writhing from terror, I scribbled on a scrap of paper the name of the bank where the BMW was registered.

This dream chased me down another time, when I was out walking (morning, after a rainfall—the damned rain kept coming down) and I saw that the road teemed with worms and remembered that this had already happened once—a long time ago, when I was a kid (my left arm held tight in my mother's warm hand), staring in wonder at the Worm Kingdom: you couldn't take a step anywhere.

Stepanych didn't call; from time to time I began to doubt myself, my plan, fearing that basically this was all raving nonsense and that I had come tearing to Petersburg on business, that Stepanych had in fact called—until this nightmare finally ended: Yura came through with the documents. But I was worn out.

III

The last two days: all that remained was to create out of water the reptiles and so forth as set down in the Bible all the way up to man. In the morning I called Stepanych and said that I couldn't take it anymore (it was the absolute truth: I couldn't).

"It doesn't matter, Stepanych, nothing's working out. I'll tell them to prepare a press release and an appeal to the public prosecutor."

"Just a sec, Anton, hold on." Stepanych moved to a quiet spot so he could talk. "Can you hear me? Anton, my dear boy, I can't forbid you from doing anything," he said softly and persuasively; in the background, loud and smug men's voices were discussing something. "But I don't advise it, my dear boy, I don't advise it. First of all, because as I told you, a half an hour after your press release they'll start throwing money around on the market. The company will lose millions. You'll lose. And second, because we're almost there, just a little bit longer and we'll have them by the neck. Wait a little. The main thing here is control—and not to be afraid, don't be afraid."

I briefly resisted, but let him talk me into waiting one more day.

"Stay calm, my dear boy, and don't let your nerves get the best of you: if Mohammed won't go to the mountain, then the mountain can go fuck itself!" He roared with laughter, evidently trying to reassure me.

Strangely enough, I really was reassured after our conversation—so much so that when I was buying tickets, I kidded the blushing girl at the counter, although more than anything I wanted to turn around and see if somebody was listening behind my back. Just in case, I didn't say anything out loud, wrote everything down on a piece of paper and handed it to the fair snub-nosed girl.

Then I headed back home and slept, clutching my cell phone, and in the evening went to Toasted. The call found me on Labor Square, which was deserted (it's always deserted—and there seems to be something particularly appropriate about that): the unfamiliar, ordinary voice asked if I was the one they were looking for, and then gave my name and patronymic, and so on, blah blah blah. Afterward, I immediately dialed Stepanych's number.

"There, you see, what did I say! What was the message?"

"That perhaps I might be interested in their proposal."

"Where did they set up the meeting? Is that southwest? Now listen. They'll probably try to get you into their car and take you to a dacha somewhere. You cannot get into a car under any circumstances. My guys will be there"—Stepanych relayed his plan the whole time I was walking to Toasted. According to him this was going to be a full-scale military operation, only without helicopters.

"It seems overly complicated, Stepanych—you're sure nothing's going to go wrong?"

"Patience, Cossack." I'd suddenly become a Cossack.

As I pushed the glass door open, I experienced a brief fit of nostalgia from the longing seeping through from the future: that perhaps I was in Toasted for the last time. And if there's something I feel bad about in this whole story, it's that there wasn't a chance to properly say goodbye to Miss Piercing. I was thinking about this when I fell asleep. (On that last night I kissed Nadya-Isolde especially tenderly, and she responded, but the hand that had set out on the journey around her stomach was almost immediately deported back home; instead she hugged me and fell asleep.)

I also needed to ask the siren to sing her little song. I had been whistling it nonstop for the past day—it had stuck in my head, but this last day proved to be a long one. Even though I got up late, Nadya had already vanished; all that remained was her makeup bag by the mirror. I straightened up the apartment, went out to buy some bread, had breakfast—it was almost evening when I grabbed my laptop and went to the bank's website, the name of which was written down on the crumpled piece of paper. Andrei Petrovich was listed third under the heading *Administration*. For the last time, as I combed my fingers through my hair, I checked myself and my plan: everything was in order.

I told the secretary that I was from the FSB's Department of Personal Security. And I told Andrei Petrovich that I wanted to talk with him regarding a document from a large company's administrative file. And that it was possible that someone had more interesting and more realistic proposals than those that had already been made.

"In an hour? I've got a meeting in an hour, how about tomorrow?"

"Reschedule your meeting, Andrei Petrovich, or you'll end up in a ridiculous position. Like the financial analyst."

Andrei Petrovich had no choice but to agree. But he didn't drive up in a Lexus, he had a Bentley. He stepped out—from the driver's seat, of course—and, naturally, he didn't see anybody: some people simply don't see bright blue jackets with hoods, even when the jacket pockets are sticking out like they have a Glock 19 in there. He put on his coat, walked over to the parapet, clasped his hands together behind his back, and pointed his sharp-nosed head in the direction of the arch—out of old habit some scum are still moved by beauty, even while they're thinking about investments. At that moment her shadow escaped from the car's whalelike maw: she was looking straight at me, smiling reassuringly, and, growing cold with loathing that I could possibly have something in common with that dead monster, I suddenly understood that this was probably how my mother would have looked had she managed to grow old before dying, but the most terrifying thing of all was that the old woman did not walk away, until now it had only been in my dreams that she didn't walk away; squinting at me, she slowly raised her hand, at first it seemed that her hand was simply shaped like a pistol, but I suddenly realized that she was indeed holding a pistol, and now I wanted more than anything for her to shoot it, and I even mentally whispered to her, *Pull the trigger, pull*—and Andrei Petrovich carefully lay down on the slippery, grassy dung.

I put the Glock back into my pocket and glanced around: the half-dark embankment (the streetlights weren't on yet) was empty; the old woman once again merged with the shadows. Up to this point I had been acting solely according to my own precise reckoning, but now I experienced a surge of inspiration: I took the suitcase from the passenger seat—it was packed tight and heavy, it looked decadent, like all expensive leather—and I found the key (because it was locked) in the pocket of the lawyer's jacket, opened it up, and after crossing the parapet, I shook the contents out into the Moika (the second phone I no longer needed ended up there with a splash as well). And even empty the suitcase was still very heavy, as if the leather had preserved the memory of its crocodile—I just barely dragged it to the apartment, and only there, in the silence, did I call Stepanych (the phone was blinking with eight missed calls).

Stepanych was a bundle of nerves, but I cheered him up.

"Anton? I'm beside myself, I don't think they were looking out for the guy."

"Everything's fine, Stepanych, the guy was looking out for himself."

"What happened?"

I kept my silence.

"Okay, so it's not a conversation for the phone."

"Stepanych, I have the suitcase."

"What? The suitcase?" Seemed that I managed to surprise him. "How?"

"It's not a conversation for the phone. I got lucky."

Stepanych remained silent for several moments, then asked me to wait a bit—I could hear him talking on another phone about the next flight.

"Now then, Anton, I'm getting on a plane, I'll be there soon, we'll talk it over." A pause. "You know what? Your father and I were partners . . ."

"I know, Stepanych."

"In a word, you surprised me."

I couldn't just sit there in the apartment. Or go to Toasted either—not only because I shouldn't drink; the main thing was that either I would have to come back with Nadya (and thereby introduce a factor of unpredictability, which I didn't need at all), or I would have to hint to her that she shouldn't come today—and she would be sure to think that I'd paid for a girl. I had prepared everything—the suitcase was in the corner, the jacket on the bed—and I went out. It was raining buckets again, and on the embankment I took cover in a trolley—the whistling submarine was almost empty, so I took a seat by the window and observed, absolutely fascinated, how to my right over the abyss of the Neva hovered the specter of the fortress, and then the sparkling garland of palaces plunged and surfaced, and already across the river—from the broad bay of the square a trolley was dragged along into the narrow mouth of Nevsky Prospect. I still had three hours to kill: I took a seat in the aquarium-like café and opened my laptop.

When Stepanych walked into the café cheerful and guarded—the last time I'd seen him was ten years ago, but he was the same: gray hair buzzed short, fleshy face, shoulders like dumbbells, no eyelashes, wispy eyebrows, a smile as if to say that we're off to the whorehouse now, and a repulsively familiar handshake—I had collected four dozen addresses in the form of a letter. I pressed *send* and went outside with Stepanych. The rain had already stopped: I would have gladly taken a stroll, but Stepanych didn't go anywhere on foot—large emergency lights flashed by the doors of the Lexus with its tinted windows.

"So tell me, where are we going? And why not your father's place?" Stepanych seemed like he wanted to pat me on the back.

"I can't go there," I said, turning away. "I rented an apartment. On Line 1."

"We heard. Mikhail Viktorovich?" Mikhail Viktorovich looked like a trained bear: from under the hair on his hands you could see the blue of his tattoos. "The boss said that it was Line 1?"

"That's right, Comrade Colonel."

"Yes," and now this was directed at me, "I understand you: alone, after something like that . . . You know, when it happened, I couldn't believe it. Your old man suffered depression, now and again, but it never got so bad that he . . . He took on too much, you understand? But still, money can't buy happiness, you agree?"

I said that I agreed. Nothing was reflected in the tinted windows. A wave of disgust and terror began to envelope me: thank God, it wasn't far to go—we were practically the last ones to make it across the bridge and a minute later we were turning on to Syezdovskaya Street. I showed him where to park.

The whole time we were walking through the courtyard and climbing the stairs, I averted my gaze from the shadows and corners, so as not to see the old woman. Stepanych's joking became more and more forced.

"You're just like Lenin in Razliv." I was already opening the door. "Guess only a communal apartment could beat this." His voice filled the brightly lit room.

There wasn't time to think whether I had turned off the lights or not—I stepped into the room, pointed at the suitcase in the corner, and walked to the blue patch of the jacket on the bed. I was on autopilot, acting according to my plan, which I had run through a thousand times in my head, but everything was swimming before my eyes and my hands became weak: the makeup bag wasn't by the mirror and the jacket wasn't in the same position as I had left it.

"Did you already open it?"

"What? I'll give you the key right now."

The key was in the pocket, but the Glock was gone. I tossed Stepanych the key, sat down on the bed, and, while he was fiddling with the lock, I listened to my heart beating so hard it seemed like it was hitting the bottom of my chest. My mouth was dry, sounds seemed to be coming to me from underwater, blinding light penetrated everything. Stepanych's hulking figure appeared to take up half the room, he opened the suitcase, wheezing and swearing: from out of the suitcase a dead, bloodstained head with a sharp nose was looking at us, I felt sick, Stepanych took out a pistol from his jacket and aimed it at me, his mug was red, like a piece of raw meat, his eyes narrowed and had become predatory, he asked me what the fuck kind of game I was playing.

I forced myself to unstick my lips. "You know, Stepanych, when I realized it was you? I suspected you as soon as you offered to help, but I understood for sure when I put out that feeler here, and you called two days later to see whether I had told anybody. You couldn't just sit tight. Well, and of course you thought that I was just a little fool"—I understood that he was listening, and if that was the case, then I needed to keep talking. "Everything worked out quite easily for you: you intimidate me, you show me a '90s-style shoot-out, evil Andrei Petrovich would hardly seize the company, and then good Uncle Stepanych would hint that it wouldn't be a bad thing to sell everything off cheap, because after all we needed to hold onto the business to be a Stepanych, and Uncle Stepanych legally takes over the business of his old friend for a ridiculous price, and I don't know anything about prices, so it's the right thing to do. The funniest thing is that you were right about everything. Only I started feeling disgusted. How much would you have offered me, Stepanych? Would it have been enough to buy a Lexus? All the fall guys here ride around in a Lexus."

"You psychotic little mongrel."

"I don't need all this crap, Stepanych, and my father didn't need it either, only he didn't understand that. But it would have made me sick to give it to the likes of you."

"Where are the documents, you son of a bitch?" Stepanych yelled.

"You thought that you were hunting me, but I've backed you into a corner, Stepanych. And the papers are in the Moika. The documents are gone."

Stepanych shouted for me to stop jerking him around, that I was a dead man, that I should tell him where the documents were, and that he was going to fuck me up good.

"Wake up, Stepanych," I managed to say to him before I closed my eyes, signaling to Nadya, who was standing in the doorway, and she, as pale as a white bathroom tile, pressed the trigger and a shot rang out. "Wake up, you're a dead man now."

Laughing, I rolled out from under Stepanych, who was falling on top of me.

IV

I was getting ready to ask Nadya to leave with me, not knowing whether she would agree or not, but now she didn't have a choice: I calmed her down with cognac and handed her the passport. She opened it and looked at her photograph.

"Isolde?"

"Don't you like it?"

"It's not that . . . Will they come looking for us?"

"Yes. But they won't find us."

"I just wanted a look, I was curious. Was it very expensive?"

"A passport is just a piece of paper. Passports aren't expensive, people's trust is."

We were sitting in the kitchen on the windowsill, the city was emerging from darkness, and you could see that overnight yellow fluff had covered the lindens in the Rumyantsev Garden. The first cars were streaming along the embankment: it was time. Nadya took a look at the tickets.

"I've never been to Sweden. And where do we go afterward?"

"Lisbon," I joked.

"Why?"

"*You must remember this . . .*" I sang. She took up the melody and sang it almost in a whisper, while I put our things in the backpack.

It was icy and clear outside. Somewhere high up you could see white archipelagos of clouds against the blue ocean of the sky, and right overhead, just barely clearing the roofs of the houses, flocks of large grayish fish floated westward. We walked to the embankment and down to the water by the Krusenstern monument— I threw the package with the pistol and phone into the water. As we were climbing the stairs back up, I gasped in surprise—a hunchbacked old woman with a three-corned kerchief on her head was shuffling along the embankment, and when she turned to get a look at us, I saw her kind, round face and her big plastic-framed glasses. She was simply an old woman, she was feasting her eyes on us. Holding hands, we ran across the street and hailed a car to take us to the sea terminal. The radio was on in the car, and the news was about "*the branch of a large company, whose owner three weeks ago . . .*"—the yokel switched stations.

As we made our way—registration, passport control, security—to our cabin, exhaustion was transformed into a light emptiness in my head, I finally had a drink, we undressed and crawled into bed. I kissed her and embraced her; she resisted until the last and became tender only when there was no place left to go. Then she embraced me—the way you embrace a beloved being.

With thanks to the group Pretty Balanced for their remarkable song.

THE WITCHING HOUR

BY ALEXANDER KUDRIAVTSEV

Dostoevsky Museum

Translated by Marian Schwartz

T hey sussed him out immediately.

The slutty mermaid by the bar gave him a lurid smile. The dark, bony vamp "accidentally" brushed her bare shoulder against him when she passed. Two underage Barbies drilled their gaze into him. The bitches could smell the aroma of large round numbers at a distance. Whoever said money had no scent?

He nonchalantly loosened the neck of his Dolce & Gabbana and looked around.

No, this was all wrong. Your typical club lemmings who inhabit the institutions of the night and sleep it off by day in their office cubicles. What a drag.

Although . . . his gaze latched onto a figure dancing madly in the crashing, colorful gloom. The tall bitch was swinging her mane and slithering to the music like liquid flame. He examined her round ass, narrow waist, and high breasts with approval. When she emerged from the crowd, he walked up and asked for a light.

"Have a light!" She grinned, holding out a lock of her tousled hair. A rough voice, as if she had cigarette smoke in her throat.

He smiled. "I'm afraid of burning myself."

Her ruffled, bright red hair really did remind him of a bonfire.

"My name is Anatoly."

"Zlata." She offered a curtsey.

"You'll have a drink with me," he said assertively, and he ordered two daiquiris from the bartender. "I love this swill," Anatoly added to get the conversation going.

Zlata squinted her eyes, which held a hint of green, and sloshed her glass with a chuckle.

Up and down.

Puffy lips and fat straw.

Up and down.

Anatoly swallowed and nearly choked.

"Did you know that daiquiris are the preferred drink of Havana whores?" she shouted over the club's din, but the hammers in Anatoly's ears were drumming too loud.

"What?"

She repeated herself. Her hot mouth was now next to his ear. He tried to feel up her bare knee, but she flicked the impertinent hand away.

Anatoly stared blankly at his glass of yellow liquid. She bubbled with laughter; in the chic ultraviolet, her teeth were blue pearls.

He felt like hitting her in the face till she bled. She was laughing at him. Him! This close to becoming a deputy in the city parliament! A year away from becoming the second capital's deputy governor! Yeah, he could always make a call for a girl.

They'd come. The best were from the massage parlors. Black, white, yellow. Thin, fat, pregnant, whatever. And for free. Hadn't he once provided them with protection? Just let them whine . . . But that was low-hanging fruit. It didn't hang any lower . . . It was interesting to toy with them, track them down, a trap here, a trap there, bring them to bay, attack . . . Now that was a hunt. The cleverer the beast, the sweeter the victory.

Caveman was sweating and grinning. She looked at his large

head, meaty ears and cheeks, and red neck—Nozdrev's spitting image. They were all alike there at the feeding trough: the Russian power breed. An oily little smile and a dash of money grease in his voice.

"This little skirt of yours . . . I adore minis," he said, making eye contact.

"And I don't," she replied. "You know when women's dresses started getting shorter? After World War I. After all that lead decimated the supply of men, there was competition for the ones left over. Miniskirts were invented after World War II. There's a man's death in every millimeter of bared female leg."

"Gothic," Anatoly attempted to recall the young people's slang.

"No. But I know where it really is gothic." She held out a shiny key.

"What's this?"

"Have you heard, the Dostoevsky Museum opened an offsite exhibit?"

"A museum?" Anatoly felt himself tuning out.

"An offsite exhibit from the torture chamber"—she smiled broadly—"like at the Peter and Paul Fortress, only more naturalistic. I lead tours there, and the guard is my good friend. Sometimes I get the keys from him for the night. When I really want to let my feelings go"—Zlata shot a glance at him and gazed down—"and my body."

The bitch was a little twisted. All the better. They say redheads are hurricanes in bed. We'll just see about that today . . . He thought it over briefly and beamed the best smile in his collection.

"I have an idea!" he said, a little too enthusiastically.

"I'm listening."

"I'm inviting you to dinner. Dinner in a torture chamber. Sound good?" He snuck a glance at himself in the mirror and was satisfied. "You provide the key. I'll take care of the rest . . ."

She hesitated a moment before answering.

"What are you blushing about?" he cackled.

"Fact: redheads blush very easily."

Anatoly had a hard time restraining the urge to lunge and throw her down right on the table, sweep the glasses aside with a crash, and . . . Settle down . . . What's that the Arabs say? Anticipation whets the appetite.

She finally nodded. "Okay."

A gold-toothed Tajik in a rusty Lada 6 picked them up and drove them down Petersburg's deserted night roads. Anatoly couldn't take his eyes off her, while Zlata gazed out the window at the underlit hulks of the old buildings flashing by and smiled at something.

"Charming little spot!" he said when the metal lock clanged behind him. Swaying, he walked through the narrow slit of a door. "What stinks?"

"Ethyl alcohol. The very impressionable start feeling bad and they have to be brought out of their Turgenevan faint. A little alcohol-soaked cotton wool under their nose—and they're good."

The museum lobby greeted them with an enormous plaster executioner with a beard. An ax gleamed in the hands of the red-smocked man. Anatoly playfully touched the steel with his finger. Dull.

Zlata flipped the switch in the first hall. A thin yellow light bathed the predatory exhibits, which had frozen piranha-like behind the display glass. Anatoly thought some of them may even have stirred impatiently. He felt a chill, ran his palm across his forehead, and burst out laughing.

"Hello!" Anatoly amiably flicked the nose of a mannequin nicely set on a spike and spotted with stage blood. It didn't answer, and Anatoly laughed even louder. His head was spinning pleasantly from the adventure and the daiquiris.

"Where's our food?" She walked over to a prep table where a broad hatchet had been wedged in a corner. "I propose we raise our glasses."

"You really are something!" Anatoly gave her a slap on her rear and immediately received a jab in the chest in return.

"Remember your manners, boy."

"Of course, of course!"

He raised his hands in jest and pulled out a flask he'd bought at the bar.

"Are we going to have a tour?" Anatoly winked, splashing them fresh drinks.

"All night long," Zlata responded.

"It's beautiful," Anatoly clumsily changed tactics.

The young woman frowned. Zlata was getting noticeably drunk. It's time, Anatoly thought, as he always did in these instances. I'll lay her out right on this table, next to the shiny hatchet, and I'll watch the nervy bitch squirm naked in the broad blade, bellowing with pleasure . . .

He had trouble pulling off the Hugo that crackled under his arms and tried to free the Versace over his tightly belted belly.

"Easy now, wild man." She grinned. "Take your seat in the audience. Have you ever seen a striptease in a torture chamber?"

Anatoly jokingly folded his sweaty palms into a submissive stack on his chest.

"Oh no." She wagged her finger at him and undid the top three buttons of his checked shirt. "That's not how to get me off."

"Then how?" Anatoly took a deep breath.

She pulled him by his tie toward the wooden beams.

"This hand here, this one here . . . your head like this . . . Fine . . ."

He was on his knees with his hands poking through the rough openings in the timber walls and his head held by the neck a little higher. His wrists were firmly gripped by thick leather straps.

"Begin!" Anatoly commanded.

She bit her lip and slowly freed her taut white breasts from her shirt. Her small pink nipples stared at Anatoly, making him moan in anticipation.

"See?" she said with a quick intake of breath, moving nearer.

"Yes . . ."

"Look closer," she whispered in his ear. "This is the last time you're ever going to see these tits. Or any others."

Her knee crunched into the man's jaw and his drunk vanished. A completely sober Anatoly understood. The torture chamber's walls started closing in like a frightened sphincter, and the bloody tattooed mannequin opened its eyes, raised its head, and laughed a plastic chuckle. Anatoly spat out a tooth and shouted, and she immediately slapped tape across his smeared mouth.

Zlata glanced at the platinum face on his left wrist.

"It's midnight, the witching hour! It's time!" she proclaimed. She tore off his shirt and deftly lowered his trousers and boxers, turning his hairy butt toward the dim museum lamp. She examined her victim critically.

"Honored ladies and gentlemen!" she announced to the mannequins frozen in eternal convulsions at the back of the hall. "Witches and warlocks! Brothers and sisters! Before you is a fellow seeker of justice in the lynching court of Anatoly Nikolaevich Kvadrat. A leader in making campaign faces for his deputy portfolio, a model family man, yesterday's athlete, today's bard, blah blah blah. My God, how tedious! Much more interesting is his unofficial dossier and the way it stinks . . ." She gave a loud laugh. "We will accompany this with color illustrations. Especially since our ward, as his last wish, expressed an interest in a brief excursion into the history of executions and torture."

The witch walked up to the display glass, which was crowded

with exhibits that from a distance resembled a surgeon's time-darkened instruments.

"Am I right, Tolya, that you left the Young Communist Workers to join the Democrats? An old dog doesn't give up its bone easily, huh? You wouldn't surrender your power just like that . . . Did the budget cut you out? Honestly, did it? I know it did . . ." She was concentrating on smearing a black marker across a small steel object that was quite frightening to Anatoly at the present moment.

"And so, the time has come to become acquainted with the first item in our exhibit." She walked slowly toward the naked man. He made a muffled sound and shook his head.

"The brand! The prototype of the prison tattoo!" she exclaimed, and energetically pressed into Anatoly's sweat-shiny forehead something resembling a large razor with a studded plate on one end. He screamed under the tape and his legs started squirming again.

"Exactly the same principle. Studs with alcohol-based paint are driven under the convict's skin. The most widespread brand in Russia was a word." She took a compact mirror from her bag and brought it up to her victim's pale face.

He read the inscription in the drops of blood emerging on his forehead: *THIEF.*

He bellowed and jerked but soon tired and coughed muffledly. His bugged-out eyes followed her every movement.

"Scared, Tolenka? Desperate? Don't be. You don't know what that is. Despair is when you're young and healthy and you don't want to live. Because you work ten jobs and can't buy a friggin' corner to lay your head down. And do you know what it is to be the lowest trash? The lowest educated trash with honest, educated parents who are also the lowest trash? You don't know, bitch. Guys like you don't know, but now you're *caught* and you're going to answer and pay for everyone's sins, and more than likely this will be the sole beautiful act in your whole fat, point-less life . . .

"The knout!" She took a leather lash off the wall. She raised her eyes to the ceiling and quoted in a sing-song, *"For his first pilfering the guilty man was sentenced to punishment by the knout and loss of his left ear* . . . Pilfering is stealing, and this is how it was punished under canon law in the seventeenth century. Now this is going to hurt a little . . ."

She flicked the knout and a frisson of terror passed through Anatoly's body. He squealed and jerked. The straps held him tight.

After the tenth lash she threw the knout in the corner and did a few exercises, trying not to breathe hard. She was flushed and under her tousled hair her eyes shone with dilated pupils.

"Ivan the Terrible came up with a curious method of punish-ment for those who had absconded with the state treasury," Zlata said. "As a man of power with a Swiss bank account, Tolya, this should interest you. The czar hung the embezzler of state funds upside down, brought in his relatives, and made them watch the paterfamilias be sawed in half with an ordinary rope. It took a long time, a very long time."

She burst out laughing again, sweeping a few fiery locks off her damp forehead.

"One other item in our exhibit has a simple, boring name, the 'pear'"—Zlata moved on to the next display case—"but sometimes an executioner could make silent heroes quiver at the mere mention of it. Pay attention. There were pears to be intro-duced into the mouth and the rectum, and there were vaginal pears. As we know, what makes man different from an animal is his abstract thinking and his ability to create."

She came up close to Anatoly, playing with a device that resembled a metal beetle whose belly was decorated with a large screw.

"Upon being introduced into a person's natural orifice, the pear opens up with the help of the screw mechanism. Just like an iron flower opening its daisy petals. The internal organs pop like balloons. And you know who the first people who used the anal pear were? Lovers of small boys . . ."

She raised her voice, again addressing the silent mannequins: "And who would have thought, honored gentlemen, that this model family man, the father of two children, by the way, and this close to becoming a legislator . . . It's shameful, Tolik, how painstakingly you've hidden from the electorate your love for little-boy ass . . ."

He closed his eyes. Somehow this witch knows everything about me. Everything . . . She's insane, truly off her rocker, and that means she's capable . . . of anything. But what exactly? What did I ever do to her? What? . . .

A deadly anguish turned his arms and legs to cotton. Anatoly shuddered a few times on the floor and fell quiet. The pear lay there beside him.

"Adultery is a mortal sin," the witch sang out, "but death by pear sometimes comes too quickly. Therefore, we'll leave the fruit for dessert."

She busied herself with something at another display, then walked up to Anatoly and disdainfully touched his small, shriveled member with the tip of her shoe. A blade resembling a table knife gleamed dully in her hand.

"Spousal betrayal, Tolya, was punished mercilessly, regardless of the defendant's regalia. I also heard that before you were in state service you used to traffic in young girls, right? So you see, the same fate awaited procurers. Do you understand what I'm talking about? Plain old castration. Point of fact: as autopsies of eunuchs' corpses have shown, the castrate's cock was small and underdeveloped. The hair on his body was sparse and absent altogether from his limbs and anus. There was almost no hair in the armpits or on the genitalia." Suddenly, she winked. "But if they got to you younger, castration might help preserve your luxurious head of hair. The hair on eunuchs' heads grows beautifully. But now, alas, it's too late."

The knife clattered next to the metal pear. Anatoly whimpered, slowly shaking his head.

"I'm tired," she confided, resting her hand on his big head, "but you and I will be done soon. How would you like to conclude our graphic tour, after the practical part is over, with our trial of the pear and a couple of other things? The stake? The noose? The ax? Forgive me, the axes here are props, so we have at our disposal only two options. Although, wait . . . I've got an idea of how we can combine it all! We'll start with impaling. Look what I have here! Every bit as good as a spike."

The candidate for deputy looked with horror at the fat black dildo in her fingers. Zlata took her time pulling out a tube of lubricant and squeezed a generous stream on the plastic.

"You now have a real chance of finding out what Havana whores experience in their thankless work . . . Don't squirm, please. You're making it hard for me . . . There we go . . ."

A muffled squeal ripped from under the bloodied tape.

"Hello, Stas? The deed is done. Where we agreed . . . Yeah, he's lying there half-dead. Awaiting his promised death . . . Yes. Gather those hacks of yours, the TV guys, and any other gawkers you can find, and hurry over to the scene of the crime. You've got the duplicate key and the cash as agreed?"

She turned off her cell phone and pulled out the battery and SIM card. She locked the museum door, turned her face into the cold night wind, and dove into the dark alleys.

The order had been fulfilled: one down. He was a candidate—and now he was fucked. Not a bad performance. That monster was going to be sinning on the down-low now. It had been worked out so precisely. True, it was too bad about the bribed museum guard. On the other hand, why sell yourself out for a case of vodka? That's cheap . . . And now he was going to be looking for you. A wild goose chase. Hah! I'm hard to track down; I never repeat myself. Never. Remember that, my fine friends. Past and future candidates . . .

She came out on a small square by the favorite church of Rodion Raskolnikov's father. She stopped, looking at the cupolas' black kernels hovering above the earth. Their crosses scratched the night's low clouds, but you couldn't hear them sliding across the dark sky. She shut her eyes and listened closely, just like when she was a child and someone seemed to be walking around up there, in the sky. All you have to do is squint and be perfectly still—and you'll hear steps . . .

It was quiet in the sky. She chuckled and opened her eyes. She had to get out of town and be quick about it. She could milk the cash she'd made for a good six months—until the next election. Somewhere in the Far East. Or Kostroma. Oh, fuck it.

The fact is, everyone makes a living as best he can.

Your work should bring you satisfaction.

PART II

A WATERY GRAVE

PEAU DE CHAGRIN

NATALIA KURCHATOVA & KSENIA VENGLINSKAYA

Rybatskoye

Translated by Marian Schwartz

This story began when Kolyan, who lived in a redbrick house right under the Vantovy Bridge, found out that the homeless little towhead by the Rybatskoye metro station, where mainly unemployed punks, gypsies, and profiteers collected, was his own daughter Shurka.

In case you don't know, in his younger days Kolyan was the king of the neighborhood lowlife. Later, by means fair or foul, through an inheritance or a grab, he acquired a small structure right on the Neva, where it still hadn't been hemmed in by embankments and flowed freely alongside the weed willows, poplars, and mountains of beer cans leftover from the freewheeling picnics of the local proletariat. At one time on this spot there had stood the village of Rybatskoye, whose inhabitants had been given a stela by Empress Catherine the Great in gratitude for voluntarily providing recruits for one of her Swedish campaigns. That's what the whole district had been called ever since— *Rybatskoye*.

Kolyan's little red house was one of the few structures that had survived on the riverbank when the new Vantovy Bridge went up. Unlike older bridges, it had enough clearance to let vessels under, so the Vantovy was never raised. It was also linked by interchanges with the ring road and Obukhov Defense Avenue and formed the basis for an entire transport system. On top of that, it was very beautiful at daybreak, when from the east, from the direction of Lake Ladoga, fluffy peach-colored clouds sailed in; and when they didn't it wasn't half bad either. To this day, Kolyan's little redbrick house clings to the sloping bank, facing the belly of the Vantovy Bridge, which bounces under the transport stream, one of the first in the city to meet the barges going into the gulf from Ladoga, lining up to proceed along the river on a summer's eve.

Ever since he glimpsed Shurka among the grimy Tajiks and Gypsy kids, Kolyan had become despondent. The thing is, Kolyan hadn't seen his wife (Had she ever been his wife? Not likely!) for years, and had every reason to believe her dead. More than likely that was the case—but a shadow of doubt lingered. Kolya and Nastya got together in their teens; she was barely fifteen and he had six months until he went into the army. Young and stupid, Nastya got knocked up pretty quick; her mom and granny threw her out and said they'd throttle the baby. Soon after that, Kolyan was called up, and there he had some luck. He didn't serve in the war but was sent to the Southern Federal District, with the same black guys he'd been beating up on his own turf. Well, he hit the jackpot, raked it in big time, and came back an invalid, with a withered left arm, because he wouldn't stoop over for the Dags.

He came back and tried to check in with Nastya, naturally. His homeys said that after he left she'd started shooting up and went out in a blaze of heroin. Died of an overdose, crapped-out in a ditch. She'd been living a crummy life, going from one dump to the next, lying down under anyone for a hit. The usual fairy tale in these parts.

Kolyan didn't grieve for long. Why should he? There was plenty of ass around, and you had to live. He did some driving, did the odd job for a gang, tried all kinds of things, and now, at thirty, found himself the owner of a small redbrick house and his own business.

And then—Shurka. She'd flashed by like a vision in front of the metro station—a skinny teen with grimy knees, torn jeans, and a bright crown of hair. Hair like her mother's—flaxen curls, a rare breed these days.

To confirm his suspicions, he walked up to Auntie Alla, a Gypsy who sold weed near the station and who knew everyone. "Whose is she?" he asked.

"Oh, that one," she replied, "that's Nastya's daughter, the one who works at the wheelchair factory."

"Where can I find this Nastya?" he said.

"I won't tell you the address," Alla toyed with him, "but you go on Friday, Kolyan dear, to the old textile institute dorm. They sell booze at the entrance, and Nastya's always there on weekends tricking for cheap."

Kolyan got the picture, but on Friday he still went to the dorm—a yellow building with windows so narrow that the fat weavers couldn't jump out to end it all. The freak parade was already starting, but slender Nastya with the flaxen curls didn't seem to be among them.

"Nastya!" Kolyan shouted on an off-chance.

There was a rustling in the line. A skinny female croaked back at him: "Whaddaya want?"

Kolyan threw his crushed pack of cigarettes on the ground and started back home, under the Vantovy Bridge.

He had nothing left but his kid. He locked himself in his little house for a couple of days with his best friend—a dog named Voldema—and his secretary Zoyenka, who brought him Jack Daniel's and ham on rye. Kolyan dispatched his faithful muscle—Arif the Uzbek, and Roman, who was half Chechen—to keep an eye on the street kids who hung out by the metro.

* * *

A colorful balloon, a scarlet blow-up heart in the little tramp's hands . . . The muzhik seemed okay, not scary at all. Offered her some khachapuri. "Come with me," he said.

He didn't sound Russian, but had the usual look—broad face, a light stubble up to his eyes, a jersey and tracksuit pants. On the other hand, that babe of his was the ideal for any teenage girl. Miniskirt, black tights (maybe even stockings), a top with rhinestones, the most expensive kind they sell at the market. And, of course, blond. But not straw-dry, just right . . . an elegant honey color. And made-up. A beauty, in short. A fairy.

"Don't be afraid, we'll go together," the woman said to her. What was she supposed to be afraid of? It's not like they were going to cut her. Maybe they'd even give her a bite to eat and a dress or something. She was still young, of course—she wasn't going to smoke or drink vodka, just Jaguar, like the really cool kids in their crowd. Beer was awfully bitter . . . but Shurka had great respect for Jaguar and other drinks in colorful tin cans that opened with that unmistakable, delicious *pssh*. In short, she agreed to go with the beautiful lady and the black guy.

But she began to get scared when they drove up to the red-brick house on the edge of the district, practically right under the bridge . . . There was a time when she loved walking around here—the pretty, shimmering bridge covered in diverging patterns of light, like a piece of sun—and the river, boats big and small, the barges and passenger ships. Shurka was entranced by the loud music and laughter that came from them, the reflections of bright lights dancing on the water. Then a rumor went around about creepy things going on in the red house, and everyone stopped hanging around near there. A few guys did try to take a look, but they never had any stories to tell afterward. A couple of girls a little older than she was had been there. They never did say what went on, but afterward they had money and they started going somewhere in town "to work."

Inside, the house wasn't at all frightening: in the big living room, to which the kitchen was attached, all four walls were painted a different, very bright color, and there was equally colorful furniture against each wall. In the middle of the room there were tall lamps with big white umbrellas. And the windows had black film over them.

The pretty woman's name was Zoyenka, and her companion was Roman. They really did feed her, as promised, and Zoyenka gave her a pretty scarf that was saturated with a yummy tobacco smell and some kind of sweet perfume. From time to time Zoyenka would go into another room, where she would shout at some drunk. Later, Zoyenka brought him into the room. She told Shurka that this was Nikolai . . . Kolyan. He had a puffy face and inflamed eyes with narrow slits. Nikolai was standing, swaying, and holding his head with his hand. His clothes were clean and crisp—a white jersey with the portrait of some dude, and pressed jeans. He looked around, as if here for the first time, and his glance ran into the towheaded girl sitting on a chair, her hands folded tensely on her pretty little knees. Suddenly he grunted, emitted a drunken roar, and staggered first toward Zoya and then toward Shurka, muttering something unintelligible about "my little girl." One of his arms, twisted, hung next to his body, but the other bulged with muscles.

And so Shurka began living in the red house on the bank of the Neva, practically under the sunny bridge. Sometimes she thought she'd acquired an excellent family. Zoyenka showed her how to do her makeup, got her off the Jaguar, explaining it wasn't chic, and in general treated her like her own daughter, something Shurka had never seen from her mother, who had been lost to the bottle a long time ago. A couple of times, after figuring out where Shurka was living, her mother did come to the house and demand they give back her daughter. She and Nikolai would yell at each other for a long time and then Roman or Arif would lead her away—staggering, smelling nasty, and sobbing for all to hear—to the nearest bar. For a couple of weeks her mother would calm down.

And there were days when Maxim, a cameraman, would drive over to Kolyan's (Shurka couldn't bring herself to call him *Papa*), and then Zoyenka would take Shurka to the other half of the house and they would sit there all night. They watched television and ate pastries. Maxim always brought something delicious like chocolate "potatoes"—éclairs or bouchées in cardboard boxes—and talked, trying not to listen to the sounds from the other half of the house. Then, at dawn, once Shurka had drifted off cozily on the sofa, Zoyenka would hurry to move her back to the other side before going to work. The whole next day Kolyan would sleep. His favorite dog Voldemar, fed his fill by Zoyenka, would sleep too. On days like that at Kolyan's, when morning came, Zoyenka would already have dashed back to make breakfast. Kolyan grumbled that she'd practically moved in there and forgotten all about her own apartment, to which Zoyenka lightly replied that she and Shurochka had found a common language, and she was thinking about renting her little apartment out to someone.

Shurka never did see Kolyan as drunk as that first day again. When Maxim came, then Kolyan didn't drink at all, but in all other instances he was usually a little high all day, though never tanked.

Sometimes, sitting in the living room under the huge plasma screen (this was the best place to watch cartoons), or at the kitchen table, or on the rug by the fireplace, next to a peacefully snoring Voldemar, Shurka would catch the pensive and rather unpleasantly heavy gaze of the master of the house. Then she felt not fear but something truly creepy. But Kolyan never said or did anything, instead just ruffled the dog's velvety coat with exaggerated gaiety, calling him his "golden boy." Why Voldemar was "golden," Shurka could not understand—he was black with rusty spots—until Zoyenka explained to her that this was a very expensive dog and brought his master a lot of money. These evenings always ended with Kolyan falling silent, an awkward quiet hanging over them, and him going to his room, at which point Shurka would calm down and convince herself she'd imagined everything.

It was Thursday. A gentle, sunny, and especially quiet day. Lulled by the soft rays of sunset, Shurka was sitting on the riverbank that lovely evening feeding a roll to the greedily quacking ducks. The grasshoppers were making such a racket that the sound wedged under her skin. Brushing the bread crumbs off her shorts, Shurka started toward the redbrick house, looking around out of habit—just in case her mama was getting ready to leap out from somewhere and spoil her mood again.

Maxim's car was at the house. Shurka as usual thought of cake and pastries and started smiling. The door to the house was locked, but Shurka had taken a key when she left. She opened the door, walked down the hall, and entered the living room. A very bright light blinded her, and the first thing she took in was the sound. Voldemar was whining and yelping in a silly way and a woman was groaning. Then she saw it. She did not throw up and somehow made it to the hall, and she instinctively fled.

Kolyan bellowed helplessly, "Zoyenka!"

She heard the clicking of heels, and Zoya's soft hands kept Shurka from running outside. She led Shurka to the other half of the house, where the TV was turned on and there were pastries— bouchées and éclairs, her very favorite, damn it all to hell.

"Your papa's making money . . . Don't take it too hard," Zoyenka muttered rather guiltily. "We all roll any way we can. And we don't live badly . . . the plasma TV, the éclairs. Hey, your papa's got his eye on a car for you and now he can even afford a driver. And he'll buy it for your eighteenth birthday, have no doubts about that. What kind do you like, girly ones or bigger ones? Red or white?"

Shurka was hiccupping and fighting off waves of bile, but she listened and consented. Why should she be so surprised? This was better than shooting up junk . . . The sounds in the living room made sense now and for that reason she could hear them better. Her imagination obligingly brought up a picture: her former classmate (they'd dropped out at approximately the same time, only Svetka had mysteriously come into money right away) down on all fours under the Doberman Voldemar . . . Voldemar was an aristocrat, of course, but he jerked on her just as ridiculously and clumsily as any guy, and he was also grinning and whimpering.

Shurka quickly made her peace with Kolyan's secret and even decided it was good, creative work, not like sitting in some shop or at some construction site. But something changed imperceptibly in Kolyan himself. His demeanor became even heavier and more intent, and sometimes at supper he would put his good hand on her knee. Under the table, naturally, so Zoyenka wouldn't see. At first he just let it lie there, then he started stroking, pushing between her knees. This scared the shit out of Shurka.

Then Kolyan lost it. He got ripped with his faithful comrades Arif and Roman on cheap swill from the nearest bar. They howled songs and smashed furniture. Shurka slept in her own room, Zoyenka either in Roman's or Kolyan's—they both liked her, though Kolyan was cooler, of course. Kolyan barged into Shurka's room and started confessing. Still barely awake and not understanding a thing, she huddled at the corner of her bed, pulling her blanket up and trying to hide behind it. Kolyan grabbed her by the feet and started stroking her ankles and begging her for something. Then Zoyenka ran in and she and Roman led him out into the living room. Shurka heard Arif give Kolyan a serious and stern talking-to about Allah. Soon after, Zoyenka returned and hugged Shurka around the shoulders, rocking her.

The next day the house turned into a besieged fortress. Kolyan drove Arif out, Roman left on his own volition, and Zoyenka and Shurka were locked up in the half of the house where they used to eat pastries at night. They sat there like scared little mice, but in the evening he came to them and with a wave of his arm ordered Zoyenka: "Get out." She shook her head, locked gazes with him, and stayed put. Then he simply grabbed her around her body with his good arm and flung her out the door, slamming it behind her.

"Look, child," he said, perching on the edge of the table. "No one but them knows that you . . . that we . . . well, you understand. Without me, who are you? Homeless, the spawn of a lush. Before you know it they'll be carting you off to an orphanage, assuming you don't fuck yourself up first and start getting handed around. I'm suggesting that we live together. And I won't rush you . . . I'll wait . . . a little while. You'll live here as always. You'll be in charge of the house. I'll give you a fur coat. I'll buy you a car. Ask for anything you want. Then, when you're of age, we'll register. Cross my heart! The Uzbek says Allah ordered us not to . . . but what's Allah to me? I sent him fucking packing. Who does he think he is? But me—I'm king here, and I'll throw out anyone I want. If people love each other, what's the difference? . . . You do love me, right? Do you love me . . . ?"

He leaned toward her abruptly and grabbed her face, drew it closer, and stared at her, crazed. Shurka got blasted in the face by the reek of alcohol.

"Anything you want, all you have to do is ask, child, dear child, my little sunshine . . . Do you love me . . . ?"

The door swung open and Zoyenka appeared on the threshold holding an electric drill. Tear-stained. "All right, back off, you goat! You horny shit!"

Nikolai started laughing and cleared out, landing a good swing at Zoyenka as he left. She went flying into the room, and the drill fell from her hands.

Shurka was sucking a hard candy and listening to Zoyenka, whose eye was gradually swelling shut. Zoyenka wrapped ice from the refrigerator in a napkin and pressed it to her face.

"You said it yourself—he's going to buy me a car," Shurka objected soberly. "And later we'll get registered. That means he'll buy me a dress too. He said anything I want."

Zoyenka looked at her as if she were a space alien. "Fool! You haven't even started your period. He'll rip you in half. And he's your papa, for god's sake!"

She started crying again.

The next day Nikolai came.

"Well," he said to Shurka, "what have you come up with?"

The girl was sitting on the sofa with her legs folded under her. She clicked the remote. The channels changed on the screen—MTV, cartoons, all kinds of news in Russian and other languages. "A fur coat," she said. "I want one."

Kolyan positively glowed. He rubbed his palms and pressed them between his knees. "A fur coat! What kind of fur coat? My little girl . . ."

"From Voldemar. His fur is so . . . nice to touch."

And she shot her blue eyes at him, the bitch.

Kolyan gritted his teeth. "Well, all right."

To be honest, she thought he would just drown her now. Under the bridge. Because she hadn't seen Zoyenka since yesterday, and instead a new guy had come—another Azeri, only with lackluster eyes and swollen veins. She recognized the expression right away. A druggie, a goon. He grabbed her by the arm, just the way she was, wearing a T-shirt and shorts, not letting her take her hoodie, or skirt, or jeans, and led her into a small, windowless cell with a mattress on the floor and locked her in.

She lost track of time, but several days passed for sure. There was a cooler in the room and she drank water. Then the lock clicked, the door opened, and Kolyan was standing on the threshold. He was swaying. Shurka backed up toward the wall. Kolyan grinned and threw something at her that smelled of beast and blood. Voldemar's hide fell heavily on the mattress.

"Tomorrow," he shook his finger at her. "I'm coming for you tomorrow."

Zoyenka returned to her that night. She had been thoroughly abused, beaten, and she was missing some teeth. But she had the key.

As she spirited Shurka out of the house under the Vantovy Bridge, she lisped slightly: "You can't rithk Rybathkoye. I don't have any money. Go to town on foot . . . or . . . there'th a boat in the th-thed. Ith really thkinny . . . it'll cut right through!

Zoyenka's thoughts were confused. "Write me a letter when you get there," she said. "My name'th Rybina, to Rybathkoye, general delivery. Or find me on v-Kontakte, I've got a page there."

Together they dragged the boat out of the shed, an old Pella. They even found oars. They waited for a barge, and Zoya went into the river up to her knees and gave her a push. Shurka sat in the boat until she was carried off, and then she started rowing. She was strong, little Shurka. The long barge's sidelights lay on the water and trembled in it. The poplars' crowns and Catherine's stela were reflected in the river. Jaguar cans and other trash floated with the current.

On the morning of the second day they made out something stirring in the load of coal. The captain sent Styopa to investigate.

"What is it? Some kind of hide . . . A dog's, looks like."

Styopa gave the hide a kick, and a grimy little towhead crawled out from under it.

Hi, my deer byuteeful Zoinka. Our barge arrived at the port in Vysotsk. It's on the Finland gulf, not very far from Vyborg. You remember, I terned foreteen in August and got my passport. But I rote down I was sixteen. So now I have a rezidence permit, for the provins. Styopa sez he'll marry me too, but I like him more than Kolyan. They lode cole and oil here, and I werk in the cafeteria. There's the sea here, and pine trees, and even more ships than in Rybatskoye. I like it heer. Sending kisses and wishing you luck. So dos my Styopa.

DRUNK HARBOR

BY LENA ELTANG

Drunk Harbor

Translated by Marian Schwartz

T he money ran out before I knew it, as if I hadn't stolen anything. I kept it in a heavy, striped model lighthouse somebody I knew gave me—back in the old days, when decent people still came over. One morning I stuck my hand in the lighthouse hoping to pull out a few bills and came up with nothing but greasy dust and my old stash—a joint that had lost even the smell of pot.

Last fall the lighthouse had been stuffed and the money'd been poking into the pointy roof with the mica window. They'd counted my cut honestly, in cash and stones, and I immediately started paying back my debts, even bought my ex-wife's apartment, which I'd taken a mortgage on in '07. I got myself a couple of suits and a belted cashmere coat, the kind I'd wanted for so long, light-colored, like Humphrey Bogart had in *Casablanca*; then I met this Latvian girl from the consulate and took her to the shore and rented a cottage for the summer so we could traipse around the Jurmala casino. I sent money to my creditors in small installments, but strictly and regularly, and so as not to raise any suspicions, I told my Latvian that I'd inherited money from a relative abroad and couldn't spend it in Petersburg—I said I didn't want to pay taxes to the Russian treasury. The Latvian's name was Anta, which in the Incan language means copper, but she was a strawberry blonde, not a redhead, and blushed crimson at even the mildest swearing.

But less than a year had passed and the money'd run out, the valuable stones dissolving in bills and interest-owed like a candy emerald in boiling water. I'd put the smaller stones in a fruit-drops box long before and left them with my wife along with the keys to her place; I'd stopped by when she was on duty. She was happy to work the nightshift because she was banging some surgeon from oncology, though it was up to me to support her. I had no desire to see my wife, who would have started harping on about *other possibilities*, which drives me nuts. I don't have any other possibilities.

Ever since I broke into the jewelry shop and killed the owner, who showed up out of nowhere, my possibilities have narrowed to the dark slit in the mailbox. My own mailbox, at 22 Lanskaya Street. I'd rented a room on Lanskaya before spring began, and the diamond tucked away for a rainy day lay there under a kitchen floorboard, in a piece of cork. Before I'd kept it in the model iron lighthouse I'd bought in Riga, then Anta zeroed in on my hiding place and I'd had to find somewhere else. Now that rainy day was near, and the time had come to sell off the ice, but my reliable fence wasn't answering my calls and I was getting nervous.

I knew that one day I'd find a subpoena there and I'd have to clear out of town; I thought about this every morning, waking up in my room with the mold drips on the north wall and the mirror broken out in a greenish mercury rash. There might not even be a subpoena, two guys from the slaughterhouse could just come, handcuff me, force my head down like a stallion at the veterinary, and shove me into a barred van.

The day they came for me I was walking home and I just had a bad feeling; damp clouds were gathering over the roofs, and the January sun had rolled way up where it shone dully, like a czarist coin. I was walking from Kamenny Island, where I'd been to see this scam artist who'd been doing passports since the '90s and now lived behind a solid fence not far from the Kleinmichel dacha. I wanted to offer him my last stone—the purest, pear-cut—in exchange for a clean passport with a Schengen visa and twenty thousand cash. Not finding the owner at home, I gave his guard a note and started on my way back, thinking how I could've been living in a place like that, with a fountain and brass herons, if I hadn't frittered away last year's loot. A sparse snow was falling from the sky, like down from an old lady's feather bed. It got into my eyes and mouth and even seemed warm to the touch.

Right by my building I slipped on an iced-over manhole and barely kept my feet, almost dropping the paper bag with two bottles of sauvignon I'd bought for the Latvian—I don't drink wine myself, diligent Jah not taking kindly to rivals. After the thaw the frosts had struck, and the ice in the untidy city turned into black rolled-out paths for sullen pedestrians to plod along, arms out to the sides like tightrope walkers. I didn't notice the Toyota by the front door right away; it was so dirty it blended in with the sooty yellow façade. Sitting behind the wheel was some dummy in a knit cap who'd cracked the window to tap his ashes in the snow. I might not have recognized him if it hadn't been for the familiar sleeve poking out the window, and it's true, he was a dummy if he went on a job dressed in fiery-red nylon. There was no point trying to figure out who my guests were—police or former accomplices. The nastiness would be different in kind but identically leaden.

I decided to wait it out at my neighbor the conductor's place, hoping she'd be on a run. Once I'd crashed at her place for a few days, and since then I knew where she hid the extra key. Things had taken a bad turn. No matter who these people were, they could move into my attic and sit around drinking tea, waiting for the moment the apartment owner's patience ran out. Picturing the Latvian sitting on a kitchen stool with tied hands, I could feel my throat smarting, like from cheap tobacco. If it's cops, then Anta's sitting on the stool, but if it's my old friends, she's lying down with her skirt pulled over her head. I pictured her legs in blue stockings, like the two blades of a split Ottoman saber, and my throat dried up.

Last winter, when I put some of my loot in the mailbox, I did it not in a fit of generosity but as a reliable investment; whatever fell into my wife's hands could only be wrested away along with her hands. That meant I was free of her letters, phone calls, and fits of insanity for a few years. Now she'd think twice before coming to look for me; she'd slip her take under her shirt and make herself scarce. I locked the mailbox with the key that had been lying in my coat pocket for six months, tossed the key through the slot, thought a second, and threw the apartment key in after it. Now I had one home, one woman, and one stolen crystal of carbon that I planned to sell so I could leave town. The home was someone else's, the woman was a slut, and there was a wet job hanging over the stone—so if you thought about it, I didn't have all that much. I had to get away as fast as possible. Some guy I didn't know who wore a red quilted jacket had shown up more than once and hung around the courtyard trying to look nonchalant. At one time I'd thought he was visiting my neighbor the conductor, who sold a little grass on the side, but when I stopped by and asked her a couple of questions it turned out the guy wasn't one of her clients, he was some stray wise guy. Or a cop.

I turned into the courtyard, opened the boiler room door, went down the steel stairs quietly, nodded to Timur, the stoker, who was sitting there in a scorched quilted vest, and went out through the janitor's door on the other side of the building. The conductor's apartment was on the third floor. Climbing the stairs

I peered at the gray Toyota, which was already sprinkled with crumbly snow, so it must have been there at least two hours. No one answered the bell, so I stood a little while on the landing, waiting, and then went to the railing by the elevator, twisted off the cap of a cast-iron snake, and stuck my hand in deep, all the way to the tail. The key was lying there, right where it was supposed to be.

The apartment smelled of stagnant water and rotten stalks. I went on into the bedroom, found a vase of withered roses there, and threw them into the trash can. The roses were long so I had to bend them in half, and a stray thorn poked me in the palm; I saw a drop of blood, and I suddenly remembered how a year before I'd stood in a strange room watching the blood turn black in the small, beady holes on a dead man's face.

I hadn't planned to kill the jeweler. I'm a burglar, not a killer. I'd been told the shop would be clean, no one in the apartment above—the owners had gone to their dacha in Pargolovo—and the security system was connected to the local station, Chinese junk, a plastic box with ten buttons. The shop entrance was protected by a corrugated iron curtain, but as often happens, the owner had arranged for one more entrance, from his apartment on the second floor, and one was simpler—a steel door, two rods, and a hole in the floor. The alarm didn't take me long, and I'd noticed the camera's dim crimson pupil back on the street when I unlocked the door. It was easily taken off its hook and showed me the wire to the server.

If I were a jeweler buying stolen goods, I'd install a German system with a satellite signal, but the dirty jeweler was a ballsy old man—he even kept his safe in view, under the counter, so he wouldn't have to go so far. I searched for that safe for half an hour—took pictures off the wall and books off the shelves in the living room, poked my head under the bed, sneezed after getting a noseful of soft gray dust, and felt like a movie gendarme tossing a female student's room in search of a hectograph and subversive proclamations.

The safe was way under the counter, and I opened it in no time after playing with the last key. There weren't that many options. The fence who'd cased the job was sure of the first nine numbers, only he hadn't been able to get a good look at the tenth. I opened the little door and raked up two velvet sacks, a clear one with pale yellow stones, a long box with the necklace promised to the fence, and a fat stack of cash. I got on my knees and was starting to distribute the loot in my pockets when I heard heavy asthmatic breathing, like the creak of a floorboard, and turned around. The old man was standing right behind me holding something shiny high over his head. Whatever it was looked heavy, the size of a bucket, and I glimpsed a chesty shepherdess in a glade with high pointy grass. He was planning to hit me with it but didn't get the chance.

I remembered his face, even though I only ever saw him for less than a minute—spongy cheeks, folds on his shaved skull, the dim eyes of a deepwater fish, round from surprise. He shouldn't have been surprised. The stones were of an old-fashioned cut, and they hadn't been in that safe two days. I grabbed his arm and tried to take the bucket away, but the old man yelled and sank his surprisingly strong teeth into my wrist. That made me see red and I pushed him down on the floor as hard as I could; the shepherdess broke off and stayed in my hand, but the silver glade with the sheep fell on the old man's face, right on his wide-open, yelling mouth. Silence fell so unexpectedly that I didn't realize right away that the owner had choked on his own blood, and for a few moments I tried to stop up his mouth with my jacket sleeve.

The old man's eyes were open and gazing past me at the ceiling, which was thickly overgrown with plaster molding, and I spotted one more camera eye hiding in the leaves. There was no point worrying about the camera because I'd turned off the server, removed the disk, and put it in my pocket. The shop owner, however, was a problem. There was nowhere to take him out, and nothing to take him out in—the old man was a big guy and he would only fit in a trash bag in pieces. I left him lying on the floor with the silver glade jutting out of his smashed mouth, the price tag white on the velvet glade: 299,999. I stuck the shepherdess into my jacket pocket, closed the safe, examined my footprints on the granite floor, grabbed the mop from the storeroom, splashed water on the floor from a pitcher, and gave the dirt a good smearing.

I got out through the apartment over the store, the same way I'd gotten in, went down the back stairs, which for some reason smelled like apples, stopped on the first floor, turned my jacket inside out, pulled my cap down over my eyes, and walked quickly down the street. There wasn't a soul on the avenue, four in the morning is a dead time, the leaden Petersburg dusk, even the ice underfoot seemed soft and gray.

By the fish store on the corner I came upon a sleepy janitor who asked me for a cigarette. I swayed, grabbing his sleeve, put a whole pack into his hand, and complained about whores in a purposely Eastern accent. That accent and my three-day beard stuck in his mind, so that the sole witness would say he'd seen a tipsy Caucasian walking away from a local girl that morning.

That was late last fall; in the winter I sold my cut to someone I trusted, managed to pay off my debts, bought Gulia the apartment, and spent the rest, and now the day had come when my money was gone and the lighthouse was empty.

Rouser? Rover? Roarer?

I stood on shore trying to read the boat's name, but in the dusk all I could make out were the first two letters: *R* and *o*. Fine, who cares, this was obviously the tub the lush at the station had told me about.

"Going toward Drunk Harbor, turn at the old Lenvodkhoz wharf," he'd said. "You head down the shore from the datsan, and as soon as you pass the Elagin Bridge turn toward the water, and there it is, it's got bushes around it and you can barely see the boat, but it's there."

The bushes were young and prickly and looked like barberry. I tore my coat sleeve while I was pushing through them in search of a ramp or a gangway, but I couldn't find anything. The boat was twenty paces from shore, locked in the filthy gray ice, and there were no footprints or boards leading to it. There were long puddles on the surface of the ice, and it was spongy, like bread crust. The hull of the boat wasn't all that old, but it had rusted through from stem to stern, and the bottom had had concrete poured on it, the former owner probably hoping to take care of a leak. At one time the pilot house had been painted white with three red doors, but all that was left of the white paint now was flakes that resembled shredded eucalyptus bark, and the door latches had been sliced off. I rolled my pants up to my knees, took off my boots, tied them by the laces, hung them around my neck, and started out over the snow barefoot, it being harder to dry footwear than feet—and not only that, these were my only boots and there was no knowing when I would come by another pair.

When I left the conductor's apartment I already knew I wasn't going to get in my place. I had almost no money with me, and actually there wasn't much left at home either. I could forget about picking up the stone. Whoever paid me that visit had left in their scratched-up Toyota, but they could easily have left an ambush in the building, or just planted a bug so they could come back the moment I opened the door. They'd dawdled a long time—I'd sat on the windowsill for two hours until I finally saw my Latvian coming out the front door with two guys. The one on the left hoisted the iron lighthouse on his shoulder like an antiaircraft gunner carrying a rocket launcher. Anta had clearly spilled the beans and now they wanted to smash my hiding place to smithereens. You're going to have to sweat, archangels.

It didn't look like they were dragging Anta by force. I couldn't get a good look at her face, but her walk was easy, and she got in the car smoothly, showing her leg in a high boot. If these were cops they'd let her go quickly, as a foreigner, and they probably wouldn't bother recording her information. If they weren't, they'd taken her in addition to the diamond, which they were hoping to find in the lighthouse. Then she'd be back a little later. I left my cell on the table, stuffed my pockets with bread and cheese from the conductor's refrigerator, took a flat bottle of brandy, and rifled through her dresser but didn't find anything unusual. Though I did snag a baggie of grass, which I found in a wool sock, didn't write a note, slammed the door, and tossed the key back in the snake's tail.

By seven or so I was on Primorsky, and forty minutes after that on shore, a kilometer from Drunk Harbor. The wind was at my back the whole way, and I counted that a good sign.

"Boat's nobody's," the homeless guy told me. "Don't wet your pants, I spent all fall there until it got chilly, and if no one was using it for sailing then, now I'm sure no one'll come. Sometimes the locals throw some work my way, loading and unloading, but I can tell you're a strong fellow, you won't break. Best not to argue with the locals—if they ask, help, and you'll have a quieter time of it. In November I dragged a stove onto the boat, plenty of firewood in the forest, only it smoked something awful. I went to the datsan for chow, Buddha Balzhievich's the abbot, they started feeding people there—only kasha, of course—but at least you don't have to go scrounging in town."

I'd ended up at the station, where I met the homeless guy, out of stupidity. Not only did I have no reason to leave Petersburg, I didn't really have anywhere to go, I had next to no money, my mother in Gatchina wouldn't let me cross the threshold, and in the last year my buddies had become few and far between. Habit kicked in—hit the station and get out of town—but now things were different, and all I needed was to crash for a few days, keep an eye on the apartment from a safe distance, and somehow get to my kitchen. I was sitting in the station snack bar pecking at a cold omelet with my fork when this guy in a camouflage jacket sat down at my table and asked me to treat him to a drink—preferably two. I bought us each a shot of vodka and shared my omelet with him, and at that my change ran out, and my only thousand left in my wallet I'd stashed safely away that morning, for a rainy day. That shot got the man so muddled that he started calling me Stasik, grabbing my sleeve with his calloused paw, and dropping his face in his hand with a mournful look. This last part I understand, actually—I myself might as well have dropped my face in my hand, only I would've had to have drunk ten times as much.

I glanced at him and thought about the cops at my place on Lanskaya. It could be the people I worked for a year ago, for a whole winter, and in the spring I said I was tired and jumped ship. I cracked four safes for them like Easter eggs. The last job was a surgeon, a collector of precious stones, that was quite a haul, but they held back my cut, said I'd done messy work at the jewelry shop, botched it, and they'd had to pay off some people. Perhaps my accomplices came to Lanskaya, deciding that if I hadn't worked for a whole year I'd stashed away a tidy sum, and if they cleaned me out I'd come crawling to them faster for a new assignment. In retrospect, they must've worked Anta over a long time ago. In the fall I'd noticed her asking incoherent questions, looking around furtively, and basically acting like an Estonian washerwoman. Of course, she'd searched the place long before—*the pig with the white face rooted up the whole place*—but I let it go, deciding I wasn't giving her enough to cover expenses, and started giving her more.

Anta was a minor pawn at the consulate, one step above cleaning lady, but she knew how to parlay her sweet diplomatic butt, which she brought to work by noon, carrying her office shoes in a paper bag. Anta did have kind of a big butt, but her legs were made for basketball, they went on forever.

Skirting the boat, I saw a tree trunk to port that had one end resting on a stack of icy debris and the other on the iron railings. There was also a line of six small portholes to port, sealed tight, and there were old tires strung on a rope along the side. I grabbed onto one as I was pulling myself toward the railings, but it slipped out of my hands and I nearly collapsed back on the ice. I climbed on deck, sat on a coiled towline, and put on my boots, though they slid on the iron like skis down a mountain slope. There was a gaping black hole where the wheel had been, and the searchlight looked like a tin can—though a Chinese alarm clock jutted out of the compass niche, probably left by the previous lodger.

I couldn't open the door to the deckhouse, I just smashed my fingers for nothing, not that there was anything to do there—the glass had been shattered and inside was a slab of gray ice. I lit one of my last two cigarettes, and standing at the stern surveyed the shore. Far off, to starboard, loomed Krestovsky Island, looking like the face of a sperm whale; straight ahead was Elagin, black; and from the park past Drunk Harbor I could hear the lively metallic voice of a carousel.

While I was scoping out my new quarters, the wind died down and wet snow started to fall, more like rain. My fleece soaked straight through and became heavy, like a greatcoat; I'd put it on in the morning so I wouldn't look like a bum at my meeting with the passport dealer, and now I regretted not choosing something sturdier. Remembering the bum had said something about a cabin, I threw my cigarette overboard, walked across the deck, and discovered, next to the capstan, a hinged hatch on three busted bolts, and an iron rod stuck between the hatch and deck to keep it from slamming shut.

I dropped into the hold and saw a basket of firewood on the table in the galley and an army stove squeezed into the cabin, and I burst out laughing. I'd had the exact same stove, loud and stinky, in my tent during muster outside Lisy Nos in the late '90s, when I was a reserve captain, not a thief. I found a stack of greasy girly magazines in the cabin, lit the iron stove, though not easily, shed my coat, and covered up head to toe with a prickly blanket, thinking about how if anyone pulled out the rod, for laughs, say, the hatch would shut and they'd be carrying me out in a tin box. Then I thought that it really didn't matter, was surprised at the thought, and conked out till morning.

I was able to shave in front of a shard of mirror attached to the galley wall, a rusty Gillette blade with dried foam lay in the soap dish, and when I saw it I remembered my train station friend repeating, stammering insistently, "Shave before you go to the datsan, you've got to look neat, not down and out." The morning was chilly and dry, the gray ice sparkled in the sun, and about ten paces from the boat there was a black hole in the ice, like a mercury puddle, left by fisherman, and poking up around the hole were stakes with a metal net stretched between them. Ducks, half-crazed for lack of food, were jostling by the hole, trying to stick their beaks through the net, and I rejoiced to think maybe a box of fish had been left there. It would be nice to fry up a couple of whitefish for breakfast, I'd seen a bottle of congealed oil in the cockpit and an iron skillet.

It was odd, I was two steps from Primorsky Avenue but I felt like a shipwreck survivor cast on a deserted shore. I found a pot in the galley and dropped a pipe down to the ice and walked over to the hole for water and someone else's catch. The spiky net had been dropped deep into the hole—hell if I knew why, maybe so the edges wouldn't cover over; I don't know, I never liked fishing. I tried to pull out the wire, but it was frozen solid to the thick ragged edges, so I knelt down, leaned over the hole, and jumped straight back. Looking up at me was a man's face, his mouth spread in a smile, dark river water in his eyes.

I pulled out one of the stakes, perched on the edge of the hole, and armed with it, like a boathook, I snatched the scarf off the wire and tried to push the dead man back under the ice. If he'd floated here from Drunk Harbor, the current might carry the drowned man farther, toward Krestovsky Island, and the cops could fish him out there, at the Chernaya River. The scarf unwound and was left hanging on the wire net, but the body bumped into the icy edges and floated meekly onward, trailing light hair, like wet yarn. He was wearing an expensive jacket, which meant whoever'd thrown him into the water wasn't a thief, a local showdown most likely, the Lakhtas against the Olginos. That was how I was going to float if I fell into my former companions' hands, only I didn't have a scarf and had nothing to snag, I'd float off leaving nothing behind.

I didn't feel like collecting water in that hole, so on my way I filled the pot with dirty snow and put it on the stove, which heated up amazingly fast. I'd picked up a piece of wood before climbing aboard, used it to replace the iron rod keeping the hatch from slamming shut, and stuck the rod under the folding cot because somehow my quarters didn't seem quite as peaceful to me as they had the night before. My breakfast of cheese, smelly after sitting overnight, and stale bread didn't exactly thrill me, so I decided to try the conductor's joint, which turned out to be so strong I didn't wake up until dusk, and then not on my own but because someone was tugging at my shoulder.

Half-asleep but snapping to, I pushed the uninvited guest away, dropped my feet from the cot, rummaged on the floor for my rod, and only then unglued my eyes and took a good look at the guy, who seemed large and saggy in the dim light leaking through the open hatch.

"Why'd you do that?" the person said in a reedy eunuch voice. "Are you shitfaced? Put down the stick, Luka, or you'll kill me by accident."

"I won't kill you," I said when I was fully awake. "Where the fuck did you come from?"

"Have a drink?" The person reached for something, making me jump up, but just pulled out a bottle of vodka, waving it in peace and hiding it away again.

"Why don't you come out and we'll talk on deck?"

The person wheezed and climbed up clumsily, and his coat was too long so the hem kept catching on the narrow, corrugated steps. When he reached the top of the stairs, the stranger swiveled around, gathered up his hem, and sat at the edge of the hatch, placing his feet firmly on the last step. Now I could see his eyes—long and a little puffy. His hair was gathered under a wide fur hat, but by now I'd realized he was a woman and relaxed. After I'd climbed two steps I caught her smell, sharp, lemony, a little like the furniture polish my Latvian used. Polishing furniture and combing her hair, those were the two things she could do from morning till night, humming her monotonous "Kas to teica, tas meloja."

"My feet got soaked getting here—what did you do with the logs? Use them up for heat? I have to dry my boots now!" My visitor swung her feet in front of my face, leaned over, took a good look, and gasped.

"Holy moley! Who are you, muzhik? And where's Luka?"

"Gone. I live here now," I said cautiously, holding onto her boot tops so I could pull the woman down in case she had a mind to do something foolish like slam the hatch. But the beggar's girlfriend never even thought to be nervous, she just went silent briefly, then got out her lighter and shined it in her face.

"Let me in and get warm. I'm pretty. I can't go back to Primorsky with wet feet. I've got a bottle!" She pulled her present out of her shirt and licked her lips. Her mouth was conspicuous, with bright turned-out lips, a working mouth.

"I've got my own bottle." I hopped back into the hold, signaling for her to come down. "Be sure you close the hatch carefully, you've got to slip that branch in there."

"I know," she responded gaily. "It's not my first time. Are you going to be here now instead of Luka? That bastard didn't say a word to me. He and I agreed on noon, but I got held up at the datsan, they had Sagaalgan there at dawn and fed everyone pot cheese and sour cream and afterward my girlfriend and I stayed to clean up. I even put on my nice dress and got all dirty with ashes!"

"Why do you go to the datsan? Are you a Buryat or something?" I tossed some twigs in the stove, the fire came up and started hissing, and the woman laughed and began undressing. The smell of lemon polish got noticeably stronger. She disrobed silently and efficiently, shaking out her hair—she turned out to have quite a lot of hair, a whole heap of it, I can't imagine how she tucked it all under her cap. The Buryat turned out to be naked under her dress, no underwear, the ashen fur on her pubis reminded me of a crow's nest. Tossing her rags on the other cot, she climbed under the quilted blanket and crooked her finger at me.

"Let's do it quick, Luka, climb on in, I missed you. It's putting out so much heat I don't feel the cold!"

"Woman, have you gone blind or something? I told you, he's left, gone."

"That means you'll be Luka now." She pulled the blanket down so I could get a glimpse of her breasts, which looked like two cantaloupes, and her taut belly with a tattoo, but there wasn't enough light and I couldn't make out the drawing. "Come here. The other one, the one before, he had another name too, only I didn't ask."

The cantaloupes, when squeezed, turned out to be overripe, and the Buryat's uncombed hair kept getting in my mouth, making me spit. The woman was at least forty, and she creaked and tossed and turned like a millstone—two days before I would've thrown something like that out of my bed, but now I couldn't be choosy. Not only that, she had nothing against smoking a joint and even showed me how to make a pipe if I ran out of cigs but had a ballpoint pen. Toward morning, having smoked up all the grass, I told the Buryat about the dead man in the hole, and right then, at last, she surprised me.

"You mean you left him floating?" She got up with a jerk and sat down at the foot of the cot we'd fallen off long before; we were now lying on our spread coats. "Drag him out and bury him! Luka used to do that—did you see the ash crosses on shore? That's where he did it."

"Go to hell." All of a sudden I felt cold and I got up to bring in firewood from the galley. "Am I your local gravedigger? He's clearly been floating a long time, this corpse. Where do they come from, Drunk Harbor or something?"

"I don't know where," my guest said sullenly. "I know it's often. You have to bury them."

She stood up and started collecting her rags, muttering something under her breath. I got dressed too, took my heat-warped boots off the stove, and struggled to pull them on. We climbed on deck and the wind off the gulf struck us in the face. The snow slurry hanging in the air was so solid that at first I took it for snatches of fog that obscured the shoreline, but it plastered my face and hair, and very quickly I was having a hard time breathing.

The Buryat wouldn't go down by the pipe, she climbed over

the railing near the radio cabin, sat on the edge of the boat, low-ered her feet to the guardrail, swiveled around familiarly, stood on a tire, and hopped down to the ice, holding onto the line. I followed her, trying to repeat her movements, but the hem of my coat caught on a rusty plate and I went flying, the ice cracking underneath me. The blow killed my buzz immediately: I felt as naked as a dog, my coat was soaked, and my back under it was instantly covered in gooseflesh. The woman was walking so fast that by the time I got up and shook myself off she was already at the hole and standing there, bent over the wire net, from a distance resembling a fisherman in her stupid fur hat.

"Luka!" she shouted, waving the yellow scarf at me. "He's here! Come on . . ."

I couldn't make anything out after that, her voice drowned in the viscous snow, which blocked up my ears and nostrils. When I reached the hole I knelt and saw that smooth face hanging in the water. There was no hair on his head, which meant it had been a wig and the current had carried it away. I remember I also thought that the drowned man had been hiding from someone too, poor devil. He never did find his boat.

There was nothing to grab onto. He had lost his jacket, and the sweater I tried to grab with two stakes, like a two-tined fork, immediately disintegrated into rot, revealing the dead man's hairless, puffy, baby-doll chest. We messed around for half an hour or so, and in that time the body went under the ice a few more times, slipping from view, but by some miracle came back. Finally I made a noose out of the scarf, caught the dead man's head in it, and dragged the body onto the ice, nearly breaking his neck.

At dawn the wind died down and the shore was again marked by an even line, with a black, shaggy chaff of barberry and alder, and between the bushes I made out a few crosses, which from a distance looked like a pet cemetery. We dragged the dead man on shore and dug a shallow grave—just in the top layer of snow because it made no sense to try to dig the frozen ground. His face was clean, the fish hadn't yet touched it, and the Buryat tried to shut his eyes but his lids popped back stiffly. I threw snow over the body and poked a cross tied with the yellow scarf into the drift.

In the cockpit even the walls were covered with hoarfrost, and there was an old burnt smell coming from the stove. I had to find firewood to dry our clothes, but I was so wrung-out that I picked up the boathook and made splinters of the plank partition separating the galley from the cabin.

The woman gathered the pieces, deftly heated the stove, stripped naked, pulled an opened bottle of vodka from a recess, sprawled on my cot to get warm, and immediately fell asleep. I stuffed stale bread into my mouth, grabbed her fur cap for camouflage, and went to town as I was, in my wet coat. I didn't feel like kicking the Buryat out, and sleeping with her was rough going: in the light of day I got a good look at her worn face and flat cheekbones and the two scars that slashed her cheek crosswise.

No sooner had I emerged onto Primorsky Avenue than my morning troubles dissipated, and when I got to the metro I caught myself thinking that I was rejoicing at the sullen stream of underground people I used to pick my way through, choking on longing and stench—though this happened no more than a couple of times a month, when the city was stuck in a traffic jam and I was late. I bought a hot dog and scarfed it down without leaving the stand, and then I bought another and finished it in the train car, dripping grease on my coat, and then accidentally saw myself in a darkened window and laughed: I looked like a beggar despite my clean-shaven face.

Fine. The worse, the better.

Emerging at my station, I circled around along Torzhkovskaya so as to approach the building from the other side, loitered on the square, slipped into the school, went up to the fourth floor, and checked out my windows. The kitchen window was open, the same as two days before, and the green curtain was flapping in the breeze at the sill, which meant Anta had not returned—she couldn't stand drafts. I went down to the school cafeteria, stopped a kid of about thirteen at a table of trays, slipped him a hundred, and promised him two more, since that was all I had. The schoolkid wrote down the apartment number on his grimy wrist and ran over to my building, and I followed him, pulling the cap lower over my eyes.

After standing by the front door for a few minutes, I went in after the kid, heard him ringing at the apartment and kicking the door, as he'd been told, and then talking with the neighbor who came out to see what all the noise was about. The kid came down, extended his hand for the money without a word, and flew out like a shot, apparently because I looked pretty shady. It was cold in the apartment, like outside, and there was a puddle on the floor where water had come in from the windowsill. The furniture was turned over, the chairs thrown around, books and clothes piled in a heap in the middle of the living room—a search is a search. The whole kitchen was sprinkled with broken glass, like tooth powder, and the Latvian's torn bra was on the table, her panties nowhere in sight—either they'd managed to have a good time with Anta, holding her blond head to the table, or else they'd just undressed her to scare her, it didn't matter now.

I pushed the empty china cabinet aside, lifted the floorboard, pulled out the piece of cork, snagged the diamond with a fork, removed my boot, and shoved the stone in my sock. Then I went into the bedroom, where there was a spot in the middle of the bed that looked like a wine stain, wrestled on two sweaters, collected money from all the drawers, and headed back out, crunching on the glass dust. Turning onto Aerodromnaya, I called the fence from a pay phone, but he didn't answer, and I had to leave a message, although in my position it wasn't terribly intelligent. I said I'd call tomorrow at the same time and that I had a pear for anyone who had twenty well-done steaks. An idiotic code, but he liked it, the crappy conspirator. Saying this made me hungry and I quickly hit a shawarma stand, then went back to the harbor on foot, through Serafimovskoye cemetery.

The woman wasn't on the boat. There was an empty bottle on the table in the cockpit, the stove was stuffed with firewood, and there was a lipstick heart on the hatch leading to the fore-peak. I fired up the stove, smoked a couple of reefers, threw the stinking rags off the bed, wrapped up in the blanket, and fell asleep. I had a hunting dream, though I wasn't the hunter or the prey but someone else. Before I woke up I dreamed of a vixen, a dazzling vixen being chased across an empty white field by hounds. It was heading for the forest, racing. It wasn't going to make it, I thought, when I saw the pack getting closer, but then the fox stopped short, swiveled around, dug its front paws into the snow crust, let out a howl, and turned into a small dog. The hounds ran up to it, sniffed the snow-covered dog face, and rushed on. Opening my eyes, I saw the light was already oozing through the crack between deck and hatch, the February wind droning on the other side of the iron wall, and it felt as though the boat was rocking, ready to set off, and I quickly climbed out. The weed was still clinging inside my head, and scraps of fog were floating before my eyes, but when I glanced toward the is-land I saw the hole and sobered up instantly.

The yellow scarf was fluttering on the wire net. Huh? Walk-ing up to the hole I already knew who I'd see there, and I wasn't wrong. I peered at the drowned man's tranquil face and slowly walked toward shore—there was no cross in the drift, there wasn't even a drift, just level ground, a little trampled, they could have been our own prints, mine and the datsan cleaning woman's. I managed to break off a thick branch from a bush close to shore and poked it through the middle of the grave. There was nothing under the snow.

Had the dead man returned to the water? Or was this a different dead man? Or did he jump in the water like a white-throated dipper to escape a hawk, walk along the bottom, and then calmly climb out from under the ice? I returned to the hole, knelt, and poked at the floating body so the face would appear from under the ice crust. The face was just as smooth, and the hair was fair, only instead of a shirt this fellow had a clown's black bow tie on his bare neck. It looked as though he'd been killed at a party, or after the party, during a friendly orgy on a yacht. They might well have been killed simultaneously, only the second one didn't get here right away and got snagged somewhere else on his scarf, at some other fishing hole. Damn, they couldn't have identical rags on their neck. Where was the first one? No, this was the same guy, no question.

The Buryat decided to play a little joke on me, that's all. She'd hooked the drowned man's bow tie and dragged it back to the hole. She'd had her revenge for my not wanting to wind her beastly hair on my hand and go at it with her on that narrow cot in the unsqueamish Luka's place. All right, woman, do this again and you'll be the one floating with a bow tie around your neck. I went back to the vessel for the boathook and rope, pulled out the drowned man, who looked bizarrely fresh, dragged him over the ice to the shore, and buried him in the same place but didn't stick a pet cross in, and tied the yellow scarf to a handrail on the gangway. When I'd brewed the last of the tea, I heard voices near the boat and climbed on deck, went into the latrine, and peered out through the porthole. Fishermen were standing a few meters from shore, examining the hole, but they were reluctant to move any closer. One of them, wearing a down coverall, gestured and I heard something like *honeycombs* and *yellow.*

* * *

I spent the day in Lakhta, there was no point showing my face in town, and by now the boat made me sick. I bought brandy, drank it on the shore sitting on a solidly frozen log, relaxed, and tried to call the Latvian a few times, but she apparently had either turned off her phone or just didn't want to talk. A couple of months earlier Anta had told me that they had a program at the consulate that could pinpoint the location of any employee, therefore she took the battery out of her phone when she played hooky from work. This had made an impression and I'd surrendered to a moment's paranoia, leaving my phone in the conductor's apartment. At least I didn't toss it in a ditch.

It was too cold to sleep, I had enough wood left for a couple of hours, and toward morning I picked up what was left of the partition and used it for heat along with the wood carving of Esenin that was hanging over the bed. When I woke up, I went to the hole and checked out a new dead man. This one had the scarf wrapped up to his ears so all you could see was his smooth, celluloid forehead and whitened, pruney cheeks. His hands were in his jacket pockets, as if he'd been searching for his wallet or cigarettes before dying, and in general his look was bizarrely matter-of-fact, sullen even.

Load-unload, that meant. There's the job the locals have thrown your way, you sorry-ass beggar, I thought, observing the long scarf bobbing in the water like a floater on a giant's fishing rod. He cleaned up after criminals, sly old Luka, founder of the seasonal cemetery. In a couple of weeks the snow would melt and your burials were going to go floating down the Greater Nevka past Elagin Island. I'd like to know where they sunk them so cleverly that they all landed here, near the harbor. Though who said I'd seen them all? Maybe they'd released an entire excursion under the ice and I was just getting the guides in identical scarves.

All right, boys, I'm done being your gravedigger. I'm clearing out of here in a couple of days and you can catch your own rotten smelt. I took a walk as far as the shore, examined the footprints in the snow next to yesterday's grave, collected a bucket of snow, and returned to the boat. After I'd started making breakfast I suddenly realized I couldn't eat and drank some hot water with sugar I found in the galley. Then I shaved in front of the shard of mirror, cleaned my coat, and walked down the shore to Staraya, to the Datsan Gunzechoinei.

"You sit alone too often," I was told by the monk I asked about the slant-eyed woman, showing him the cap she'd lent me. "You sit alone and think about women. You're already late for the khural, it ended at noon. And if you came for the seminar of the venerable lama, then get your five hundred rubles out and go to Malaya Pushkarskaya. Not now, in two weeks."

"What seminar's that?" It was clear I wasn't getting past the gates.

"The practice of samatha and vipassana." The monk was hunched over in the wind in his robes, but he spoke with me willingly. "Or maybe you want a lunar calendar? You'll know your bad days."

"Lately that's been pretty clear without a calendar. Maybe you do remember the woman after all, she looks like a Kalmyk, rosy-cheeked, with lots of hair. She was at the New Year's celebration, and before that she cleared the snow from the courtyard."

"Women come to us to help with the housekeeping, but I don't know their names." The monk frowned. "You can leave the cap here and she'll see it herself. Come at three o'clock, we'll pray together. For a favorable reincarnation and for the departed."

"I've got stacks of departed," I said mechanically, and all of a sudden I bumped into his attentive gaze. The monk's face was ochre and doughy, and for some reason I imagined him shaving his head with a curved, ivory-handled Tibetan knife. He turned and started down the alley toward the sloping stairs with the columns, signaling me to follow. Hanging above the datsan entrance was a wheel that resembled the wheel on my boat, only that had been hacked to pieces and was lying on the floor in the pilothouse.

"Have you ever dreamed that bamboo was growing out of your head?" the monk asked. "Or a palm growing out of your heart? . . . Why are you limping?"

"I broke the heel on my left boot at a train crossing. I'm living on a boat," I added for some reason, "and I dream of dogs chasing a vixen."

"You spend too much time alone," the monk repeated, leaving me by the doorway. "You should see people. Take a walk here, look around. We need a boilerman, a jack-of-all-trades. The roof leaks, there's lots of work."

"Oh no, lama, I'm not here about that." All of a sudden I felt cheerful. "I may not be a church thief, and I don't rob temples, but I don't advise you to let me into the cabbage patch. I might not be able to help myself."

"I'm not a lama," the monk said, turning away from the doors, "and you're no thief. You're Luka, the man from the boat."

I had no desire to tour the datsan, so I waited for the monk to go inside and then went back to the street in search of a phone booth, cursing myself for ditching my Nokia so hastily. The fence was home, but he was reluctant to speak to me—even the description of the ripe pear didn't excite him, and eventually he told me to meet him at the French café on Petrogradskaya, but he immediately added that I'd have to wait awhile for my steaks. Not only that, twenty was a bit much, the trickster commented gloomily, I'd have to make do with sixteen, since they were looking for me all over town. I said we'd talk there, but as I hung up I already knew there was no point talking, his type had an animal instinct for other people's troubles.

The city stretched on like a solid snowy canvas, my ruined boot had taken on water, and I had to drop into a cheap cobbler and buy whatever they had—loafers on a ripple sole. In the repair shop I spent a long time looking at the guy, who seemed familiar, he was obviously the shop owner because he was chewing out the salesman for some cracked window. As I left the store I realized what had made me stare at him. The owner had a yellow scarf wrapped around his neck, kind of dirty, as if it had been pulled out of the river.

Reaching Petrogradskaya in my new boots, I went into the café, took a free newspaper from the counter, ordered a brandy, and got ready to wait for the fence. There were only two people and the waiter, who was wearing an idiotic getup with braids. The floor was sprinkled with sawdust, in the Parisian manner, to make the mud easier to clean up. The second customer was sitting by the window chewing something, he had a mug of mulled wine in front of him, and the light from the window fell on his hair, which looked like soaked linen thread. The guy must have been wandering around town all day without a hat, I thought, but then he turned around and I saw his face.

"You're not missing anyone?" I myself don't know what power lifted me from my chair and made me walk up to the blond guy. "You look like a dead man I know . . . sorry, like someone I saw recently. He looks an awful lot like you, like your brother really. Are you looking for him?"

"You want money?" He raised his eyes to me, dark and quick, like the river water under the ice.

I'd already raised my arm to punch him in the nose, but the waiter appeared beside the table with another steaming mulled wine, and his scornful look told me that I hadn't shaved for two days and I looked like a tramp in my damp, ash-spattered coat.

"The alms seekers have multiplied. Here, take it." The guy dug up change from his jacket pocket and sprinkled it on the table. I recognized the jacket too, and my mind went dim. Blood surged to my temples, I leaned on the table and looked into his eyes. His face was smooth and welcoming. I remembered how two days before I'd thrown spongy gray snow on that face, trying not to look at the snow-dusted eyes and the dark depression of his sunken mouth.

"Listen, buddy." The waiter put his hand on my shoulder. "You need to get out of here, leave the man alone."

"He's a dead man," I said, pointing to the blond man. "Touch his hair, it's linen yarn. My granny would hang some like that on her fence to dry, and then she'd straighten it with a steel comb. He's a drowned man, I buried him, but he dug himself out and ran away."

"I see." The waiter let go of my shoulder. "Get moving, sicko. Don't worry about the brandy. It's on the house."

"Hey, look." I reached out cautiously to tug at the man's bangs. "He's going to be bald now, and if you give him a swift kick he'll fall to pieces."

The guy moved my hand away, stood up straight, proving taller than I'd thought, pushed his chair back with a rumble, and started for the exit. I followed him, hearing the waiter's voice behind me.

"Kind gentleman, your two mulled wines and croissant?"

The blond guy pulled a five hundred out of his pocket and threw it on the floor, on the dirty sawdust. I walked out after him and tried to grab his sleeve, but he pushed me with such unexpected force that I flew back into the café's window, slipped, and struck my temple on the stone sill. Blood gushed into my eyes, I sat down, leaned against the wall, and wiped my face with my sleeve. The drowned man sped off, and for a while I could see the shiny blue dot of his jacket in the crowd, then I lost it. I tried to get up but couldn't, and I remained sitting. Pedestrians gathered around me, a fellow in a leather jacket started clicking his cell—I think he was photographing me, the bastard—the curious waiter stuck his head out the door like a lizard, some girl chirped something about the police, and I gestured that I was fine—but it was too late.

"Can you stand?" A cop who had come out of nowhere leaned over me. "The van's on its way, I called it. Do you have your ID? Citizen, can you hear me?"

I could, but I couldn't speak, the air was thick, and I had a hard time pulling it through my windpipe. I've got to get out of here, I thought, feeling the bills in my pocket, small change. I had to get out of here, I had the diamond in my sock, they'd find it if they searched me, and this would all get many times worse. I couldn't go to the station.

What would I tell them? That I was a fence? That the river was giving birth to monsters? That for the first few days they were helpless and couldn't climb out of the hole? That I had to drag them out so that they could rise after a few hours, shake themselves off, and head to town?

That this was the cycle of dead water in nature? That Petersburg was in danger?

The first thing they would do would be to pull my file, then they'd beat me in the kidneys, and then they'd call the orderlies. That was at best. At worst they'd find that dodgy old jeweler with knocked-out teeth and the glade with the silver sheep. The blood was pouring down my cheek and now creeping onto my neck.

"Listen, friend," I said with difficulty. "Lean over. I have a stone worth twenty grand in my sock. Take off my boot, take the sock, and put me in a taxi. And do it quick, before your guys come. Come on, before I change my mind."

After getting all this out, I heaved a sigh, stretched my leg out, and shut my eyes. An eternity passed, the cop was in no hurry, I could hear the street noise—the rattling windows, the streetcar rumbling, the radio muttering, the shuffling of soles over the wet snow—but still no sirens. The gawkers seemed to have started to disperse, and I no longer heard their alarmed voices.

"What, are things really that bad?" the cop whispered, leaning toward my ear. "Stop it, this is just a scratch. It would be different if you'd been smashed in the head with a silver ingot."

He smelled palpably of slime and diesel. I unglued my eyes. Or rather, just my right eye because the left wouldn't open anymore. The cop's smooth, welcoming face spread like an oil spot in water. Behind him there was some lady with a string bag looming, and behind her the young woman who had shouted about the police, a linen fringe covering her forehead all the way to her eyebrows. Behind the young woman was a snow-covered square with a view of Kamennoostrovsky Prospect. There were people walking down the avenue, a lot of people, a whole lot of people, more than usual in this part of town. I couldn't make out their faces, but I knew that many of them were wearing yellow scarves. I looked at them with one eye until the siren went up at the corner of Avstriiskaya Square.

"Get up, Luka," the cop said, holding out his hand to me. "The van's here. Very well, we'll drop you off at work."

BARELY A DROP

BY ANDREI RUBANOV

Liteyny Avenue

Translated by Marian Schwartz

T
he writer headed off an hour before midnight.

Usually he took the sleeping car: he liked his comfort and did not care for traveling companions. In fatter, richer times he might take a whole double. For the sake of solitude.

His best friend once said, "Don't confuse solitude and loneliness."

Now leaner times had come upon the writer. He wasn't poor, of course, but he had no desire to pay extra for solitude. Thirty-nine. At that age you no longer feel like paying the world extra; it's time to arrange things so the world pays you. And the sleeping cars were worse now. The creak of cheap plastic, the gray sheets. The brown railroad dust. Last time he'd traveled with his son. He'd wanted to show the boy springtime Petersburg; it had been a cold May, and the heat on the train wasn't working. (The conductor apologized nonchalantly: "It broke; we're fixing it.") The writer froze and promised himself he would never travel in sleeping cars again. The cold and dirt—that was no big deal. He'd known worse in prison and barracks. Only there it was part of the rules of play, whereas here it just added to his irritation. A train plying between the two capitals and made up of "luxury" cars should be heated on cold nights, right?

So this time he took a regular compartment. He tossed his meager backpack on the rack, went out into the passageway, and waited for his neighbors: first an unshaven guy with an ordinary man's ordinary face; then a young woman with a light smile and a heavy ass skillfully raised on too-high heels. *She might have worn simpler footwear for travel*, the writer thought censoriously, and he headed for the dining car without lingering.

He had found muddle-headed, unintelligent women annoying since his early youth. For some reason, though, he was drawn to the muddle-headed types more than the others. Muddle-headedness has its own energy and charm too.

One day he chose the least muddle-headed of all the muddle-headed women he'd met and married her.

In the dining car he immediately felt good. He had a shot of vodka, turned on his computer, and started working. The vodka had nothing to do with it. He liked his work. And travel. Spatial displacement was stimulating. The writer valued detachment. To describe something, you have to detach from it.

He wrote for two hours, then was tired and had another drink—not because of his weariness but in order to prolong his pleasure. A little later the young woman came into the dining car with the same heels, the same smile, and the same ass, and sat down opposite him. The writer—an experienced night train passenger—had gone to the dining car earlier than the others and now occupied a four-seat table; he had set up his smart electronic device among the coffee cups and not a single hungry person had sat down with him all evening. Everyone had appeared in groups or pairs and found free seats without disturbing the writer; or, more likely, they had taken the writer not for a writer but for the restaurant manager tallying his debits and credits, since the table was the last one, next to the kitchen. Whatever it was, the writer was not surprised at the stranger's proximity. It is fairly risky, when you have such high heels, to sit alone in a dining car at two in the morning when four traveling salesmen—wet brows, ties askew—are dozing in one corner, and two crew-cut alpha males, together weighing five hundred pounds, are drinking beer in another. If the writer were a young woman in heels, he would have sat with someone like him. Short, almost sober. Computer on his left, notebook on his right.

And so, she was on her way to see her lover. She was free, he was married; she was in one city, he was in the other. He didn't want to divorce (his kids? the writer asked; his companion nodded), he paid for her weekly trips and hotel (generous, the writer said; his companion shrugged).

The writer introduced himself as a writer and added that the titles of his books were scarcely known to the general public.

She livened up a little.

He bought her alcohol.

"I feel like a fool," she admitted, relaxed after her third shot. "The relationship has no future. I don't want to be wasting time. He's much older and I don't love him. But he's nice. Respectable, strong, and smart. High-ranking," she clarified, slurring a little. "I don't know what to do."

"Have another drink," the writer suggested.

"No, I've had enough," she responded. "I want to but I won't."

"What should you do?" he repeated. "It's very simple. Relax. You're young. Enjoy yourself. You want to sleep with a man—do it. You want to drink some more—do it. Be happy. Do you feel good now?"

"Yes," she answered after thinking it over. Her drunken gravity and the gaze into nowhere of her well-fogged eyes cheered the writer up.

"That's just great," he said. "Hold onto that feeling. Savor your pleasure. I'm forty. I got married at twenty. I dropped out of college and got a job. I haven't stopped ever since. I kept thinking like you. I worried about the future . . . I was afraid of wasting time . . . To hell with that. Live in the here and now and don't be afraid of anything. Youth is given to be enjoyed."

"Yes," the young woman said, and she gave him a grateful look. "Ask them to bring more vodka . . ."

He excused himself and went out on the platform to smoke a cigarette. When he returned, one of the alpha males was leaning over his companion. Evidently he had made a vulgar suggestion. The other was waiting at their table sucking on a pale shrimp.

The writer thought ruefully that he had no chance. If, say, he smashed a bottle and jammed it into his back or shoulder . . . In any event, the only way to beat the square-shouldered heavy-weight was by surprise and cunning. He'd never last in hand-to-hand. The young woman, however, politely and curtly rejected the solicitation, and the alpha backed off before the writer could come within striking range.

"It must be time," she said.

He nodded and asked for the check. As they moved past the alpha males, the writer turned away, and a few seconds later thought that he shouldn't have walked by as simply as that, and he felt a primitive vexation.

He didn't want the girl and didn't care whether the girl wanted him. He should have jammed something sharp into the alpha-giant's shoulder for his own sake, not the girl's. The writer had grown up in a small factory town and from his early youth had known that a girl sitting at someone else's table was some-one else's girl. It didn't matter who she was, who she came with, or who she left with. What was important was who was pouring for her at that moment. This simple thought should have been brought home to those alpha-jerks, preferably with the help of a blow to the head. But the writer didn't strike, didn't even throw them a look. He was afraid. He had the good sense not to look for adventure.

Good sense has a nasty aftertaste, he thought sorrowfully as he climbed up onto the top berth and turned toward the wall. When his new acquaintance returned from the bathroom and wanted to continue their conversation, the other neighbor, now awake, joined the conversation desultorily, and she started talking about love (what else?); the writer thought with relief that the girl just liked to chatter, and he fell asleep.

The hotel was a five-minute walk from the train station. The writer had stayed at this hotel a few times before, and when his wife asked him to recommend a decent place, he not only told her the address but called and reserved a room himself. The same one he usually stayed in. He reminded them that he was a steady customer and they immediately took care of everything. By all accounts, the minihotel belonged to intelligent people; the staff was good-natured, and they valued steady customers. And the writer valued those who valued him—if not as a writer, then at least as a steady customer.

A private five-room hotel, a former communal apartment in an ordinary apartment building—no, not ordinary, the real deal, a classic Petersburg building with a series of mercilessly asphalted courtyards linked by arches. Iron roofs, sprawling staircases— special twists for those in the know. Around the corner, three local cafés right there, each with its own local color: alcohol and bikers in S&M leather in one; ladies with cakes and no smoking in the next; and in the third, the food was good and cheap. Fifty paces away was Nevsky Prospect.

The damp immediately grabbed hold of his face and hands. Cold and humid; the writer was shivering even before he reached his destination.

He watched the dark, curtained windows of the room for a long time. Eight in the morning. Either she'd already run off on her affairs, which would be bad, or else she was just about to wake up and turn on the light, which would be good; then he could see the silhouettes. He could tell his wife right away by her lush, long hair. If there was someone else in the room, the writer would try to tell if it was a man or a woman. If it was somehow clear that the second lodger was a man, the writer would head back to the station and leave on the very next train.

For instance, if the room's other guest pulled back the curtain, opened the window, and lit up.

Although his wife couldn't stand tobacco smoke and would scarcely allow him to smoke.

Or did she love him and allow him anything?

His best friend once said, "They should love us smoking, drinking, and poor."

When the windows lit up the writer panicked a little but quickly calmed down.

In his youth he'd done a bit of surveillance. He would get hired to find people who had borrowed money. Strange though it seems, in the early '90s the business of collecting debts was considered boring and not very profitable; smart people who began working on these cases switched at the first opportunity to something more interesting, like selling candies or trousers. The writer did exactly the same and subsequently recalled his street exploits without the slightest pleasure. Surveillance requires someone with an unremarkable appearance, and the writer was a skinny, mean kid; when the time came to send someone to prison, the citizen victims would have easily identified the writer.

In any case, he quickly realized he had overestimated his experience. Shapeless shadows moved behind the curtains; he watched for nearly an hour, but all he could tell was that there were two people in the room.

She had said an entire delegation, four of them, were going. The writer didn't try to pin down the details.

The lights soon went out and a few minutes later his wife

emerged. With her were two women and a man. Encouraging each other, the foursome headed toward Nevsky. The writer was standing too far away to form an opinion of the man's appearance. Regardless, he was young, not badly dressed, and strode broadly, boldly, ahead of the three ladies.

They went on foot, the writer thought, didn't even call a taxi; they were economizing.

He cursed softly and dove into the nearest café.

His wife liked noisy crowds. Business over, she wouldn't go to the hotel to shorten the long evening away from home. Why should she if she was surrounded by a big, handsome city, with all its theaters and restaurants?

The writer drank his coffee and two shots of brandy. He would have to wait.

For some reason he'd thought he could simply peer in the windows, watch her coming out of the hotel or going into it— and immediately *know*. And if he got a look at her friends, he would know especially. He would pick up on the signals, waves, impulses. If there's a connection between two people, the careful observer will scope it out immediately.

Now he was sitting there shivering, almost sober, and angry at himself, the way he'd been angry sometimes in his youth when two or three days of nonstop surveillance of some oaf was yielding no result, or, rather, a negative result: the oaf who'd borrowed a large sum of money was not visiting casinos and strip clubs or wearing a shiny new jacket, wasn't chowing down at expensive restaurants, wasn't blowing the dust off his vintage Ferrari hidden in some secret garage; he was just dragging out his sad philistine existence. What he had done with the money was unclear. He so wanted to go back to the client paying for the surveillance and say, "I've got it! He's living a double life! He's secretly building his own brick factory . . ."

At the time the writer was twenty-two and hadn't written

anything yet, but his writerly imagination was already playing nasty jokes on him.

He thought people lived interesting, vivid, stormy, full lives. Whereas they actually lived boring, languid ones.

He didn't believe it. He spent fifteen years trying to find people who lived interesting lives and as a result discovered that the most interesting person he'd met in a decade and a half of continuous searching was himself.

Downing another shot, he turned his anger on his wife now, not himself. Had she bounced out of the hotel doors, beaming and laughing, wearing heels and expensive stones, arm in arm with someone powerful with square shoulders and white teeth, then he, her husband, would have felt pain but also admiration. This way, all he felt was irritation. Once again, nothing was happening. Once again, nothing was clear. Only shadows behind curtains, only vague suspicions.

He ate very slowly, and killed nearly an hour and a half. Killing time is a great sin, but sometimes a murderer simply has no other option.

He came out on Nevsky and was going to start wandering around, gawking like a Western tourist at the ponderous granite façades, but all of a sudden he got scared he might run into his wife by accident; he turned onto a side street and hid in the first bar he came to.

The city was gray, chilly, and indifferent, created not for people but for the sake of a great idea, though there were plenty of establishments for every taste and pocketbook. As a small boy, the writer had come here twice with his parents—to visit the museums and soak up some culture—and even then he'd noticed the abundance of cafés and snack bars. In answer to his question, his mother had shrugged and said, "They lived through the blockade. People starved to death. The fear of famine must have etched itself into their memory forever. They're led by fear. It makes them open little restaurants in every suitable half-cellar . . ."

Even then, actually, the writer thought the people of the city lacked all fear. Constructed of massive stone, the city felt solid. And now, thirty years later, the local residents resembled calm Europeans; naturally, it wasn't fear that had compelled them to create so many restaurants and bars but healthy Baltic hospitality.

The writer pulled out his laptop, but he didn't turn it on. His vexation had the better of him. There was no possibility of actually working. It was stupid. Very stupid. A jealous man had come to follow his wife but had taken along his computer so as not to waste time. Stupid, bizarre, and ridiculous. That's how jealous men always behave.

Go to hell, he told himself. *Jealous men are all different and they behave in different ways. Are you such a specialist in jealousy? You aren't jealous at all. You just want to know. You think it's important to know whether anything happened or not. The very fact . . .*

The bar was stuffy and bleak. It had begun to rain outside. People quickly packed the narrow space and the writer found himself trapped. He could get up and leave—outside it was cold and windy. If you didn't find a nicer place you'd come back and your table'd be taken. He could stay—and breathe the sour smells and listen to Finnish, German, and English. The writer didn't know any other languages and was now ashamed of his lack of education.

He asked for another dose of brandy and decided to relax.

It was easy. The writer never forgot that he'd been created, begat, by cheap, smoke-filled dives just like this. He'd spent half his conscious life in smoky, dim establishments where customers from the lower-middle class went to unwind in the evening. He'd eaten, worked, and held meetings in smoke and liquor fumes. He'd smoked a lot. And drank; sometimes a lot, sometimes a little. He'd always eaten very little. And written a lot.

At some point—it might have been three years ago—he realized his wife was tired of that life. She didn't understand him. She'd ask him to go to Rome, Prague, Barcelona. He'd agree, but a couple of days into their stay in any European capital he would find a smoke-filled dive, and once he had, he would calm down. And when he had calmed down, he would realize that European dives were much more boring than Russian dives.

The rain stopped and he stepped out under the low sky.

He was considered an interesting man, and his books were full of interesting stories. Only his wife knew that in fact the writer was a taciturn, boring creature and all his entertainment boiled down to television. He drew his plots from his salad days; so much had happened that now he could write his whole life without getting distracted by anything else. But his wife grew weary, and one day he realized she had another man.

Not realized—suspected.

Surveillance requires a car. When dark fell, the writer hailed a cab. Finding himself in an oddly clean car, he asked whether he might smoke. "As you wish," the driver replied in an even voice; it was immediately clear that this guy would not do for today's purposes. The writer had to laugh. Usually cab drivers irritated him with their informality, dirty sock smell, and rudimentary musical tastes, but here was rare good luck—behind the wheel was a true intellectual. And so? That's not what he needed. He needed your typical rogue, a worker reeking of gasoline. A proletarian of the pedals. *It's always that way with intellectuals*, the writer thought. *They always show up at the wrong time.*

He asked to be let off at the corner of Nevsky and Marat. After paying he realized he had to reallocate his money. He took a few bills out of his wad and put those in his pants pocket and the rest in his jacket, next to his heart. Laughing at himself, he crossed the street and caught another cab, this time quite successfully. The cabbie was young and smirky and looked like a lazy scoundrel. The writer liked scoundrels, he'd spent many years among scoundrels and knew how to behave in their society. He showed his money and explained what he needed to do. The cabbie's gray eye and gold tooth flashed gamely. He was taking no risk. Better to stand around than drive. Better to do nothing than something. Naturally, given a previously agreed upon payment; money up front.

They idled across the street where they could see both the room windows and the hotel entrance. The wait could take hours; the writer relaxed and lowered his seat back slightly.

Bored, the cabbie inevitably struck up the usual, fairly pointless conversation, but the writer immediately interrupted him and started talking himself, and it was a monologue. He had long known that you could calm any idle chatterer if you immediately sucked up all the air. And forced him to listen to you. The writer had a few monologues at the ready, each of which could be made to last as long as needed. The total corruption, war, gas prices in Europe and Asia, weapons, prison, the outrages of traffic cops, air travel, games of chance, cars and motorcycles. Once I was in Barcelona; and once I was in Amsterdam. Generalities were not advisable—the chatterer would interrupt you right away. You needed concrete stories fashioned in keeping with the rules of dramaturgy, with a beginning, middle, and end. Mentions of large sums of money go down well. One time, there I was giving someone fifty thousand German marks—that was before the euro came in—and the man arrived for the meeting with a rubber belt under his shirt to hide his riches on his person, and he was amazed when he saw a thin stack instead of lots of raggedy bills; he didn't know there were thousand-mark bills . . . And so on. The stories leapt out of the writer by themselves, one led to another, the episodes were recast in decisive criminal slang, rough curses, and minimal gestures.

Thus passed nearly four hours. The driver was tired—chatterers don't know how to listen—and had smoked all the cigarettes the man had given him. And then the writer saw his wife.

Basically, the earlier arrangement was repeated, only in reverse. First, in lively conversation and even with little explosions of carefree laughter, the three persons of the female persuasion passed by; the male person, by now tieless, coat flapping open, was bringing up the rear of the procession. His left arm dragged a solidly filled package bearing the logo of a cheap supermarket. Tensing, the writer managed to make out his perfectly ordinary face in the light of the streetlamp. The heavy cheeks of a thirty-year-old not inclined to adventures, moderately charming, inoffensive. The writer managed to glimpse the gentleman checking out his female companions' figures. *He's choosing,* the writer thought angrily. *Three of them, one of him, and the whole night ahead . . . But if it's her and him, that's a disaster. He's boring. He has boring hair, boring ears, boring boots. What's he got in that package? Kefir?*

The windows lit up, and again vague shadowy patches began to move behind the curtains. The writer got out. After the stuffy car the air seemed prickly and sweet. He took out his phone and called.

"Everything's fine," his wife said matter-of-factly. "I just got back, I'm tired, and I'm going to bed. What are you doing?"

They lobbed a number of everyday questions and answers at each other and said goodbye. The writer paced back and forth. A car passing through a puddle gave him a good, stiff splashing.

The light in the room went out, and the curtains were lit up blue from the inside. She'd turned on the television, the writer realized. Or had she? A television masks noise well. For instance, in prison, if you had to break some idiot's bones, first you turned up the volume on the television and only then called the idiot in for a chat.

Who is the idiot now? the writer asked himself. *Me, naturally.*

*On the other side of that wall, in their room, they're watching televi-
sion. They have a blanket, pillows, and tea. Maybe even wine.* Actually, his wife barely drank. *Whereas I have a heavy sky, icy damp
creeping under my collar, and next to me a greedy fool with yellow
nails on his short fingers.*

The light went out, eleven o'clock—what should he do?
Where should he go? Tomorrow afternoon she'd return home.
He hadn't seen, hadn't understood anything.

He went back to the car and immediately caught a familiar
whiff that called up a number of the most varied associations.
The driver was looking in his direction.

"I could go for a joint myself," the writer declared. "Got
anything?"

"Not on me."

They quickly came to an agreement and drove off. In the
process of making the deal they'd had to find out something
about each other. The driver's name was Peter.

"Bear in mind, I'm not the pusher," Peter warned. "But I can
introduce you. It's nearby. Liteyny Prospect."

The apartment—huge, in an old building—turned out to be
something between a squat and a lair. The young guy who led
the guests in looked like Jesus gone to drink. A lump of gray ash
hung in his beard. While the writer was considering whether to
take off his boots, a petite young woman in an alcoholic's tank
top and outsize camo pants emerged from the depths of a dark
hallway on her way to the kitchen, holding onto the wall, which
was covered with pieces of different-colored paper instead of
wallpaper; her left arm was adorned with a badly wrapped gray
bandage. The writer decided to keep his boots on.

Entering this place, the driver was subtly transformed and
became both looser and cruder. He curtly reproached Jesus for
being hammered again and looked at the girl with undisguised
hatred. The writer picked up on this immediately and tensed. He

himself had not experienced hatred for many years and hoped never to experience it again.

"For you," Peter told Jesus, and he nodded at the writer, who straightened the strap on his backpack, making it clear he was a guest, a stranger, he'd come on business and would leave right away, as soon as he got what he needed.

"Follow me," Jesus responded in English, and he smiled at the writer and stepped into the hallway's dimness. He moved slowly and smoothly. He threw back a blanket covered in large fuchsia flowers that served as a door and led the writer and driver into a room hung solid with watercolors of flowers, eyes, and clouds in various combinations and even symbioses: some flowers had pupils and lashes, while the clouds looked like blossoms with partly opened petals. The illustrator didn't have much talent but was obviously a very passionate creature, and the writer chuckled to himself; he himself wrote books that had passion but not much talent.

"I'm not the pusher," Peter repeated, flashing his tooth. "Talk to him." And he pointed to Jesus.

Jesus smiled again, calmly and shyly.

The writer didn't like dealers; he silently pulled out a large bill and set it on the edge of the table, which was covered with dirty glasses and cups. Jesus nodded and left the room.

"This is my pad," Peter announced carelessly, moving the clothes off the couch and taking a seat. "Well, nearly mine. Two rooms out of five. My granny dies, I'll have three rooms. Some businessman already bought the other two. Granny dies, I'll sell him the third. My sister and I'll be left with a room apiece. We'll split the money"—he snapped his fingers—"and I'll buy a boat. In the summer I'll take tourists around, and in the winter I'll go where it's warm. Rostov, Sochi . . ." He fell silent, then added, "But Granny isn't dying."

"That's all right," the writer said. "She will."

Jesus came back and set a baggie on the table with a delicate motion. "Hydroponic," he explained quietly. "Organic, made in the European Union."

The writer opened the baggie, sniffed, and handed it back to Jesus.

"Fire one up. Let's see about this European Union."

Jesus shrugged; the motion was brief and helplessly bohemian. *Great dealer I've got me*, the writer thought contemptuously, but then he glanced at the psychedelic watercolors and decided not to judge the stranger. There are a hundred reasons why a talented young man suddenly drops from the level of artist to drug dealer. *Don't judge*, the writer repeated to himself, accepting the joint from Jesus's dirty fingers. *Don't even try*.

He pulled the smoke into his lungs, making sure not to produce a coughing fit. He handed it to Peter, who took it readily.

Suddenly, on the other side of the wall, they heard the crash of something breaking, something small and solid, like a sugar bowl or cut glass; Peter whispered a curse, entrusted the joint to Jesus, and went out.

"Yours?" the writer asked, nodding at the watercolors.

"Hers," Jesus replied. "I work in oils."

There were muffled cries. Jesus neatly placed the roach on the edge of the table and headed for the sound of the scuffle. The writer started to wonder whether he ought to remain alone in the room or put his buy in his pocket and retreat, dispensing with formalities; or, on the contrary, was the right thing to wait for Jesus's return and close the deal and only then clear out? At that moment he understood that his doubts—excessively philosophical—were the result of the marijuana's effect and that the drug itself, naturally, had to be left right here. And he had to disappear immediately.

He finished off the joint in two drags, threw his backpack over his shoulders, and made tracks.

Through the kitchen door he saw Peter sitting on the floor; he was holding his side with one hand and examining his other— bloody—hand. Jesus was standing over him scratching his greasy head. The girl, her legs tucked under her on the stool and her face covered with her open palms, was moaning softly and peeking out through her fingers wild-eyed. Right there on the floor, in a pile of white shards, lay a paring knife.

The writer walked up to it and bent over.

"Where are you going?" Peter asked, turning swiftly pale.

He's about to pass out, the writer thought. *I'm sure they don't have smelling salts. If I slap him they won't understand. Especially the girl. She'll immediately think I'm starting a fight . . .*

He sat down, took Peter by the shoulders, and cautiously lay him on the floor. He pulled the driver's shirt out of his pants and turned it up—after that came a dirty undershirt and below that a shallow cut.

The wounded man was emitting muffled groans and cursing incoherently. The writer looked at Jesus and said, "A cut. Nothing serious. You can stitch it up right here. Or take him to an emergency room. But bear in mind—it's a knife wound and the doctors might call the cops . . ."

"I hope he croaks!" the girl hollered, squeezing her knees to her chest.

"Your decision," the writer said, shifting his gaze from Jesus to Peter.

"Well . . ." Jesus said. "I don't know . . . Are you a doctor?"

"Nearly," the writer answered, taking off his pack. "Bring vodka, a clean cloth, and a needle and thread. Quickly."

"I hope he croaks, the bastard!" the girl shouted.

Jesus went into the hallway.

In principle, it doesn't have to be sewn, the writer thought. *It could be cauterized. But he would scream.*

"Sit," he ordered Peter. "And undress. It's nothing, a scratch."

"Did it nick my liver?" the wounded man rasped.

"Your liver's on the other side," the writer said. "Come on, off with it."

Peter slowly raised his hands and with clumsy fingers started unbuttoning.

Jesus came back and held out a sewing needle and towel. "There isn't any thread."

"Pull some out of something."

The author of psychedelic watercolors looked at him uncomprehendingly. The writer told him to undress the victim. He went out into the hallway, quickly studied the garments hanging on the coat rack, found an old coat with a shabby fur collar—obviously belonging to the old woman who didn't want to die—and neatly pulled threads from the lining. The thread was rotten, but folded twice it would do just fine.

There was no vodka to be found either, but there was brandy. The writer told Jesus to calm the girl and neatly closed the wound with two stitches. Peter—he had a gray body with thick rolls of fat at his waist—moaned faintly and writhed.

The writer poured half the bottle into Peter's mouth and half on his bare flesh. He wanted a sip himself, but judging from the smell, the brandy was some wretched fake.

The girl spoiled the operation's conclusion. Breaking out of Jesus's weak arms, she leapt up—the shards crunching—and tried to kick the wounded man. He bared his teeth and floridly promised his attacker a speedy and agonizing death.

The writer stood up.

Peter means stone, he remembered.

He found the bathroom at the end of the hall. He liked it—large, good acoustics, a window with a broad sill. The writer thought that it would be nice to immerse himself in water here on a warm summer's day, say, up to his chest, and turn his wet face and shoulders to the fresh street breeze.

He washed the blood off his hands and carefully examined his fingers and nails. He could only hope the wounded man didn't have hepatitis or something similar. He looked at himself in the mirror. Suddenly he felt a chill. *The adrenaline's washed out,* he thought. *Or the drug's kicking in. In Moscow they sell southern grass, from Kazakhstan or Tajikistan, but here it's the north, Europe; damn if I know where they get it. Maybe it really is from Holland. Or they grow it themselves . . .*

He buttoned his jacket as he walked, now in the hallway; he checked his pockets. He turned by the door. Peter was leaning against the wall, and Jesus was stroking the sobbing girl's head. A thin blue flame was burning peacefully under the iron kettle.

"Go to the pharmacy," the writer said as he turned the door handle. "Buy a bandage. And antibiotics. Bandage him up."

"Fuck yourself!" the girl shouted, pushing Jesus away and rolling her eyes, white with rage.

The writer nodded in agreement. The advice was perfectly sensible.

On the stairs he checked his pockets and the contents of his backpack one more time; his money and documents were where they were supposed to be.

Barely a drop, he thought, letting go of the massive door and plunging into the rain.

The wind was strolling down Liteyny Prospect. The streetcar rails glinted like dagger blades. The writer remembered the paring knife among the china shards. It was a foolish shiv, no good for killing or even seriously injuring someone. He saw the lit windows of the twenty-four-hour store and headed for that.

He didn't like to warm up with alcohol. He considered the method lowbrow. But sometimes, in lowbrow circumstances, lowbrow acts were exactly what he needed. The writer bought a flask of whiskey, raked the change, a few coins (he had never respected copper money), into his palm, turned into the very first entryway, and downed half.

If you were a real, old-school writer, he told himself, *you'd find an open bar now, perch at a table, and get down to work. Right now, at three in the morning, when your hands still smell of someone else's blood, not an enemy's, but the blood of some random clown, some philistine who doesn't matter. When your head's filled with marijuana smoke and your mouth with the taste of fake Polish whiskey. When icy drops are rolling down your neck and back. And you wouldn't write about the cold and graveyard damp. Or about fools, jealousy, greed, and poverty. You'd fill your story with sunshine and the scent of tropical flowers. Salty ocean breezes would fly at your heroes' tanned faces. They would love each other and die young.*

He set out, feeling a surge of strength. He knew for sure that if he found an open bar he would do what others had done before him. Sit down and write. Moreover, if he didn't find an appropriate establishment he'd grab a ride to the train station—or even walk—buy a ticket for the first morning train, and then find somewhere to sit in the waiting room and write anyway.

He couldn't come here and not write anything.

This city consisted of black water and black stone. The water below, in the canals and rivers, and above, in the air.

Walking, he caught himself feeling as though he were breathing water.

The local inhabitants could probably use gills; especially now, in late fall. Or special breathing organs made of stone. Granite alveoli and tracheae.

The writer liked to fantasize after he got out of scrapes. He found contemplating abstract topics gave him a sensation of the fullness of life and was very calming.

His best friend once said, "Don't look for peace, let peace find you."

He walked to the station without finding a single open establishment.

Entering the warm, booming hall, he immediately felt a weakness. He no longer had any desire to work.

He bought a ticket. The cashier yawned mightily and glanced at his sleeve. The writer stepped aside and looked—there was someone else's blood on his cuff.

Then he sat down on the plastic bench and composed a brief story about someone who loved people but not himself.

Twelve hours later he was home. That same evening his wife arrived, and the writer caught himself thinking that he was sincerely glad to see her.

The shirt he'd had to throw away; the blood wouldn't wash out.

SWIFT CURRENT

BY ANNA SOLOVEY

Kolomna

Translated by Marian Schwartz

I'm not getting ready to die . . . This ridiculous plastic thing gets tossed too—who gives that to a little girl? . . . I'm not getting ready to die, that would be a waste of time. I'm moving. Very soon. Where, I don't know yet, but there's no staying here. Why would I do that? And don't look at me like that from the wall. If only you could see . . . Hey, what is it with these photographs? Whoever invented photography ought to be shot . . . There's one more sheet on the sofa, the last one, the rest are neatly folded and stacked. I'm moving and I don't need anything now—when you don't have it, you do without. There's a kettle and a glass, so drink!

"Before, love sucked up all the air and I never did move anywhere. All those nights we fought and it always won, fell on me with its heavy, slippery body, its damp fog crushing me, squeezing my heart so hard it could scarcely beat, my breathing shallow, and until I smeared into a white cloud under its carcass, it wouldn't stop making love . . . and it always said, *I love you because you want to die.* Anyone who says it's chilly and youthful and its eyes are the color of a wave has never fought with it in bed. This city—Peter's creation—always was the victor, smothering me with its embraces, so by morning I'd be brimming with the fatal poison of his seed.

"In the mornings, as I was walking across the Kryukov Canal to Theater Square, it would gradually reveal itself, like a vision, the cupolas of the St. Nicholas Cathedral piercing the gray fog. It would pretend we were strangers and just tickle me with its quivering air, flirting with everyone at once, the cheap stud! As if I weren't the one who'd carried all its countless embryo-germs in my womb, as if I hadn't coughed through its winters trying to spit them out. I crossed that little bridge on countless occasions, and each time admiration stopped me dead in my tracks, and I forgot all the darkness and reveled in the blue.

"But then I slipped away . . . I ran and ran . . . and I stuck out my tongue, teasing them! . . . I don't go there anymore. But every day I try to describe . . . Here's this stack of papers, I packed everything away in my chest and wrote for days and days, sometimes even at night. There's heat coming from the tips of my fingers, and that heat gets transferred into the letters, my soul drains into the ink. I don't like computers, I'm made of other blood, loftier blood, and my handwriting is like runes . . . open the chest and hocus-pocus—an empty chest, yes . . . because I had to condemn the words to fire for them to fly. It was because of the fire that they locked me up, my neighbors. Fire can burn everyone. That's clear, that the fire burning inside can burn everyone. They decided I was crazy and rejoiced. Rejoiced that my room would free up sooner. They don't have far to take me. Pryazhka's a stone's throw from here. A cheerful trick. They're good neighbors, not mean. And you can see they're poor. Who else lives communally now? They don't have a car either. It's enough to make you cry. Their boy sits on the steps with his friends all the time smoking weed. Could you really invite a girl up to an apartment like that? Poor people, their hearts seethe and have nowhere to bubble over. They themselves left, and shut me out, in case I burned the building down, set fire to it. They think they'll be living in my room. Fools, fools, I have Mashenka . . .

she's not here now, but if anything happened to me she'd hop right to it and come running, my darling."

Mashenka was walking across the bridge. Plié, plié! Knees out. Jeté forward, assemblé to the side! Rond de jambe, plié, extend! Fondu sur les demi-pointes! Your back!

What was the point? She hadn't been there very long, but she still couldn't get the words out of her head. Her heart started beating fast, though why should it, really? The Vaganova school . . . her dream . . . all that time not eating, not drinking, training until she dropped, leg cramps, and her ardent daily prayer to her home icons: Ulanova, Pavlova, Nijinsky, Lopatkina . . . and then—ta-da!—the envelope, please. The letters make it simple and clear: corps de ballet. Chin to chin, nose to nose, left-right, fire—dive, little soldier . . .

Masha was still foggy about what would happen to her afterward; she had dreamed only of victory. Roses by the basket and admiration. So there'd be none of that? She didn't care if she had to slave twenty-four hours a day, didn't care if everyone in the theater hated her, didn't care if there was blood in her shoes every day, that didn't scare her. What did? Being like everyone else, going around in Turkish sweats like everyone else, talking about television, trembling to save up for an apartment in Kupchino with her beer-swilling old man. Then going to a job her whole life, coming back in the evening, choosing wallpaper, hanging lights, closing the doors on people coming off the streets so the lobby wouldn't stink, doing homework with her children, occasionally breaking free and going abroad to stroll in a crowd. What for? She hated all that, hated it. After all, times had changed. Anything was possible! Leave and find a job dancing? They would appreciate her there! But where? In a strip joint? Or one of those classical-cabaret kind of ballets that does *The Birch Tree*? Wait for some fat sugar daddy to make her his mistress? But she'd dreamed of creating a world of beauty around herself; she loved art, the audience, and she loved a city—Petersburg. She didn't care if it was dark there nearly year-round. Its lights lit at night, its golden spires aimed for the heavens, the festive crowd on Nevsky, the Hermitage, architect Rossi's street—their names alone made it worthwhile!

She found being ridiculous humiliating. She bathed for an hour in the morning and an hour in the evening, washing away the dirt, transforming herself into a pure angel twice a day. Because of the washing, she moved out of the ballet dorm and in with her aunt almost immediately. You can't bathe for two hours a day in a dorm, and anyway she was afraid of being on her own while still so young. Her aunt and uncle loved her as if she were their own, and she even called her aunt Mama. Only they tried too hard to feed her, always pushing fish oil on her, and this irritated Mashenka. She struggled mightily over each extra bite.

Of course, Masha idolized the ballet, but not to the point of oblivion, not to the point that she could stand in a single line her entire life. And who said you could hang on in the first row? You'd be trampled there too. Proud but poor—that's the only way for primas—your success is your applause, your seething blood, your power over the audience.

Mashenka seemed to wilt utterly. She walked around in a funk, and if you called out to her she didn't call back. She was used to working hard, and she expected recognition for that, her teachers had praised her for that, and now everyone had betrayed her, she had no one to count on, and only she herself knew how special she was and that she definitely had not come into this world for the corps de ballet. The others, anyone who didn't understand this, became her enemy. She threw the portraits of her idols in the garbage. Masha raked her aunt's collection of porcelain ballerinas off the shelf and hid them under a pile of linens. Her aunt bit her tongue, but she wept all night with pity for the girl. She and her husband loved their niece very much, but they had not discerned her morbid pride and did not worship her great talent, so she found their consolation utterly banal. Masha's aunt had herself been a musician. She taught at the conservatory and played violin in an orchestra. She'd never aspired to being a soloist, but then she wasn't wracked by a passion like Masha's, or perhaps she'd left it behind, somewhere in her past. This weakness stirred Masha's contempt. What could you explain to a spineless jellyfish? That was why Masha was sweet and polite with her relatives but kept them at arm's length. She danced in her corps de ballet and took sedatives after each performance to ward off hysterics—yes, after the performance, because the applause took the worst toll: the harsh pounding of hundreds of palms that had nothing to do with her, the unlucky, persecuted ballerina . . .

The pills helped. Little by little she began making kopeks on the side writing about ballet and fashion for a magazine. Because she had a head, as well as legs up to her ears. Then suddenly things started going well for her, swimmingly, marvelously. She started getting invitations to receptions with stars, designers, and directors, but she wasn't making enough money to dress for them. She couldn't make that kind of money at the magazine, of course—there weren't enough fees in the world for her to go to a dressmaker. Somehow certain fine gentlemen just approached her and suggested that she might do well to write a letter and expose the unsightly truth about their prima ballerina, and they also asked Masha to stop by the makeup room for a moment while the star was working onstage.

These services, which made trouble for their prima, fetched decent money. But Masha was willing even for free. This prima was a shrew, and she'd been seducing other women's husbands! Her stage triumphs weren't enough—no, she had to get her grubby paws on it all! They should be punished, people like that, which was why Masha had no regrets or remorse.

Also at that time she had an unusual romance, something she had waited for for a long time. Only she'd pictured it rather differently. She'd thought she would come down off her cloud for this love and allow him to kiss her knee, but the reality was otherwise. It didn't matter, though. This happiness's name was Vsevolod—Seva—and he was a somebody. He didn't just have money and connections, he didn't just have power, he had all three, and he was a celebrity in the city and beyond. He was respected—not that he blew his own horn. Seva could do a lot, a whole lot, almost anything, and it was he, a man like this, who was inspired at first glance, who immediately "got" Masha—that she was special, one of a kind—and he promised the world would soon know it too. You shouldn't be so afraid of the corps de ballet. It's a start, a jumping-off point, and with him she would become a golden girl, a sovereign over men's minds, and looking at all this riffraff, these ballet stars, would be like looking at charwomen, at the staff, but Masha still had to select a field of endeavor.

Seva began taking her to serious gatherings and introducing her to the powerful of this world. He gave her some valuable stones, so she would look more confident. Masha calmed down and left the theater—and sat down to her books, feeling she lacked education. To distract her, Seva let her dabble in power—run charitable balls and various formal ceremonies. People sought her advice, flattered her, and she started feeling her lack of money, which she needed, of course, to keep up appearances. She wasn't some errand girl who could feel comfortable in sweats with pimples on her nose. Since she and Seva still maintained separate households, she didn't think she could ask him for money. And Seva seemed not to notice that creating an image—stylish, festive, elegant, and at the same time with the most maidenly innocence and a light transparency to her face— meant hard work, hard work every day. And money.

She'd not stopped writing since she discovered she had this talent. Her range of topics had expanded and now touched on business and politics, though all that was of little interest to her personally. But when Seva's people suggested what might be good to write about, she did it without a second thought. She interviewed one public figure and they had a marvelous chat. A witty fellow, what was his name? Dima . . . true, he dressed kind of like a tramp. Then Seva told her to make an appointment with this Dima so they could go over the interview together. It could have been sent by e-mail, of course, but Dima didn't refuse to meet. Why shouldn't he hang out one more time with a girl like Masha? They set a time and place, and then Seva said, "Don't go." And she didn't, of course, and Dima was accidentally run down right where they'd agreed to meet. And killed. Run over totally by accident. She didn't know and had no desire to know these affairs of Seva's. And that Dima shouldn't have poked his nose where it didn't belong . . . The main thing was, why? They were just making publicity for themselves, but they made it seem like they were so honest, fighters for justice . . . it was sickening . . . He took her by the arm then, and laughed: "You're an odalisque, not a journalist . . ." And for a moment she actually wished he'd put his arms around her, but Masha paid no attention to that, or rather, she was able to pay no attention to that because she had an iron will and discipline.

She didn't want to think about death. Later, someday later, she'd decide what she felt about it. Even when her mama died she hadn't reflected on mortality. She simply forgot it all instantly, as if nothing had ever happened. That was when her distant relatives sent her to ballet school. The girl had been saying since she was five that she was going to be a ballerina, but her mother wouldn't hear of it, and now her mother was gone, so why not? She boarded the train and was off, especially since her aunt, her mama's sister, lived in magical Petersburg. And at school Masha had hard work to do, and she had to survive among strangers. And survive she did. She even pulled off that whole business with the corps de ballet. Only because heaven sent her a miracle. Sent her Seva—a gentle, smart, kind, courageous warrior who feared no enemy. And who believed in her.

Only why wasn't he here yet?

All of a sudden she remembered and actually staggered. How could she have forgotten? Well, yes, she could have because yesterday it was said through laughter and drunken eyes . . . The girls from the theater all lied, they were insanely jealous, but yesterday they dropped blatant hints that he'd found some other dancer—some corps de ballet louse, a pale moth . . . with freckles to boot . . . third in the back row . . . What if it were true? Was her life ruined? My God, oh my God . . . though why, why was she getting herself so wound up, why was she blowing things out of proportion?

Masha grabbed the railing of the bridge and jerked her hand back—cold, nasty metal. Just as she loved to touch granite, she hated metal. Her hands would smell of it for hours.

The round lamps lit up and shone on the turbid, swirling water. Here it was, the canal's icy ripple. Only now it was summer and it was still icy . . . A pleasure boat rammed through the water and the laughing, tipsy tourists waved to her. Masha turned away. Why did Seva want to meet here? Now she had to jut up on the street like a column, to the amusement of the rare passersby. On one side of the Kryukov Canal loomed the Mariinsky; on the other, a ridiculous construction site that in the uncertain future was supposed to be the theater's second hall. When the Mariinsky was still her theater, she'd waited anxiously for what would happen when they moved to the new building and renovations began in the old. Day after day she'd watched them clear the ground for the new one and wreck the First Five-Year Plan Palace of Culture, a fairly dismal example of Stalinist empire style. For a while, like a graphic illustration of the empire's fall, only the huge czarist columns rising out of the mountain of wreckage and debris were left standing. Masha imagined that before she knew it they would be putting in stone benches here, like an amphitheater, and instead of actors they would bring in captive gladiators—and the new theater would be ready. But they dynamited the columns, razed a couple of other old buildings, and for a long time the construction didn't even begin; they probably hadn't been able to find the money. Still, in that time, the time of Masha's maturation, an eternity passed! The building put some meat on its bones and was gradually transformed into a boring concrete box with the bare ribs of its framework poking out indecently. Instead of captive gladiators, migrant workers showed up and scurried from floor to floor like ants from morning until night. And now, despite the late hour, the figure of some detained construction worker stuck up in a window. He might be sleeping right here. He might have nowhere else to go.

People just keep coming, as if the city is totally elastic, so you can't walk calmly down the street anymore, Masha thought with irritation.

But if you hire someone like that, you don't have to pay him a lot, and when this moth leaves the theater he'll push her off the bridge and no one will notice . . . What thoughts! What evil thoughts! But it was true, no one would see. At night . . . but he's just the kind you shouldn't get mixed up with . . . he'd spill the beans. But if this young lady were to walk up . . . She rented an apartment a little ways down, on Masterskaya . . . maybe she just rented a bed, not an apartment . . . and if no one were around then, Masha herself could ask her for a light : . . Oh, what nonsense. After all, if the girl were pushed, she would cry out . . . and then—stop. After all, Masha didn't know for a fact whether Seva had anything going on with her. Insanity, that's what passions lead to. She closed her eyes and thought she could see that pale freckled vixen go flying into the cold water—a split second, and that would be the end of her.

Masha leaned slightly over the railing. Why, it was so low . . . No mesh whatsoever, just two crossbars . . . Yes, yes, my life is ruined . . . Take Dima, for example. Where is that Dima now? Before him there'd been someone else, Sergei Pavlovich. She'd forgotten all about him until now, all of a sudden . . . She wrote something about him on Seva's orders, back at the very beginning, when they'd just met, and that Sergei Pavlovich—no, Konstantinovich, definitely Konstantinovich, like her prodigal father—jumped out a window . . . Enough! If she didn't go tomorrow and get a decent pedicure and if she couldn't pay Lastochka for her hair, then she couldn't go on living. She had to find a way out somehow. Lastochka charged so much now. The nerve of her! On the other hand, you weren't going to find anyone better . . . Seva had no idea how she put herself together every day, starting early in the morning, her weekly purchases were expensive—or did he think she washed her hair with rosemary and covered her hands with sunflower oil?

She'd promised to stop by her aunt's a month ago, but no, she wouldn't go. Those visits sunk her into an awful depression, she felt like hanging herself, and then it took so much time, and Masha didn't have any money for the psychologist now. The psychologist would squeeze her dry. Her aunt could sit there alone and fancy herself a widowed duchess. When Uncle Pasha died, she'd exchanged the apartment at the favorite niece's wish. Masha got a room, which she now rented out, while she herself rented a decent separate space, and her aunt got a room too. It was her own fault for ending up in a housing project. Masha had tried to talk her aunt into agreeing to an apartment outside town, where she would have fresh air to breathe and could lead a circle at the club. They were easing her out of her job anyway. No, she clung to her city, but why? Here, they wouldn't even let her pick up her instrument; her neighbors immediately started making a fuss.

Masha found all this depressing. No, nothing like that was going to happen to her. She would age beautifully, maybe have a child—one—not that she was particularly eager, but men needed that . . . Why wasn't he here? Where *was* Seva!

Maybe he was with that mangy vixen and had forgotten about her altogether. Lord, my God, my heart's really beating . . . No, I can't leave it like this.

"Look, there's water coming in under the door. They shut me in but forgot to turn off the tap. There wasn't any hot water for a couple of weeks so the taps were all left open. But if I'm not going where my Masha is now, where the rivers meet, what's the big surprise if the water's running like this, flowing like hot blood, turbulent, and the little boats darting this way and that through it, like the needles in the neighbor boy's veins, the needles he pokes into himself in the kitchen, thinking I don't notice. I wanted to ask him, but I was scared of frightening him. What do I need a needle for? What about lighting this airshaft—what if it lit up all of a sudden? Somewhere where there's no light at all, just a wolfish-gray longing . . . This is how I dreamed of hell: I'm sitting in a deep but narrow hole looking up the whole time, at a dim light very high up . . . but I'll never get there. Never.

"Dreams are the only reason I'm still moving, because I started having terrible dreams. Once I dreamed I was in a well, not an airshaft like this one, but a real well, only without water, and up above vampires were reaching for me with their long feelers. But I'm not afraid. I know if I start playing it will all pass, but the neighbors say it's too loud. I could now—no one's there . . . but today I actually shouldn't play. Under no circumstances should I, since someone else is already playing, and playing beautifully. I just don't know who . . . somewhere, up above . . .

"The water is flowing and flowing, nonstop. Oh well, if I'm not going where the rivers meet, it will play a trick—a cheap trick!—and arrange a trap, so that it can always play cat-and-mouse with me—catch and release . . . catch and release."

Vsevolod parked his car rather far away. He was walking in no hurry, though he was late for his date with Masha. A real piece of work, but a foolish piece of work; a useful piece of work, but a stultifying piece of work. To tell the truth, he'd been attracted to dancers practically since he was a kid, but the kind without ambitions. He didn't care for ballet stars and never went after the big names. A no-name little ballet girl—that was as good as it got, that's how he'd come across Masha. Long neck and big eyes, she bat her eyelashes and caught his every word; she was always hungry. She was afraid of making any unnecessary movement, so as not to disgrace herself. After all, she came from the sticks to live with her aunt at someone else's expense. She called her aunt "Mama" and her uncle "Papa" because she had no mother and she'd only seen her father a couple of times in her life. As skittish as a hare, and she did everything without a murmur, no matter how you posed her. He took full advantage of that—lying, standing, upside down.

She turned out to be useful in other ways too. She turned out to have a brain she could flex when she needed to, and could bare her teeth at strangers, show some muscle, protect her master, and he appreciated that. On the one hand, he liked it . . . but on the other, it had started to bother him. Lately Vsevolod had sensed his babe was having quite a hard time—he guessed her time had come for nest building. He knew those tricks of theirs, and for Masha he was prepared to put up with a lot. Maybe he should give her, oh, thirty thousand bucks. That would be quite a lot for her, and he wouldn't feel it, he could bring more. He could, but there was no point spoiling her, so . . . for starters, he had to come to his senses. He could keep her longer, he'd grown used to her, but there was one new circumstance . . . this gentle eighteen-year-old circumstance . . . and Masha . . . she wouldn't understand, though she should . . . she could have caught on by now: let him, Seva, get away with stuff and accept the world as it was. He wondered what she'd do without him.

Right then Seva got a stab in his side. It was his matchless, famed intuition talking to him. She knew an awful lot, and no good could come of an injured woman, especially Masha, who was something special. You couldn't buy her off. She needed something else . . . He could pawn her off on someone else . . . someone good—that was something they did too, but with her, that trick wouldn't work, she'd get even nastier . . . but so what? What about wiping her out? The concept appealed to him: wipe off the face of the earth, from memory, as if she never existed and everything was starting fresh, and no one had ever set foot there before . . . Wipe her out. This thought didn't surprise Seva. It was as if he'd been expecting it. He started tallying up his material and moral loss in the one case or the other—if he wiped Masha out or left her walking the earth.

Seva was an old campaigner. He'd started his career small, gone through fire and ice at the very peak of gangsterism, and now he lived peacefully and quietly, or so it seemed. He came from a civilized family, was cautious, sly, beautifully educated, and generous when he had to be, and he had charisma. Seva held a respectable state post and in interviews said proudly of himself, "I'm a creator." If dirty work was required, he didn't have to get himself dirty anymore. Obliging hands were always found for that, but he had experienced that animal horror he'd known in his youth during brawls (and he'd been through all kinds) and never forgot it. Sometimes, to unwind, Vsevolod Mikhailovich would take a break and pay tribute to his old enthusiasm for the arts, which dated from his school days: photography and painting. He organized exhibits and went pub crawling with art students, touched by their childish bluntness and their modest demands on life. "Like bugs, they live on crumbs and are happy to have them, baby bugs, the muck of the earth, and we need that . . . the trees have to grow on something." He and Masha laughed so hard, and Masha understood him perfectly, she was greedy for life, but a little too greedy . . .

They met on the Kryukov near the Torgovy Bridge, as agreed.

The light was already fading, the streetlamps were on, and there was a silvery reflection in the water of the St. Nicholas bell tower flickering in the dusk.

Masha uttered not a word of reproach to her man for being late. She pretended she'd been busy examining the cranes that crossed their long arrows, as if getting into a discussion.

"Look how wretched," she said, waving her arm toward the new building.

"Check it out from another standpoint—an urbanist landscape, a clash of planes. It's going to be a lot drearier when it's all finished."

He didn't try to explain to her that at base a construction site was a clash of interests, not planes, and the loser was what was wretched.

Masha suddenly cried out. After the alarming fantasies that had overtaken her during her wait, she now imagined the water had splashed over the banks and touched her ankles.

"What's up, kid?"

"Do you have a cigarette?"

Seva held out a pack, but it was odd because she didn't smoke. Very occasionally, for photographs, she would toy with slim feminine cigarettes.

A couple of foreigners walked by. The man was lazily stroking the naked back of the woman, who was wearing an elegant evening dress. The couple were obviously counting on a long and pleasant night, a fitting cap to admiring the Petersburg landscapes.

"Well, where are we going?" Masha was hoping for a night in a good club, top-notch jazz, and she wouldn't mind a drink, her nerves were completely shattered.

"Today I feel like wandering," Seva said.

Really? Masha's friend was only rarely visited by these desires, and she'd reconciled herself, but right now it was all wrong. She tried to nudge Seva toward the center of town. But he took her arm and, jokingly ordering her, pulled her along. As always in these instances, they strolled through Kolomna, where Seva had lived as a boy and until he'd bought himself a place not far from Palace Square. From time to time they came across beautifully restored buildings, but there were entire swaths of rental apartment buildings, the refuge of the newcomers who were barbarizing the city. The Kolomna where Pushkin's poor Evgeny lost his marbles was still Kolomna, and the little Pryazhka River still bore its waters past Blok's sadly famous insane asylum, now a museum. The museum could do its museum thing, but the crazies were going to be moved elsewhere. There was no reason to be crazy in the center of town, and the freed-up buildings could be turned into VIP mental hospitals

Kolomna was probably the city's last district where lots of courtyards still weren't barred and there weren't formidable code locks on the gates. Seva dragged Masha through courtyards and secret passages for hours. She didn't like walking around here at night, even with Seva, and now the only thing that reassured her was the fact that they probably had a bodyguard following discreetly on their heels. She cursed under her breath. Where was he taking her? A man to whom all doors were open and who was received everywhere with respect was traipsing through the streets and kissing in strangers' spit-covered entryways! Why would he never ask her whether she liked doing it in stairwells when someone could walk up at any time? True, Masha herself never protested, and his swift, silent pressure was not as important to her as the relaxation that followed it and the weakness that spread over his face. Sometimes he even wept. She never told anyone about that, but she was immoderately proud of his tears. The bodily part of it barely roused her. This coldness had been in her since the very start of their romance, and she may have derived the most pleasure from the awareness that she had complete mastery, albeit not for long, over this strong, omnipotent man. How could she have known that he had never been hers for a second. His whole life had been slave to a single passion which she actually could have understood had she chosen to—the thirst for power.

It wasn't love that softened his features and brought him to tears, but the pleasure of unlimited power over her breath and life. Today, in the empty attic where he'd brought her, this passion flared up with unusual heat, for he knew the end was nigh.

At some moment in their tryst he picked Masha up abruptly and spun her around, and then, as if going rigid, dropped her on the floor. She waited for Seva to help her get up, but he stepped to the side, and without moving watched her lying on the floor, smeared in the dust. Then Seva remembered himself and gave her a hand. "Sorry," he said, and he kissed Masha's forehead.

That was it. She was the past. Like all those who had already been wiped out, all those he'd beaten.

But right then, as if on purpose—this was all he needed—a photograph fell out of his pants pocket. A photograph of the pale corps de ballet moth with freckles au naturel. Nude.

Not much to look at. Not really worth photographing. It was obvious he'd taken it himself, sitting on the couch in his kitchen, and she was covering her breasts with her hands, the tramp. What had compelled him to carry around her photograph?

Masha started screaming, calling Seva bad words that surfaced from out of nowhere, since she'd never sworn before. They fought nastily and crudely, and the worst part was that toward the end he said to her with the most genuine contempt, "Who do you think you are? Look at yourself—an ordinary trade-school girl!"

He zipped up his pants and ran out, zigzagging through the courtyards.

Masha remained there a little longer, staring straight at the wall, then went downstairs slowly and cautiously and came out on Printers Union Street. She walked home, constantly tripping on construction debris. She walked that way and farther—past Theater Square, past the monument to Rimsky-Korsakov, and for another ten minutes or so through the nighttime streets, though it wasn't so scary. She came to a halt on the Kryukov Canal. She had just been waiting here on this bridge for Seva. How much time had passed? Two hours, three?

The most terrible thing had come to pass. What she had feared most in this life. She was a mediocrity, a faded part of this gray, worm-eaten mass, a trade-school girl! This was exactly what she had hoped to avoid when she had made for the Petersburg air, rotten though it was! Why, oh why had this nightmare come crashing down on her head? Because she'd never loved her chronically ill mother? In childhood, at the sight of her, Masha had wanted to get away, flee, deny everything so as not to be saturated with the smell of illness and death . . . But she was just a child, pure and simple. Why was she being punished now?

Masha had heard many times about women getting left . . . certain kinds of women, but that couldn't affect her. She couldn't be abandoned . . . but she had been, and that meant she was like everyone else . . . Such inflated pride, such an inflated sense of herself in this world . . . and now she was a mediocrity, a nobody, and my God, she looked around—this theater and this square, the music, the dance, even the dance wasn't for her . . . It wasn't the dance that had abandoned her, though, but vice versa . . . Seva . . . Was he really to blame? He'd just noticed that the gilt had rubbed off and there was nothing underneath . . . How could there be nothing? She would show him yet. Masha tried to come up with an idea . . . maybe she would write a letter that would make him understand . . . But a terrible devastation fell over her, there was a void in her head, and that meant it was true, she was a nothing—and everyone already knew it . . . No, if she went to see him and begged on her knees, he would explain that he'd just been joking around, he'd been drunk! Yes, that must be it, he'd been drunk!

Masha had not been wrong about the bodyguard. He was watching her right now, hiding behind the construction vans on the embankment. But he was no longer guarding her body, for it had come detached and had ceased to be a part of his boss. Protector was now hunter.

There was the quick clicking of heels. Coming toward the bridge from Theater Square was a maidenly figure holding a single rose. Masha glimpsed the girl's face and wasn't surprised to encounter the very same freckles from Seva's photograph. Time had become dense, as if it wanted to gather up all events and encounters in a single night.

The killer saw that Masha more than likely had asked for a light because the click of heels stopped and the girl with the rose was digging in her purse. Then a weak flame ignited, but she couldn't get it to light for a moment because of the wind. Another minute and again the clicking of heels.

Masha took a drag, but again, as a few hours before, cold water from the canal splashed her. She leaned over the railing; the water was far away. Masha thought she saw a reflection slip by in it, or no, someone's shadow, but the water bore it away, and then another shadow, and again the current carried it off.

The hunter saw Masha slowly begin to dance, as if hearing music and trying to fall in with the beat. Preparation, sissonne, pas de chat, chaînés. . . transition to grand jeté en rond. . . No, that's wrong! She threw her arm up, as if tossing away the learned technique, and abruptly dropped it, slicing the air. The bitterness of loss in the broken and terrible movements of her elbows and knees, the spinning of freakish suffering, the impotence after birth and the flight, the clumsy, insane flight, the fall full-force, and the slow awakening. Her body was buffeted like a banner of despair, her dance was the dance of the shadow, the dance of the reflection, death dancing and an incredible revelation, so unlike anything she had known before. Too bad there was no one to appreciate the birth of this insane whirlwind that had suddenly settled in her.

There was only one spectator. He squeezed the trigger when the dancer was right at the bridge and, continuing her pas, bent over very low, as if she wanted to examine her own reflection in the water. The bullet did not interrupt her movement, and a second later the waters closed over.

Seva was walking through the courtyards alone. He had sent his bodyguard away. Let him do his job. He knew everything here, he'd grown up here. Each building was marked by a fight, kisses, humiliation, because he'd known that too, he hadn't always been on top, sometimes he'd been way down below . . . Right now he felt himself at full strength, fixed into this life like a screw, and if he was meant to go to the bottom, he would take the whole boat down with him. His fears and the neurosis that had once made his eyelid twitch were now behind him.

It was torture being a teenager with a twitching eyelid. So he had conquered that tic. His dream of becoming the helmsman in this life had come to pass, and that meant it was God's doing—if, of course, He existed. If not, all the better. That meant he had earned his helm without outside assistance. In any event, there were natural laws that were helping him make his way up the ladder. A flat-out sprint, thank God. Donkeys never advanced, capable only of obeying, unable to live without idols such as he was, without his firm hand and approving smile. He began making plans for tomorrow. He wasn't thinking about Masha.

"Look at all the water that's accumulated, I have to hurry . . . So? . . . Don't take the violin? You're sitting in your burrow, and you think you need everything. But you go out and what is this stuff for? I'll just pack up the little statue, the china ballerina, I have to wipe the dust off her and wrap her up in newspaper . . . We have plenty of ballerinas here, the Mariinsky Theater is next door, they're like windup toys there, but this one always sits here sad, lifeless, as if she were ill. Goddamnit! A foot broke off! Rats . . . And the music is too loud, my ears hurt, beautiful music, who's playing, I don't know—there, upstairs, or maybe I'm going mad because the mind is a boundary and I'm trying to erase things. This is all a joke, though. I see perfectly well that the dust has to be wiped away. But the water is flowing, still flowing, I guess I need to climb on the chair. Let not the water overflow me, neither let the deep swallow me up, and let not the pit shut her mouth upon me.

"Here they are thinking they did me in . . . strange people, as if I could be done in. See, the flood has begun, I have to hurry, I'll send for my things. Fine . . . there's been so much that's terrible I don't have to be afraid anymore. I'm going away, yes, I said I'd send for my things, only I have to tell Masha. Here's what she should be told: *Dance, Masha!*

"*Masha! Hear me, Masha? Dance! Dance, Masha, otherwise we're lost.*"

* * *

Seva had just stopped to take out a cigarette when a heavy body fell on him from above. His head struck the ground and he no longer saw anything, he just felt a swift and powerful flow pull him along.

The comic death of a big shot killed by an old woman falling from her window—actually, it's a sin to call her that since she wasn't even sixty—kept newspaper readers entertained for quite a while.

Masha never was found, and they simply wrote her off as missing.

THE PHANTOM OF THE OPERA FOREVER

BY JULIA BELOMLINSKY

Arts Square

Translated by Ronald Meyer

*"Do you like street singing?" Raskolnikov suddenly addressed the
passerby, a man who was no longer young and had the look of an
idler, standing next to him by the organ-grinder. The latter looked at
him startled and surprised. "I do," Raskolnikov continued, but with
a look as if to say that he wasn't talking about street singing at all.
"I like it when they sing to the accompaniment of an organ-grinder
on a cold, dark, and damp autumn night, it has to be damp, when
all the passersby have sickly pale green and sickly faces; or even
better, when there's wet snow falling, straight down, and there's
no wind, you know? And through it shine the gas streetlights . . ."*
—Fyodor Dostoevsky, *Crime and Punishment*

We were walking along Italyanskaya Street.

Italyanskaya Street was empty.

Four thirty—the most unpopular time for White
Nights.

All the carriages had started turning into pumpkins.

The coachmen into rats.

The crystal slippers fell off and shattered.

The ball dress turned out to be smeared with ashes.

The pumpkins rolled downhill to the bridges.
The rats readied themselves and were screwing around.
Everyone wanted to go home, but the metro was closed.
The early-morning chill had set in.
Puddles of vomit and shards of beer bottles everywhere.
The era of street-cleaning machines had not yet arrived.

But we were local, you see—guys from the district.

Long ago we had grown accustomed to the fact that if you were just going out to pay the electric bill on Millionaya Street, you'd run into Atlas holding up the sky.

Go straight—and you bump into the Hermitage.
To your left—the Capella Courtyards.
To your right—Kazan Cathedral . . .
"But why do you want to go to St. Isaac's?"

My companion Lyokha Saksofon fully realized the "happiness" of living in the city center and hanging out in the district.

And he wrote this joyful song.
Now we were loudly singing it on the empty square:

And this, my friend, is my district and my city
That's why my collar is raised high
That's why I'm not wearing designer shoes
That's who we are—that's how we do it
What are you talking about! What are you talking about!

"Come on, Lyokha, roll one. Roll a couple right away, it's pretty nice here. Pushkin is waving . . . We'll leave him the roach . . . For the best poet, the best roach!"

We were already sitting on the bench and looking at Pushkin.

The bums who hang out on the square by the Dostoevsky monument are called Dostoevskies, and the ones on Pushkin Square are Pushkins. But there's nobody here now . . . half past four, child's play—and nobody's here.

The Golden Triangle. Nothing ever happens here . . .

Two years ago, right outside the Hotel Europe, the English consul was robbed—and since then it's been quiet. Every night the Phantom of the Opera is supposed to come out onto the roof of the Maly Opera and cry out like a muezzin: "All's well in the Golden Triangle!"

Although it was precisely on that roof that something happened to one of my friends last winter.

It was Misha Bakaleishchikov—the Man from the Past.

The Man from the Past was supposed to come to the City of His Youth in search of his Past . . . It's the usual move for an idiot.

I even envy him. He had come back for good to the little town of his childhood that's green with mold . . .

Once he saved me. I was fifteen.

We had just come out on the Nevsky then for the first time— to make some money.

Three kids from the seventh grade. Sonya had a violin. Manya, a clarinet.

And I had a harmonica. And a black cap for the money. And all around us—deaf Soviet power. We managed to stand there for about four minutes. And then they took us by the hand and led us away . . . No, not the cops. Fyoka's crew. The cops didn't touch anybody . . .

So far, Fyoka's crew hadn't given them the go-ahead.

Fyoka's crew—sounds good, right?

It's like when Long John Silver in the movie version of *Treasure Island* asks, "Where's Flint's crew?"

And then later, when they're still on the brigantine:

The Jolly Roger waves in the wind—
Flint's crew is singing a ditty . . .

We all sang that song when we were in the Young Pioneers.

The brigantine—that was the most important part.

The pirates raised the brigantine's sails on the high blue seas.

And somehow that got mixed up with Alexander Grin's *Scarlet Sails*.

All the cafés were called that.

And the clubs where the young people were supposed to spend their leisure time.

Young Pioneer groups.

Scarlet Sails. Or the Brigantine. Or Romance.

That's what our romance was like . . .

But it turned out that the pirates' sea wasn't so very far away after all—it was right there in front of us, on the banks of the Neva.

And Flint's crew was there as well.

They made their journey on scarlet sails. Or grew up right there.

Out of the slime and dampness . . .

They sent the young people into ecstasy, trembling.

Flint's crew—that was really something.

The fucking corsairs! The fucking corsairs! The corsairs.

We thought that they were in opposition to the powers that be. That they weren't any worse than the dissidents—fighters and heroes.

As a matter of fact, I don't know what it was like in Moscow, but in Piter their relationship with the powers that be was precisely as if they were real corsairs.

The powers that be had been living off their thieving for quite some time.

In Piter all the cops were taken care of.

Once Sasha Bashlachov came up with this metaphor about us and the West: "You're still between the spoon and the lie, and we're still between the wolf and the louse."

The wolves, you see, were these corsairs of ours.

The KGB of those days was probably the louse. Which didn't hunt for real criminals, but for the shitty bohemians.

Catching poets was an entirely lousy occupation. And they gave you ten years for smoking a joint . . .

And the Wolves weren't your usual criminals.

It was our Young Capitalism.

Our Nascent Bootlegging.

In our Northern Old Chicago.

The people were being dressed by the black-marketeers.

The hard-currency girls were teaching the *Kama Sutra*.

Shadow capitalists were setting up factories.

Somewhere in the depths of Kupchino, simple Soviet people were making fifteenth-century Saxon porcelain. Even the fact that porcelain wasn't invented until the eighteenth century didn't stop them.

Well, naturally, the Underwater Kingdom needed poets like it needed a hole in the head. But artists and musicians could sometimes find work. Somebody had to draw all those stencils and sketches, and the musicians attended to the leisure.

The life of a corsair is simple: battle on the seas, and an end-less holiday on shore—that is, a tavern with some tunes and babes.

A lot of people worked in the taverns. And I'd been singing in one since I was sixteen . . .

It was right then, during that period, that everything was possible. Because nothing was impossible.

And the laws didn't work for shit. I started singing a year and a half after that first appearance on the Nevsky . . .

Then the corsairs took us gently by the arm and led us away.

And they led us to the Ulster, Fyoka's port of hail. Flint's crew gathered there every night.

We wept. We said that we were in the seventh grade. We said, "Guys, we won't do it again . . ."

They didn't beat us. This first time they explained that any-one who wanted to sell something on the Nevsky—no matter what—needed to come to an agreement with the corsairs and pay up. It was all very simple. Musicians were already working on the Nevsky. And the artists were pushing masks of some kind and pottery.

And everybody paid off the corsairs, while the corsairs paid off—again, not the cops, but higher up—the KGB itself. Every-thing concerned with hard cash was the fiefdom of the KGB. And not the cops. Although the cops of course also got in on the action sometimes.

The Nevsky started getting wild when the tourists arrived.

And when there weren't any tourists, you had the Finnish construction workers.

But we were little schoolkids, so they took pity on us and let us go after we gave our word that we wouldn't show our faces on the Nevsky with our music.

They threw us out like the trash.

We had such an immature look about us—skinny and under-developed.

But I very much wanted to be part of that life. I managed to fall in love with one of the guys, the one who held me by my col-lar as he led me there and back.

He was either Fyoka's right hand . . . or the left one . . .

And I started going there. They would chase me away right when Fyoka would make his appearance. He was a well-known sadist. But he wasn't a fucking pedophile.

He really liked manhandling girls. But all his girls were real blondes, with tits and asses . . .

These Russian Barbies. With long blond hair . . . These Barbie babes.

And then I was emaciated and tall—well, like I am now. Dark, short hair.

Definitely an underground look, just for him.

And the other corsairs found me to their liking.

Or did I simply like this circus around me?

They found it somewhat amusing that he wouldn't allow me to go to the Ulster.

And I became particularly friendly with the barmen. I was always sitting there at the bar, drinking coffee with cognac.

Later, they stopped chasing me away. Even when Fyoka was there.

I would sit quietly and watch them. And listen to music.

And of course, just like in the movies, I knew by heart the entire repertoire of the group that played there.

Then one fine day I finally got up the nerve and butted in—they were playing cards. Twenty-one.

I said that I wanted to play one-on-one with Fyoka.

That was me showing off in front of the guy I was in love with. He didn't give a fuck, but he laughed at the situation along with everyone else.

Fyoka said: "Let's play. But if you lose, we'll take you with us today. And then we'll really play . . ."

There were rumors that they had taken one girl to some wasteland, poured gas on her, and set her on fire . . . I'm not sure if that's true, but their working girls were always walking around broken and shattered and ending up in the hospital—those weren't rumors.

I knew all that. Since I was fifteen.

And I didn't need to brazen it out.

But in general there was no stopping me.

It was probably the effect of the coffee and cognac.

Of course I lost.

And then our Captain Flint said, "You're a very brave girl. But now we're going to test you and see what you're made of. You don't want us to take you with us? Well then, we can try this: our brave girl puts her little hands on the table now and we'll put out our cigarettes on them. If the little girl doesn't yell, we'll let her go home. And if she yells—we'll take her with us."

There were seven corsairs besides him, and of course each one applied his cigarette for a second. Only for a second. But nobody refused to do it—they had their own rules.

And then the captain said: "Now I'll show you how to put out a cigarette." He touched me with it and held it there, well, for what seemed like a hundred years. Probably all of a minute. But I didn't cry out, I was determined to remain silent, like a partisan . . .

This scar here, the big round one from the captain's cigarette, is always visible, while the other seven are small and faded.

But the point is, I didn't cry out. And Fyoka said that I could go wherever I damn well pleased . . . since I'm such a brave girl.

My teeth were chattering, but I still had the strength to make out that I was okay, and I said that I'd sit for a bit and drink my coffee.

And I still had enough strength to get to the women's bathroom. And there the girls started shouting at me: "Piss on her hands! Quick, piss!" Then they wrapped my hands in napkins soaked with urine. I felt such pain that I let out a howl and collapsed to the floor.

And there and then the barman flew into the women's restroom, picked me up, got me outside, and took me to his place.

He lived with his mother, Larisa Mikhalna.

Of course, that wasn't typical of the real corsairs, or of those who were simply real criminals. Well, just like in the Russian classics.

Here in our Petersburg swamp mafia—strange as it might seem—almost everybody had parents. After all, there were a lot of Jews and half-Jews. And a lot of Armenians among the newcomers to the city. Not so much your military peoples as your trading ones.

The Russian boys, on the whole, were from the intelligentsia. The hard-currency girls also somehow turned out to have mothers—hairdressers, nurses, teachers, shop assistants . . .

And this barman was none other than Misha Bakaleishchikov.

I lived with them for two weeks, and Larisa Mikhalna nursed me back to health. She smeared me with some special creams. My mother was at the dacha. And in general she didn't pay much attention, since she was busy with her latest affair.

But Flint's crew started to respect me after this incident. And they accepted me not as one of the girls, but something like Jim the cabin boy.

In 1937, in the worst fucking time of the Stalin era, a Soviet version of *Treasure Island* was released. The plot was changed a great deal: the heroes were now Irish rebels. For some reason, the action was switched from Scotland to Ireland. They didn't need treasure, they needed to buy weapons to fight the English imperialists for the freedom of Ireland, their homeland. And the main hero is a girl named Jenny.

This Jenny loves Dr. Livesey. She gets fixed up as a cabin boy on the *Hispaniola*, after dressing up like one, and now they call her Jim the cabin boy. Some red-headed girl wearing trousers is clearly playing the part. And like all girls playing trouser roles, she's got short, fat legs and a fat, round butt.

In general, it's first-class. And the script had to be like that. Because in a romantic society—and under Stalin, society was superromantic—heroes couldn't love money for the sake of money. They had to love more important things, like freedom, the Fatherland . . . It was impossible simply to love cold, hard cash.

And, well, it was stupid simply to love cold, hard cash. Even though a lot of people do love it . . . And one could also love power. Fyoka probably loved the power he wielded over his schooner more than the girls. Many of them loved the game. The process of the game. And of course it was precisely the bucks that the shadow capitalists loved. I don't believe that any of them loved manufacturing Saxon porcelain or those Japanese kerchiefs . . .

And there, on this Petersburg pirate schooner of ours, I turned out to be Jim the cabin boy. My idiot's dream had come true—I was proud and happy.

These scars on my hands were like my initiation—they had accepted me, they had taken me aboard the schooner.

And they had accepted me not for my cunt, but for my bravery and determination. Me and lots of my peers had made a cult of these guys. I was fifteen and they were victorious heroes to me.

Not victors over the KGB, not the Wolves who were victorious over the Louse, but rather the Wolves from Vysotsky.

They'd jumped over the fence, knocked down the flags, victors over the hunters.

Victors over the system.

That's how it seemed to me then. About the Louse, it's only now that I understand. But then, when I was fifteen: "The Jolly Roger flaps in the wind."

And another old song, this time from Jack London:

The wind howls, the sea rages
We corsairs will not surrender
We stand, back to back, by the mast
The two of us—against a thousand!

Now isn't that super?

* * *

Well, so that's when I started singing. First there, in the Ulster. And later at the Troika. And then in various places . . .

At the same time we were going to school somewhere, and received our superfluous Soviet diplomas. I had studied for a period at the school of the Ministry of Culture.

There was this young dude who played the Fano in the Ulster . . . Simply a phenomenal ear. And he was studying engineering. Because his dad wanted him to.

And Misha and I are still friends; well, he helped me to get on board the schooner—my singing is all thanks to him.

All the more so as I was still a minor. And he had been a student at some point in that same institute of the Ministry of Culture, only he was seven years older than me . . .

We'd run out of pot . . . And the sun had already started to shine through Pushkin.

Small birds perched on Pushkin's head: sparrows and pigeons. While large birds flew around: crows and seagulls. And all of them were crying out in their own language. So let's say the sparrows chirped, while the pigeons squawked melodically. But those large birds were making monstrous sounds, particularly for a person who'd just had a good smoke and wanted some peace. All that wailing and moaning and horror. It seemed astonishing that the language of birds is called "song." But we still didn't want to leave the nice little square. We of course had a serious case of the munchies, though we were too lazy to do anything about it, particularly since all the places open at night were so unappetizing. So it made sense to be patient and wait until Prokopych or Freakadelic opened up, right here on the square.

Although it was clear that we wouldn't make it here in this little square till nine.

Lyokha had some more grass in his little Indian jar . . .

The seagulls and crows had ascended and flown off to the roof of the Maly Opera . . .

* * *

Misha Bakaleishchikov, the Man from the Past, made his appearance then like a bolt out of the blue.

In late February.

And not from the States, but from London for some reason.

He found me—he'd searched me out specially.

We were sitting in a café—at the Hotel Europe, on that very same square. We were in the midst of a terribly slippery winter thaw—black ice.

We talked about the Past.

We said to each other, "Give me a cigarette . . ."

Misha's wife had left him.

The fifth one or the third.

"It's because you smoke grass from morning till night!"

In London he had been working at some mythical Russian radio station.

But he vaguely hinted at his close ties to personages out of favor. Either Gusya or Beryozy (a.k.a. Gusinsky or Berezovsky) . . .

"In general, I can do anything! Well, I can make your any wish come true! What do you want? Do you want me to take you to London tomorrow?"

"I want . . . London is too easy now. Let me think a minute . . . In fairy tales they always give you three wishes. And here you're giving me only one. So that means I need to come up with something really fucking hard . . ."

"Well, come on, think up something hard. If I make it come true, will you marry me?"

"Why the hell do you want to marry me? I'm forty—"

"Five. I remember. Well, I already married a young one. Sveta, the last one, was young. I'm tired of her. And I never married you . . ."

"And you always dreamed of it?"

I started laughing. And so did Misha. He'd never dreamed

of it. He's always been married, as long as I've known him. First it was the deputy director of the Beryozka store. Then a Finn, a Swede, a famous ballerina, and a famous model. All his marriages facilitated the "machine of social advancement," as he put it.

In bed, handsome as he inhaled the obligatory cigarette: "You understand, my girl, that I can't marry you. I long ago turned into a machine of my own social advancement . . ."

There was a time when I would get excited by the frequent visits of the elegant Bakaleishchikov—driving either a Mazda or a Honda.

Restaurants and cafés, spending the night in expensive hotels, carefree sex of an athletic bent with all kinds of interesting foreign doodads . . .

I said, "Come on, knock it off, roll us one."

And he sang me the song from *Easy Rider*:

Don't bogart that joint, my friend
Pass it over to me
Don't bogart that joint, my friend
Pass it over to me

And he explained that contemporary English has this verb "to bogart."

"It comes from Humphrey Bogart—I swear! It appeared after the movie *The Roaring Twenties*. Bogart is in a foxhole with Jimmy Cagney, and Cagney lets Bogart have a puff of his cigarette, but Bogart smokes it down to nothing with one draw and doesn't leave anything for Cagney . . . It's a verb from the hippie days: don't 'bogart' that joint, pass it on to the next guy . . . *The Roaring Twenties*. But for some reason here it was called *The Soldier's Fate in America*. Even though they're soldiers only for the first five minutes of the movie, it's just that one scene in the foxhole. And then all of sudden they're fucking bootleggers . . .

But you probably didn't see this movie . . . By your time it had probably already disappeared from the rerun theaters. But I remember it . . . Still, there's a seven-year difference—that's a lot. And it's particularly noticeable when discussing movies . . . oh, and music too . . . And *Easy Rider* wasn't screened in the Soviet Union until we had VCRs . . ."

"Come on, knock it off, roll the joint . . ."

And here we are together once more. And he even has a room in the Hotel Europe again. And the bed as before is more of an athletic field than a meditation space. It's a strange setting for smoking weed . . .

He started talking about old movies again. Turns out he has an uncle in America.

"Go figure, Anya, he's got the same name—Misha Bakaleishchikov! And he worked as a composer in Old Hollywood, composed music for movies Bogart was in. And Lauren Bacall. Real first-class film scores . . . They showed them in the rerun theater on Vaska, remember? Some were spoils of war, others came from Lend-Lease . . . And I taught you how to raise your eyes when you're getting a light . . ."

Then we reminisced about our old gang, made up of various inhabitants of the square.

The times when we were all hanging out in the inner courtyard of the Maly Opera.

The scenery model studio was in a former admiral's apartment—an enfilade of communicating rooms, and there was a corridor on one side as well. The theater had appropriated the house; there were empty, uninhabited rooms above and below. You could enter this courtyard simply through the gate—there wasn't any security.

In the mid-'80s a whole group of artists worked there.

And they all dragged along their friends. Other artists would

go there, and musicians too . . . Actors from the nearby theaters—
the Operetta, Komisarshevskaya, and Comedy theaters . . .

And the corsairs would go there . . . the blackmarket guys,
hard-currency girls . . . prostitutes from the Hotel Europe.

And the artsy bimbos—the girlfriends of the poets—always
to be found in this sort of gathering . . .

The artists had funny names: Nemkov, Nemtsov, and Nemchinov. And another two were named Tabachnik and Pasechnik.

The arrival to the studio of a guy named Bakaleishchikov
made everybody's day, for sure.

Tabachnik, Pasechnik, and Bakaleishchikov were close
friends. Nemkov, Nemtsov, and Nemchinov, fought constantly.
And Kit would pull them apart . . .

Kit bound the whole gang together, he made models for all
of them.

And they often fought to get closer to Kit. In the very first
room stood an enormous bathtub, and Kit kept his axolotls there.
One day he had an argument with the fire inspectors, who came
back later and poisoned his axolotls.

Kit also collected old irons.

I once got mad at Tabachnik and threw an iron at his head.
Thank God I missed, because it could have killed him.

I was always throwing and hitting people over the head with
bottles—for nothing at all.

Since childhood. Why did I do it? Life is a battlefield.

Sometimes fights would break out there in the studio—
drunken artists having it out, no worse than the corsairs.

But not because of Kit. And not because of some dough. The
fights, more often than not, were on account of girls. You know:
don't bogart that joint, you son of a bitch—pass it to your friend!

"Anya, do you remember that time when you went to Odessa
with Afrikan and his whole gang, and you were doing some

bullshit music for some nursery or something, and you pretended to be a singing teacher who taught kids jazz and rock, and Kit was in love with you and called you every day from the studio on the office phone, and you explained to him that somebody had swindled you, that you didn't have anything to eat, so you were going to sell yourself because you were starving . . . ?"

"No, that's not how it was! I said very nicely that I was going to live according to the laws of the front line, and to put out for anybody who would feed me supper. And in general there in Odessa, and that year in particular, it was a fucking disaster. That was the year when the sailors were forbidden from selling things to the secondhand stores. And they closed the flea market . . . There wasn't any food at all in the stores in Odessa!"

"Ah yes, the decline of the empire . . . And you, you singing bitch, were having a gay old time in your hotel with film directors and Moscow artists . . . You even bragged later on that you fucked that old guy who filmed *Bumbarash.*"

"Yeah, that was Felya, our cameraman, he was wonderful . . . Fed me and then dropped me, said he didn't have long to live so he couldn't hang around with one girl, he still needed to fit in a lot more . . . And then there was that old actor from Kyrgyzstan, he was great, you know, the one who played the Tatar prince in *Andrey Rublyov;* he also played the teacher in that movie *First Teacher* . . . But he was really old and a complete drunk, and I up and left him . . ."

"And then, you sordid gerontophile, you told poor Kityarushka that you had to betray him with seven different Chuvaks . . . and he would tell us everything. We reminisced that since you were fifteen you were nicknamed Nyusha Zeppelin because you were so out of control . . . And then Kit stared at us with his drunken rabbit eyes and muttered something like: *So what is it that you want to tell me? That Anya's a whore? And that you all slept with her? But you all slept with her before I even knew her. While I, on the other hand, slept with all of your wives, when they were already your wives* . . . So then the troops got a bit jumpy . . . Kolya Punin took offense and left right away, and never had anything to do with any of us ever again, and the rest of them turned out to be some serious businessmen and started to fuck with Kit . . . But for some reason I was on his side . . . I already had Yukka then, and would have been only too happy for her if one of my friends had given her a good fuck, because I was having a hard time of it . . . Anya, I don't remember, did Kit get high with us? Or was it strictly booze with him . . . and a bit of snatch?"

"Listen, he was such a hard drinker that he barely had the time to smoke pot with us."

"But he didn't really drink that much; it just seemed that way to you. He gambled left and right, so booze was the easiest thing to get." Misha burst out laughing. "He was two-timing you all the way. Said that he'd fallen asleep drunk somewhere, and you, fool that you are, believed him."

"No, I didn't, but I could always find him when I wanted to. Sometimes he'd be held up because of the bridges, but I could still show up at his place at five in the morning, as soon as the bridges were down. Once I really did lose him, but it later turned out that he'd fallen asleep in that very same studio and they simply rolled him under the sofa so he wouldn't get in the way of the dancing and so that nobody would stumble over him. No, Kit didn't spend his nights sleeping with other girls in a comfortable bed. No fucking way . . . His cheating on me was heroic, accomplished under difficult circumstances: in cars, bathrooms, upstairs—above the studio, in an empty apartment . . . on the 'fucking' chair. Remember the 'fucking' chair? Tabachnik brought it for one of his girls. And then we all used it . . . In general, Kit was a fine, one-of-a-kind drunk. And his golden fingers would shake in the mornings . . ."

"In your diamond cunt, and you liked that a lot."

"Everybody goes on about something, for the soldier it's a cunt . . ." Misha wanted to talk about love. But I'd started thinking about Kit: "And they killed him in a drunken fight!"

"Anya, what are you saying? What, do you still believe that it was a drunken fight? Come on now, you're not a complete fool!"

"What do you mean?"

"Anya, it was all for show. I thought you knew . . ."

"For show? What had he done that was so terrible? Was it because of some bimbo? I remember there was one of Fyoka's lady friends, some Marinka Zhalo or other . . . Was it because of her? The whore . . . The opera *Carmen* . . . with fucking tramps . . ."

"I don't know for sure. Maybe it was girls . . . No, it couldn't have been because of girls . . . Must have been on account of the knock-offs. They all sat there in that studio turning out fakes. That whole group—all those lefties forging fleas. The guys were making money hand over fist. There were a lot of orders for restoration jobs, and right after the restorations there were the orders for knock-offs . . ."

Of course, I remember this "Restoration" period. It was like being in a DIY club. There were ornaments, paintings, sometimes furniture. I once even helped cut out a rose from a sheet of veneer for a marquetry side table. Petals and leaves. The veneer was multicolored, I used a stencil. They even trusted me. And Linas came separately to pour the bronze angels . . . There were also some antique models from the museum, drawings . . . I remember the girl Tabachnik bought the chair for there too, and she was painting old drawings with delicate watercolors . . . And there were even arguments, it was either Nemkov or Nemchinov who said that they should be done with pastels, but she insisted that no, only watercolors, and she painted them according to the album that she had of these drawings—scenes of St. Petersburg . . .

* * *

"Misha, but why Kit in particular? Nothing happened to the others . . ."

"Because he was, like, independent. The others all worked for particular people. And everything went far away to somewhere in Georgia . . . I don't know exactly. And suddenly he had his own client. As a matter of fact, they met here in the Hotel Europe. You can't reconstruct now what happened then. But it seems like it was somebody else's dough. And, consequently, different rules. He crossed somebody, something went over there, and it turned out that good people ended up in a tough spot. I'm talking some serious bucks. I don't know the details, but it was something like that . . . But when they killed him, you weren't living with him anymore, were you? You were already with the next one . . . Who was it? The King of Jazz?"

"The Phantom of the Opera . . . It was the Phantom of the Opera! Once and forever."

Later we were sitting downstairs again in the cafeteria that they now call a "lounge."

We were chatting again and remembering the Past. Some different Past now, either afterward or before . . . Turns out that there was a lot of this fucking Past.

Misha grew sad. "You don't change, Anya—why don't you change?"

"I changed in the middle. At thirty, thirty-five. And then after forty I somehow lost weight again . . . It's old age. The end of my blossoming."

"Your old age looks like youth. Your legs are spaghetti-thin again, and your face is just like it was then. Come on, let's go . . . It's lonely for me there . . ."

"Hey, don't bogart that joint, friend, take a puff and pass it on to your friend . . . But I did come up with my wish: I want to go up on the Maly's roof. Like we did then. Remember how we liked to go out there on summer nights? You could easily climb up from the roof of the studio."

"Well, that's a fucking stupid wish. Not even interesting, roofers probably working there now. And it's slippery. And easy as pie."

"No, it's not as easy as pie. It's hard to get in the Maly now. There's a serious security system."

"I can't get in? Are you kidding?"

Misha's last job before going abroad was assistant administrator of the Maly State Opera Theater. It's called the Mikhailovsky now.

"They've got an ID card system to get in now. Electronic cards. Different kinds. With one card you can go certain places, and with another card to different ones; most of the cards don't let you go everywhere. So if you're all-powerful, take me to our roof, that's my dream. If you take me to the roof, I'll go with you to London."

"Easy, Anya, that's easy! . . . If you want to go to the roof, we'll go to the roof—I'll be your Phantom of the Opera!"

I didn't believe that it would be possible.

But there we were—standing on the very same roof.

We entered the building like theatergoers. And there at the coat check we ducked behind a hidden door; he opened it with a card, we ended up on a hidden staircase and walked up it for a long time, and then we hid in a little closet. We had to wait until the performance ended and everybody left.

It was all quite complicated. There in the theater, besides the ever-watchful old biddies and ushers, you had the security guards with their Tasers.

The degree of security in the theater under the new director reminded me of a military factory in the USSR. Bakaleishchikov proved to be a real hero. He had managed somehow to get a card that gave him unlimited access.

And he remembered all the hidden doors and rooms.

"How can you remember after so many years?"

"I'm usually quite scattered."

"That's the weed."

"Well, yes, Sveta said the same thing. But it's the opposite with unnecessary things, you see—those I remember."

"Why the fuck are you smoking grass from morning till night . . . ?"

While we were sitting in the closet, we once again reminisced about our Maly Opera life.

I was a Petersburger and so was Misha Bakaleishchikov.

And the whole gang was made up of artists who had come from elsewhere a hundred years ago to study scenic design at the theater school.

They'd all become friends in the dorm.

Nemkov, Nemtsov, and Nemchinov were from the Urals and Siberia, and Tabachnik and Pasechnik were from western Ukraine.

Nemchinov, however, was a Tatar from Kazan. Misha was the one who remembered that. How does he remember everything after smoking grass first thing in the morning?

We walked up the concealed flight of stairs and came out onto the roof. Like we used to. Only then it was usually summer and White Nights.

For some reason it doesn't occur to anyone to clamber onto the roof in winter. This was the first time on the roof in winter.

There wasn't any wind.

It wasn't cold.

"It's a few degrees above freezing today."

There wasn't any of Petersburg's bewitching beauty.

There wasn't any hyperborean ice.

All around there was streaming, squelching, crunching . . .

On the square lay lumps of black snow.

"Careful, Anya, don't slip."

"It's okay, there isn't any ice. It's all melted. Come here, I want to show you something. Come on, step over that railing, otherwise you won't see anything . . .

There was an empire-style minifence lower than your knee, and beyond it a little piece of open roof about a meter and a half wide—it was from there that you could see farther.

Bakaleishchikov was absolutely fucking blown away by the view from here of the dreadful square, made a shambles by black snowdrifts and mud . . . Although to me it was still beautiful. But on the whole, a terrifying sight. You expect more from Petersburg. Even in winter . . .

He presented a monologue. Classical in all respects. About how all of us who live here are assholes.

He stood on the edge of the roof wearing his black overcoat, flapping in the wind, and was shouting almost hysterically, and his scarf fluttered like a red banner . . .

"All our life here—it's a fucking Dostoevsky nightmare! One big czar asshole named Nastaysa Filippovna! Humiliation stronger than pride. Allegedly there's beauty here. Anya, what kind of fucking beauty is there here? Anya, there is rot here, this fucking Piter is rotting, do you understand, it's rotting just like Venice . . . only Venice is rotting in a civilized manner, but this, this spawn of bullshit is decaying at will—in the broad expanses of the north. And nothing can stop it from fucking rotting, not UNESCO, not DICKESCO . . . Snow, Anya, ought to be white! White, do you understand? Bears are white and brown—and that's normal. But snow should be white! And only white! Here we have the kingdom of fucking black grime and slime. Nothing but fucking, fucking, fucking, damned fucking noir!"

My heart was pounding. And my head was pounding. From

fear. *He's not coordinated. He smokes grass from morning till night. He won't manage. He'll lose his footing. He won't grab hold of me.*

I pushed him hard in the back with two hands—forward.

He didn't manage to keep his footing. He didn't grab hold of me. Nothing was "like it is in the movies."

He flew down, like a deer, with a shout.

Smashed to smithereens.

No fucking good smoking weed from morning till night.

I didn't care what happened to me afterward.

They didn't keep me for very long.

The investigator was young and handsome.

The medical expert was young and lazy.

They could have done some special tests and come to the conclusion that he wasn't responsible, that somebody had pushed him from behind. But they could also choose not to do any tests.

And not come to any conclusion. And that was clearly more expedient.

Seems I'm a born actress.

I wept naturally and said that he was my friend and what a terrible thing it was! And they found absolutely no motive whatsoever for my doing it.

The prematurely deceased guy was a Russian citizen, he didn't even have a European passport, just three different "places of residence."

So why go to a lot of trouble?

Misha left behind seven children from five wives. The youngest son was already fifteen.

Of course, I'd like to be able to tell all this to Lyokha Saksofon. My comrade-in-arms in the group Anyuta and the Angels. He's the main angel. And even more of an archangel with a heavy golden trumpet.

Lyokha Saksofon probably couldn't have pictured me as a

murderer. I was a heroine to him. Just putting together my group Anyuta and the Angels, and somehow managing to feed myself and four musicians—that meant a lot in our closed and stagnant city. Everybody was pushing and shoving here on our little square—there wasn't much money, or much fame. And you needed to somehow elbow your way in and squeeze out the others.

Lyokha could never do that. The only thing in life he knew how to do was to blow into his pipe, into the archangel's gilded trumpet.

And I became legendary for surviving the '90s with two small children, and how when I was left a widow I sang in gangsters' hangouts and clubs.

Once I was shot at by the owner of some casino who was high on cocaine, and he was hauled away by six guys . . .

Well then, even if Misha had performed a completely different monologue, one about his love for Piter, I still wouldn't have spared him. I had sentenced him to death, and had led him to his personal place of execution. Onto the stage set of his personal death . . .

Because the Man from the Past always has some story like that . . . about the Past. From which it becomes clear that he is not long for this world. That he's already lost.

Everybody mixes up who's the father of my children. Because there were two fathers: my first daughter was with Tabachnik, and the second one was with Kit.

But since Kit practically raised the first one from birth, she was also considered Kit's girl.

Kit always had a hell of a lot of work. At the Maly Opera he was on staff as a modeler. And there he only needed to make Tabachnik one official model a season for the current production.

But all the rest of the models were made to order—for Tabachnik, if they were going to other theaters, and for the rest of the merry band. Later there were also military models, which in the late '80s brought in orders from collectors, when the theater business became superquiet as the result of the usual revolution.

Kit of course was a drunkard. The most natural drunkard. The classic Russian master drunkard. His heart belonged to the tavern.

He spent most of his time in the Maly Opera studio, which according to the theater's inventory, both movable and immovable property, was the "modeling" studio. But he divided the rest of his time among three restaurants of the All-Russian Theater Society. One was upstairs—formal—one was in the basement, and the third was simply a little café-buffet. He didn't like the Hotel Europe. Not because our corsairs went there, but because his clients went there, particularly during those final years. Refined, elegant collectors who ordered one-of-a-kind models of famous battles. With all kinds of little soldiers and machinery. And all this was on a scale of one-to-twenty. And sometimes even smaller. And they paid a lot by the standards of those days.

For some reason this made him nervous.

He would probably have become an alcoholic, but he didn't have the chance.

And perhaps I would have left him; on the whole I was reckless.

But I didn't have the chance to leave him.

They often started fighting when they got drunk. And one day he got killed in a fight.

Foolishly, accidentally. They punctured his spleen.

Bang! . . . and the boy's gone. And this was before all the big guns came to Petersburg.

That's what I thought for twenty whole years.

And would have gone on thinking.

Were it not for that conversation with Misha.

When it happened, among our group only he, Bakaleishchikov, was married, to the Finn, and he was already, like, living there, and would rush back and forth.

And it was so obvious that he had set this all up.

This superorder, for a super-knock-off, for superbucks.

And he surrendered Kit. Nobody else could have done it.

And to surrender meant to . . .

It was very much accepted among the corsairs.

In general, to surrender your own is accepted in any criminal milieu, going back to the real John Silver.

The wind howls, the sea rages
We, the corsairs, will never surrender . . .

What a fucking lie, what a big fucking lie . . . We'll surrender, and how!

And so I thought up this complicated punishment to be executed from that roof.

I decided that God would be the arbiter. That it was almost a bit of a duel.

I consider it to be a duel, because it's a miracle that he turned out to be so uncoordinated. He didn't grab onto me at the last moment and drag me with him.

Although he did grab me and drag me with him. Because now I am a murderer and betrayer just like him. The evil in the world has increased because of me . . .

But all the same, Kit won't come back. And Misha of course had no idea that Kit was such an important person to me. Misha thought that he was still the main man in my life. And Kit was considered a loser, at least according to the standards of the corsairs . . . And for the artists he was a loser too, poorly educated, merely a craftsman . . .

Not one of them understood that Kit was my Phantom of the Opera. Once and forever.

And it doesn't make any sense to tell this story to Lyokha Saksofon.

He never knew Kit or Misha Bakaleishchikov.

He's twenty-five, and he's being tormented by Kira. Or is it Lera . . . ?

We sat on the bench, looking at Pushkin.

Little birds and fliers for our group Anyuta and the Angels were flying all around.

The Man from the Past was dead.
The Woman with the Past was rolling a joint.

Don't bogart that joint, my friend
That one's burned to the end,
Roll another one
Just like the other one . . .

Author's Note: Sanya Yezhov wrote the song "This, My Friend, Is My District and My City."

PART III

CHASING GHOSTS

THE NUTCRACKER

BY ANTON CHIZH

Haymarket Square

Translated by Walt Tanner

The White Night, a night without darkness, fanned out into early morning. Leaden clouds, pregnant with June rain, hung over St. Petersburg like a thick shroud, threatening to break into a deluge. Roofs and houses, empty streets, and lone passersby all merged in a gray gloom. The wind had abated, but the chill air seemed to ooze through to the bone. Indistinct rustlings floated in the air, like the pitter-patter of claws on tin. A grubby burgundy house loomed over Griboyedov Canal in the fog. The stucco was coming off in chunks, and the jointed sections of the rain pipes met in rusty rings. The building was in dire need of repair. Despite that, someone had hung up a sign that read, *Hotel Dostoevsky*. Although the grim classic of Russian literature had no connection to the building, tourists seemed to like the name. But other than its name, nothing else distinguished this hotel from any one of the dozen or so such lodgings in the Haymarket Square area.

A black car marked with a taxicab checkerboard shot out onto the canal embankment, darting past randomly parked cars until it came to a screeching halt under the letter *D*. The cab driver demanded one hundred dollars. He was politely reminded that the fare agreed upon beforehand was half that amount. But the driver remained adamant until he got the green bill he wanted.

He refused to help carry in the luggage, saying that wasn't his job. The cab took off into the fog, raising a cloud of grit in its wake. A young woman with a backpack and large suitcase was left standing on the sidewalk with a twelve-year-old girl, who perched exhaustedly on the luggage, ready to sleep standing up.

The woman glanced around. The embankment, the closest intersections, a partial view of Haymarket Square—she examined them all carefully, as though checking them against a mental map. Rousing the sleepy child, she shouldered her backpack, grabbed the suitcase, and mounted the small flight of stairs to the hotel with a light step.

In the dark lobby she woke the receptionist, a moonlighting student who was dozing on the keyboard of the laptop in front of him. He yawned without bothering to express any stock pleasantries. Scratching his T-shirt, with a picture on it of mice drinking beer, he said there were no vacancies. The woman gave him her reservation code. The receptionist tapped his nail on the keyboard and, yawning again, asked for her ID. He copied the Russian surname from the American passport, refused to take American Express, accepted Visa, and tossing a key, as ancient as the building itself, onto the counter, promptly lost all interest in the guests. Taking the luggage in one hand, and her exhausted companion in the other, the woman went up to her floor.

The reservation website had promised a charming place in the very heart of St. Petersburg, "where every stone is saturated with history." The other virtues it extolled included comfort, coziness, reasonable prices, and a lovely view.

The door opened into a tiny narrow room, permeated by the smell of dirty socks. The windows, which looked out onto a dull courtyard and a garbage heap, were haphazardly covered with tattered tulle curtains. Pushed up against the wall were two beds, each covered with a gray blanket. The bedsheets, laundered to a dirty yellow, lay folded in a pile on the windowsill. Hanging from just one hinge, the door of the wardrobe gave out a plaintive squeak. A note had been taped above the hot water faucet that read, *Off until September*. The room, however, did not strike the requisite horror in the guests. The child dragged herself over to the bed, where she collapsed without undressing. This was the very hotel the woman wanted.

She sat down on the edge of the mattress. She had hardly noticed the twelve-hour flight from Chicago, or the terrible bout of turbulence over the Baltic Sea. Now she had to be sure of herself, for there would be no turning back. She had to see it through all the way, or she would never be able to forgive herself for the rest of her life.

She took off her wristwatch and gave herself exactly 120 seconds of restful quiet to take control of the nervous tension that was building within her. She breathed deeply, just like she'd been taught, to clear all thoughts from her head.

Her name was Kate. Ekaterina Ivanovna by birth, but for as long as she could remember, she was just Kate. She'd wanted it that way. She came to the United States at the age of one with her parents, who were trying to save the family from the debris of the collapsing Soviet Union. She had grown up like an ordinary American girl. The language was the only thing she'd held on to. At home they spoke Russian to her and forced her read the classics. Kate had always considered this a whim of her folks: knowing a difficult Slavic language in the modern world was totally useless. Unexpectedly, however, that language had now come in handy. Otherwise, she might not have dared.

Time up. Kate opened the suitcase, trying not to wake Annie. She dressed in a pair of jeans and comfy sneakers, put on a thick T-shirt and a sports jacket over it. She felt the left sleeve, as though there were something inside it, put on a baseball cap, and turned into an ordinary girl in the crowd, just one among thousands. That was the best camouflage for this city, they had explained to her. She left the room and locked the door, turning the key as far as it would go, but didn't drop it off at the desk.

A humpbacked bridge led over Griboyedov Canal to Haymarket Square. Kate walked slowly, looking around. Returning to the city of her birth did not stir any emotions in her. She was neither touched nor excited. All of her senses were poised for another vital task: Kate was getting a feel for these real streets, which she had examined before on Google Earth.

The square was empty. The occasional car cut across the paved area, paying no heed to traffic lights. Kate stopped on the corner of the square and closed her eyes so that nothing would distract her. She waited for the signal; it was the thread that had led her this far. The secret voice made her wait, but did finally answer. Weak, barely audible, but clear. That was a good sign after so many long weeks of waiting.

She opened her eyes.

Kate recalled reading Dostoevsky with distaste. It was on this square that the killer Raskolnikov fell to his knees, begging forgiveness from the people. He wouldn't have been able to do that anymore: all the open space had been turned into a parking lot. The view was stunningly unreal. A mall in the far corner of Haymarket Square towered like an iceberg of mercurial glass. The red ruins of brick walls were visible just behind it. A Roman mansion with columns from a neoclassical epoch abutted the square at the other end. Nearer to her was a multistory monstrosity from the beginning of the last century. A building with a corner tower, recalling the boulevards of Paris, stood opposite. Round-roofed trade pavilions huddled underneath it, just as they had a century before when the market bustled and carts of hay stood all around. It seemed as though holes had been ripped in the fabric of time on the square, connecting various eras and centuries.

Both power and enmity lurked there. That was what Kate

sensed, anyway. There was something about it—what exactly, she couldn't say. It was as though some unknown force was hiding behind every corner and observing her, an uninvited visitor. She shivered, as from the morning chill.

By then it was seven a.m., and still the square was almost empty. Just an old man dressed in rags, with a pushcart stuffed with grimy bundles of paper. A shadow darted past his feet; Kate didn't realize what it was at first. She wasn't afraid of mice or hamsters, but it was shocking to see a live rat in the center of a European city. The little gray creature pressed itself to the stoop of a meat shop, then, sniffing the air, it casually went on its way.

Moving around the sprawling square in a circle, Kate overcame her fear of the unfamiliar space. On her way back to Griboyedov Canal she dialed the secret number. For a long time there was no answer. Then, finally, the ringing cut off. Someone coughed on the other end of the line and a husky male voice said, "What do you want?" Kate said the code word. There was a hacking cough at the other end again that went on for some time, followed by the gulping noises of a throat swallowing something with difficulty. The line fell silent. Then the same voice, but in a completely different tone, started arranging their rendezvous. No unnecessary questions. They would recognize each other.

Strolling around, Kate arrived at the venue ahead of time. In an all-night café, she sat at the far table. There were four customers there besides her, tending their mugs. Instead of the aroma of fresh coffee and cream, the place was permeated by a mix of chemical scents used to mask the smell of decay. Rousing techno-pop was piped through the loudspeakers. The waiter, with a hairy wart on his lip, took a long time writing down her order but returned almost immediately with a large coffee and glass of water. Kate did not so much as sip the murky water: she was keeping her eyes on the door. Nevertheless, she missed his arrival. He had been at the café for a long time, observing her and making his assessments. He stood up swiftly and seated himself at her table.

Porphyry looked exactly as he'd been described to her: a week-old stubble, rheumy red eyes, and the persistent fumes of a heavy drinker. Even in the summer, he wore a fur jacket with a greasy shirt sticking out from underneath it. He was a tramp, a lowly nobody. Yet he was the one her Facebook friends had recommended. They said that this unpleasant person reminiscent of a polecat could take care of any problem in the city. He could deal with any kind of trouble. Even something as serious as Kate's situation.

"Who told you about me?" he asked, swallowing a mouthful of her coffee.

"You helped some friends of mine." Kate recalled a few names.

Porphyry accepted her explanation with a curt nod. He fixed her with an unblinking stare, as though testing her mettle. Kate kept her composure and said, "I have a serious problem."

"That's the only reason people come to me."

"My sister is missing."

"Since when?"

Not long ago her parents had been seized by the idea of showing their youngest daughter, Sonya—who was born in America and spoke no Russian—the country of her roots. A gift of sorts for her twelfth birthday. They got their visas and had arrived in St. Petersburg one month before.

"Then what happened?"

Sonya had just disappeared. According to her parents' incoherent account of events, she asked to go out for a walk around the hotel and never returned. Their parents only noticed her absence when the girl had been gone for a full three hours. They called the police, who refused to help, saying they couldn't do anything unless she had been gone for more than a week. Dad paid the lieutenant a bribe to persuade him to start the search immediately. The officer came back the next day to say that nothing could be done: Sonya was gone.

Kate listed many more relevant details, but she didn't divulge the most important one of all. When her parents had broken the news to her, she immediately knew it was her mission to save Sonya. It was like a revelation. Kate dashed to the Russian embassy, but despite her Russian name, tears, pleas, and an envelope with a hefty bribe, they said that the procedure for issuing a visa would take a month. She decided then and there that she would spend the intervening time not on prayer, but on preparation: she took leave from her job at a law firm and hired a trainer, a former marine, to teach her skills that would come in handy for rescuing someone. Killing, in particular. She trained with a desperate zeal. Now she could finish off the slight man sitting in front of her using nothing but a teaspoon. Except she couldn't let anyone know. The trainer had said, "Never let your enemy know your real strength." And Porphyry looked more like a foe than a friend.

He snapped his fingers nervously. "Got a photo of your sister?"

In the last picture of her, taken at the airport in Chicago just before their departure to Russia, the child stared with grudging severity into the camera lens. Porphyry wanted to keep the picture, but Kate refused to let it out of her grasp.

He scrutinized the image for a long time. Then he said, "You know my rates?"

Kate quoted a price.

"Half up front. No refunds. No matter what the outcome."

Ten bills were counted out for him. Porphyry carelessly shoveled the pile into his pocket and made to leave: "I'll keep you posted."

"No." Kate said it with such conviction that he sat down again. "I am going with you. I might be able to help."

"Oh yeah? How?" Porphyry sneered.

"Sonya is being held somewhere on Haymarket Square."

"How do you know?"

Kate had only accepted the news of her sister's disappearance because she was certain that Sonya was alive. She couldn't explain it, but she could sense her sister even at a distance. It had always been like that. They could never play hide and seek: Kate always found Sonya instantly. An inner voice whispered to her.

"Sonya is somewhere nearby," she said.

"Just keep in mind that I haven't promised I'll find her alive. Got it?"

"She's alive."

"Hope is a good thing."

"She's alive," Kate repeated obstinately.

"We'll find out soon enough. Listen up, now. Here are the rules: You do exactly as I say. No objections, no questions. Keep a cool head no matter what happens. No hysteria. Got it?"

Kate accepted all of his conditions.

"Oh, and uh . . . pay for my breakfast," Porphyry said, walking out of the café.

A low-vaulted underpass diving into the bowels of the subway cut across the insides of Haymarket Square. Even in summer a wind blew from within it. Kate was told to keep her distance.

Porphyry descended the stone steps and headed for a motley pile of rags. He stopped beside it and said something. The pile began to stir, as though there was a mole burrowing within it, and a human face emerged. It was a swollen, cadaver-colored lump. Staring at Porphyry, the creature belched. Then the cast-off clothing began to rustle, and a paw appeared, clutching a new iPhone. The face muttered a few short, incomprehensible phrases into it, switched off the phone, and disappeared once more into the heap of rags.

Leaning back on the wall of the underpass, faced for some reason in white marble, Porphyry lazily lit a smoke, paying no attention to what was going on around him. Close by, a couple of swollen-looking men of indiscernible age were sitting on their haunches. One of them produced a bottle of Coca-Cola, into which the other fellow poured some varnish from a can. Some alcoholic tinctures contained in pharmaceutical vials were also added, and the concoction was shaken. They drank the "Haymarket Square Cocktail" straight from the bottle, passing it back and forth, gulping greedily and wincing.

Kate turned away, waiting.

A tall young man dressed in a leather jacket and leather pants approached Porphyry. On one hairy finger, adorned with a massive diamond ring, he twirled a Mercedes keychain, which made a soft whirring noise. A thick gold chain glinted on his furry chest. The cocky young man's angular face broke out into a smile.

The men talked. The hairy dude gave Porphyry a friendly left hook on the chest. They summoned Kate with an imperceptible nod. Looking the woman over, the hairy man smirked.

"Let's see the photo," he said.

Kate didn't let go of it. She didn't want the greasy macho fingers touching Sonya's little face.

Giving it just one glance, he said, "Nope, not her."

"What about the neighbors?" Porphyry asked.

"I'd have heard something. A good specimen like that, I'd have taken her for myself. Could've made some good money too."

"You can make some good money right now."

"No. Never seen her."

"Come off it, Alik. She disappeared in your territory. You know everything that goes on here."

Alik just shrugged. "There's no telling. Maybe the Nutcracker got her." He gave Porphyry a clap on the shoulder and withdrew, whistling and twirling his keychain.

"Who's that dude?"

"He's the lord of the local beggars," Porphyry replied sternly. "Very rich. If children go missing here, chances are they end up with Alik. He makes them into good workers. Although sometimes he maims them. Makes them sniff glue, gets them hooked on vodka and drugs. To keep them in line. But girls are usually put to different use."

"He could have been lying,"

"There's no reason for Alik to lie. He's not afraid of you. And a doll like your sister he would have gladly taken for himself. He loves kids in his own way . . . You ready to go on?"

Kate was ready for everything. She only said, "Who is the Nutcracker?"

Porphyry screwed up his face. "Don't take it seriously."

"I want to know."

"It's total bullshit."

"Please!"

"You really want to know? Fine. Supposedly there is an old man who lives in basements and kidnaps children to feed them to the rats. It's just an urban legend."

Kate was ready to believe any story she heard. "Why do they call him that? The Nutcracker fought rats, and in Tchaikovsky he was a good guy."

"Tchaikovsky or Dostoevsky, it's all the same. This is Haymarket Square, and it's a whole different ballgame," Porphyry said darkly.

"Where are those basements he lives in?"

"Not my line of work."

"I am paying you to find my sister."

"It's not about money. It would be like looking for a ghost. You got time to waste?"

She had to desist.

Porphyry led her away from the square to where the pass-through courtyards began. They traversed these for a distance of several blocks. Kate tried to remember the way, but the dirty yellow walls seemed to run together into one turbid stream. She had lost her bearings and had only a vague sense of the direction of the square.

In one courtyard, Porphyry yanked open a shabby stairwell door and went up to the fourth floor. Kate was allowed to do as she pleased: she could wait outside or go in after him. She followed, close on his heels. At an unmarked apartment door, Porphyry made a call on his cell phone and growled something into it. The bolt clicked and the door opened to reveal an obese fellow in a bathrobe hanging shamelessly untied. The next moment a little face, caked in heavy makeup, poked out of the doorway. Her eyelashes were stuck together with blobs of mascara. The little mouth was swollen under a thick coating of lipstick. Dressed in a transparent nighty with wine stains all over it, she was no more than ten years old. She licked her lips and she asked in a hoarse voice: "Hey, handsome, could you buy me some ice cream? My throat's all dry."

The fat man kicked her away with his knee, sending her sprawling. Her nightie flew up, revealing her stomach, which was covered in yellow bruises. She got up, straightening the flimsy garment, and hobbled off, tunelessly singing a nursery rhyme: "*Quiet, quiet little mice! The cat's on the rooftop, she'll leap in a trice.*" The smell of chlorine and vomit wafted out from the apartment hallway.

"Porphyry!" the fat man exclaimed, smiling sweetly. "You haven't been over here in ages, buddy! Want to try something fresh?

"I'm interested in used goods."

"Anything you wish. What exactly are you looking for?"

"This one." Porphyry waved a hand at Kate as though summoning a waiter.

She approached them but did not let go of the snapshot. The fat man squinted like a well-fed cat and made clucking noises with his tongue.

"What a honeybun! Wouldn't mind snuggling her myself. Sorry, Porphyry, that one didn't come my way. I wouldn't have let her get away if she had. What a doll! May I offer you another one? Perhaps your lady friend would like something? Some of the boys I have are pretty good. I highly recommend them." He snapped his fingers in affirmation of the high quality of his product.

Kate went downstairs without saying a word. A sudden downpour detained them in the stairwell. The rain came down in torrents, as it does in the tropics, pounding the asphalt with its coarse watery arrows and clattering on the rooftops. Porphyry lit up, exhaling the thick smoke.

"Doesn't look good," he said, flicking the ash underfoot.

Kate waited for him to elaborate.

"Liolik runs all the child prostitution rings. Eight out of ten will end up with him. Girls are always in demand. Sometimes he'll take care of an order personally, if the client is after something in particular. But she's not here. Even if you broke his neck, it wouldn't get us closer to what we're looking for."

"Why do you take his word for it?"

"Liolik would sell your sister back to you. If he had her."

"That's good news."

"You don't get it. That asshole Alik could easily have been lying, like you said. Sonya could have ended up with him. But after a month, he would definitely have sold her on to Liolik; he has no need for used goods. That way, at least your sister would still be alive. But if Liolik doesn't have her—"

"She's alive," Kate said, repeating the words of her spell. "We just have to keep looking."

"Whatever you say."

"What's our plan?"

"Keep doing everything we can."

The rain subsided sharply, tapering off to a fine spatter.

Haymarket Square turned out to be just behind the building. It was highly likely that Porphyry had been walking around in circles intentionally, so that she—an outsider—could not find her own way back. He was right to do so. Kate wanted to go back there and wring Liolik's fat neck. And she had stopped trusting her partner.

Inside a glass kiosk, a pyramid of meat rotated slowly on a skewer. A swarthy young man wrapped in a dirty apron was cutting off slices of the roasted meat with a long knife. Eastern music and the stench of burning oil floated from the open window. Resting on a low stool beside the counter was a gray-haired man in a black shirt. Prayer beads clicked; his face betrayed an inward gravity. He opened his eyes and rose to greet Porphyry. They hugged and pressed their cheeks together. The woman was told with a gesture to keep her distance.

Porphyry spoke with exaggerated politeness. He respectfully inquired about the state of Aslan's health, and received a cordial reply. Then he muttered something abruptly and, moving in close, whispered in the man's ear. Aslan listened to him attentively. Then he answered: "All right."

Now she was allowed to approach.

Aslan examined the girl's picture carefully, running his fingers over the beads, and spat out: "No."

Kate didn't know who he was or what he did, but she understood the obvious: this was her last chance. She didn't have anything to lose now.

"Could the Nutcracker have gotten her?" she asked pointedly. "Do you know where I might find him?"

Aslan looked as though he'd seen a ghost. "*Inshallah*."

Without saying goodbye, he recoiled into the booth, grazing a saucer of milk that stood on the threshold for some reason.

Porphyry gave her arm a sharp tug and dragged her aside.

"Who told you to speak?" he hissed. "Do you know what you've done?"

Kate pulled away. "I want to find my sister."

"You won't be able to, now."

"Why?"

"At Aslan's kiosks, they make shawarma. You know what that is? It's a pocket of bread, stuffed with fried meat. Real cheap, because they fry up everything from rotten chickens to stray dogs. Sometimes people bring Aslan dead bodies—they don't let them go to waste either. Human meat really hits the spot. If your sister was killed, it is more likely than not that she would have ended up in Aslan's shawarmas. But you just ruined everything. After your rude behavior, Aslan won't bother asking his people anything. That's it. That was our last chance. End of story."

"She's alive," Kate repeated. "How do I find the Nutcracker?"

Porphyry slapped his palms together and brushed them off. "Our contract has just expired. Don't call me again."

The fur jacket disappeared into the bustling throng of people.

Kate stood by herself amid the crowd filling the Haymarket. People hurried about their business, and nobody cared about a missing little girl. The wind got rid of the few remaining storm clouds. The sun came out, and it became as humid as a Turkish bath. Shiny puddles dried up right before her eyes.

Porphyry hadn't worked out. She was going to have to use Plan B.

She dialed a new number (also recommended to her by Facebook friends) and gave the code word. In less than an hour, she handed over two thousand bucks right there on the square, in exchange for a heavy metal object that fit snugly behind her belt.

Annie was still asleep.

Kate sat down on her own bed. She did not feel any need to rest, nor did she want to eat or drink. Yet she was faced with the most difficult task of all: three hours of waiting. Then she would reenact the events of a month ago, every last detail, up to the moment Sonya disappeared.

Kate spent the next few hours killing time, letting her fingers get used to the grip of her new Walther. The weapon had been used recently. Kate had learned how to tell by the smell. That was why it had been sold. But she didn't care how many people had died at the end of the barrel of that gun. All that mattered was that it work without fail when she needed it to.

She also decided not to let Annie in on things. She had sworn to protect her just as she would her own sister. In order for the whole thing to work, Annie couldn't have any idea what was going on. Otherwise, she would get scared. It had not been easy to persuade Annie's parents to allow the girl to go with her. But after all, she and Sonya had been best friends. Sometimes you just have to back up your friendship with deeds.

The wait was over. Soon the hour would strike.

Kate was ready. She stood up, touching Annie's shoulder gently. "Wake up, honey, it's evening already. Time to take a walk."

Annie blinked rapidly, and smiled. "Kate, do they have hamburgers here?"

"Let's go and find out."

"When are we going to see Sonya?"

"Very soon, I hope."

Yawning noisily, Annie jumped up on the bed. "Ready when you are!"

Kate opened up the big suitcase. "First, we have to change."

A McDonald's took up the ground floor of a large building on the far side of the square. At around ten o'clock in the evening, a little girl came out of it. She was wearing a white polo shirt and light-blue jeans. A backpack hung from her shoulders and she had a camera around her neck. A funny-looking pair of glasses nearly slid down her nose. She was holding a large milkshake and drinking it through a straw. The little girl stood in front of the restaurant, turning this way and that, then strolled leisurely about the square. A month before, Sonya, a girl of similar height and build and dressed in similar clothes, had found herself at that very same spot, without her parents' supervision, for approximately half an hour. Kate's empathic powers told her that this was where it had all begun. She was certain of it. They wouldn't let such appetizing bait give them the slip, would they?

Kate was on the lookout for anyone who moved close to Annie. So far, the young tourist had gone unnoticed. Annie walked halfway around the square, then something in her gait changed abruptly. She paused for a moment, as though straining to hear, then bowed her head, walking in a manner that seemed somehow too rigid, like a windup doll. Kate took note of the change, but couldn't figure out what had caused it. There was no one near her, and she hadn't been approached by anyone either. Then Kate thought she heard someone cracking his knuckles close by. The sound was so soft that it dissolved into the hubbub of the square.

Dropping her milkshake, Annie seemed to quicken her pace, pressing her head to her shoulder. She made a large circle, looping her way back to McDonald's, then turned sharply onto a side street. Kate lost sight of her. She'd been taught not to hurry when tailing someone, but now she had no choice. Darting around the corner she was just able to catch a glimpse of Annie going into the nearest archway. Kate made it to the stone entrance in three bounds. The stench of stale urine assaulted her nose. She had a partial view of the courtyard from the end of the tunnel, yet Annie was nowhere to be seen. Slipping through the gate, Kate found herself in what looked like a jail, surrounded by rows of windows reaching five floors up. Opposite were the large kitchen windows of McDonald's, and employees scurried to and fro. The courtyard was dirty and empty. Someone had nailed a handmade sign on the side of the building that said, *NO EXIT*.

No sign of Annie.

Kate dashed to the door of the stairwell and tugged it. It was locked. She peered into the kitchen, which was buzzing with activity. She had lost Annie. The girl had disappeared right from under her nose. She'd been outwitted. She had wasted her last chance to save Sonya. This really was the end.

Stifling a fit of panic and the desire to scream at the top of her lungs, Kate forced herself to think. This was the only way to get the situation under control. She had to take a good look at everything around her.

A shadow darted along the base of the wall. Then another one. Two more were not far behind. The rats were all moving toward the same target—a crack between iron shutters that covered the basement trapdoor. Kate jerked the rusty handle with all the strength of her despair. The massive lock barring entry swung open easily. She'd blown its cover.

Kate dove down inside.

The concrete walls of the basement ceiling forced her to keep her head low. Above her was the floor of McDonald's. She searched around, moving in the direction of a flickering light. Small gray bodies scampered right alongside her sneakers. She had taken no more than ten steps into the basement when she caught sight of Annie. The girl was walking as though hypnotized, following a tiny creature that was whistling softly, snapping its fingertips in a ragged rhythm, as though coaxing a frightened little dog to come nearer.

Snappity-snap . . .

"Hey you, boy, what do you think you're doing?" Kate shouted. "Stop!"

His face was eaten up by deep wrinkles. Kate couldn't make out anything else. Something came crashing down on the back of her head and she sank into blackness.

The pain brought her back to conciousness. Her wrists had been bound and the skin beneath was burning. She shook her head and was overcome by a wave of nausea. When it subsided, she was able to take a look around her. The shallow space had become more crowded. Sitting there cross-legged on the floor were Alik, Liolik, and Aslan. There were other men she didn't recognize, including one dressed in what appeared to be a police uniform. She was the center of attention.

"Damn busybody," said a familiar voice.

Porphyry was sitting beside her, smiling. "I told you not to go after the Nutcracker, but you wouldn't listen. Now you've only got yourself to blame."

Stretching cautiously, Kate felt that the thick rope holding her wrists behind her back was bound so tightly that it offered no possibility of escape. They hadn't bothered searching her, though. The barrel of the gun had slipped deep between her buttocks. The Walther was still with her.

"You're lucky. You get to witness something few people ever live to see."

Bending her fingers down to her wrist, Kate groped the edge of her sleeve, where her trainer had taught her always to keep a razor hidden for just such a situation.

"Only you won't live to tell anybody about it. Too bad." The joke was followed by sinister laughter.

With the tip of her finger, she pressed the edge of her sleeve until a thread gave way.

"What an excellent specimen you brought along with you! The Nutcracker will be very pleased."

The seam ripped. A strip of metal slipped out.

"You stay quiet or we'll have to sedate you," Porphyry said, fiddling around with a set of brass knuckles.

Kate slowly leaned back and felt the wall with her shoulders. No one would notice what she was doing with her hands. And who would pay much attention to a girl whose hands were tightly bound?

The boy with the face of an old man came out of the darkness. He closed his eyes and whistled softly. The floor began to move. A pack of rats crawled out in a dirty stream and then froze. Letting out a thin, barely audible whine, the midget bent over in a low bow. Everything went so quiet that Kate held the razor in place, afraid that her rustling would betray her.

There was a soft tapping of claws in the distance, as though someone was snapping pieces of brushwood in half somewhere in the darkness. It grew nearer and nearer until a rat the size of a large cat appeared next to the boy. Its bushy whiskers stuck out, and the fur on its snout was gray with age. The men bowed their heads. Lifting its nose, the rat studied Kate intently with its black beady eyes. The boy bent down even farther.

"The Nutcracker is talking with the Mother," Porphyry whispered solemnly. "He is finding out what she wants . . . Oh, beautiful! The Mother is prepared to accept his offering. It's going to happen now!"

The razor was making slow progress.

The Nutcracker disappeared into the darkness and reemerged carrying Annie, who was completely naked. The girl was unconscious but alive. The Nutcracker whistled, then declared, "In honor of our eternal union, we bring offerings unto you, O Mother Rat, the gift of innocent flesh."

He set the body on the stone floor. The rat raised her whiskers and nodded. At least Kate thought she had. She couldn't be sure of what she had seen. Her head was throbbing, the razor was cutting into her finger, and the rope was not quite giving way.

Following some secret signal, a furry wave of gray-coated beasts lunged forward and began devouring the child. Greedy gnawing and the sucking pop of meat being ripped apart could be heard amidst the frenzied hubbub. Annie disappeared beneath the fangs.

Kate winced, closed her eyes, and went at the rope frantically, with redoubled energy.

When she opened her eyes again, it was all over. The last of the rats were busily picking over the remains. Their snouts were coated in a thick layer of blood.

Porphyry was ecstatic.

"The offering has been accepted," the Nutcracker intoned. "Our union is strong."

The announcement was greeted with a buzz of approval from the men.

"Now, for the most important part of all," whispered Porphyry.

The Nutcracker disappeared again. When he returned, Kate guessed right away what he had brought with him. It was Sonya. They had put her in what looked like a doll's dress. She was in a deep sleep, but still alive. Kate had no doubt about that. She knew.

Brushing away the remains of his first victim with a sock, the Nutcracker put Sonya down in a pool of blood. "Today is a great day," he said. "Our union with the Gray Tribe has lasted for over three hundred years. The time has come to pass it on. Many years ago, Mother Rat rewarded me with her bite, so I can understand the language of the Gray Tribe and speak her will. Soon, the hour will arrive when I must leave. We have waited for so long for someone fit to continue in my place. Finally, we have found her: a blond girl with green eyes!"

The men let out cries of adulation.

With a sharp gesture, the Nutcracker commanded utter silence. "O Mother Rat! Favor the chosen with your bite, and I vow to bestow all my knowledge upon her, so that she may take my place honorably."

Kate worked in furious haste.

"What an honor, you should be proud of your sister," her former partner whispered to her.

Mother Rat twitched her nose and fixed the newcomer with a stare. Did she suspect something?

Please, not yet.

The rope gave way. Trying not to change position, Kate shook off the knots that bound her, and eased her palm under her belt.

"May the great union with the Gray Tribe last forever!" screamed the Nutcracker.

Her fingers slid down to the grip of the gun. The safety mechanism went up ever so softly. Now, in one fluid movement, just as her trainer had instructed her.

Mother Rat sniffed Sonya's wrist and licked her chops.

Scraping the skin on her back with the clip, Kate placed the cartridge into the chamber and withdrew her arm, straight out, extending it so that it became one with the weapon, and gently pulled the trigger. A nine-millimeter bullet smashed through the rat's snout, spattering the Nutcracker in blood. The thunderous shot was enough to shake the basement. No one dared move. Five more seconds of shock.

One . . .

Without bending her hand, Kate aimed the gun at the stunned face of Porphyry.

Two . . . *Crack!*

A fountain of brains and shards of the skull once belonging to the specialist at solving other people's problems spewed upward.

Three . . . *Crack!*

The bullet pierced Liolik's belly. The fat man moaned as his face hit the stone floor.

Four . . . *Crack!*

Alik's hairy chest was ripped to pieces with a juicy burst.

Five . . .

The muzzle of the gun was trained on the graybeard. Aslan's chin was trembling slightly.

"If you want to live, run! Get out!"

People and rats scattered every which way in the smoke from the shooting spree. Only the old man-boy, drenched in blood, remained motionless. He was sitting on the floor with his legs spread wide apart, stunned.

"Who are you?" he whispered.

Slowly, shaking off the last coil of rope, Kate stood up on legs that had grown numb and her knees cracked. The ceiling was low enough that she had to stoop. She disengaged the Walther peaceably.

"I'm her big sister."

"What have you done? People and rats live in peace. Once a year we bring them sacrifices. I communicate with the Gray Tribe. I know their language. It's all over now. You killed Mother Rat. Now chaos will reign!"

"That's your problem. You kidnapped my sister. She belongs to me." She picked up Sonya, soft and warm, and pulled her against her chest. She was with Sonya; Sonya was here. No one would ever be able to separate them again. Even if the horde of rats attempted a counterattack.

"Rats are everywhere! You can't hide from them. They'll never forgive you!"

"That may be, but I can shoot 'em up real good."

The Nutcracker wanted to say something, but suddenly his wrinkles seemed to draw together into one, he began to whisper quietly, and his parched fingertips started snapping out a rhythm. *Snap-snap-snap* . . .

A sense of calm surged through Kate's exhausted body. She felt like sitting down to rest, or maybe even lying down. That would feel so nice, wouldn't it? After all, the boy was so sweet.

Snappity-snap . . .

Enervated and drowsy, Kate extended her arm mechanically, then pulled the trigger, almost without aiming. Faster than lightning, the Nutcracker was blown away into the darkness. The midget's brains seeped out of a hole in his forehead. His body twitched in the convulsions of death, then grew still. Lying on his back, his arms spread wide apart, he looked like a discarded toy.

Kate's swoon burst. Pain and clarity returned.

"If you can snap, you should know how to crack," she whispered. "You rat."

She hugged Sonya close to her. "Time to go home, sister."

Kate carried Sonya with one arm, not noticing the weight. With her other hand, she hid the Walther in the folds of the doll dress. She was ready to kill anyone who crossed her path. Her sister, lolling on her shoulder, was floating in deep sleep. They had strung her out on sleeping pills, but her breathing was regular. She had not even lost weight in the month she had spent in captivity in the basement.

Haymarket Square was bathed in the soft light of the White Night. The passersby glanced back, startled at the woman dressed in sports clothes carrying a large doll in her arms, all smeared in blood.

Dashing past the new receptionist on shift, who couldn't be bothered to notice her, Kate hurried up to her room and locked the door behind her. That was unnecessary: who would dare come in? Still, she didn't have much time. She changed the clothes of the sleeping Sonya, ripping the doll's dress to shreds. Only then did she wash the remnants of Porphyry's brains off her face. The rest took almost no time at all: leave the suitcase behind, toss the backpack over her shoulder, carry her sleeping sister under one arm.

Running out onto the street, Kate flagged down the third cab that drove by, just like her trainer had told her to do. Casually opening the door, she said, her voice calm and confident: "One thousand dollars to the border with Finland. Three if you take us all the way to the airport."

The driver agreed without a moment's thought. He only noted politely, "Your jacket has some spots on it. Looks like blood."

Kate settled herself in the backseat with Sonya on her knees, and said, "I was taking care of a rat problem."

The taxi driver stared at her in the rearview mirror.

She managed to muster a weak smile. "Just kidding, it's all right. You mind your own business, and I'll mind mine. Just steer the wheel and earn your three grand." Kate didn't want to waste another bullet. "Excuse me, but we're running late for our flight."

The car sped through the empty streets of a city that would forever be alien to her. Haymarket Square dissolved into the soft pale gray of the White Night.

Sonya stirred lightly and opened her eyes. "Hey, big sis! You know, I had a dream about the Nutcracker."

"Don't worry, sweetie, it was just a dream. There is no such thing as the Nutcracker."

"No? Where did he go?"

"He burst."

"Like a balloon?"

"No, like a rat. He went *kaboom*!" She made a loud snap with her fingers.

Sonya sighed and settled down more comfortably. "I missed you."

"I missed you too."

"The Nutcracker fed me Big Macs. It was nice . . ."

Kate was calm. Absolutely calm. She still had four bullets left.

Crackity-crack . . .

PARANOIA

BY MIKHAIL LIALIN

Lake Dolgoe

Translated by Margarita Shalina

But the main distinction lies in this, that whereas wine disorders the mental faculties, opium, on the contrary (if taken in a proper manner), introduces amongst them the most exquisite order, legislation, and harmony.
—Thomas De Quincey, *Confessions of an English Opium Eater*

Eighteenth of August in the year 20—

Help yourselves."
Three-mile-long lines. Uh-huh.
"Walk your mile."
Amphetamine. The rush begins.
"What do you suggest?"
"You can put it up your nose. I'll put it in my coffee. I don't like to snort—get a runny nose after."
K sweeps his line into a mug of coffee. I turn to C.
"What do you say?"
"Snort half, the other half—with coffee."
"That's what we'll do."
C rolls a tight straw out of a hundred-ruble note after a few tries. Checks it, makes sure it fits in a nostril. Divides my line into two parts. Passes me the straw.

"Well . . . your substances reflect your money."

I put the bill in my right nostril. The paper squeaks. I inhale. Pass the bill to C.

K throws the remaining half into a mug. I take the mug and begin to drink slowly.

We've cleared the glass tabletop. We sit.

"Nah-nah, nah. Absolutely no way."

K takes the used hundred-ruble note from C, sticks it in the center of a wad of cash. Adjusts it, turns it over, and folds it in half. "This'll be the first thing they see."

C crawls to the computer, puts on music, a video.

The room we're getting loaded in is located on Komendantsky Prospect. It's K's apartment, he's painted the room all white. A wardrobe lines the entire side of a wall, which has a big heart drawn on it.

We sit on a sectional sofa near the window. There's a table in front of us, holding up a monitor, mugs, a rolling kit, tobacco, a brown cube of hashish.

There are shelves in the corner on the wall behind us. K claims that he gathered the wood for the shelves from the shore of the Gulf of Finland. The boards are nautical—veiny, warped, the grain is gray.

There are a lot of things stacked on the shelves. There's a bust of Pushkin in the corner. K tells of how he dug it out from under a heap of trash last spring. The bust is primed for painting. Across from us is a carpentry table. K works with wood professionally.

It's midnight by the clock. The three of us came here in a Deo Matiz. They picked me up at Petrogradskaya.

A small terrier walks around the room slowly. The first thing its owner did upon entering the apartment was put a bowl of food down. The dog's called Rogue.

K cuts hashish into thin squares on the tabletop. Gathers

them into a spliff, mixes them with tobacco on rolling paper, rolls with a filter, seals it, and passes it around the circle.

I'm not feeling the speed. "Nothing so far."

"Yeah, there was a little something there."

The hashish dulls any reaction, I move over to the leather armchair beside the sofa. It's deep. I slide down the back, stretch out. Feel a small spark in my cerebellum, which flows down my cheeks to the heart.

"Fellas, let me tell you that it is friggin' awesome to have sex in that chair," K says.

He takes a scale out of an extravagant ebonite case. Next, a blue parcel with white substance. He places the parcel on one side of the scale, a counterweight on the other. The scales are even.

"Thirty grams." K takes a lighter and seals the parcel.

We sit drinking coffee.

"Well, should we talk about why you're here?"

I get up, go into the hallway. K has stacked books to the ceiling and painted them silver. The books reach the top of my head. I take a napkin that's been folded several times out of a bag. Return to the room.

"My grandma called her friend and said: *Get here as fast as you can! My K has gone crazy—he's drilling into books*. That's when I was making that sculpture."

I hand the napkin to K. "You've even got Marx in there."

K unwraps the napkin. In it are sugar cubes that I swiped from home. K takes an insulin syringe and expels a small amount of antiseptic or iodine. Fills it and checks it in the light. Holds it over the two pieces of sugar. Carefully lets drops fall. Checks the syringe. Wraps the pieces in foil, each one separately, puts the instrument away.

I had handed over the money to C for two drops of English LSD while we were still in the car.

"Well, there it is, it's ready."

K throws himself against the back of the sofa. His shirt is open and his athletic torso is visible. Although he's thirty-five, K looks more like twenty-five or thirty. He's short, swarthy, lean, but somehow exceedingly slow and graceful in his movements.

The mug of coffee is half empty. I recline in the chair.

C is still rooting around the Internet—putting on different songs and videos. C is also athletically built, but it's a different kind of athleticism. In his youth he played basketball profession-ally. C is blonde with blue eyes. K is a brunette with brown eyes. C's big, almost childlike lips betray his sensitive nature.

It's nearing one a.m. We sit smoking a second joint. Watch a funny video. Finish up the coffee.

On the glass tabletop are the two little parcels wrapped in foil.

K walks into the room with a pistol. Black, heavy, big. K walks up to the carpentry table and with a strange contemplative expression he holds the pistol up to eye level.

After that he throws it on the table. The sound is abrupt, loud, unpleasant.

I get up, come closer. "Is it real?" I break the tension, point-ing to the barrel.

"Yeah, don't be afraid, I filed down the hammer."

I can feel the room exhale; even C brightens up.

"What do you need it for?"

"I have to make it inoperable."

I take the pistol, twirl it in my hands. "That's funny, a gun that can't shoot. It's lost its destiny."

K takes the barrel from my hands and with white plaster he tightly stops up the openings beneath the screw with a palette knife.

The doorbell rings. C and I flinch. Rogue barks.

Two enter. One is red, tall, with a full beard, his eyes are rac-ing. The second is shorter, a bit heavier, with gray circles under his eyes. His name is P, I crossed paths with him in the Siberian city of U. He's a musician.

We greet each other. The fellas sit on the floor. K takes the sealed parcel of speed, places it on the edge of the table.

"You got lucky, fellas. Seriously lucky. The goods are pure. This hasn't happened in a long time."

The fellas nod. They stare at the little blue bag with hungry eyes. Especially Red.

We sit, lazily talking things over. K lights up a new joint. We pass it around.

"I think I'll pass," Red says.

P takes the joint from my hands. I put my legs up on the armrest of the chair. P passes it along, sets his smartphone on the table. Presses it. The glass tabletop and this device merge into one another. P places the little bag of amphetamines on top.

"So you, like, make music?" K asks.

"Something like that," P replies.

"Well, put something of yours on for us."

P becomes flustered, but then gets up and heads to the computer. "Here, this is from the old demo."

An IDM beat begins to play. I hear a recorded voice from the radio. I focus my eyes on the screen, try to read the name of the band. *Aurora Baghdad.*

We finish smoking the joint.

"Well, I guess we'll go."

The fellas get up. We say our goodbyes. C and K go into the hallway to see them off, I remain in the room.

I hear: "We rode here on kick-scooters."

"It's the first time that I've ever ridden a kick-scooter."

"How did that go?"

They walk out the door, continue talking there.

I move over to the sofa. Try to find something online.

K and C return. K rolls another joint.

I tell you, it's really cool here at his place.

"All right, you haven't even seen the whole apartment."

K's converted half the kitchen into a carpentry workshop. He's got a workbench there, a carpenter's vise, a lathe. The floor is covered with wood shavings.

"Before, I used to make lots of little things and give them away as presents. I called them *pleasantries*. But then I realized they were much more dear to me than anyone else." K stares off somewhere beneath the ceiling, lost in thought. "So now I make them for myself."

We return to the other room. K leads us to the wardrobe with the heart. Opens it. There's a small illuminated nook in which miniature items are arranged on red velvet. K removes a perfectly smooth egg from a stand.

"This is what they look like."

Among the items are a box for wedding rings and Escher's staircase made of wood.

K returns the egg to its place and closes the drawer.

I take a seat on the sofa and lift my arms out across the shelves that begin where the back of the sofa curves.

"Feel it. Doesn't it feel like the wings of an angel?"

There's definitely something to that. I throw my head back. Pushkin's turned upside down. My arms on the nautical boards, I'm ready to start flapping them and fly away.

K sits down, rolls yet another spliff.

"What do you think? Should we trip?" I offer.

"Why not?" C responds.

The original plan was different. Drop in on K, take acid, and go see P and company. They rent a studio apartment right here on Komendantsky where they record music. Half of the group came here from E especially for that. There's a boom in the Urals right now of new music with a slant toward reggae.

But it's evident that something didn't line up with C and P.

C and I unwrap the foil, toast symbolically. Let's ride. It's one thirty.

C's at the computer again, searches, finds, puts on.

I notice a female mannequin in the far corner with a replica of the heart from the wardrobe on its left breast.

"Cool," I say. "You've even got your own mannequin."

"That's my ex-girlfriend's." K walks up to it. Studies it a couple of seconds, then turns abruptly on his heels. His black shirttail lifts up, revealing that solid torso. "She sat indoors while I worked all the time. I just needed a couple of pieces of scotch tape. I love creating something out of nothing."

The conversation turns to *The Portrait of Dorian Gray*. K leaves the room, but quickly returns with a book.

"Here, I haven't thrown this away only because of the cover." Against the soft yellow of the cover is the white profile of Wilde. The book is passed from hand to hand. "These are the little pleasantries I'm talking about."

The book is laid on the carpentry table next to the pistol.

K takes a baggie from the shelves, unseals it, sprinkles white powder onto the table, divides it into three parts, and goes off to the kitchen. We sit terrified of blowing away the powder.

Rogue climbs up onto the sofa and lies down next to me. She starts to lick. Her rough tongue goes up and down my arm. I close my eyes. I feel the tongue with a thousand granulations on it. Open my eyes.

"Good, Rogue."

The dog stops, looks at the body prone on the couch, and continues running its tongue here and there. It's not unpleasant, it's good. Rough. C and I chuckle lazily.

K returns. In his hands are mugs of coffee. He sprinkles the lines one after the other into the mugs.

"Gentlemen, coffee's ready."

I add three spoonfuls of sugar.

K gets up, leaves the room, and returns with a seven-branched candelabra. He places it on the carpentry table in the corner in front of the mirror. Turns off the overhead light.

Rogue doesn't stop for even a second.

"Why don't you give her a rest?" C says.

"She's doing it herself. It's not like I'm forcing her."

"Take your hand away."

Warmth is radiating from the dog. I don't remove my hand.

"So how are you both doing? Good?" K distracts himself from his activity.

We nod.

"It's hard to enjoy yourself if your guests aren't happy."

We slowly pull at our coffee. Two in the morning. Time for the LSD to show itself.

"I know what you need," K says, and leaves again.

"So how are you?" I ask C.

"Not bad, I'm starting to feel it already. That was a great idea K had about the candles."

The flames break apart as soon as I try to focus my attention on them.

We deliberate about what film to put on.

"Have you seen *Baraka?*" C asks.

"Obama?"

"No."

"Then no."

C burrows through the Internet, finds it, reads the description.

"Listen," I say. "It sounds a lot like this one film that I've wanted to see for a long time. I can't remember the name. It starts with a K."

We search. The director of *Baraka* leads us to *Koyaanisqatsi.*

"That's it."

We read about the thirty-five thousand meters of film used on the movie.

K returns. "Here, this should be just the thing for you both right now." Two jam dishes appear on the table, filled with white globs.

"What's that?"

"Fruity ice cream. Little cocktails."

We try it, a soft sweet taste, it flows smoothly into the stomach.

"C, pass Alexander Sergeyevich over."

C climbs onto the sofa, lifts the bust of Pushkin. "Behold the power of art," he says.

I take the bust, it really is heavy. Pass it over to K.

K places Pushkin on the carpentry table, starts painting the white poet. C puts on *Koyaanisqatsi*. We eat the fruit cocktail, drink the spiked coffee. Rogue finally calms down and falls asleep.

"*Koyaa-nisqatsi, Koyaa-nisqatsi*," a voice repeats against the background of mournful ceremonial music and clouds of fire.

After a minute we understand that a rocket is taking off in slow motion. It's the beginning. Time passes quickly and imperceptibly. Hours fall away, leaving only perfunctory minutes behind them. The echo of *Koyaa-nisqatsi* traverses the entire film. The final scene. A rocket goes skyward. So does the mournful ceremonial music of Glass. Something has gone wrong, the music only reinforces this sensation. A torrent of air flows over the body of the rocket in a white plume. A second, then an explosion. The camera watches for falling debris. One piece stands out. It falls, tumbling and burning. For a second it seems as though it could be the astronaut's seat. But no, it's a piece of the rocket. Twirling in a final dance, it slowly falls to earth.

"*All is senseless and futile*." I'm quoting Mujuice here.

K sits at the computer, searches for a color picture of Pushkin. In the time it took to watch the film, black kinky hair has appeared on the bust of Pushkin on the table.

I register the change. Colors have intensified. Trails have begun in my peripheral vision. I think of Kesey and the Pranksters' tests. Put the jam dish with the fruit cocktail to the side. C finishes eating it to the very last.

"How tall did you say your ceiling is?" K ask unexpectedly.

"It's, like, normal," I reply. "Average."

Outside the window we hear a guitar being played, singing.

"It seems our musicians didn't get far."

I go up to the window. A seaside neighborhood. Komendantskaya Square, at the center of which is a shopping center that resembles a flying saucer. Right beneath the windows is another big shopping center, overlaid in gray paneling. The frightful tastelessness typical of a residential neighborhood. Seemingly the only signs read, *Secondhand*. Beyond it, bunched together, are high-rise homes.

A young man sits on the grounds of the shopping center and strums a guitar. Beside him stands the yellow-green Deo Matiz. I step away from the window.

K has printed out several color images of Pushkin, and C is at the monitor again. He finds and puts on *Baraka*.

"I'm going to the store," K says. "Got to buy food for Rogue. Anyone need anything?"

We shake our heads.

C closes the door. *Baraka* begins with the same images as *Koyaanisqatsi*.

The film is more vivid, the colors more vibrant. The camera moves along the corridors of a temple, a mosaic appears all around the monitor. It's literally like looking through a kaleidoscope at the center of which you find yourself. You open all of these doors, walk through all of these corridors. You're on the inside, while your eye is a camera. The music is extraordinary, it blends with the landscape in a very soothing way.

I grasp at something important. There's something encased in the center of the universe. Some sort of simple and at the same time fundamental truth. Another second and I'll understand it, seize it.

I need to get rid of this sensation. I recall the story of the banana. The story goes like this: Friend K faithfully wrote something on a scrap of paper during a moment of insight in the middle of an acid trip. The next morning K discovered the scrap. On it was written: *The banana is cool. But the peel's thick.*

C sits with his legs tucked beneath him, and has gone quiet. I want to talk, share my perceptions with him. But something interferes, some strange and unknown barrier. It could be that the whole matter lies with K, since we've never had problems like this arise before.

K has now returned from the store, filled the dog's bowl, cut up fruit in the kitchen, and brought it into the room on a big tray along with other edibles.

C goes for the pretzel sticks.

I try one too. The taste of salt is very pleasant. Words can't begin to describe. It fluidly dissolves into the walls of the mouth. Even the cheekbones take it in. It's also interesting to just gnaw on the pretzel stick. To bite into it, feel as the stick crumbles in your mouth, as crumbs from sharp edges scratch at your tongue, cheeks. As they slowly lose their rigidity.

I'm discussing this with C, whose attention is taken up mainly by the grains of salt, before he grabs an apple. The apple is undergoing a metamorphosis too. It's succulent, spraying sweet juice along the walls of the mouth cavity. Biting, chewing it gives pleasure, bordering on ecstasy.

"There it is, fellas. That's what I'm talking about. Now acid is going to eat away your entire brain."

Hmmm, strange. Eat away the brain . . . The white jam dish. The fruit cocktail. Orange juice. Kesey's tests.

Baraka culminates in a scene with cave paintings, also shown at the beginning of the film. I observe: "It looks like the director made another *Koyaanisqatsi*. He realized this and decided to mix in different scenes."

Pushkin's face is beginning to reveal itself. K works with inspiration, he periodically sticks out his tongue without noticing it.

It's five thirty. The sky slowly grows light at the window. Soon it will turn turquoise, a pleasant color in every sense.

K pulls himself away from the bust and rolls a joint.

"Was that your girlfriend saying goodbye to you? I mean, when we drove up?" he asks.

"Yes, that's her."

Why is he asking this?

Rogue has eaten her fill and jumps up onto the sofa again, lies down next to my arm, gives me a reproachful look, and goes at my hand anew.

We pass the joint around. How many has it been tonight?

C puts on a video of Jefferson Airplane from 1968. The band performs on the roof of a building. Judging from the architecture, people, and taxis—it's somewhere in New York. But something's not right. The music is wondrously good. It's reminiscent of contemporary "desert rock." Yeah, even cooler! No, there's something conspicuously not right here.

"Look at how it's filmed," I say. "How contemporary the camera angles are!"

I wait for a reaction, but it seems that no one is paying attention to this anymore.

"They've even got Bonham on drums. Perhaps it's an omnibus show. Or maybe he's replaced a sick drummer."

"Perhaps," C responds.

I look at him, he's completely lost in the video. He sits right in front of the monitor with his feet tucked up beneath him.

The people in the video look as though they're cut out and pasted. They jump off the screen toward the viewer. The background is glued to a wall, but it's the opposite with the musicians— they move about their environment freely.

There, Polanski just walked behind the musicians.

"No doubt! This is a new video, styled after the 1960s. With all the attributes of that era. Even Polanski's there. The music is a giveaway—it's got a contemporary beat."

C shrugs his shoulders. The video ends.

"That must be it," I say. I get up, start to walk around the room. "Did you see Polanski there? It was so cool how they did that, and I was all ready to believe it. And Bonham's planted there. It's like, he who knows will understand. A subtle hint for us. Plus it's only a year before Manson murders Sharon Tate." I cut off the verbal fountain. Stop in the center of the room, throw my arms wide open, and say: "Now tell me, how is it possible to kill anyone in a state like this?"

It was worth it to voice this thought—the idea of murder no longer seems so absurd. Suddenly the urge arises to grab a knife and cut someone. Not out of hatred, but out of love. No, that's not it. Out of an irresistible desire to show the world in my eyes, though such an attempt would be total depravity.

I go to the bathroom.

It's good here, cozy. A soft glow comes from below, having something to do with the toilet. There are reeds on the red walls. Glassed-in pipelines of communication. Hieroglyphs.

I exit.

The top pocket of the bag that I came with is open. I remember that I retrieved the napkin with the pieces of sugar from there. What about my keys? The keys have been here the entire time in the pocket of a green Adidas Original jacket.

Knucklehead! I grab the jacket, feel the pockets. The keys are in their place. I retrieve them. The metal shines. But of course someone could have made a copy while I was out of the room.

All right, calm down. Right now it's important to not show what you've figured out. Just go back to the room like nothing has happened, sit down, and think everything through all nice like.

All right, go on and think: You were sitting here, they arrived. You didn't like Red from the start. His eyes were racing. What do they live off of? Music?

"C, what do those fellas live off of? Red, for instance?"

C slowly (way too slowly!) turns, he's beet-faced. What's wrong with him? Is he afraid of something?

"Well, he put this website up overnight."

Spoken unpersuasively. Is he lying? Or does he just not know?

Fine, go on then. Next they got up and made their way to the front door. How much time did they spend in the hallway while they were saying their goodbyes? Enough to pull off the deal with the keys.

I have to ask where they went. The answer will calm me down. If they went to record music, then everything's okay. However, if C lies, then I'll know it right away. And then I'll have uncovered their plan. They'll know that I know. No, that's not the way to do it. I have to be more careful.

Fine. They made a copy. Then what? They went to my house! No one is there but my sister, and she's totally helpless. They're drug addicts, after all. What did Hunter S. Thompson say? *You can turn your back on a person, but never turn your back on a drug.* They hold nothing sacred, they have no qualms.

To try to ease the trembling, I head back to the bathroom. Wash my face. K walks by.

"Well, is that helping any? It usually calms me down."

Calms me down? That means he knows something.

The water is definitely pleasant, velvety.

I return to the room. Begin walking around in it. I notice that the pistol is no longer lying next to *The Portrait of Dorian Gray*.

K gave the barrel to those two drug addicts. He took it out of commission, so that they wouldn't misfire at something. But now they're at my house with a pistol and my sister . . .

The height of the ceiling. K asked me about the height of the ceiling. They want to go through the window. Of course, that's it! They've got it all planned. There are cameras everywhere over there. They must have planned it all in advance. And they need to know the height of the ceiling, so as not to get the apartments mixed up.

I have to call my sister right away. It's six thirty. I'll wait until seven, then call her, wake her up for work.

What was up with the questions about M, my girlfriend? They want to kidnap her. Or rape her? Rape her. God, how did I not figure this out sooner? They want to ravage her. There were some characters hanging around the place where they picked me up. Stop. She sent me a message as soon as she reached home. But they could have forced her. They want to take it all away from me in one go.

All this is how clowning around with acid, amphetamines, and hashish affects a body—it is making me stupid, shutting off my brain so that I can't comprehend.

And there sits C, all gloomy. He definitely knows the truth, which is why he won't look me in the eyes.

"C, everything okay?"

"Yeah, yeah, everything's good."

I don't believe him. Could it be, e tu, Brute? You're embroiled in this mess. But of course! Why didn't I think of this sooner? They forced him. He alone knows where I live. He knows everything about me. Trust no one. He needs money just like everybody else. He doesn't have a job, his mother has probably stopped sending him money. He asked to borrow two or three thousand from me not long ago. E tu, Brute!

K is all well and good. Him I can understand at least, I'm no one to him. But you! I trusted you, you and I lived in Siberia together for a month.

And Rogue. She was looking at me as though she wanted to say: *Oh, you! You've squandered your good fortune. You've been blown full of hot air.* They say that dogs possess a certain intuition about these matters. So she wasn't just casually licking my hand.

It's all good—I try to focus and make sense of everything. Quit being so jumpy!

Facts, only facts are needed here.

What do I know about K: he made a cross for a local church in the small Siberian city of U and at the age of thirty-three carried it throughout the entire city.

But how does K earn a living? Could it really be from those piss-away-the-day handicrafts? It's not possible to live off of things like that now. He's a drug dealer. People like that are dangerous, and you trusted him without even knowing him. All the clues were right before your eyes, he was just toying with you. And the pistol, and the amphetamine sale . . . Amphetamines! That was payment to those drug addicts for their services. Remember what their eyes were like when K gave them the blue package? Craving, thirsty. They couldn't wait to use. That kind will be up for anything. That whole charade about "music" . . . it was really clever how they managed to cloud my brain.

K—that's brain surgery. He thought this all up. He's the one who's maintaining contact with them, that's why he keeps going out, that's why none of these questions are lining up.

He went out to the street and passed them something. But what? The barrel? The keys? How long was he gone? Long enough. You can't trust how time passes while on LSD.

Or maybe this is all because of a robbery. They went to attend to their affairs. I dropped out while on acid. So much time passed, but I didn't know how to occupy myself. I've only watched two films. They've mugged someone, and they want me to take the fall for it. It's obvious that I'm on drugs, I can't argue against that. My statement will be nullified after they test my urine. God, what a drug combo I have in me right now!

Stop! All of these quaint little jam dishes with cocktails, little bits of fruit on trays—all this was intended to keep me calm. Distract me. While they . . .

Oh God!

They've broken into my house, raped my sister, taken anything of value—they could even still be there. I can only guess what they've done with M. And I can't do anything about it. Because if I go to the police, they'll just arrest me. I'm a drug addict, after all. They've thought of everything.

"Let's take a walk," K suggests. "It'll be good for you right about now."

He's read everything on my face and he's going to hand me over to those drug addicts. I shouldn't have stomped around the room like that. Idiot!

Seizing the moment I tell C: "It seems that I've stepped into a web of betrayal." And I tell him about Manson, about the keys, about the copy. I'm telling him, while laughing myself.

It gets better. Or does it?

"Do you know what one of the most popular questions asked on Google is?" C replies.

"No."

"What do I have to do to come down?"

A good attempt at changing the subject. Still, I need details about a few things. "How much did P purchase the goods for?"

"Twelve bills for everything. He'll take it to E, sell it there for three times the price."

Sounds good, but he's not very convincing when he says it, his intonation is off. It's too precise.

"Did they definitely go off to rehearse? And where's their space?"

"Yeah, not far from here. Let's go for a walk, you definitely need it."

We head out onto the street. The sky is turquoise. People are rushing to work. It's beginning to rain.

Rogue runs ahead, K and C follow a short distance behind.
I hang back, call my sister.

"Hello?" Her voice is drowsy.

"Get up, it's time for you to go to work."

"Yeah, yeah."

Her voice is strange somehow. It's hoarse. Could this be a consequence of the night?

It's starting to get chilly. The only thing that calms me down is this rain. It's fine, practically dust, a fog. Drops of it land on my face. They soothe an inflamed brain, a body feverish with paranoia.

We walk along the green stripe that divides Marshal Novikov Prospect. Overhead is a power line, stretching its veins through the body of the sleeping neighborhood. Underfoot is wet grass. My Adidas Originals are quickly getting wet, they're suede. But you don't pay any attention to this. Look at how green the grass is. Wet, luscious, bright. It's such a color that you just can't avert your eyes. And it matches the color of your jacket so well.

In one of the yards we find outdoor exercise equipment. It's painted wild yellow, blue, red. K and C throw themselves at it and attempt to try each one out.

This would be a little weird if seen in passing—three grown men with a dog at seven in the morning in a playground dressed in tracksuits.

"You've got to try this," says C. "Stand over here."

We try the treadmill. I slide off it fast. "Somehow I really think I'm stuck in a web of betrayal. C, tell me that everything is all right."

C gets off the treadmill. "No, everything's bad."

I walk off to the side, call my sister.

"Hello?" That hoarse voice again.

"Get up. You have to go to work."

"Yeah, yeah. I'm up already."

That frog in her throat. If I wasn't sure it was her . . .

We walk around the neighborhood. I feel a little better out on the street. K walks ahead with Rogue.

"You look like a baseball player from the '60s in that Adidas jacket."

"C, I have such intense paranoia. I can't shake it off."

"A sleepy neighborhood. No matter where you look everything is gray. It's totally depressing. Everyone here's paranoid."

"Listen, you said that P and company have a rehearsal space in this neighborhood. Where is it?"

"Over there." He gestures in an offhand manner to a building with a round tower just beyond the high-rises.

Rain and grass—that's what soothes. And also this bright green jacket. The acid jacket of a baseballer.

We return to the apartment. I sit in the easy chair. Rogue settles down on the sofa next to my arm and begins to lick it.

As a force of habit—K packs a joint. We smoke ourselves out. Next K makes coffee, spikes it, hands it out.

I need to call M, but it's too early, she's still asleep. Maybe if I hear a loving voice, it'll save me. Or ease the suffering.

The next hours pass unnoticeably, they flow one into the other. We drink coffee, smoke spliff after spliff, play a game of finding the wildest video on YouTube. We end up with an Italian commercial for window blinds and East German agitprop. After that we get bored.

Some of the videos are frightening in their wildness. I cower in the easy chair. I want to be on the street, it was better there. The enclosed space is intensifying my paranoia. I want to leave, but it's still too early. I might get rounded up. Shaken down.

"Pushkin and I don't see eye to eye," says K. "I lost a girl who I was in love with, to him."

Pushkin continues acquiring color.

"Of course, not to the poet himself. His distant relative." K approaches the window. "That sign over there," he points out beyond the window. "It makes me crawl out of my skin every time."

I approach, look. It's the big signboard in lights that reads, *Secondhand*.

"We have to go there right away," he says.

We get ready, go out.

For ten in the morning there are plenty of people in the store. Items are hung in a strict order, which distinguishes this shop from similar places, where the merchandise is typically piled up in heaps.

C and K browse through the hangers. The average price of merchandise—two hundred rubles. For a bill you can get an entire ensemble. C tries on some checkered pants and grabs a cloth bag with a logo for the 1980 Olympics. K gets lost in the rows of clothing. Above the aisles two heads can be seen moving about, each with a white earpiece. The heads look around and monitor the surroundings. They move to intersect with us.

I rush C, but he's soundly carried away with shopping. I'm starting to feel ill at ease. I have to leave right away. But what if they're out on the street waiting? What if they take us away right on the street? Two-two-eight. From four you get eight.

Of course, that's the arrangement! K got busted on a sale, he cut a deal: K and C pump out drug addicts, they lure them onto the street, they pass them along. Statistically, the neighborhood does not suffer from this.

The two heads tighten the circle, I rush to the exit. The cashiers watch me go. Even they are involved in this? You've thought this through on a grand scale, fellas. I hold my breath and exit.

Rain. Nothing's happening. No one is ambushing me, throwing my hands behind my back, pressing me into the concrete with a massive knee, removing baggies of gray-yellow powder from my pockets, yelling in my face. There's nothing but the rain. I walk around in it, and then I return again.

The two with the earpieces cruise through the aisles of clothing as before, scanning from side to side. It's in these moments
that you start to understand Philip K. Dick.

I find C in the fitting room, we go to the checkout. C's total
is rung up as half the value of what he's purchased. What's that
about—plain negligence or payment for services? We'll find out
as we exit. I hold my breath anew.

Nothing.

We walk beneath the cables of the power line. I look up, the
black cords blend with the gray sky. The rain intensifies, but I
don't get a pleasant feeling from it. Since the grass has lost its
succulent brightness, I want the rain all the more. Perhaps it's
capable of cooling an overheated brain.

We separate. K goes off to buy some things. C and I walk
around the neighborhood. People look sideways at us.

"It didn't turn out so well this time," I say. "I'm not on the
same wavelength as K. Although he's pretty generous. What's
that about?"

"Yeah, I don't know. Next time he needs to drop acid too." C
doesn't look me in the eyes. What could he be hiding?

"I'm going to ask you one last time. But please answer me in
all seriousness. Is everything all right? I don't have anything to
worry about, right? And P went off to rehearsal, and not to some
other place?"

C looks sideways. "Yeah, everything's all right. P went to rehearsal after he left us."

"Then why didn't they take us with them?"

"I guess they didn't want anyone interrupting them. They
wanted the speed for themselves."

C's answers calm me, but not for long.

"You and I have had trips that have turned out awesome.
Remember, on New Year's Eve?"

"Yeah. We must have a soul connection, we're a good

match when it comes to these things. We're on the same wavelength."

We walk in the rain, we're soaked through. We stumble upon K. Go home. I beat my hands in the pockets of my jeans.

At home, K returns to Pushkin, C heads to the kitchen to write a poem.

I go to the bathroom, wash my face. The water carpets my face with velvet. I look in the mirror. Something's changed in my face: either the cheekbones have grown sharper, or there's a diamondlike glint in my eye. Something subtle, it scares me.

I call M. She picks up, answers cheerfully. I ask if I can come over tonight.

"Of course, come over. I'll be waiting."

Calm. There it is.

I try to write in my notebook, my hands shake, some food for thought about love and self-sacrifice comes out. Then I unexpectedly make a note: *Looking in the mirror, you never know what kind of creature you'll see.*

K rolls a joint, spikes coffee. I'm sick of having to run to the bathroom but take the mug anyway. K asks that I check the Internet to make sure he recites the poem "The Bronze Horseman" correctly. He reads the opening.

I search for poems more to my own taste. I read Mayakovsky (*At the very least allow this final tenderness to pave your departing step*), Brodsky (*Neither country, nor graveyard . . .*), I finish with Okudzhava: *He knew how to sully the page by the glow of a candle/ So what did he have to die for at Chernaya Rechka?*

It's two in the afternoon. Still too early to descend into the metro. But it's imperative to rejoin the living. It's become stuffy and cumbersome here. We say our goodbyes.

C and I go to his place, he doesn't live far from here. We walk down veinlike streets. The drug doesn't want to leave my body, it's giving me the shakes. My hands are in the pockets of my wet jeans.

Before we settle in at C's we move along the wasteland surrounding Lake Dolgoe. This wasteland borders the new multistory homes, although just two years ago the city ended here. Clay swims about at our feet from the rain. A lone car, the driver of which looks back in bewilderment. Ducks. The ripples on the water turn into the ripples of the sky.

At C's we drink it off with green tea, have conversations on near-literary topics.

P comes over with a girl, looks in on us. She's a poet in one of the groups from the Urals who are ushering in a wave of new music. I'm still *very much* on speed, my pupils take up the entire rainbow of the iris. I study P closely—the last thing he looks like is a human capable of doing anything horrible.

"Want an amphetamine?" P asks in the hallway.

"No. I'm loaded up to my ears."

We speak of music, of Shulgin's acid, of enlightened states of being. The girl spiritedly speaks of her own experience with substances.

I go to the bathroom, check my pupils. At least I don't look like a person who's had a blood hemorrhage in his eyes. I can go.

On the street along the way to the metro I've gathered myself together, I'm oriented and prepared for anything. In this green jacket with my brain dried out after the acid I feel like an ancient Viking, one who's just gobbled down mushrooms and is making his way through uncharted land.

I want to get home as fast as possible and make sure that everything is all right. But I can't show up there in this burned-out state. I go to M, on Petrogradskaya. That's the lesser of two evils. I text C from the metro: *We're superior to single-celled organisms. People in the metro aren't real: typical specimens for a drug addict. Let's be superior to this.*

I think: *That's my "banana."*

* * *

It's nine at night. M joyfully greets me at the doors. We go to her room. She sits on my lap. Looks into my eyes.

"You have pretty eyes."

I'm silent.

"What did you do for fun?"

I'm silent.

"How did you spend the night?"

"I haven't slept yet."

"Uh-huh." She carefully studies my face. "Well, how many hits did you take this time?"

"Two."

"Uh-huh. Understood." M turns away. Her wavy hair conceals her face. She brushes it away. I want to hold her, but she's distanced herself. We sit in silence for a long time.

"I haven't had anything to eat since our dinner last night at the café."

"Let's go. I'll make you something to eat. Demon spawn."

M wipes away tears. In the kitchen she prepares an extraordinary omelet with white bread and tomatoes. I pour myself cognac.

"This will help me come down."

M is silent. I take a big swig and am barely able to finish the omelet. I begin to conk out. I drag my body to the bed, undress, collapse, and fall asleep immediately.

Several hours later the smell of tobacco wakes me. I cautiously open my eyes.

Quiet. The dead of night. The table lamp has been turned on. The window is thrown wide open. M sits on the wide windowsill and slowly and very seductively smokes a cigarette. The scarlet tip is visible through the billowing half-transparent curtain. I can't remember the last time I saw her with a cigarette.

THE HAIRY SUTRA

BY PAVEL KRUSANOV
Moika Embankment, 48

Translated by Amy Pieterse

*"The pentagram," said Semion Matveev, halting at the table and
pressing his hand against the globe. "Swear upon the pentagram,
for the devil's sake! And I shall reveal a great secret."*
                              —Boris Pilnyak, *The Naked Year*

Demyan Ilich had a good grasp of the essence of man: he
looked at a peach and saw the pit. That was the way
he was. Some are preoccupied with the question: what
kind of man are you? While for others, it's: what are you capable
of? Demyan Ilich wanted to know: who is inside of you?

As for who was inside of this young maid, he, of course,
knew. She had the following cast of mind and habit: with strangers and those she took a liking to, or at least didn't dislike, she
was kind and friendly. But with everyone else she was given to
caprice, and if her upbringing did not allow her to slap someone
across the face with no good reason, nothing prevented her from
kicking them from behind. Demyan Ilich was disgusting to her.
He knew she was a graceful and obtuse creature; but he couldn't
help the way he was.

What was she to him? When Demyan Ilich saw her, he was
beset by strange, conflicting thoughts and emotions. Evil has ma-

tured in my mind, he thought, smiling to himself. Yet at the same time he wanted to touch her tenderly, to stroke her, maybe even try to lick that girlishly plump cheek covered with dainty apricot fuzz. It was so easy, so frightening . . . Such thoughts made Demyan Ilich's heart throb dully; his blood ran thicker, and his chest grew tight and hot. Oh well, if they couldn't be together, they could still be close. In his head a plan began to hatch. A whim? No, the curator never acted upon a whim—that was against his principles. But this was a special case: Demyan Ilich could not control his feelings. If they couldn't be together, they could at least be close to each other . . .

The plan fell together piece by piece. People in whom unrestrained passion lets loose become terrifyingly resourceful. The plan ripened, writhing in his brain amid heated thoughts like a sterlet in a broth of fish soup. The plan fell into place inexorably. And, finally, it was ready. No, Demyan Ilich did not wish upon her the same fate he had dealt so many others. But what else could he do? She must stay and be with him. This way or another, he wasn't going to give her up.

"Ahem." The curator cleared his throat. And picking his way through the mess reigning in the house, a mess grown familiar and cozy to him, he went off to the bathroom to freshen up. For even the best news could be ruined by the foul breath of its messenger.

Take the platypus, for example. It was no doubt in deep trouble, which is why it was on the IUCN Red List of Threatened Species. This meant that it was next to impossible for a museum to acquire that beast (stuffed) for an exhibit by legal means. First, hunting the platypus in Australia is illegal and severely punishable under Australian law. Second, the export of the platypus, procured by illegal means on the territory of Australia, is outlawed. Third, in accordance with a plethora of international conventions and agreements, any attempt to import a platypus that has been illegally procured and exported from Australian territory to most any country that abides by the laws of the international community is also a highly punishable offense. It is a three-tiered system. Naturally, one could always try to obtain a stuffed platypus on the secondary market, but the availability is rather limited, and chances are that the platypus would already be moth-eaten and gray with dust. There is, of course, the practice of museum exchanges, but this is a privilege of larger institutions with better funding. Finally, there is the shadowy world of illegal commercial zoology—but how legitimate would the exhibits be? And at what price . . .

Here, in contrast, they had no less than three stuffed platypuses adorning the glass display cases. Not bad for a small museum—just one crowded hall, really—at the Zoology Department of a university bearing the name of a perfectly respectable writer. (His life had been wrecked by the Decembrists, who had awakened the revolutionary democrat within him.) The museums's collection was started almost two centuries ago at the Lohvitskay-Skalon Gymnasium for Ladies, and in 1903 the museum moved here to the then brand-new Imperial Pedagogical College for Ladies on the Moika Embankment. Since those bygone days, the display cases of the museum had housed two particularly rare exhibits: a stuffed Cuban red macaw (*Ara tricolor*), an extinct species of parrot, the last of which was shot in 1864 in the Zapata Swamp; and a gigantic Taveuni beetle (*Xixuthrus terribilis*), housed in a glass entomological box. The beautiful macaw had suffered for its splendor: its feathers were used in ladies' hats, and when at last people thought to replenish the population or at least preserve a small number of the species in captivity, it turned out to be impossible. The Taveuni beetle, brown and branchy as a mandrake root, has since become extinct. It once inhabited Fiji, where natives stuffed themselves with its thick, oblong larvae, which looked like sausages carefully and obligingly prepared by nature herself. In the end, not knowing when to stop, the natives gobbled up the entire population of the species.

From the year 1909, and for a quarter of a century to follow, this Department of Zoology was chaired by a renowned professor, an academician whose name was recognized throughout the world. During his tenure the museum was able to augment its collection and become one of the best university collections in the country. Among the rare exotic objects that an astonished visitor would encounter was an African pangolin, covered with brown boney scales like a huge pinecone, a lesser hedgehog tenrec, a seven-banded and a nine-banded armadillo from the pampas of South America, a short-beaked echidna, a three-toed sloth, and a *Tamandua tetradactyla*. The imaginations of medieval bestiary writers would have paled at the sight of such creatures, just like a jellyfish, pulled from the deep, pales in the sunlight.

The list of exotic species was not limited to the aforementioned exhibits, however. Inside antique showcases, and upon the shelves of glass-covered oak bookcases, the round eyes of lemurs and capuchins bulged, and patas monkeys, drills, colobuses, and marmosets smirked and pulled faces. Not to mention polar bears and brown bears, sea otters, koalas, flying foxes, monitor lizards, crocodiles, walruses, manatees, and dugongs. Birds? Indeed, they ranged from the green woodpecker to the marabou stork. How about the ascarids preserved in alcohol, and tapeworms in thick glass flasks? Mollusks, you ask? Hundreds of shells, from the giant clam to the rapana, spiky and smooth, bivalves and twisted, with nacreous curls and opaque gaps. And what of the echinoderms and starfish . . .

And the Entomology Department itself? There you would find a hundred square feet of one wall were occupied by boxes of various collections, plus entomological cabinets and drawers, and a large glass cube with exhibits of insects and arachnids from Southeast Asia. And fish? Sponges? Here, among other things, was a glassy sponge, which according to Japanese tradition is given to newlyweds as a symbol of eternal love. The sponge was occasionally inhabited by two shrimp of the opposite sex. They crawled inside through the pores of the sponge as larvae, and when they grew into adulthood were unable to get out. And so they lived inside the sponge, feeding on the plankton that the sponge itself fed upon; and when the sponge died, they had no choice but to die with it. And reptiles, amphibians? What of marine arthropods? And the horns and heads of ungulates on the walls just beneath the ceiling? The senses and imagination were overwhelmed, and taking in the entire collection at one go—a collection that numbered more than three thousand items— was out of the question. By the same token, it would have been impossible to squeeze the collection into the limited space that was allotted to it, so some of the less valuable exhibits were displayed in the lecture halls and auditorium. For some museums such numbers would be undeserving of notice, but here it was a source of discreet pride.

These premises were not often disturbed by mere members of the public. Groups of curious students would visit from time to time. The exhibits amused guests taking part in the occasional scientific conference, and once in a while someone from the chancellor's office would show off the museum to an important person, as one of the college's most valued and prestigious assets—but that was about it. The rest of the time, the museum's doors were kept firmly shut, and the key was kept by the gloomy Demyan Ilich, who had held the position of collection curator for the past three years.

Also under the supervision of the curator was a tiny closet with a workbench, tools, and a spacious freezer. At the workbench he performed small maintenance jobs on the exhibits, and in the freezer, waiting for their turn under the taxidermist's knife, he kept his materials—pelts and carcasses of beasts and fowl, which he had come upon by chance or which were presented as gifts by the chair of the department, who was an occasional hunter. Demyan Ilich spent his working hours in primeval solitude like Adam, surrounded by the deathly somnolence of Eden, opening only at the knock of a teacher who had stopped by on some matter that needed attention, and venturing out himself only now and then to get water for the electric kettle.

And yet . . . although the museum covered an area of no more than two hundred square yards, one could get lost there. Not simply get lost: one could disappear altogether.

"I just don't know what came over me. I must have been in some kind of fog," said Lera, the laboratory assistant, and behind the lenses of her glasses her eyelashes fluttered up and down like the feathers of a large fan.

"You weren't in any fog," thundered Tsukatov. "It was pure negligence, which is far worse!"

"Off with my head. It's my fault."

"Of all the parasites that eat away a human from the inside, the only one worse than treachery, and the one I most despise, is slapdash work—a careless job trying to pass itself off as something up to the mark," said Professor Tsukatov to Lera, as he examined her poorly composed request for reagents, materials, and laboratory utensils. "Watching those nature programs with names like *The War of the Giant Beetles* fills me with black bile. Yes, technically, the series is impressive. Yes, the camerawork is flawless. But that's where it ends. They have spiders and crickets, praying mantises and scorpions, they have wasps and ants, giant centipedes and grasshoppers. Damn, they even have crabs and tiger leeches! What they *don't* have are giant beetles! They don't have *any* beetles. And instead of informative commentary they have some half-witted blather. They are professional go-getters out to make a quick buck on the side. They have been eaten away by the parasite of slapdashery, corrupted by audiences of ignoramuses, who not only no longer wish to educate themselves, but insist on bringing knowledge down to their own paltry intellectual level."

Doctor Tsukatov, professor of biology, was a parasitologist, and a well-known specialist on nematodes. He saw worms everywhere and in everything. Throughout years of work, nematodes, those tiny creatures, had made nests in his thoughts and had grown to unbelievable proportions. They had gained so much weight that they—his thoughts, that is—sailed heavily along the smooth surface of his consciousness, much like the barges that used to float along Lake Ladoga centuries ago, loaded with travertine for the construction of the then newly-founded city of St. Petersburg, ponderous and inexorable. His thoughts themselves seemed like worms to him, parasitizing their host and forcing him to act according to their own wormy demands.

"I understand. I'll rewrite this," the stately Lera said, fluttering her thick eyelashes. She was in the wrong, but believed that she deserved leniency. She was exhausted by the remodeling that was underway at her home, which she blamed for this little slipup. "Two desiccators, pipettes, test tubes with sixteen-by-eighteen caps, paraffin strips, ethyl acetate, diethyl ether—"

"No, we don't need diethyl ether," Tsukatov corrected her.

Outside the window of the chair of the Zoology Department's office, the year's first snow was falling. It powdered the courtyard, stuck to the trees, and swirled above the black waters of the Moika, afraid of touching the twinkling dangerous gloss of the surface. In the summer, the green treetops partially obscured the view, and the water wasn't visible. Now, before it would be covered in ice, the black water of the river could be seen through the tree branches and the embankment railing, snaking slowly along. Set off by the fresh ocher color of the buildings, the clean snow looked festive, like a childhood memory.

Farther down, past the Red Bridge, the green Jugendstil steeple of the S. Esders & K. Scheefhals Trading House, topped with a caduceus, could still be discerned through the falling snow. Right behind it the gilded cupola of St. Isaac's Cathedral shimmered dimly. The boat weathervane on the spire of the Admiralty had vanished—the northwest wind had turned it sideways to the viewer.

Tsukatov's eyes were still smoldering, but he himself had already started cooling off—the spirit of righteous anger had left the professor in his usual state of pedantic severity, which did not seek a victim intentionally, and was even kind by nature. Tsukatov was the chair of the department, but he was also a man, still strong and not old, and as a man, he was prepared to forgive a woman her little foibles because of her nice figure.

"Microscope slides and cover slips, filter paper," muttered Lera, "smooth tweezers and serrated tweezers, alcohol, diethyl ether—"

"No diethyl ether, we don't need that," Tsukatov corrected her once again.

The door of the office opened without a knock and Professor Chelnokov appeared. He was stocky and thickset, and despite having long ago entered the sixth decade of his life, he looked youthful and energetic. He had just finished giving a lecture and he was excited by the vivacious spirit that had poured into him. A renowned ornithologist, Professor Chelnokov enjoyed talking to young people, and young people answered him in kind—he had been called Chief Bird by at least four generations of students. Chelnokov could boast of having a fine memory, but with time, the fullness of detail began to fade, and although he remembered many stories from his life and the lives of others, he couldn't recall to whom and how many times he'd already related these stories.

In his day, Tsukatov had been Chelnokov's student, and he too had affectionately called his teacher Chief Bird (though not to his face, of course). Now Tsukatov shared the office of the department chair with him. Their desks stood near each other on a low platform by the window, hedged away from the rest of the space by a bookcase and a short wooden banister. Although obliged to become neighbors due to circumstance—Chelnokov's office was in a perennial state of reconstruction—they both sincerely enjoyed one another's company. Besides, Chelnokov himself had recently been the chair of the department, but had to abandon the post due to his advanced age.

"Y-you know, we don't have a single decent primate in our m-museum. I mean, an anthropoid," said Chelnokov, stuttering elegantly, resuming the conversation they had been engaged in before he had gone off to give a lecture. Their discussion was about how to utilize the unexpected funding that had been allotted for the museum's needs. "We have macaques and other short-tailed monkeys all over the p-place, but not a single gorilla. Or an orangutan, b-beautiful and orange, like a tangerine. It's just not right."

"There are many things we don't have yet," said Tsukatov. His personal preference was to augment the reptile collection, and he was considering acquiring a Galápagos tortoise. A thought he shared with all present.

"Who is the Galápagos tortoise to us, anyway? A son-in-law? A brother?" Chelnokov countered, producing a can of coffee from the bookcase they had adapted into a cupboard. "Now, a ch-chimpanzee is basically family. A distant relative, at the very least." And then to Lera: "Care for coffee?"

Tsukatov pursed his lips into a fine line. A supporter of hierarchies, he preferred not to mix ranks, assuming that as long as he remained on formal terms with both his subordinates and his superiors, neither of them would feel emboldened to indulge in chummy manners with him. Especially his superiors. Why on earth should they? Professor Tsukatov wasn't looking for their approval. He knew what he was worth, and he knew he was worth a great deal. Hence, his deeply held belief was that laboratory assistants ought to drink their coffee back in the laboratory.

"No," continued Chelnokov with gusto, "the first thing on our list should be a decent primate . . . Uh, an anthropoid. Perhaps we could even section off a c-corner as something of an ancestral temple, like a Chinese fanza." He was playing the buffoon. "My daughter was in Jiangxi. Uh . . . in their houses the Chinese have a special c-corner they use as an altar, with the ashen remains of their ancestors where they b-burn incense. And they talk to their ancestors in Chinese about everyday matters. Girls talk about their beaus"—Chelnokov winked at Lera who was stifling her laughter with her palm—"and the paterfamilias might talk about the harvest or consult it on matters of monetary investment."

Chelnokov's arguments were flippant, empty, and unfounded. In fact, it would be unjustified to call them arguments at all. But as Tsukatov listened to his colleague, he felt that in fact he really had nothing against the idea of a stuffed ape, and that perhaps it would be a better idea than getting a tortoise. After all, the vice-chancellor of science had moved to the administrative position from the Department of Biology. While he was still a practicing zoologist, he had participated in some ridiculous project for acclimatizing chimpanzees to the Pskov region. It stood to reason that he would still feel affection toward anthropoids. This also meant that it would be easier to get the paperwork through.

Ever since the university's reputation had improved and the Ministry of Education had named it one of the leading institutions in the country, their financial situation had changed for the better. The department's scientific projects won grant after grant, and they were able to rig up a new laboratory. Some tidbits even trickled down to the museum itself. That was when they realized that they needed a museum *curator*—a specialist whose obligations, among other things, would include replenishing the museum's collection, restoring old exhibits and museum furniture, as well as any other matters that came up.

Demyan Ilich had excellent references and extensive experience working at various institutions, including the Russian Academy of Science's zoology museum. Tsukatov made a special trip to the spit of Vasilievsky Island to make inquiries about the applicant with the assistant director of the zoology museum, who was an acquaintance of his. The latter attested to the fact that Demyan Ilich was an impressive specialist with a deep understanding of his field, although, as a person, he was a handful: gloomy and unsociable. His coworkers found Demyan Ilich difficult. He had a way of putting people on their guard, which is why he changed jobs frequently. He had his own secret (albeit quite economical) ways of obtaining materials for exhibits. He could get hold of some of the rarest, most improbable exhibits, and his taxidermy skills were held in high esteem by the museum staff.

Tsukatov was not put off by the gloomy nature of his future employee. For him, a supporter of hierarchical discipline, warm relations with coworkers meant absolutely nothing. The most important thing to him was how well they did their jobs, and he was certain that he knew how to get them to do their jobs *well*. Tsukatov was one of those people who didn't have to play around, gnashing his teeth and crunching the knuckles of his clenched fists. Everyone could see full well that he was a heavyweight. Demyan Ilich's ability to get hold of whatever was needed was nothing to turn up one's nose at, either. As a matter of fact, it would prove very useful for replenishing and expanding the museum's collection. The only problem was that the materials he managed to get hold of—pelts, corpses, and even complete stuffed animals—often lacked the necessary paperwork. But even this did not deter Tsukatov. During the course of his work with the for-profit organizations that delivered the museum its collection of shells of crustaceans, and the glass cube with the display of insects and arachnids from Southeast Asia, their employees had offered, rather unambiguously, to produce the necessary papers for just about anything—any beast, even a diplodocus, hunted in a safari in the swamps of equatorial Africa. For a reasonable fee, naturally. Through their fly-by-night branch offices he could also cash the official funds earmarked for acquiring new museum exhibits, since the suppliers used by Demyan Ilich accepted cash only.

Since hiring the curator, Professor Tsukatov had already used the services of these fly-by-nights twice. First, when at his request Demyan Ilich obtained a wonderful, brand-new stuffed female alligator so large that they had to set it on the highest shelf, just beneath the ceiling, opposite the Steller sea lion, which had been placed in a similar fashion. The second time was when, on his own initiative, Demyan Ilich suggested that they acquire a new stuffed peacock to replace the old one, which had become tattered and frayed during its hundred years of service.

Professor Tsukatov went over to the window and gazed out at the snow, the trees that had turned white, the glass dome of the atrium of the trading house behind the Red Bridge, the chains of black footprints made by students trudging through the courtyard, the sky that promised an early twilight, no longer murky, since the downy winter had already spread itself all around. The calm of the snow-covered earth slowly spread within him.

"Chinese cuisine is also quite p-peculiar," said Chelnokov, removing the bubbling kettle from its base without interrupting himself. "I'm rather afraid to go to their restaurants. Have you ever noticed how m-many of them live in our cities? Yet they don't seem to have any cemeteries. Why do you think that is?"

"Call Demyan Ilich in," Tsukatov said to Lera, who already knew she'd been forgiven, and was poking about in the cupboard searching for a coffee cup. Then, turning to Chelnokov, he said, "Yes, a chimpanzee. I suppose a chimpanzee would be best after all."

The untidiness of Demyan Ilich's abode did not concern its mas-

ter in the least, and was in fact merely a semblance of disorder—
every item here had its place. Just reach out, and the necessary
tool was in the palm of your hand. Toss it, and it would fall into
position. Joiner and furrier tools, vials with acids, salts, alkali,
alums, varnishes, and arsenic solutions, molds for plaster casts
of the slim ankle bones (distal limb sections) of some ungulates,
piles of glass eyes with hand-painted irises and highlights on
the pupils, cans of construction foam, glue, rags, bits of hide,
feathers . . .

Demyan Ilich was to the business of taxidermy what Stradivari
and Guarneri were to the art of violinmaking. He had invented a
special solution for preserving fresh materials, a wonderful lotion
that worked for pickling bird pelts, and a brilliant tanning solution for animal hides, which changed the qualities of the inner side of the hide, making it flexible and resistant to decay
and fungus. He had solved many a riddle of the trade, and he
knew quite a few special tricks that were unfathomable to others. Soaking, cleaning the inner side of the hide from any leftover muscle tissues, quill preparation, rinsing and fat removal,
pickling, drying, and softening—he had his own secret recipe
for every stage of the process. The fur of the hides that he had
dressed remained glossy and didn't wear thin, and the feathers
never fell out. The recipes of his shadowy secretive art quickened
the dressing process, making it five or ten times faster. No other
taxidermist could complete the process so quickly. Assembling a
beast or bird with unfinished hide would mean that it would rot,
develop a foul odor, and lose its fur and feathers. And if it didn't
rot, then the hide of the stuffed animal would dry up, become
deformed, the seams would rip, and the edges of the hide would
curl up on the bare mannequin, which then couldn't be rectified
by any number of bandages or clamps. Demyan Ilich was able to
get excellent results in a short time: the gloomy bliss of genius
had chosen to descend upon him.

"Involution . . . Ahem . . ." The curator's index finger shot upward. "Involution . . . yes. A serpent shall give birth to an angel."

He talked to himself when he was in a colorful mood. Demyan Ilich had finally come up with a plan for luring the little devil into his lair. She would come of her own accord. She had all that remodeling going on at home, and he had offhandedly set her up with a ceiling plasterer. The man was a spurious wretch from the joiner's shop of the museum on the spit, who was greedy and dumb as a cork. He would bring her to Demyan Ilich, as if to show her his work: *I did the ceilings over there a few days ago, come and see for yourself what a great a job I did.* Demyan Ilich would give the handyman his due later—he'd invite him over to pay him, and then he'd awaken the polecat within.

Lera didn't like the museum curator, and was even a little afraid of him. Demyan Ilich's gaze was sharp and piercing, his eyebrows thick and disheveled, his face sallow and bony, his character unsociable and nasty. Once, seeing him in the hall in front of the genetics kitchen, where students in thrall to science brewed porridge for fruit flies, Lera automatically smiled at him with her large mouth and fluttered her eyelashes. Only after she had passed him had she heard him mutter, "Ahem . . . Quite an ostrich." Lera's ears blushed scarlet and her back became covered in goose bumps. What a weirdo!

Then Lera studied herself in the mirror. Yes, she was tall, slim, wide-hipped, and, well, yes, she had a long neck, large mouth, and large eyes beneath her contact lenses. She was young, healthy, beautiful, and lively. In a word, Artemis. What did he mean "an ostrich"? What nonsense!

Demyan Ilich was in the museum. He answered, "Yes, yes," from far off, but didn't open the door right away. He was a long time shuffling behind the closed door. When he finally opened it, he gave her a sullen look. His white lab coat was stale, his hair unkempt, his shoes dusty and worn to the point of indecency.

Coldly, without hiding her aversion to him, Lera conveyed Tsukatov's message to the curator. Without waiting for his reply, she turned around haughtily and headed off to the lab assistant's room, high heels clicking, to rewrite the letter of request for reagents, materials, and laboratory utilities. Her shoulders felt cold from the gaze that followed her from behind.

"A little flea went walking in the garden, the louse did bow, and that flea did swagger . . ." Demyan Ilich muttered to Lera's back. His eyes, which had been sharp as an awl a moment before, were now glazed over . . .

"I need an answer now; will you take this on or not?" Tsukatov was talking to the curator, who looked at the professors with a gray, imperturbable owl-like gaze, as though it was already in the bag. "There's not much time. We need to spend the money before the end of the year. So we have one month left."

There was a long pause. Tsukatov stretched the truth. On several occasions he would submit the paperwork for equipment that had been purchased but hadn't yet shipped out. It would ship eventually, but no one checked and Tsukatov was clean. The chair of the department wasn't afraid of responsibility—he had made the choice between what was necessary and what was easy once and for all. It didn't matter how many living beings had to be killed in the name of science to develop an elixir of immortality—he would kill them all without hesitation.

"Ahem." Demyan Ilich's voice grated on the ears as though it was an old machine. The curator grimaced, his face clearly unused to smiling, and wriggled his furry brows uncertainly. "I'll have to look around . . ."

Another pause. The silence in the curator's presence was so heavy that it took on an almost physical weight, producing an effect that was even more intolerable than conversation itself.

When he was silent, it was as though he became all-powerful. There was no doubt about it: if you asked that man to get you a platypus, he'd get a platypus. Never mind the platypus, he could even summon out of nonexistence the extinct red macaw.

"Well?" If Tsukatov deemed a matter important, he could be patient.

"Ahem. It's not really enough money." Demyan Ilich's brows undulated like two furry caterpillars. "Yes, well, I can ask around. Maybe something will turn up." His nostrils flared as though he had already caught the scent of his prey, hiding nearby.

"How soon will you know?"

"I'll get back to you in two or three days."

When the door closed behind the curator, Professor Chelnokov exhaled as though he had just surfaced from a murky darkness, where he would surely have suffocated had he hesitated for even one more moment. He had a hard time dealing with forced silence. Chelnokov felt that when he was silent he no longer *existed*. And even if he did still exist, he was becoming ever smaller and more insignificant, like a devaluing currency.

"Getting him to talk is like pulling teeth!" Tuskatov said testily.

"A very difficult fellow," Chelnokov agreed, taking a sip of his coffee, already grown cold. "I'm dumbfounded. If one were to believe Lombroso's anthropological c-criminology, he'd be nothing less than a serial killer. Those students of ours—could that be his handiwork?"

Two years prior, a female student had disappeared, and half a year later a male student went missing. The latter, however, was from the Physics Department, which had some of its classrooms on the same floor as the Biology Department, in the right wing, opposite the Genetics kitchen. At the time there were numerous rumors floating around—that a cannibal maniac was on the loose, or that the victims had been sold into sexual slavery, or that they had been butchered by surgeons dealing in human organs. For a while the chancellor's office was full of police operatives who questioned teachers and students; but soon things quieted down. The victims weren't found. In fact, it never became clear exactly when and where they had disappeared—at the university or off the premises, somewhere in the city.

"Being difficult isn't a crime." When Tsukatov deemed someone useful, he became lenient. "It's not like we're getting married to the guy."

"Him?" Chelnokov cried indignantly. "What do you mean *married?* I'd be afraid to turn my b-back to him. He'd just as soon b-b-brain you!"

People don't talk about things that are important; things that are important are *felt*. Those feelings burn the heart, and the heart tosses and turns like a rose chafer beetle inside a closed fist. Demyan Ilich knew his materials and was rarely mistaken. That kid was definitely suited for the job. Of course, it would take a lot of work, pressing, crushing, and occasionally giving him a good shake to awaken his true nature, forcing the sleeping essence to hatch and crawl out of its eggshell . . . But he looked very promising. To himself, with his distinctive brand of humor, the curator referred to this process as *awakening the beast*.

Demyan Ilich stopped him in an empty hallway. Lectures had already begun, and the fellow, it seemed, had arrived late, or had perhaps shown up earlier than necessary. He was an ordinary student, with loose pants hanging from his buttocks, a sweatshirt with a hood, and a bag hanging across his stomach. He had a backpack, and his movements were loose, as though his joints had too much play. He had dark fuzz on his upper lip, pimples, and shifty eyes. The curator asked him to help bring the reagents for the laboratory class. The fellow agreed. Why not? Demyan Ilich let the boy go into the open storage room ahead of him, closed the door, and *click-click*, he turned the key, locking them both inside.

One moment there were two people in the hallway, the next moment there was no one at all.

After the third class had let out, Lera took the key to room 452 and went off to rescue the wild boar's head. A hunter, a general who was an acquaintance of Tsukatov's, had given his hunting trophy to the department a year ago. It was the excellently dressed head of an enormous male boar with terrifying fangs. There wasn't enough room for it in the museum, so they hung the head in the lecture room. From that time on, unable to rely on the vigilance of instructors, Lera was responsible for unlocking room 452 before class and locking it after class was over. Otherwise, the students, due to someone's forgetfulness and/or lack of supervision, might give way to their curiosity.

Lera locked the room, plowed her way through a crowd of vociferous sophomore girls, passed the wide stairwell that veered off sideways, and went into the laboratory, where she picked up the IKEA catalog she shared with her friend, a graduate student. They chatted briefly about this and that, the trouble and inconvenience of the remodeling and so on, before she headed back to the lab assistant's room. As she passed the storage room of that loathsome Demyan Ilich, above the noise in the hallway she seemed to hear a muffled voice coming from behind the door. That was unusual, since the curator never let anyone into his lair. Lera stopped, hesitated a moment, and then carefully put her ear to the crack between the door and the frame. The door was well fitted, but what if . . . yes. That is, no—she couldn't have been mistaken.

"*We're gonna friggin' acquire some new habits now.*" The custodian's muttering growl came through the closed door, almost indiscernible, as though from underwater. "*We're gonna do it one friggin' step at a time. Ahem. First we're gonna make a real guy out of you. Then . . . Sure you are. What did you think? I'm gonna grab your throat and hold it like that a little, and then you will . . . What was that? How's about I kick your balls? And your Adam's apple? Don't bitch out on me. Ahem. Yeah, that's the lesson we're gonna learn now—we're gonna have a little talk and learn how to behave. Yeah. And eat sunflower seeds too. It's called the Hairy Sutra Awakening. Ever heard of it?"*

Lera recoiled from the door, her ear burning. What was this nonsense? She could only hear one voice coming from inside. Even if there was someone answering the curator, that voice was inaudible. And who could be in there? No one. No one could stand Demyan Ilich here . . . Suddenly Lera's thoughts stood on end like iron shavings on a magnet: *Why, he's a maniac! He can't even be trusted with a fork! My goodness, he's really lost it. He's talking to himself . . .*

But unable to stifle her own curiosity, Lera put her head to the door one more time.

"Are you gonna make trouble? Don't just stand here, sit down on the floor. Ahem . . . No, damnit, not like that! Not on your ass, you moron. That's for our next lesson. Squat down . . . Yep, now we're talkin'. Tuck your knees below your underarms and let your arms just hang . . . Good. Now spit. Spit between your legs . . . No, not that much. Count to seven and then spit. Ahem . . . Good boy. You're almost a real man now. Now, let's eat sunflower seeds . . . No, who told you you could get up? Stay put. Here's your seeds. Wait! Gotta learn how to eat them right. Empty the whole bag into your pocket. That's right. Now grab a fistful . . . Okay. You take a seed from your fist with your thumb, and use your nail to stick it between your teeth. Like this, see? Now, snap it open with your teeth. And keep your nose to the grindstone. Say if you're at a watercolor exhibit, or the subway, or at somebody's house or whatever, and you can't spit the husks on the floor, you're gonna have to put them into your other hand. But if you see that no one cares, you spit them anywhere you want to . . ."

Lera thought that the voice was getting closer. She sprang

away from the door of the storage room and hurried away, clicking her high heels and glancing back over her trembling shoulder all the while, then rushed into the lab assistant's room. Jesus! There was a whirlwind of thoughts in her head. *He needs to be locked up! What is Tsukatov thinking? I'm scared to work with him!*

There are usually two paths for man to choose from: the path of truth and the path of lies. Lera had always preferred the third path: somewhere in-between. The chair of the department wasn't in that day. It was time to renew his hunting rifle license, so he had gone off to see the license inspector. That was too bad. Lera was desperate to report what she'd heard. It was no use telling the Chief Bird—he was spineless and just as scared of the curator as she was.

The snow that had fallen the day before hadn't stayed. The Baltic wind had licked it clean with its rough tongue. First from the roofs and cupolas, then from the ground. There wasn't even any slush left, except perhaps on the asphalt of the courtyard and on the Moika Embankment, where a few damp dark lines could still be seen. It wasn't uncommon for the green grass to still linger and buds to come out on the trees around New Year's. The boat weather vane on the golden spire of the Admiralty sailed bravely through the turbulent skies over the Neva River. The southwest wind had turned it ninety degrees.

Three days passed and Professor Tsukatov called Demyan Ilich into his office again. Lera, the impressionable lab assistant, first made another blunder with the request form and then started imagining things. The girl seemed to have gotten entirely carried away. Shivering uncontrollably, she wrapped a light scarf around her shoulders, and demonstratively drank a few drops of herbal sedative. Instead of the sedative, thought Tsukatov roughly, you should have a hot water bottle on you from head to toe. To calm Lera down, Tsukatov had to promise her that he would personally test the curator's sanity. It just so happened his acquaintance, the hunting general, had invited him to go on a bear hunt. Tsukatov had never hunted bears before, and he needed a consultation on how to skin prey in the field, just in case. Down there in Vologda, where the general had invited him, everything was covered in snow, and had been for some time. The bears were hibernating, and the huntsman had found a den.

"Ahem. If the skin is for a rug, then you need to take it off in one layer," croaked Demyan Ilich, and his thick brows stirred. "First you cut it straight from the chin to the scrotum. And if it's a female, then take it down to her privates. Start from the jaw, about a palm's length from the edge of the lower lip, and cut down. Make sure you start all cuts from the underside of the hide so you don't mess up the fur. Ahem. Well, you're a hunter yourself, you know what I'm talking about. Right, then the paws."

Tsukatov seated Demyan Ilich at the large desk in the middle of the office, and sat across from him. He listened carefully, occasionally jotting something down on a piece of paper. Chelnokov, who was at his desk in a nook separated from them by a bookcase and the wooden banister, put on his glasses and pretended to be reading an article in the *Journal of Ornithology*.

"Ahem. The cuts on the paws all have to come together in the same spot by your main cut." The curator made a gesture with the nail of his protruding thumb from his throat to his belly. "And you finish coming out at a straight angle. The front paws, from the palm callouses to the elbows and then across the armpits . . ." To illustrate the point, Demyan Ilich pointed out where to cut on himself. "Right. The hind legs you cut from the heel callouses to the knees, and then from the inside of the hip to here." He got up from his seat, bent over, and demonstrated. Then he sat down again. "Ahem. If you're taking the hide to a taxidermist right away, you can snip the paws off right at the carpals, and you don't have to skin the head—just chop it off at the last vertabra and you're good. Ahem. But if the hide is going to be lying around for a while, then you cut the callouses from three sides and take the paw out. Just leave the last phalanxes of the toes. Right. And the head . . . you'll have to take the hide off the head too." Demyan Ilich fell silent in yet another unnecessary pause. "Then you salt the hide thoroughly. Where there are muscles and fat, make incisions and rub in some salt. Then fold it, the inner sides facing in on themselves, roll it up, and hang it on a stick so the brine can drip off. Ahem. It's best to freeze it."

"What if I want it mounted? Full-size?" said Tsukatov, "How do I go about it then?"

The curator went silent—as usual, for longer than was comfortable.

"Then you're not going to want to take it off as a single layer. Ahem. You make a cut from the back. Then the seam on the belly won't show. There's usually not much fur on the belly. It's hard to hide the seam. Right." Demyan Ilich spoke weightily, as though he was moving rocks, but Tsukatov listened without prompting him. "And it's best to take the beast's measurements if you want to stuff and mount it. From the tip of the nose to the corners of the eyes, and from the tip of the nose to the base of the tail. One more thing: once you've skinned the bear, measure the girth of the neck—behind the ears—and the chest, right here, around the stomach. You need the measurements so the taxidermist knows the right proportions." As before, Demyan Ilich indicated on himself where exactly the bear's stomach was. "So, we cut along the spine from the tail to the back of the head. Right. And the paws, from the callouses to the elbows and knees. Ahem. Then you skin it. Right."

"I'm not quite clear on the head," said Tsukatov. "I've never had to take the hide off a head before."

"Now that's tricky. Right. First you make a deep cut where the lips and jaws meet. You pull the lip back with one hand and cut with the other, so that the knife slides right along the jaw-line. Right up against the jaw. Ahem. If you don't do that, you'll rip the lips when you remove the skin from the head." As De-myan Ilich spoke, he became more and more excited, which was unusual—for three years everyone at the faculty had known him as a gloomy, silent man. "Ahem. Cut the auditory canals as close to the scalp as you can, and make sure you slice the skin around the eyes right up to the sockets, so you don't damage it. You'd be better off with a scalpel instead of a knife. Right. Cut the nose off whole, along the cartilage. Ahem. Next, the ears. The ears will be difficult." He ran his fingers through his hair, and then simulated some careful handiwork. "From the back of the ears you separate the skin from the cartilage, slowly turning the ear inside out. Then, of course, you salt it. Make incisions in the lips and the nose and rub salt in."

"What about the tail?" asked Tsukatov, jotting down the in-structions. "Do I dissect the tail too?"

"Naturally. Ahem. Open it up along the inner side, starting a little ways down from the hole, and pull out the vertebrae. And then you salt the inside again."

"Thank you, Demyan Ilich." Tsukatov was pleased. "Now what about our ape? The chimpanzee. Any news?"

Demyan Ilich went dead silent. "You'll get it," the curator finally said in a Spartan manner. "Money up front."

When Tsukatov and Chelnokov were left alone in the office, Chelnokov tossed his *Journal of Ornithology* aside and popped out of his nook as quick as a flash. Of course he had listened to the en-tire conversation, and of course he was tormented by the silence.

"The girl is just imagining things," Tsukatov said, surprised. "He's all right, damnit!"

"As healthy as the goat-legged Pan," Chelnokov agreed. "Al-though, if you think about it, we all have our idiosyncrasies. The Chinese, for example, they have no interest in b-bear hide. They only take the spleen, and the paws for some reason. P-peculiar p-people they are. By the way, do you know why there are no Chinese cemeteries here?"

"You already said they serve their dead in their restaurants." Normally Tsukatov listened politely to Chelnokov's stories over and over again, but today he didn't have the patience. "Lera is the one who should get checked. I once brought my dog to the department, and she got so scared she nearly jumped up on the table."

"As a rule, women are more wary of d-dogs than men are," Chelnokov said. "And there's a reason for it: women are cats at heart."

Three weeks later, Tsukatov, who had just returned from his vacation in Vologda, was telling the story of the bear hunt in Chelnokov's office. The story was colorful, adventurous, epic, and unbelievable, like the *Iliad*. The synopsis of his tale is as follows:

They approached the bear's den on skis. Tsukatov stood behind a tree, not more than a dozen paces from the entrance. Behind him was the hunter, with two huskies on a leash. The general moved cautiously counterclockwise around the den, to get an idea of the surroundings. If you didn't kill it right away, the bear would attack the dogs and run around his den from the entrance in the direction of the sun. So the general set out, and Tsukatov took off his skis and began packing down the snow beneath him with his feet—when you're near a bear's den, you want to feel solid ground beneath you. The bear must have heard them approaching—perhaps it was sleeping lightly, though the hunter had taken care to tread quietly and keep downwind. The hunter hadn't even had time to let the dogs loose, when suddenly the bear emerged. He was shaggy and enormous, his head pressed to the ground, his chest hidden. Even if you shot, you wouldn't kill him with the first bullet, and Tsukatov didn't even have his rifle cocked. Fortunately, the bear didn't attack them, but instead followed the general's ski tracks. The hunter let the dogs loose, and Tsukatov finally fired his rifle, although the bear was already escaping. As it turned out later, the bullet hit the bear in the behind. Then the huskies got in on the action, nipping the bear in the haunches. The bear was enraged. The general didn't let them down: he fired the fatal shot. Tsukatov had brought bear meat back with him, and the hide went to the sharpshooter as trophy.

Chelnokov listened greedily. He had the habit of reconstructing other people's stories and telling them as his own in other company. He was like that.

Outside the window, everything was white again, except the black water of the Moika River, which had still not succumbed to the icy clutch of winter. Snow lay on the roofs and the glass dome of the atrium. The wings of Hermes's caduceus on top of the trading house were also covered in a fine web of snowflakes. Yet St. Isaac's and the spire of the Admiralty shone a bright gold against the gray skies.

"By the way," said Chelnokov, apropos of nothing, "another student d-disappeared. A freshman. It happened ten days back but they only began searching a little while ago. Everybody thought he'd gone back home to Slantsy, but it turned out he wasn't there either. Police inspectors came to see the dean."

"This time it's definitely a UFO." Tsukatov's thoughts were still at the bear's den.

"And Demyan Ilich inquired about a van yesterday. The stuffed animal was delivered to his place, so it's ready to be p-picked up. We should ask someone at the garage to drive over there."

"Why didn't he tell Lera?" said Tsukatov.

"Lera and Demyan Ilich don't really g-get along very well," Chelnokov reminded him. "And then again, she's been so busy with her remodeling: first it was the plumber, then she had to choose the laminated floorboards, then the ceiling. Remodeling," Chelnokov sighed, remembering the ongoing work in his own office. "That's no beetle sneeze for you."

Tsukatov drew in the corners of his mouth sharply, as a sign that he understood. No, no one could be trusted to do anything in his absence. Throwing his sheepskin coat over his shoulders with the firm step of a man who knows his own worth, Tsukatov headed down to the garage without delay.

Demyan Ilich dreamed that an ostrich nipped him on the finger. He gasped and woke up from the pain. His finger was intact, but somewhere within, underneath the skin, was a memory of that recent ephemeral adventure. The memory, though still pulsing, was quickly melting. It was indeed a most nonsensical dream.

For some time Demyan Ilich lay still. Then he turned his head to the window. At that instant his neck started throbbing with a burning sensation—the scratch, disturbed by his movement, seemed to be actually on fire. "My, some claws are just too nasty," Demyan Ilich said aloud, wincing. Nothing would be nipping him now. She would stand there, beautiful, proud, and foolish, and he would stare at her. In the closet, wrapped up tightly, the *material* was shifting quietly. Demyan Ilich had no plans to give his would-be project away to some third party. Of course, he wouldn't make any good money on it, but this was a special case. Really special. It wasn't the first time he passed up the opportunity for profit, but he was pleased that he had decided things for himself.

Carefully turning his scratched neck, Demyan Ilich examined the room, flooded with light from the streetlamps—pale, cold, no discernible colors. The room was a mess. There were objects strewn everywhere, unrecognizable in the twilight: clothing, tools . . . and a mounted stuffed animal in the middle. Baring its teeth, it sat slightly back on its hind legs, leaning on the knuckles of its forepaws. The room seemed like some sort of un-inhabited utility space, and looked more like a workshop than a living room.

"Ahem," rasped Demyan Ilich. Examining his finger, he thought about the ghostly nature of suffering.

The next morning, in the interests of edification, Tsukatov de-cided to send Lera, along with two young men from the Student Scientific Society, to Demyan Ilich's to pick up the stuffed ani-mal. But she wasn't in the lab assistant's room, and no one had seen her at the department since yesterday. The van left without her.

Dismissing the matter from his mind, the chair of the depart-ment disappeared into his office and sank his teeth into writing an article full of new ideas about *Dirofilaria* nematodes—completely unprecedented ideas. Tsukatov had been working on the article for *Parasitology* for a long time, and the end, it seemed, was now in sight.

In the middle of the second lecture period, under the guid-ance of Demyan Ilich, the students brought in a large object, tightly packed in bubble wrap. They worked quickly, like grave-diggers. Demyan Ilich's neck showed red around the coagulated crust of an angry scratch.

Having brought the parcel into the museum, they sent for Tsukatov. The chair of the department came in, accompanied by Chelnokov.

The parcel stood in the passageway by the oak cases hous-ing the primates. In solemn silence, Demyan Ilich cut open the adhesive that held the bubble wrap with a pair of scissors and set about stripping it off the bulky exhibit, taking his time. A minute later the bubble wrap was lying on the floor. Chelnokov threw up his hands in rapture, and the severe wrinkles on Tsukatov's face relaxed; for he had seen things, but this exceeded all his expec-tations. The chimpanzee's fur shone. Each hair seemed to have

been combed individually. The figure, frozen in motion, radiated
a gush of fury. The teeth gleamed with moisture, the yellow fangs
were bared threateningly, the skin of the face seemed alive and
warm, the dark lemurlike eyes burned in watchful fury. The ape
looked even better, brighter than it could have when it was alive.
It seemed as though it wasn't a stuffed animal at all, but rather
a pure idea, the very essence of a new creature, as the Creator
had imagined it before giving it life. It looked as fresh, as new, as
clean, and as perfect as a beetle that had just emerged from its
chrysalis, before having tasted the dung of life.

Chelnokov regaled it with superlatives. Tsukatov walked
around the animal, staring at it, touching it, kneeling beside it,
and stroking it. He didn't try to conceal his satisfaction: excep-
tional mastery had obviously gone into the making of the piece.

"Ahem," Demyan Ilich croaked behind his shoulder. "I have
another offer from the same source. Right. A bonus. From the
manufacturer."

"Oh?" Tsukatov now felt trust and respect for the curator.
These were things not inherent in a person, the way having red
hair, protruding ears, or a nose like a duck was. One had to keep
on earning them, again and again. Having won them, these qualities would begin to melt away. And one had to start all over from
the beginning. Now Demyan Ilich had won Tsukatov's trust and
respect, at least for the time being.

"Ahem. I can get you something special. Right. If you make
the decision sometime this week, it should turn out pretty cheap."

"Cheap? How cheap?"

"Ahem. Almost free of charge."

"And what is it they're offering?"

Demyan Ilich grinned, the scratch on his neck turned crimson,
and a chain of indescribable emotions ran across his sallow bony
face. He came close to Tsukatov, and uttered in a whisper like a
conspirator: "An excellent, ahem, an excellent African ostrich."

A CABINET OF CURIOSITIES

BY EUGENE KOGAN

Kunstkamera

Translated by Margarita Shalina

1.

"Mama," Ilka's heartbreaking cry rang out. "Ma-a-a-a-a-ma!"

Olya bolted to the nursery. She was much too young, skinny as a reed, with long black hair and enormous eyes that seemed to take up half of her face. "What is it, my son?!"

"Mama, he's back again." Ilka sat pressed into a corner of the bed with a blanket he'd gathered into an enormous heap—that heap was supposed to barricade the child from whatever it was that his eyes fixed on.

"Son, Ilyusha." Olya sat down on the bed and embraced her child. "There's no one here."

Immediately, Ilka began to wail, pressing himself to his mother.

2.

Peter Alexeyevich disliked the journey from the very start. The second week of March was well under way by the time the delegation had arrived at Riga, which found itself under Swedish ascendancy. His mood had been ruined by General Erik Jönsson Dahlbergh, the regional governor—who'd refused Peter's request to visit a fortress and survey the construction of fortifications.

"Damn this place," muttered the czar as he cast off the city.

The mighty delegation moved along slowly, and Czar Peter Alexeyevich was traveling incognito. But to not notice him was difficult—his enormous figure stood out among the rest. It was practically impossible for the czar to conceal his own presence.

3.

Ilka had just turned five. For his birthday, his mother baked him a very beautiful pirog with chocolate filling and she even drizzled it with chocolate icing. Six candles stood atop the tort. Ilka knew how to count to five and was very proud of the fact that he was able to tell everyone about his age. "There was four, and before that three, and before that two, and before that one, and now five," he declared, laughing at how big and bright he was, and all those around him laughed as well. But the candles turned out to be incomprehensible. Ilka counted up to five and realized in astonishment that something else did indeed come next, but what was a mystery. "Mama," Ilka looked at Olya questioningly.

"After the number five comes the number six," smiled Olya.

"Six," repeated Ilka and calmed down. He liked six as well.

Ilka was small. At a glance, he seemed no more than four years old. He was smart, cheerful, found a common language with other children easily, always shared his toys in the court-yard. When he was three, he gave a shovel and a red plastic bucket as a present to Sveta, the girl next door. But all the neigh-boring children were taller than him, and Olya worried. Ilka, however, hadn't yet noticed that he was smaller than everyone else, he didn't dwell on it—such foolishness is not dwelt upon in childhood.

4.

By August they'd reached the Rhine and descended to Amster-dam. They didn't linger there though, and carried on further to

Zaandam. The czar spent over a week there under the name Peter Mikhailov, a junior officer of the Preobrazhensky Regiment. In Zaandam, Peter Alexeyevich stayed on Krimp Street in the little house of the nautical blacksmith Herrit Kist, whom he'd become acquainted with back in Russia; the handy Dutchman had been at the wharves of Archangel, sharing his expertise. Now Peter Alexeyevich worked in the Netherlands on the wharves of the East India Company—everything had changed, however he did not share his expertise, but drew from others, attentively observing how the clever Dutch shipbuilders labored at their craft.

News inevitably spread that the Russian czar himself resided in that unassuming little house belonging to the nautical blacksmith, so visitors from all countries were drawn to Zaandam. Peter Alexeyevich was forced to quickly leave the city behind—beneath the sail of an acquired iceboat he reached Amsterdam in just over three hours and remained in the capital for some time, carrying out excursions to Utrecht, Leiden, and other places.

5.

Olya dropped out of university when she was in her second year. She was alone, with her small son. At first she'd wanted to continue her education after a year-long maternity leave. She did return, but couldn't keep up—there wasn't enough money, work had to be found, the child demanded attention. So, she forgot all about university.

That first year, Ilka was horrid—he bawled ceaselessly, surpassed all the rest when it came to being sick, anything imaginable, he didn't sleep nights, refused to eat, and generally created a merry life for Olya. Olya feared that his behavior wouldn't improve. Her mother helped however she could, but she didn't have the strength either—who can argue with a job and an ailing heart? And there were no men in the family.

But later, when Ilka turned one, everything changed. With

what seemed a wave of a magic wand, the likes of which Olya occasionally dreamed of when she forgot herself in a restless dream during the breaks between Ilka's hysterics. Once, in the middle of the night, the child became dreadfully frightened—either he'd dreamt of something horrible, or perhaps he'd seen something, all he did was wail the whole day, finally he couldn't even wail—he was hoarse. Then he abruptly calmed down and everything changed. Ilka began to sleep, eat with an appetite, and caused a scandal only with good reason—like if he'd painfully knocked against something or lost his favorite toy. Olya was able to exhale in relief.

6.

In Utrecht, Peter Alexeyevich became acquainted with William of Orange—ruler of the Netherlands and king of England, a vast reformer and navigation enthusiast. Enthralled by shipbuilding, the Russian czar gazed with delight upon the foremost European wharves and scaled one of the whaling vessels himself.

Then, by accident really, he found himself in the anatomical cabinet of Frederik Ruysch, a botanist and professor of anatomy. A specialist in the embalmment of corpses and proprietor of a renowned anatomical museum, Ruysch stupefied Peter Alexeyevich with his art. Once, upon entering the professor's laboratory, Peter saw the body of a child on a surgical table—the child was dead, but it looked as though it was alive. The talents of the Dutch professor captivated the Russian czar, and Ruysch was extremely pleased.

7.

Olya did calm down somewhat, of course, but then she'd regard this change in her child's character with disbelief all over again. What would cause a one-year-old to exchange rancor for sweetness in a single day? But the weeks passed and Ilka continued to behave himself well, or as well as a child who had just recently turned one could be expected to behave.

After a month, Olya asked her mother to babysit Ilka and set off to her girlfriend's—they had drinks, gossiped about everyone, like before when Olya didn't have a child. A little later, Olya said that she needed a job—it would be ideal to start off working from home, some modest freelancing, then later she could think about something more serious. As things go, money was badly needed. In three days time her girlfriend called and offered her work transcribing text; precisely the kind of work that she was best suited for had fallen into Olya's lap. Some money began to appear, and life began to improve.

8.

Under the guidance of Professor Ruysch, Peter Alexeyevich got so carried away with anatomy that he forgot about shipbuilding for a time. Being who he was, or course, he didn't forget for a second that that the czar of a superpower must spend every minute thinking about vital matters, so he continued to call on fortresses, shipyards, meet with heads of state and engineers, but Peter Alexeyevich's thoughts were always there, in the anatomical theater.

In the anatomical theater of Herman Boerhaave in Leiden, Czar Peter participated in the dissection a cadaver, and then another. He was good at it, and he liked it. In his diary he wrote of being struck by the sight of a dissected human body—the heart, lungs, kidneys, the "tendons" of the brain . . . There remained one last thing to do—establish something similar at home, in Russia.

9.

When Ilka turned two Olya found steady work as a typist. She wasn't paid much, although she supplemented this by freelancing. Plus, the daily trip to the office forced her to take care of herself once again, and interacting with people was really quite pleasant.

During this time Ilka continued to behave like an angel. He was indeed an angel for the most part, only with dark hair. He and his mother had the same face—thin, with big eyes. He'd attentively monitor the world around him, feeding on information. Because he didn't know how to speak yet, he would point his fist at whatever interested him and peer up into his mother's eyes. Olya loved explaining everything to him and couldn't wait for him to begin asking questions. More than anything in the world she wanted to speak with her son.

10.

Having purchased several collections from various biologists and anatomists across the border, Peter Alexeyevich returned to Russia with steadfast resolve to establish Kunstkamera in the motherland—a cabinet of curiosities following the example of his new friends in the West. In St. Petersburg it was decided that the collection would be housed at the Summer Palace, and Peter personally supervised what went where.

But the collection kept growing and growing. The last time he set out for Holland, Peter Alexeyevich made the acquaintance of the well-known apothecary and collector Albertus Seba—the very one who drowned in one of the canals some twenty years after meeting the Russian czar. Peter Alexeyevich had the opportunity to purchase an enormous collection—an entire pharmaceutical assemblage—from Seba. The collection was moved to St. Petersburg and it became clear that the Summer Palace alone could not contain it.

11.

Ilka had a breakthrough as soon as he turned two and a half.

He literally spilled everything that had accumulated onto his mother. Everything interested him—a lamp, a door, the wind at the window, the neighbor's cat, droplets on glass, a mirror, a television, a sandwich with butter and kielbasa, the chamber pot, day and night. He posed hundreds of questions and listened attentively to every answer.

Olya was happy. Finally, she didn't just get to read her son a story for the night or sing him a song, but could carry on a more or less comprehensible conversation with him. She got the impression that Ilka was attempting to dig down to the truth of the matter. He didn't just listen to everything that his mother told him, he comprehended, and it seemed that he even analyzed. Olya occasionally marveled at how Ilka remembered what she told him. That's how it was—her son didn't ask the same question twice, though often the next question followed the prior for the most logical reasons.

Olya and Ilka would have long talks now. Ilka would ask, and Olya would start explaining whatever it was that interested him with pleasure. Neither he nor she grew weary of this.

12.

They began to search for a place. Various suggestions were made, but Peter Alexeyevich didn't care for them. The only thing that could be agreed on was that the future museum must be located somewhere on Vasilyevsky Island. The question was where.

One day Czar Peter was strolling around Vasilyevsky. The weather was fine—a rarity for Petersburg, which is accustomed to rains and the low-hanging gray sky. Only a gnat pestered him, but nothing could be done about it. Peter Alexeyevich was lost in his own thoughts when two pines, the likes of which he'd never seen, suddenly appeared before his eyes. The pines grew very near, and the fat branch of one had grown into the trunk of the other. Peter stopped before the trees—Siamese twins that had grown into one common bough; he touched the trunk with his hand, circled it, and grinned. The question of where the cabinet of curiosities was to be located had been decided.

13.

When Ilka was almost three, Olya decided to place him in daycare. Out of two daycares located not far from home, she chose the one that seemed best to her—anyway, there was no money for anything specialized, private, or extravagant, but here at least the nursery-governess who had a name found in stories and jokes, Maria Ivanovna, smiled in a kind way and Ilka seemed to like it. At the very least it didn't scare him, even though he understood right away that Mama was handing him off to someone else.

Ilka looked at Olya with woeful eyes and asked: "When are you coming back?"

"Soon, my son, soon." Olya suddenly had a feeling that her heart would tear apart.

"All right," Ilka said sadly. Taking Maria Ivanovna by the hand, he went off into a large playroom to join the other children.

Olya wasn't herself at work. It was one thing to leave her child with his grandmother, but another matter altogether to leave him with some nanny who is a stranger, even if she did have a kind expression. Olya was perpetually distracted, jumped each time the phone rang, made a ton of mistakes, and as soon as the workday was over, she sprang from her seat as though she'd been stung and raced in the direction of the daycare. Ilka was already waiting for her—calm, carefree, and full of new information. Olya calmed down.

14.

The future Kunstkamera building was placed under the direction of a German, Georg Johann Mattarnovi, who'd had a hand in the finishings of the Summer Palace where the collection was being housed for the time being. For some reason construction moved along slowly; it wasn't easy. The years passed, yet still there was no building. For Peter Alexeyevich, the erection of Kunstkamera was one of the most important works of his life, but he didn't live to see the completion of construction—he died seven years following the laying of the foundation stone, even though by his death just the walls had been completed. Then the architect died as well, and others carried on construction.

After another year, they began moving the collection from the Summer Palace. Yet construction went on and on. Rumors spread that the Nevsky land was refusing to house a collection of dead monstrosities. But enlightened people didn't pay attention to such rumors—they'd say the collection had been in Petersburg for years already, so there was nothing to talk about. And soon, the rumors dissipated to nil.

15.

In no time at all Ilka became Maria Ivanovna's favorite and the soul of the daycare gang—as much as three- and four-year-old children can become a gang. An inquisitive, courteous, smart boy, Ilka never vexed anyone, knew a great deal, and was always polite and even-tempered. He took part in merry and noisy group games organically and happily, enjoyed racing around during outings, and didn't really separate from those around him. He never caused mischief, nor raised a ruckus, nor cried without cause, behaved calmly during naptime, and ate whatever they served in the daycare cafeteria. Barely a day passed that Maria Ivanovna didn't sing his praises to Olya, and Olya was utterly overjoyed.

It was only later that she noticed her boy wasn't really growing. Of course, he didn't stay the same small size that he'd been the day Olya had brought him to daycare. But his height had radically slowed—when he and all those around him had turned four years old, Ilka was considerably shorter than the others. This was definitely something to worry about.

Only then did Olya realize that she was recalling the nightmare that had changed her son's character overnight all too frequently. But why she was remembering it was unclear.

16.

Soon after laying the foundation for Kunstkamera, Peter Alexeyevich decided to construct a special building in Petersburg specifically for the growing collection of anatomical and other curiosities. For research purposes, he visited the French port city of Calais, located directly on the strait of Pas-de-Calais. There, he met a man who was so tall that his height left the czar in a state of shock; Peter Alexeyevich was over two meters tall himself. In no time at all, Peter Alexeyevich prevailed upon the Frenchman to relocate to Russia in private service to the czar—he was appointed the position of chasseur.

The Frenchman died in seven years' time. By the decree of Peter Alexeyevich the giant's skin was removed, tanned, and stuffed—the result was something like a tarantula. The Frenchman's gigantic skeleton was situated next to it—and both the tarantula and the skeleton were immediately absorbed as components of the future museum.

The Frenchman was called Nicolas Bourgeois, or Nikolai.

17.

Olya waited a long time—maybe it would right itself. But it didn't. It seemed Ilka had stopped growing, just dead stopped. They decided to see a doctor. Through friends, they found a good endocrinologist—a gray-haired old man with attractive hands. He examined Ilka, ran every possible test, then disappeared. After a week he called—Olya felt as though the stress had caused her heart to stop beating. The endocrinologist said no pathologies had been found as far as health was concerned, and from a medical standpoint he had no explanation for the growth problem. That is, speaking strictly from the perspective of his own specialty. He advised not to waste energy worrying about it: "Ilka will probably begin to grow—this happens with children sometimes, they don't grow, don't grow, then suddenly they erupt, and then there's no catching up to them."

The doctor's words didn't make Olya feel any better. Again and again, throughout the course of the next year, she took her son to various endocrinologists, each one better than the last, but all the doctors spoke as one—there are no problems with the boy's health, he's healthy as an ox, and it's totally possible that his not growing is just the individual predisposition of this particular developing organism, and it could happen to anyone. Olya began to calm down a bit, although she occasionally cried at night—very softly, so that Ilka wouldn't hear.

Then the nightmares began.

18.

Over twenty years had passed since the death of Czar Peter Alexeyevich when a terrible fire occurred on the premises of Kunstkamera. The cupola burned atop the steeple, both the collection and library were badly damaged. Among the pieces lost was the skull of Nikolai Bourgeois. Time passed and the museum's curators began to speak of strange occurrences. They recounted an enormous headless figure that wandered through the corridors of Kunstkamera by night, no doubt in search of something. And it was clear what he was searching for, the museum's curators said, nodding.

The specter of Kunstkamera, and that's precisely what they called him, spent many long years wandering the dark halls of the museum finding no peace. Just as he'd disappear for a time, compelling his own existence to be forgotten, so he'd reappear.

Later he began venturing beyond the confines of the premises. Not very far at first, but with time he ventured ever farther into the city, appearing here or there. True, no destruction came from him—he harmed no one, just frightened them. How they pitied him, this wretched one. Finally they decided something had to be done—they found a skull with no owner and attached it to the skeleton of the French giant. And the giant calmed down. At the very least he no longer appeared to people. Or perhaps it's just that no one has spoken of it since.

19.

The first time it happened was almost immediately following his birthday, after they'd celebrated Ilka turning five. That night Olya was awoken by a blood-curdling howl that emanated from her son's room. Olya sprang up and threw herself headlong at the cry. Ilka sat wailing on the bed, crammed into a corner. He couldn't speak, only trembled.

Olya got him to calm down with some difficulty, remaining nearby until he fell asleep. First thing in the morning her son explained that he'd awoken in the night with the sensation that someone was in the room. He'd focused his eyes on the wall and seen an enormous shadow cast by a strange figure. And he was scared that this person would take him, Ilka, away—but where was a mystery. He was afraid to go to sleep alone for several nights after and asked Mama to sit close by. Olya sat, stroking his head, gazing into the darkness.

20.

"Mama, he's back." Ilka sat, pressed into a corner of the bed with a blanket he'd gathered into an enormous heap, which was supposed to barricade him from whatever it was that his eyes were fixed on. "Son, Ilyusha," Olya perched on the bed and embraced her son, "there's no one here."

Ilka pressed against his mother and started to sob, his hand pointing to the wall across from them. "There he is."

Olya gazed into the dark—and was horror-struck. The enormous figure of a man was suspended midair before her. Olya screamed and covered Ilka's eyes with her hand. At first the figure didn't stir, but then it began to sway and, slowly, with seeming difficulty, float in the direction of the bed.

"Don't move!" Olya yelled. "Don't move! What do you want?! Why have you come here?!" She was so frightened that she couldn't figure out what to do. She was only aware that Ilka had stopped crying. "Go away!" screamed Olya. "Please, go away." Then she began to cry, repeating through tears, "Go away, go away, please, don't touch him, go away!"

The figure stopped for a moment, hovering in the center of the room. Then it began moving in the direction of the bed again. Olya was crying, shielding her child, but there was nothing else she could do. What could she have done?

Meanwhile, the figure had stopped very close by. The giant floated above the floor, so that he had to bend his head to keep from knocking it against the ceiling. Ilka didn't stir, only shuddered occasionally. Olya didn't stir either; she'd stopped crying and it seemed that she'd folded into herself from fear. The figure hung in the air a bit longer, then slowly circled around the bed and stopped again. He extended his fleshless hand and touched Ilka's head. Ilka noticed nothing; Olya's hand covered his eyes, and Olya thought that at any moment her heart would burst from her chest. But it didn't burst. The figure of the giant hung suspended in air another moment, then dissolved. He never appeared again.

After that Ilka began to grow, and everyone knows what people say is the cause.

HOTEL ANGLETERRE

BY VLADIMIR BEREZIN

Hotel Angleterre

Translated by Amy Pieterse

He was staring at the ceiling, his feet up on the desk. It was an absurd habit he'd picked up from the Americans, but had now come to love. The plaster molding overhead had started to crack in the seventh year of the revolution, forming an intricate pattern that seemed to augur something. Whether it augured well or ill was unclear. The longer he stared at it, the more it resembled a man with a sack and bludgeon, or a rider with a sword.

He lived in the middle of an enormous city, in a hotel whose windows were beleaguered with monuments. Nearby was a church that had taken many years to build. Now that it was finished, time sought to undo its fate, and everyone said it would soon be closed down.

In light of all that had already happened in this city, it seemed a new life was in store for the church. And he had heard about life here during the siege and the civil war.

Shpolyansky was the one who had told him. A well-known graphic artist had drawn Shpolyansky right here. In the portrait, one of Shpolyansky's buttons is loose, hanging by a thread. He had grown bald, and quite suddenly. He talked about the city abandoned by the government in 1918. Demoted as the capital, the city continued to live according to its old habits for a time.

Then its most illustrious inhabitants started leaving. It was that old law of nature: when the lid is removed from a pot, the fastest molecules of water begin to escape, and the pot cools down. During the recent war, the city cooled down quickly.

And so he lived in a hotel, built by an unknown architect. The building had undergone reconstruction several times, but one thing didn't change: the architect was still unknown.

Obscurity seemed to consolidate the mystical power of the place, so nobody was surprised when a famous industrialist—a foreigner, one of the wealthiest people in the empire—died in one of the rooms.

Now the empire was gone, and the golden epaulettes of the capital had been torn from the city. It stood before enemy fire like a demoted officer on the breastwork.

The city was still enormous, but it had been dying for several years.

A crazy old woman had wandered the streets, announcing to all and sundry that there would be three floods, the first one in 1824. One hundred years later, a second flood would occur; and a hundred years after that, a third would submerge the domes of the doomed city once and for all. Then the floodwaters would subside, taking everything with them: the cupolas, the crucifixes, and the buildings themselves. Where the city once stood, there would be flat marshland, overgrown with osier for the rest of time.

And the old woman went up to one of the statues, the one prancing on the square, its back turned to the river. Twirling about in her foul-smelling skirts, she ate something from the palm of her hand. The hotel's inhabitants watched her in fear, as belief in the prophesy grew within them like grass through pavement.

Grass had indeed sprung up in many streets after the revolution, especially those paved with hexagonal wooden tiles. The grass grew tall, and goats grazed here and there, as they did in the

Roman ruins. The goats were especially numerous in the outly-
ing districts.

Shpolyansky told him about those times, and his stories were
permeated by a foreboding of flight. Later, Shpolyansky did in
fact flee. He escaped across the ice on the Gulf of Finland to a
different part of the empire, which had gained independence.
Many fled that way, and the first to do so was the father of the
revolution himself. Now he was the one they were fleeing. The
city was empty, and the grass grew taller.

Shpolyansky spoke feverishly, saying that in the demoted
city people's wounds did not heal and women had stopped
menstruating.

All around the hotel, new times were afoot and streets were
being renamed. No one knew for certain what the street beneath
his feet was called.

Shpolyansky's friend Dragmanov liked to quote two poems
about the large church that was visible from the windows of the
hotel.

"This temple serves two kingdoms: above, of brick; below,
of marble." But they rebuilt the church almost immediately, he
said, so the words had been changed: "This temple serves three
kingdoms: marble, brick, and devastation."

Dragmanov included these poems in his novel, and the novel
seemed very promising. The church had long been a place of
central importance to the city. The square derived its name from
it, the massive black church looming through the cold mist. But
the man with his feet on the desk in the hotel room couldn't
think about the novel.

He felt changes in the air acutely. And change was definitely
on its way. The city that floated past the Angleterre like floodwaters was pliant and soft—always the case before a change of
fate. The city was fluid like the dark waters of the river, or the
shadowy water of the gulf pulsing beneath the ice.

It will flow for another hundred years, until the prophesy is fulfilled and the bronze horseman rides on the water as though on solid ground, until the waves swallow the Finnish rock beneath him.

And the hotel—a beehive for the masters of these new times—was ideally suited as that point of fracture.

He had just tried out some new sleight of hand, as was his habit. His friends always found his tricks amusing. Once he concentrated on a mug for so long that he actually made it disappear. "Where's the cup? Where did it go?" his mother had said, perplexed, as she stood in the middle of the room, waving her arms in dismay. Even then, he didn't share his secret with her. And to think she's still alive, my old lady; and I too am alive. There is probably a wisp of smoke coming out of the roof of her little hut right now.

In any case, he had performed for her so often that the trick with the mug would have seemed like a childish prank.

Spoons, as it happened, succumbed to mystical practices far better. The world of Russian objects seemed to yield to his manipulations easily, while objects from abroad were less obedient. The same was true of Russian words: the letters seemed to line up neatly one after another, like rye in a field. The Latin alphabet was more stubborn.

A long time ago he had known Latin, but time seemed to have purged him of all languages except for Russian.

Many knew him as Seriozha, but when you're pushing thirty a nickname is embarrassing. Yet he knew he would never grow up. He simply didn't know how to get older.

In his hand Seriozha gripped a glass. A bottle of Rykovka vodka that had just skyrocketed in price stood on the desk, its contents lukewarm.

At last, the heavy fretted door creaked. The man in black leather, who had Seriozha's own face, had come. For a moment,

Seriozha was astounded at the plan—indeed, the mirror reflected twins: one in a suit with his feet up, the other in black leather and a Russian peasant shirt.

"We meet at last, Seriozha," the man in black said with a slight accent.

I wonder how they did it. Makeup? Doesn't look like it. Probably a mask.

"Your time has come," the man continued, sitting down at the desk.

The poet sighed to himself: this called for a display of terror; but how much did the interlocutor know about all of this?

He could look the man in the eye, stare him down as he had stared into the eyes of a killer with a knife in hand, the one who had accosted him at Sukharevka. He had given him a certain look, and the killer desisted, slinking away along the wall and dropping his switchblade.

But Seriozha restrained himself. "You remember Ryazan, don't you? Konstantinovo? Remember when we were kids?" That would be the perfect move. Except that Seriozha had in fact spent his childhood in a completely different place.

Ryazan? Of all the nonsense! He had been born in Constantinople.

During the second year of the revolution, Seriozha met Morozov, the Schlüsselburg prisoner who had just been released into the world. Captivity seemed only to have preserved the elderly member of the People's Freedom Party—he was fresh and ruddy, with a formidable snow-white beard. Morozov had dedicated himself to studying errors in historical chronicles. In them he had found references to him—Seriozha. He found out that the copyists had mixed up his documents (if only he knew how much this would cost him), changing "Constantinople" to "Konstantinovo."

It was here they had strolled, to their left the gloomy bulk of

St. Isaac's Cathedral, the famed church; and to their right, this very hotel, where fates were decided. The old man sought to avenge history, and decided to start with him, the poet.

Underneath their feet grew the sickly grass of the streets and squares of Petrograd.

The old man waited for an answer.

Seriozha smiled, peering into his eyes. Who would ever believe you, old man? Unless maybe one day some academic follows your lead and starts shuffling the deck of centuries and scepters—but no one will believe him either.

He himself could recall in great detail, though, that hot May, five hundred years ago, when the crackling of fire, the yelps of Fatih's warriors, and the shrieks of the inhabitants surrounded the temple. The doors were torn off their hinges with a thunderous clatter and a crowd of Janissaries broke inside. There were a few who stood out even within the ranks of Fatih's select band of cutthroats. The boy knew that these warriors who looked like dismounted horsemen were dark angels. Their faces were covered in slashes, as though carved out of wood.

The sounds of the Liturgy had not yet died away, and one by one the priests entered the stone masonry which parted to let them pass, carrying the holy gifts before them. The youth rushed in after them, but an old monk grabbed him by the arm and led him through a long underground passage toward the sea. They ran past cavernous cisterns, and heavy droplets from the ceiling beat down on their backs.

The monk put him into a fishing boat with two Greeks who watched solemnly as the city burned.

The two were brothers—Yanaki and Stavraki. They took the young boy along the coast, careful not to lose sight of land. He read them Greek and Latin poetry. The sea censored some of his words, filling the boy's mouth with the salty water of the waves. They soon found themselves in a strange land where the steppe met the water, and the boy took his first breath of foreign air. With each step toward the North, something inside him changed. He felt his soul transforming. His body would remain unchanged forever.

He became the Wandering Russian, a lonely soul attached not to earthly love, but to that of the heavens. Yet he never forgot the wooden horsemen, for it was said of them in the Holy Book: And there was a great battle in heaven—Michael and his angels fought with the dragon. That battle was eternal.

The visitor in black was mumbling something, looking at him from time to time. He must have thought Seriozha was completely drunk.

The boy who had come by the day before had thought so too. Poetry was what had led him through life; but now he would have to end this phase. He would be mistaken about time, however. The Wandering Russian had been duped. Duped like a little boy whose daddy takes him to the big city. The little boy runs away on the sly and goes to the bazaar, where he is swindled out of all his coins wrapped up in a little scrap of cloth.

Poetry was his destiny; but there would be no poetry here.

Without poetry, eternity means nothing, and everything else is meaningless too. Like the time he fought Celery, the famed poet, and suddenly felt his opponent's special hatred for him. It was only now that he realized Celery had hated not him, but fate. Fate saw to it that the Wandering Jew, the eternal Jewish poet, was not he, Celery, but the lowly Mosstamp. Celery couldn't fully comprehend it, but with his sensitive nature he felt fate's cruelty. It was fate he was fighting, not his comrade and fellow poet.

His fate was that of a man destined to die in his own bed, having known early love and late love, having suffered abuse and praise. But whereas he would die forever, Mosstamp would crawl out from under a mountain of dead bodies during his exile to the Far East, and wander the earth forever.

The man behind the door shuffled his feet awkwardly, anticipating the business at hand, and Seriozha grew very sad. He felt offended by the crudeness of it all. He recalled meeting the Wandering Scotsman at a bar in Berlin. Seriozha immediately recognized him by his wavy hair. They roamed around Berlin all night long. In his cups, the Scotsman showed him Japanese Bartitsu moves. Growing animated, the Scotsman pulled a sword out of his bag, which he waved about like a hay mower on the banks of the Oka. In one fluid motion, Seriozha dove sideways, jabbing a fork he'd stolen from a restaurant into the man's side. The Scotsman stood there blinking, hiccuping, waiting for the wound to heal.

He eventually admitted defeat and they read poetry until dawn. The Wandering Scotsman read a poem by his friend about the dry heat of Persia and doe-eyed maidens whose arms wound about like snakes. And Seriozha read the Scottish poem about a wayfarer caught out on a winter night, and a northern maiden who takes the stranger in; how she drifts off to sleep between him and the wall of her humble dwelling. In the morning she sews the wayfarer a shirt, knowing that she will never see him again. And Seriozha knew that those lines were about them, about the shelterless life of eternally wandering poets. As they parted ways on a bridge over the Spree, Seriozha gave the Scotsman the ill-begotten fork, which the Scotsman put in his sword case. Robert MacLeod, or Burns, as Seriozha usually called him, disappeared with his ungainly sword into the rays of the German sunrise, the wind ruffling his hair.

Now, sitting here in a false trap, Seriozha knew that he could kill both of the Cheka officers (for he had no doubt who they were), pluck them from life like two worm-eaten mushrooms from the soil, leaving only small, nearly invisible indentations in reality. He could carve them out, using, say, a fork. Or a spoon. No, the spoon had disappeared during his extrasensory experiments.

But he didn't need to do that. He was a poet, and so was moved by a greater aim than the bestial thirst for blood.

He had to leave his place, like a beast must leave its lair, because he had chosen the wrong word to rhyme with *revolution*.

His visitor produced a grimy book from the depths of his overcoat, and thumbing through the tattered pages began to read some filth aloud. It was probably one of Galya's tearful letters (usually a mixture of complaints and pleas). It was in bad taste, and embarrassing in the extreme. He allowed himself not to listen any further to these stories of happiness and broken arms, of wooden horsemen.

He really did know who the wooden horsemen were, who appeared suddenly in tall grass just as he was getting off the train at Konstantinovo. He had to convince his relatives of his own existence (which he did); but the wooden horsemen were always after him wherever he went. One of them he recognized as Omar, one of Fatih's warriors, who had almost killed him in the church five hundred years ago.

Wooden horsemen—now, *that* would be truly terrifying, because they alone had power over wandering poets. One of them had chased after the automobile he rode in with his wife. The wooden horseman started losing ground. He knew he could not reach Seriozha with his crescent sword, so he tugged at the woman's blue scarf, pulling her out of the car and under the hooves.

Seriozha could not forgive himself her death—though he did not love his wife. Revenge was senseless, for the wooden horsemen had special, invincible powers. He cried then, listening as the din of oaken horseshoes on the paving blocks grew fainter.

The dark angels are no naïve and trusting Cheka officers. Why, if he had heard the wooden neigh of their horses on St.

Isaac's Square just now, right under his windows, the whole plan would have been ruined! As for these two, let them think they had caught him in a hotel-room trap they had set.

At that very moment the visitor said something about some high school students, and Seriozha poured himself some vodka, spilling it on purpose. The vodka tasted of disappointment. Yes, beautiful illusions should be left behind.

All of a sudden, the man in the overcoat jumped on him, and in the same moment another man dashed into the room. Together they wrestled him down, and the second one threw a thin cord from a suitcase around his neck.

The poet stopped resisting and surrendered his body to them.

The trap they had set had worked. But then his own plan began to unfold. First let them think they had succeeded.

The man in black punched the poet in the stomach a few more times, and Seriozha felt a belated surprise at human cruelty. He waited for his death as though for an unpleasant procedure—he had died many times before, and it was unpleasant, like a coarse male nurse administering an enema.

With a dull pop, the little ventilation window flew wide open, and he felt himself hanging, the steam-heating pipes searing his side.

This won't do at all, he thought, looking down through his long eyelashes at the Cheka officers who were stamping their feet, brushing themselves off, and straightening their sleeves, as though after a snowball fight. One left, while the other began to search the room.

Hanging like this was terribly uncomfortable, but soon the man in black grew tired. He stood up, then disappeared behind the bathroom door. The poet quickly loosened the knot and hopped onto the floor. Then he slipped into the armoire.

He didn't have to wait very long. From the depths of the armoire, he could hear a wild cry from the fellow who discovered the body was missing. He listened to the halting explanation, interrupted by threats, and heard them send someone down to the morgue to look for an unclaimed dead body.

A dead body was found, but it turned out to be a suicide who had slit his wrists. By then, however, the Cheka officers had no other choice. Time had them in a stranglehold, chafing their throats, pulling them toward the open window.

The poet watched through a crack between the doors of the armoire as they smeared glue on the gutta-percha mask, which they now pulled over the face of the hapless suicide.

He caught sight of the dead man's feet, then a lifeless arm—and then a new body was hanging from the noose, and the poet listened to their unsteady breathing.

When at last they had left, Seriozha climbed out of the armoire and looked sadly at the lifeless face of his double. Bidding himself farewell, he touched a cold dead hand and left the room.

Seriozha closed the door using a copy of the key, and went out into the corridor, past the receptionist in a paramilitary uniform who was fast asleep.

Leningrad was black and still.

The damp cold struck him in the chest, honing his senses. The wolfhound had missed—and the poet's trick had worked; as had the Cheka officer's trap, for that matter.

Now he could move far away, to the east, to hide beneath Siberia's snowy quilt, where cities and towns have peculiar and wonderful names like Ol' Erofei Palych. Or Winter. Winter sounded like a good name. Why not settle down there?

A new page of his life was beginning: with the dawn snow and the pale sun—a fair copy right off the bat.

ABOUT THE CONTRIBUTORS

JULIA BELOMLINSKY was born in 1960 in Leningrad. A poet, artist, and songwriter, her cult novel *The Poor Girl* was short-listed for the National Best Seller Prize. Belomlinsky is a founder and leader of the Poor Girls movement, a member of the artistic community the Insane Madmen, and a member of the Professional Artists Union of Russia. She lives in St. Petersburg.

VLADIMIR BEREZIN was born in 1966. He graduated from the department of physics of Moscow State University and studied economics in Germany, specializing in the history of the Soviet economy. Berezin is the award-winning author of many titles written in different genres, among them the novel *Witness*. He contributes to the magazines *Novy Mir* and *Znamya*, and he lives in Moscow.

ANTON CHIZH is a journalist, scriptwriter, and head of a PR agency in St. Petersburg. He is the author of a best-selling historical mystery series featuring the criminal investigator Vanzarov, which has been adapted into a video game. Chizh also writes for a series of TV documentaries about criminal investigations that occurred in St. Petersburg in the early twentieth century.

LENA ELTANG was born in Leningrad. A journalist and translator, she has also become known as a poet and as a short-prose writer. *Blackberry Shoot*, her first novel, created a stir on the Russian literary scene and was short-listed for the National Best Seller Prize. Her second novel, *The Stone Maples*, won NOS, the Modern Literature Award, in 2010. Her most recent novel, *The Other Drums*, has been short-listed for the International Russian Prize. Eltang lives in Vilnius, Lithuania.

JULIA GOUMEN was born in Leningrad in 1977. With a PhD in English, she has worked in publishing since 2001, and started her own literary agency after three years as a foreign rights manager. Since 2006 Goumen has run the Goumen & Smirnova Literary Agency with Natalia Smirnova, with whom she also coedited *Moscow Noir*.

Julia Lismyak

ANDREI KIVINOV (PIMENOV) was born in Leningrad in 1961. Originally a shipbuilder by profession, he worked in a St. Petersburg criminal investigations agency for twelve years. Kivinov is the author of thirty books of prose, many of which have been adapted for screen, including the TV series *The Streets of Broken Lanterns* and the movie *High Security Vacations*. He is the winner of the prestigious television prize TEFI.

EUGENE KOGAN was born in 1974. He is a writer, journalist, and an editor at Corpus Publishers. He is the author of four books of prose, among them the best-selling novella *Raccoon and I*, and a collection of short stories, *The Fear of Darkness*. He also edited a collection of short stories, *Forever Yet*.

PAVEL KRUSANOV was born in Leningrad in 1961. He graduated from the department of geography and biology of Leningrad State Pedagogical Institute. In the 1980s he was an activist in the musical underground movement. He is a prize-winning author of the cult novel *Angel's Bite* (1999); his novels *Bom-Bom* (2003), *American Hole* (2006), and *Dead Tongue* (2010) were short-listed for the National Best Seller Prize and the Big Book Award.

Pavel Krusanov

ALEXANDER KUDRIAVTSEV was born in the Bryansk region in 1979, and moved to St. Petersburg in 1996 to study at the journalism department of St. Petersburg State University. He is the author of the coming-of-age novel *Never Fear Nothing*, and he is currently at work on a collection of short stories. Kudriavtsev lives in St. Petersburg and works as a staff reporter at *RIA News*.

NATALIA KURCHATOVA was born in 1977 in Leningrad. She graduated from the department of journalism of St. Petersburg State University. She writes novels, short stories, essays, and articles. Kurchatova has contributed to such magazines as *Time Out* and *Expert*. She lives in a village not far from St. Petersburg.

Ksenia Venglinskaya

VADIM LEVENTAL was born in Leningrad in 1981. He graduated from the philological department of St. Petersburg State University. As a literary critic he contributed to publications such as *St. Petersburg Vedomosti, Izvestia,* and *Sol'*. His prose has been published in literary magazines and several anthologies of short fiction. He is an editor at a Russian publishing house and is currently working on his PhD. Levental lives in St. Petersburg with his wife and son.

Masha Slepkova

MIKHAIL LIALIN was born in Leningrad in 1983. He graduated from the department of economics of St. Petersburg State University. Lialin is the author of two novels, *The Soldiers of TRASH Army* and *RST*.

Sergei Nosov

SERGEI NOSOV was born in 1957. He is the author of five novels (including *Give Me the Monkey* and *The Rooks Have Gone*), several collections of short stories, and a dozen plays. All the novels have been short-listed for various literary prizes, as has his recent collection of essays, *The Secret Life of St. Petersburg Monuments.*

ANDREI RUBANOV became widely known to Russian readers in 2006 with his self-published prison novel, *Do Time Get Time,* which was short-listed for the National Best Seller Prize and then translated into several European languages. He is the author of ten books, including the best-selling dystopian novel *Chlorophilia.* Rubanov lives in Moscow and runs his own small business.

ANNA SOLOVEY was born in Leningrad. She graduated from the Leningrad State Pedagogical Institute, and is a journalist by profession. Also a scriptwriter and a director of several documentaries, Solovey has been published in various literary magazines, and she is the author of the collection of stories *Ward #.*

NATALIA SMIRNOVA was born in 1978 in Moscow. After studying law and working as a lawyer, she moved to St. Petersburg to become the foreign rights manager for a Russian publisher. In 2006 she cofounded the Goumen & Smirnova Literary Agency, with Julia Goumen, representing Russian authors worldwide. She is also the coeditor, with Julia Goumen, of *Moscow Noir*.

KSENIA VENGLINSKAYA was born in 1977 in Peterhoff, "the town of fountains," in the vicinity of St. Petersburg. She has directed music videos for underground musicians and natural history documentaries. With Natalia Kurchatova, she cowrote the novel *Summer According to Daniil Andreevich*. She currently works at a photography studio.